WHAT THE CRITICS ARE SAYING

★   ★   ★

"If you only read one novel this year, this is it! *The Ezekiel Option* is brilliantly conceived and flawlessly executed—one of the most exciting political thrillers I've ever read. I literally could not put it down. **LIKE AN EPISODE OF 24 WITH A SUPERNATURAL TWIST.** Rosenberg has become one of the most entertaining and thought-provoking novelists of our day. Regardless of your political views, you've got to read his stuff."
> ★ **RUSH LIMBAUGH**, #1 *New York Times* best-selling author

"Joel Rosenberg is one of my favorite novelists of all time. . . . **THE EZEKIEL OPTION IS ANOTHER OUTSTANDING BOOK.** . . . What's so eerie about all Rosenberg's novels is that he brings them to life with modern events."
> ★ **SEAN HANNITY**, #1 *New York Times* best-selling author of *Let Freedom Ring* and *Deliver Us from Evil*

"Joel C. Rosenberg is a masterful storyteller, a true friend of Israel and of the Jewish people. He understands the real problems and threats in the Middle East better than any American novelist I know and turns it into a chilling, prescient, and unforgettable read."
> ★ **NATAN SHARANSKY**, former deputy prime minister of Israel and *New York Times* best-selling author of *The Case for Democracy*

"*The Ezekiel Option* is an exciting, action-packed thriller based on one of the most important end-times prophecies in the Bible. This often-neglected prediction needs much more attention as we race ever closer to the very alignment of nations the prophet described 2,500 years ago."
> ★ **TIM LAHAYE**, #1 *New York Times* best-selling author of the Left Behind series

"RIPPED FROM THE HEADLINES—NEXT YEAR'S HEADLINES."
> ★ *Washington Times*

"Better written and more complex than *Left Behind*, to which it will inevitably be compared."
> ★ *Publishers Weekly*

"Eerily prophetic . . . unsettling and scary . . . Rosenberg documents his plot with extensive research. . . . A fast-paced story packed with action from beginning to end."
> ★ *Dallas Morning News*

"Another page-turner."
> ★ *WORLD* magazine

★ **Rush Limbaugh** says *The Last Jihad* is "amazing. . . . I could not put this book down. . . . You have to read this."

★ **Sean Hannity** calls *The Last Days* "riveting to the point you can't put it down—a heart-pounding, edge-of-your-seat roller-coaster ride."

★ **Joe Scarborough, MSNBC,** says, "Joel Rosenberg is almost a prophet. . . . I would recommend you read these books. This is a guy who understands what is going on in the Middle East."

★ **Michael Reagan** says, "*The Last Days* is a gutsy new breed of political thriller— almost prophetically forecasting what you'll read in tomorrow's headlines. . . . Rosenberg is a rising new star on the American fiction scene."

★ **Steve Forbes** says, "What a timely tale. Rosenberg has written, à la Clancy, one of those rare novels that is riveting to read because it seems too real. A tingling triumph."

★ **Vincent Flynn**, *New York Times* best-selling author of *Separation of Power*, says, "A wild, rocketing read, *The Last Jihad* is Tom Clancy writ large."

★ *The New York Times* calls Rosenberg "a Washington success story."

★ *CNN Headline News* says, "J.K. Rowling may be the writer of the moment for the young and the young at heart. But for many adults Joel Rosenberg is the '*it author*' right now. Inside and outside the Beltway in Washington, people are snatching up copies of his almost lifelike terrorist suspense novels."

★ *U.S. News & World Report* says Rosenberg's novels are so close to reality he seems like a "modern Nostradamus."

★ *The Jerusalem Post* calls *The Last Days* "a fast-paced thriller, packed with the authentic details and behind-the-scenes tidbits that only a Washington insider such as Rosenberg could know. . . . Screams 'possible' from every page."

★ *Publishers Weekly* calls *The Last Days* "an action-packed Clancyesque political thriller."

DEAD HEAT

DEAD HEAT

JOEL C. ROSENBERG

Tyndale House Publishers, Inc., Carol Stream, Illinois

Visit Tyndale's exciting Web site at www.tyndale.com

TYNDALE and Tyndale's quill logo are registered trademarks of Tyndale House Publishers, Inc.

Dead Heat

Library of Congress Cataloging-in-Publication Data

Rosenberg, Joel C., date.
  Dead heat / Joel C. Rosenberg.
    p. cm.
  ISBN-13: 978-1-4143-1161-6
  ISBN-10: 1-4143-1161-3
    1. Presidents—Election—Fiction. 2. Political campaigns—Fiction. 3. Terrorism—Prevention—Fiction. 4. Assassination—Fiction. 5. Middle East—Fiction. 6. Temple of Jerusalem (Jerusalem)—Fiction. 7. Political fiction. I. Title.

PS3618.O832D43 2008
813′.54—dc22   2007046702

Printed in the United States of America

14 13 12 11 10 09 08

7 6 5 4 3 2 1

To my dearest Lynn –

You take my breath away and always have.

I love you dearly, and I am yours for eternity.

CAST OF CHARACTERS

★ ★ ★

THE PRESIDENT OF THE UNITED STATES
- James "Mac" MacPherson

THE VICE PRESIDENT OF THE UNITED STATES
- William Harvard Oaks

THE PRINCIPALS
- Jon Bennett, Former Senior Advisor to the President
- Erin McCoy Bennett, Former CIA Operative

SENIOR ADMINISTRATION OFFICIALS
- Marsha Kirkpatrick, Secretary of State
- Danny Tracker, Director of Central Intelligence
- Lee James, Secretary of Homeland Security
- Bob Corsetti, White House Chief of Staff
- Ken Costello, National Security Advisor
- Burt Trainor, Secretary of Defense

WORLD LEADERS
- Salvador Lucente, Secretary-General of the United Nations
- David Doron, Prime Minister of Israel
- Mustafa Al-Hassani, President of Iraq
- Khalid Tariq, Chief Political Aide to the President of Iraq
- Liu Xing Zhao, Prime Minister of China
- Zeng Zou, Foreign Minister of China

MILITARY LEADERS
- Lieutenant General Charlie Briggs, Commander of NORAD and USNORTHCOM
- Admiral Neil Arthurs, Commander of USPACOM
- General Andrew T. Garrett, Commander of Combined Forces Command Korea

AUTHOR'S NOTE

★ ★ ★

I pray to God the novel you hold in your hands never comes true.

Certainly not as written.

Dead Heat is a work of fiction. I didn't see it in a vision in the middle of the night. I made it up. It does not represent the future as I wish to see it. It represents a future I fear could be coming, and soon. I hope I am wrong.

Despite the fact that numerous fictional elements in my previous novels have seemed to come true, I am not a clairvoyant, a psychic, or a "modern Nostradamus," as some have suggested. I am simply a storyteller. *Dead Heat* is the fifth and final novel in the series that began with *The Last Jihad*, and like the other four, it is based on a series of very real and increasingly serious geopolitical threats facing the United States and our allies today, as well as on a series of very real and deeply sobering prophecies written in the pages of the Bible centuries ago.

So far as such geopolitical threats are concerned, it is not my contention that we are necessarily destined to see such horrors come to pass. Hopefully our nation's political, military, intelligence, and law enforcement leaders will have the necessary wisdom, courage, and sense of urgency to counter and neutralize these threats, and many others like them, in time. If we and they understand the nature and magnitude of the evils gathering against us, we could very well avoid the sort of cataclysms that some experts now believe are no longer a matter of if, but when.

So far as the prophecies are concerned, however, let me be clear: the world *is* destined to see such horrors come to pass. When? I cannot say. How exactly will such events play out? One can only speculate. I have no doubt they will happen as the Bible predicts, and they certainly could happen in our lifetime. Only the Lord Himself knows.

That said, it is worth noting that of the one thousand or so prophecies found in the pages of the Bible, more than five hundred have already come true. Indeed, a number of startling "end times" prophecies have actually come to pass over the course of the last century, including the rebirth of the State of Israel, large numbers of Jews returning to the Holy Land after centuries of exile, Jews rebuilding the ancient ruins of Israel and making the deserts bloom, and Israel creating an "exceedingly great army."

All of this begs the question: since some dramatic "last days" prophecies have come true in our lifetime, isn't it remotely possible that more such prophecies could happen in our lifetime as well?

One of my fictional characters, Dr. Eliezer Mordechai, put it this way in *The Ezekiel Option*, describing Bible prophecy as "an intercept from the mind of God." The Scriptures tell us that God in His sovereignty has chosen to give us advance intelligence of some future geopolitical events that will shake our world and shape our future so we are not caught off guard, so we can get ready, so we can help others get ready. As the Hebrew prophet Amos once wrote: "Surely the Lord God does nothing unless He reveals His secret counsel to His servants the prophets." (Amos 3:7)

Which brings me back to my first point. Though something is coming, I pray we are spared the events portrayed in *Dead Heat*. I did not write this book to predict exactly how such end times prophecies will come to pass. I wrote it to ask, *What if?*

What if the political debates that so obsess and divide us prove one day to be trivial pursuits, distracting us from the most important and pressing issues of our time?

What if in the midst of presidential campaign seasons that invariably consume so much of our nation's time, talent, and treasure we find ourselves one day blindsided by gathering evils we either do not see or fail to fully appreciate?

What if the great fortunes we are trying to amass do not protect us from the weapons being formed against us?

And what if in our never-ending national hunt for power, prosperity, and celebrity we somehow gain the whole world, but forfeit our souls?

A new evil is rising. I feel it. I fear it. Let us awaken, before it's too late.

JOEL C. ROSENBERG
November 2007
Washington, D.C.

It was going to be bloody, but it could be done, if they moved fast.

All eyes in the CIA's Global Operations Center turned to Danny Tracker. Once the deputy director of operations, Tracker, forty-six, was the newly installed director of the Central Intelligence Agency. Only he could authorize the Delta Force commander on the ground to carry out this strike, and it was he alone who would have to answer for his decision to the president, to a myriad of congressional oversight committees, and to his colleagues throughout the Byzantine world of U.S. intelligence.

The Agency had been hunting this "high-priority target" for months. Tracker watched as live video images of their prey streamed in from a Predator drone hovering—unheard, unseen—a mile above an abandoned warehouse outside of Sanaa, the capital of Yemen, where their target now entered, surrounded by scores of heavily armed bodyguards.

"How far away are they?" Tracker asked the senior watch officer beside him as he surveyed the feeds coming in on five enormous plasma TV screens on the wall before him.

"Both Delta teams are at least twenty minutes out, sir."

Tracker winced. Twenty minutes was an eternity in his business. They had to take this guy down fast. Umberto Milano, after all, was the head of operations for the Legion, one of the most feared terrorist organizations on the planet.

Tracker flipped through the file in his hands, the one stamped "CLASSIFIED—EYES ONLY" in red. Only forty, Milano, the Sicilian-born son of Marxist radicals, had already served seven years' hard time for blowing up two banks in Rome and one in Florence. Converted to Islam in prison. Escaped with two fellow inmates in 2000. Fled to Afghanistan. Trained with bin Laden. Returned to Europe just before 9/11. Joined the Legion, a loosely affiliated European arm of Al-Qaeda. Planned the Madrid train bombings in 2004. Responsible for at least eight other bombings from Casablanca to Cairo and from Jakarta to Jerusalem.

After the demise of Al-Qaeda, Milano provided financial and logistical assistance to the Al-Nakbah terror network run by Yuri Gogolov and Mohammed Jibril. What's more, the Agency had some evidence—circumstantial but compelling—that Milano had masterminded the suicide bombing at the Willard InterContinental in D.C. the previous January.

Tracker had no doubt the Legion was planning something far deadlier, but at the moment, he had no idea what. Milano had eluded the Agency for years, operating in the shadows and off the grid. They had no idea where he lived. They had very little idea who his contacts and associates were. All they had were occasional bits and pieces of phone and e-mail intercepts; this was the first time they'd ever been able to spot and track him in real time. They needed to take him down. They needed to make him talk. They needed to extract every last bit of information they could. And they needed to do it now.

"Yesterday's tip on Milano's movements—do we know where it came from?" Tracker asked.

"No, sir," the watch officer said.

"But you're absolutely certain it's him in that warehouse?"

"Yes, sir, I am."

Tracker turned to two senior intelligence analysts, each of whom had spent much of his career focused on the Legion.

"Do you guys concur?"

"I do, sir," one said.

"No question," the other said. "That's Milano, all right. And with all due respect, sir, we need to take him before it's too late."

Tracker turned back to the senior watch commander and asked, "Do the Delta teams have everything they need to bring this guy in?"

But the commander was no longer listening to the conversation. His eye had suddenly been drawn back to the live feed coming in from the Predator.

Now Tracker looked there too. "You've got to be kidding me." He cursed. "They're leaving already?"

No one said a word. The Predator feed said it all. A dozen armed men were clearly exiting the warehouse and taking up positions around the third vehicle in a line of five black SUVs.

"How much longer until Delta is on scene?" Tracker asked.

"They're still ten minutes out, sir."

Tracker glanced at his watch. They didn't have ten minutes.

President James "Mac" MacPherson was en route to Los Angeles. Tracker knew he'd love nothing more than to be able to point to a new success in the War on Terror during his prime-time speech that night at the Republican National Convention. Giving the president the ability to announce a major CIA coup to a global audience couldn't hurt his Agency's tattered image, or his own career.

The country was deeply divided over the future. The rhetoric of the campaign could not have been hotter. Both major parties were locked in a knock-down, drag-out battle over who could better protect the country for the next four years. MacPherson had served his eight years and couldn't serve again. The latest polls showed his anointed successor in a dead heat with the Democratic challenger. Perhaps an operation like this could help tip the balance, even a little, Tracker thought. Perhaps in a race this close, even a little boost might be all that was needed.

"Sir, we need a decision," the senior watch commander pressed.

Tracker felt his pulse racing. He had only two options. He could let Milano leave the warehouse, use the Predator to follow him to his next location, and pray Delta could move against him later that day or the next. Or he could forfeit the possibility—slim though it was—of bringing Milano in alive by ordering the Predator to fire two Hellfire missiles into the warehouse and parking lot, killing everyone and destroying everything inside and out.

"We're out of time, sir. What do you want to do?"

Tracker hesitated. What was more valuable—the information he might be able to extract from Milano later or the worldwide headlines

Milano's death could give them now? He stared at video feed and cursed again. Sometimes technology wasn't enough.

"Take him out," Tracker said at last. "Take them all out."

All eyes turned to the center video screen, and as the senior watch commander relayed the orders to the Predator controllers in the field, everyone in the Global Operations Center seemed to hold their collective breath. No one said a word, but Danny Tracker was sure they were all thinking what he was. Was he doing the right thing? How much actionable intelligence was he about to sacrifice? What exactly would the president say when he heard the news? Was there another way?

But it was too late now.

Suddenly they could see the contrails of two laser-guided AGM-114 Hellfire missiles streaking toward the earth below. One hit the center of the warehouse. The other hit the center vehicle in the convoy. Two enormous explosions filled the screen with a blinding light. Then thick, black smoke rose from the wreckage. Then came grisly, full-color images of a blazing building, five burning vehicles, and body parts strewn about as far as the eye could see.

The ops center erupted in cheers, but Tracker began pacing. He couldn't celebrate. Not yet. Not until they had all that they'd come for.

He stared at the Predator feed and the digital clock on the far wall and felt the acid chewing through the walls of his stomach. He clenched his teeth as two vans pulled onto the scene. Eight Delta operators, all heavily armed and clad in Kevlar and black masks, set up a secure perimeter. Four more headed straight into the inferno. It was their job to find Milano, confirm his remains, and secure any evidence they might find on or around him, evidence that could—if they were lucky—give them some idea of what the Legion was planning next. But they were quickly running out of time. Whatever didn't burn or melt, Tracker knew, would be in the hands of the local police in less than ten minutes, and their best hope for protecting against the next attack would be lost forever.

2

2:41 A.M.—A REFUGEE CAMP IN NORTHERN JORDAN

Jon Bennett had no idea that U.S. forces were on the move.

He had no inkling of the horrifying plot they were about to uncover in the Yemeni capital. Nor did he care. Fourteen hundred miles away, in a crowded, disease-infested refugee camp in northern Jordan, just minutes from the Syrian border, a wave of panic gripped his body as he held his wife in his arms and begged her to hang on until help arrived.

"Erin, talk to me. Look at me, sweetheart. Please."

But Erin did not respond. Her breathing was shallow. Her pulse was weak. Bennett yelled for a doctor, but no one came. Again and again he cried out into the scorching August night—thick with the stench of sweat and death—but amid the grotesque cacophony of the masses, no one even noticed, much less cared.

Bennett's heart was racing. It wasn't possible. He couldn't be losing her. They had been married less than eight months.

He had no idea what was wrong, but he couldn't wait any longer. He had to find a doctor, a nurse, a soldier, someone—anyone—who could help. Still, he didn't dare leave Erin alone. What if he took too long? What if he came back and it was too late? He would never forgive himself. He'd have to take her with him.

Bennett scooped up Erin's limp and nearly lifeless body in his arms and rushed her out of the small tent that had become their home. Dressed only in the shorts and T-shirt he typically slept in—he wasn't even wearing shoes or sandals—he began working his way to the medical compound on the other side of the camp. But that proved tougher than expected.

Even so late at night, large numbers of people remained up and about, congregating here and there and clogging the narrow, dusty alleyways that crisscrossed through this tent city of nearly five thousand refugees. Some begged for food. Others dealt drugs. Some smoked water pipes, while others drank away their woes. Old men talked politics. Old women gossiped. Young boys chased each other, while teenage girls roamed in packs, whispering and giggling and wishing the boys were chasing them. Anything that passed the interminable hours of isolation and despair was fair game, it seemed, and the cries of unwanted and unexpected babies—more and more each month—filled the night.

Bennett elbowed his way through the crowds, finally pushing free and spotting the camp's primary care clinic, not far from the front gate, heavily armed by U.N. peacekeeping forces in their distinctive blue helmets. His pulse was racing. The muscles in his arms were burning. His legs were ready to give way. But he pressed on for Erin's sake, racing across an empty helicopter landing pad and bursting in the front door.

"*Help, quick, I need a doctor.*"

The senior nurse on duty came over and began asking him questions in Arabic.

"*English,*" he insisted. "*Do you speak English?*"

Apparently not. She kept asking him questions he didn't understand, insisting on information he couldn't give.

Bennett looked to the right and then to the left. He called out for anyone who spoke English. But no one responded. His panic intensified. Erin's olive skin was rapidly turning gray and clammy, and he had no idea what else to do.

Suddenly, a young woman appeared through a side doorway.

"What seems to be the trouble, sir?" she asked with a slight accent that might have been British but could very well have been Australian.

"I don't know," Bennett conceded, his voice catching. "We were just getting ready for bed when she started vomiting, over and over again. She couldn't stop. Eventually she started dry heaving, and then she just collapsed."

"What did she have for dinner?" the nurse asked.

"Nothing—maybe a few crackers," he replied. "She hasn't had much of an appetite for the last week or so."

"She's burning up," the nurse said, feeling Erin's forehead and sticking a digital thermometer in her ear. "One hundred five," she said a moment later.

Jon gasped. It was so high. Too high. And it was spiking so quickly. He didn't remember her having a fever when this had begun. Where was all this coming from? What was happening? And why?

3

★ ★
★

It had been twenty excruciating minutes.

But the secure call he'd been waiting for finally came. Tracker checked the ID. Sure enough, it was the senior watch commander in the ops center.

He picked up on the first ring. "Tracker, go."

"Umberto Milano is dead, sir," the commander confirmed. "Delta just made a positive ID."

"They're sure?"

"Yes, sir."

"And they got off scene in time?"

"It was close, but yes, sir, they made a clean exit."

Tracker knew he should be ecstatic. But there was something else. He could hear it in the commander's voice, and twenty-three years in the clandestine services told him what was coming next would ruin his night.

"What else?" he asked reluctantly. "What's wrong?"

"Well, sir, we may have a situation."

"Talk to me."

"Well, sir, the Delta teams were able to grab Milano's cell phone, but it was fried. They found his laptop, too. It was badly damaged, and most of the data they have been able to recover is encrypted. It's going to take some time to sort out."

"Cut to the chase, Commander," Tracker demanded, his patience wearing thin. "What are you saying?"

"Sir, the tech team was able to recover the last two e-mails Milano sent, and they're troubling, sir."

"How so?"

"One contains detailed maps of Los Angeles—streets, subway lines, sewage and electrical facilities, and so forth. The second e-mail contains detailed schematics for Staples Center."

Tracker's stomach tightened. "The convention center?"

"Yes, sir," the watch commander confirmed. "I don't know where they would have gotten it. It's not available online. We checked. They had to have gotten it from the office of the architects who designed the place, or from a city office."

"When were they sent, Commander?" Tracker asked, racing to process what he had just learned.

"Yesterday, sir."

"To whom?"

"We're not sure yet, sir. The tech team's still working on that."

"Find out fast and call me back," Tracker ordered.

"Will do, sir."

Tracker hung up the phone, swiveled his chair, and turned to look out his seventh-floor windows at the woods of the Virginia countryside. Was he hearing this right? The evidence was circumstantial but terrifying. *Air Force One* was en route to Los Angeles International Airport. By now, it was probably on final approach. Once on the ground, the Secret Service motorcade would take MacPherson directly to Staples Center. Twenty thousand delegates were standing by for the kickoff of the Republican National Convention. The president of the United States was about to address his party for the last time before handing over the platform to the man he hoped would succeed him.

Was the Legion planning an attack? an assassination? Was it coming tonight?

He had been working with the Secret Service, FBI, Homeland Security, and local and state law enforcement agencies for months to ensure the safety of both the Republican and Democratic conventions. At this point, he considered Staples Center impenetrable. Even in the highly unlikely scenario that a terrorist or team of terrorists actually did get inside the building, there was absolutely no way to smuggle weapons in. Pre-positioning weapons inside the convention center or somewhere on the grounds was out of the question as well. Every square inch had been checked and double-checked by the best security teams on the planet. But still . . .

What if it was an inside job? It had happened before during the MacPherson administration, hadn't it? That was what eventually forced Jack Mitchell, his predecessor, to step down as DCI, wasn't it?

Al-Nakbah had been able to penetrate the Treasury Department and the Secret Service six years earlier and nearly assassinated MacPherson twice. Not long after—and maybe before—the Legion had penetrated the CIA and somehow turned Indira Rajiv, one of the Agency's top Middle East analysts, into one of the most damaging traitors in the history of the Agency. *Wasn't anything possible at this point?*

The Republican National Convention, of course, was the ideal target. Especially tonight. The eyes of the world would be riveted on the president's prime-time address. By all media reports, this was not going to be an ordinary campaign stump speech by a lame-duck president. Leaks from "senior White House sources" suggested MacPherson was going to make major news, though no one was sure what it might be.

European leaders were urging the president to cut off U.S. aid for Israel if Prime Minister David Doron continued to insist upon constructing the new Jewish Temple in Jerusalem, now rapidly nearing completion. Editorials in several leading American newspapers were urging the same course of action, and there were rumors MacPherson was growing impatient with Doron. Might MacPherson throw down the gauntlet with Israel tonight?

Congressional Democrats, meanwhile, were pushing MacPherson to back a sweeping new Middle East peace plan being crafted by U.N. Secretary-General Salvador Lucente. The central element of Lucente's proposal involved the withdrawal of U.S. military forces from the Middle East, particularly from the oil-rich Persian Gulf area. These would be replaced by U.N. peacekeeping forces contributed from every corner of the globe. Secretary of State Marsha Kirkpatrick was rumored to be sympathetic to such an approach. Was the president going to announce a "phased redeployment" of U.S. forces tonight?

If that wasn't enough, the *Wall Street Journal* was reporting that in light of the unification of Europe into the European Union centered in Brussels and the fact that virtually the entire Middle East had recently united its government in Babylon as the United States of Eurasia, several senior MacPherson administration Cabinet officials were urging the president to call for the political, economic, and military unification of North, Central, and South America into a "United States of the Americas."

What's more, the treasury secretary had reportedly had lunch with the president in June, urging him to embrace a single regional currency known as the "Amero" as a replacement for the traditional American dollar. One senior administration official who asked not to be named told the *Journal* that every government in the Organization of American States—with the exception of Cuba and Venezuela—was quietly backing such a political and economic unification, phased in over the next decade or so.

"The only way the U.S. can compete and succeed in the twenty-first century is to create a trade bloc comparable in size and muscle to the emerging economic behemoth in Brussels and the emerging oil superpower in Babylon," one high-ranking U.S. official told the *Journal*. "Will it be controversial here at home? Absolutely. But we have no other choice."

Controversial didn't even begin to describe it. *Explosive* was more like it. Such a proposal threatened to rip apart the GOP. Several prominent social conservative leaders worried openly about the loss of U.S. sovereignty and a never-ending flood of new immigrants from south of the border, even though many fiscal conservatives loved the idea of expanding free trade and enhancing economic efficiencies.

None of these ideas or the varied reactions to them was the point, however. The point was that given how close the race for the White House was, and how much heat had been generated by various rumors swirling in the press, interest in the president's speech that night was running high, making an already "high value" target that much more tempting. The *Los Angeles Times* estimated eighty to ninety million Americans would tune in to hear the president's speech, along with as many as a billion people around the globe. No one had to tell the newly appointed director of central intelligence just how devastating an attack on the Republican National Convention would be on a fragile American psyche, or on the

U.S. and global economy, still recovering from last year's so-called Day of Devastation and oil prices that remained well over $300 a barrel.

Tracker picked up the phone on his desk and hit speed dial.

"Get me *Air Force One*," he told his chief of staff. *"Now."*

4

★ ★
★

The nurse was now yelling something in Arabic.

Suddenly two more nurses and an orderly rushed to Erin's side and whisked her into an examining room. Bennett tried to follow them but they refused him entry. They insisted he remain outside, then shut the door in his face. A moment later, he watched two doctors race down the hallway and into the examining room, and for a split second he was able to catch a glimpse, however fleeting, of the feverish activity inside—the needles, the monitors, the battery of tests—before the door slammed shut again.

He had done all he could, Bennett kept telling himself. He had gotten his wife to the clinic. He had gotten her into the care of doctors with years of trauma experience. But was it going to be enough? It had to be. The alternative was unthinkable. Still, as hard as he tried to console himself, as desperately as he tried to convince himself that everything was going to be fine, the bitter truth was that he had no idea, and he hated this feeling of powerlessness that was intensifying by the minute.

Bennett stared at the closed door for a moment. He had never felt so scared in his life. Not in Eli Mordechai's house in Jerusalem the night he'd been shot by terrorists. Not in Gaza the day his convoy had been attacked by radical jihadists. Not in Moscow during the coup or even on the day of the firestorm. Those were different. Then, he'd feared for his own life. Now he feared for hers, and feared what he'd become without her.

No one had ever loved him like Erin did. Nor had he ever loved a woman so deeply, so completely. He loved the sound of her voice and the way she laughed at his jokes. He loved the touch of her hand on his face and the way the light glistened off the diamond he'd given her the night he'd proposed.

When he was in a crowd—unloading supplies off the U.N. relief trucks before dawn or feeding refugees in the mess tent morning, noon, and night or handing out toys to the children on various holidays—his eyes always seemed to be searching for hers. He loved to watch her serving others, caring for others with a love that welled up from somewhere so deep within her soul. He loved the delight she had when she caught him looking her way. And he loved how she could sense the longing in his eyes and how, as soon as she could, as soon as her task was complete, she would work her way back through the crowd to be with him, knowing that he simply couldn't be apart from her for too long without being overcome with a sadness he couldn't quite explain.

When she was away from his side for more than a few hours, he physically ached for her in a way that would have embarrassed him to tell anyone but her, and sometimes even her. It felt odd to need someone so intensely. *Was that normal? Did other men feel this way about their wives?* When they were together—private and alone—the world lost all meaning. All he wanted to do was play with her chestnut brown hair and kiss those soft lips and gaze into those dazzling green eyes until their souls sparked and sizzled, and their desire turned to hunger, and their hunger turned to passion, and their passion turned to heat, and they could finally melt again into one and drift away for hours, peaceful and secure.

To Bennett, it still defied all reason that God in His mercy had created him for her and her for him before the foundations of the world. Some of his friends didn't believe that. Bennett himself hadn't always. Not that long ago, he hadn't even been sure if there was a God. But Erin's love was living proof of the existence of God. Of this he had no doubt. She was the miracle God had used to open his eyes to the presence of a higher love and bigger plan than he had ever dreamed possible. He only wished he'd met her sooner, or that he'd allowed himself, at the very least, to fall in love with her sooner, faster, deeper.

How blind he had been—how blind and how stupid. Why hadn't he asked her out when they'd first met? Why hadn't he insisted they elope immediately? How many days had he wasted alone? How many nights had he needlessly surrendered to cold sheets and a lonely heart?

In all his life, he had never met anyone like Erin. He found himself intoxicated by her passion for Christ and her compassion for others. She didn't care about money or fame or power (Bennett's "triune god," he had joked back in the days he'd worked on Wall Street). She was constantly giving her time for those who needed her most, to a fault even. Since arriving at the camp, she'd worked twelve- to fourteen-hour days—sometimes longer—with minimal breaks and had taken only one weekend off. She always got up before he did, often before dawn, and hated naps. "Sleep is for suckers," she'd laugh and then drag his sorry body out of bed every morning. He was starting to feel his age. She never did. He was ready for the end to come. She wanted to seize every moment and make it count for eternity.

Erin couldn't balance a checkbook if her life depended on it. She had a stubborn streak that sometimes played out as determination but other times was downright nonsensical and infuriating. And every now and then Jon would see flashes of jealousy that surprised him but also reminded him how deeply she loved him and wanted him all to herself. How in the world would he survive without her? He couldn't begin to bear the thought, not even for a second.

5

★ ★
★

Air Force One touched down amid airtight security.

On an average day, more than two hundred thousand passengers flew in and out of LAX, making it one of the busiest airports in the world. But not today. Secret Service Director Jackie Sanchez had ordered the entire airport closed for the president's arrival, grounding all flights and refusing all nonessential personnel access to the premises. The airlines were furious, as were their passengers. Even the mayor's office had called to complain. But Sanchez was taking no chances. Her sole responsibility was protecting this president, and she refused to be distracted from that mission.

She ordered armored personnel carriers from the California National Guard brought in to block access to all runways and tarmacs. Heavily armed agents and bomb-sniffing dogs patrolled the grounds. Sharpshooters were positioned on rooftops, paired with spotters using high-powered binoculars. Apache helicopter gunships circled the airport and the motorcade route, as did three reconnaissance choppers on loan from the L.A. police department. And all this had been put in place *before* the latest threat intelligence from Yemen.

Tensions were running high as the gleaming blue and white 747, surrounded by an escort of black SUVs filled with Secret Service counterassault teams, taxied to a maintenance hangar. There, the president would be able to disembark out of the view of reporters and fans and would-be assassins and step into one of two bulletproof, armor-plated Cadillacs, without anyone beyond the Secret Service and his own inner circle knowing which one.

Keeping MacPherson alive had not been an easy task over the past eight years, and no one knew that better than Sanchez. She had rescued MacPherson from an airborne attack in Denver just after his first midterm elections and had been named the special agent-in-charge of his protective detail. After the recent fatal heart attack of Bud Norris, the longtime director of the Secret Service, MacPherson had promoted Sanchez to the top job. He trusted her with his life, and his family's, and she counted his trust and his friendship a great honor.

But there were days when Sanchez wondered if the sacrifices she'd made were worth it. And this was definitely one of them. She had never married. She was never home. She never felt rested. She constantly lived with the fear that this day could be the president's last. Or her own.

For the first time in her eighteen-year career, she began to seriously think about retiring. As the president came down the steps, she started to daydream, just for a moment. Maybe it was time to buy that boat after all, sail the Caribbean, and do a whole lot of drinking.

Sanchez suddenly cursed herself for losing focus. Retirement was a topic for another time. Today she had to stay sharp.

"I'm scrapping the motorcade, Mr. President," Sanchez said before MacPherson even greeted her. "I'm putting you on *Marine One*."

MacPherson nodded. It didn't matter to him one way or the other. But White House Chief of Staff Bob Corsetti went ballistic.

"Are you kidding me?" he shouted as he bounded down the steps of *Air Force One* and caught up with the president. "We're going with the motorcade. We agreed on that as early as this morning."

"Things have changed, Mr. Corsetti," Sanchez explained.

Corsetti swore. His face was turning red. "We need the TV pictures," he insisted. "We need the pomp and circumstance. Or do I have to remind you what a close race this is and how carefully I've orchestrated every moment."

"Can't do it, sir; I'm sorry," Sanchez countered. "We've got a credible threat."

"Circumstantial at best, from what I'm hearing," Corsetti said.

"We can't afford to be wrong," Sanchez replied. "The route to Staples Center takes twenty-one minutes by motorcade. By air, I can have the president there in less than six. It's really not negotiable, Mr. Corsetti."

The chief of staff stepped in front of the president and got in Sanchez's face. "Look, I fully appreciate you've got a job to do," he began, "but so do I. Getting my party elected again. Two months ago, Governor Jackson was nine points up. Now Senator Martinez has closed the gap to less than three points. I need the president out there. I need him looking presidential. I need him sucking up all the oxygen in the political universe. I need wall-to-wall television coverage. And I need it now."

Sanchez stared back into Corsetti's eyes, then turned to MacPherson and said, "Mr. President, I'm not basing my decisions on polls. The Legion wants you dead, pure and simple. They want American power and prestige neutralized. We have every reason to believe they will stop at nothing to accomplish their objectives. And honestly, sir, if I were trying to take you out, I'd strike today, with a billion people watching. Even if you survive, the country panics. The markets are rattled. Oil prices spike again. The global economy shudders. And with all due respect, sir, what if you don't survive?"

The hangar was silent for a moment, save for the jet engines of the Boeing winding down and the Lockheed Martin VH-71 revving up. But Corsetti wasn't taking the bait.

"You do your job, Director, and we'll be fine. But if you don't let me do mine, Elena Martinez is going to be the next president of the United States. You want that? She's going to cut and run from the Middle East. She's going to let the U.N. seize control of U.S. foreign policy. She doesn't have the foggiest idea how to stop China from terrorizing Taiwan. She has no idea how to stare down the North Koreans. And her approach to the Israelis? Don't even get me started."

"Mr. Corsetti, none of those are my concerns, and you know it," Sanchez replied. "I've done everything I can to make this motorcade route safe. But given the latest intel, I can't in good conscience put the president on the 105 and the 110 for the next twenty-one minutes in broad daylight with a credible threat of an imminent terrorist attack when I could have him in a secure holding room under Staples Center in precisely seven minutes. Now with all due respect, it's time to get the president onto *Marine One*. That's final. Let's move."

Sanchez could see Corsetti trying to muster another argument, but they both knew it was pointless. Not a single voter really cared how the president got to the GOP convention site. A billion people wouldn't be watching the motorcade or the helicopter flight. They wouldn't be tuning in until the president's speech began at precisely 6:07 p.m. Pacific Standard Time, or 9:07 p.m. Eastern—a little more than one hour from now.

"That's fine, Jackie," MacPherson interceded. "Do what you need to do."

Corsetti shook his head and took an incoming call on his cell phone.

"Thank you, Mr. President," Sanchez said, then spoke into her wrist-mounted microphone: "We're a go. I repeat, we're a go. Gambit's moving."

6

★ ★
★

Bennett scanned the emergency room.

It was empty. He took a seat in the waiting room, closed his eyes, and felt a gnawing, wrenching pain rising from deep inside his stomach. Grief was clawing its way to the surface, and with it the terrible realization that in the next few minutes or hours—short of a miracle—he might be utterly and completely alone.

His father was dead. His mother lived half a world away. He had no brothers or sisters. His mentor had been gunned down on the road to Jerusalem eight months before. Most of his closest friends and colleagues had been killed over the past few years, often in front of him. And Erin was teetering on the brink of eternity, a heartbeat away from joining them and leaving him behind.

Was this it? Was this his destiny—to be all by himself in the universe, until the Lord came to take him home? He knew the Scriptures. He knew Jesus said He would never leave him nor forsake him. But at this moment, life seemed terribly cruel.

Bennett tried to push such thoughts away, but they refused to leave. They clung to him, haunted him.

He'd never remarry. There wasn't time. The Rapture, he was certain, was imminent. Any moment, he and millions of believers like him would disappear from the earth, in the blink of an eye, to be with Christ for eternity, and then the end would come. But what if the Lord in His sovereignty chose to kick the prophetic can down the road a couple of months or even years? What if the Rapture was years away, or decades, or longer? Bennett knew he would never find someone else like Erin. How could he? It had taken them long enough to find each other, and now he wanted to be together for eternity.

"Till death do us part" wasn't enough for Jonathan Meyers Bennett. He wanted Erin Christina McCoy forever. They were no longer two separate people leading two separate lives. They were no longer simply best friends, walking the road of life side by side. Somehow in the last few months, he and Erin had fused together into one body, one soul, one spirit. It was a mystery. It was magic. It might sound corny to some, but it was true. And in that moment, Bennett knew that if Erin died tonight, he would not be long for this world. He simply could not survive without her. He wasn't being melodramatic. He couldn't explain it. He couldn't prove it. He just knew it.

Some people could endure the death of a spouse and go on to lead normal, healthy lives. He just wasn't one of them. Erin was, quite simply, the oxygen that sustained him, and he could already feel himself beginning to suffocate.

"*Sir . . . hello . . . can you hear me?*"

The voice startled him. Bennett opened his eyes and was surprised by the sight of a hospital administrator of some sort staring down at him. She was a large, severe-looking woman with gray hair pulled back in a bun and dark, joyless eyes fixed on the clipboard in her hands, not on him.

"I must ask you questions," she said without emotion, without compassion, in a heavy Italian accent.

"My wife," Bennett replied. "I want to see my wife."

"Later," the woman said. "Now I ask questions."

It was late. Bennett was exhausted. He was worried. He had no desire to answer a bunch of ridiculous questions for some U.N. bureaucracy or compassionless insurance company that would never pay out the trillions already claimed by the region's survivors, much less by new victims of the Day of Devastation. Millions had died from the earthquake, the pestilence, the hailstorms, and the firestorms that came just as Ezekiel had foretold more than 2,500 years before. Nearly a year later, pandemics such as the avian flu and Ebola were still claiming the lives of hundreds every day, thousands every month.

Was Erin about to be next? As careful as they had both been, had she somehow contracted one of those deadly diseases?

Ebola-Zaire was the one he worried about most. Tens of thousands of birds from Africa had come to Lebanon, Syria, and Jordan after the War of Gog and Magog. As the Bible predicted, they had feasted on the bodies of those slain during the judgment. They had brought the dreaded avian flu, to be sure. But that was not all. Bennett knew from searching various Web sites that Ebola-Zaire had the highest mortality rate of any Ebola strain, killing as many as nine in ten of its victims. There had been more outbreaks of the Ebola-Zaire strain than any other Ebola virus, and once you had it, that was it. You were finished.

The Wikipedia article Bennett had read had been particularly disturbing. The first Ebola-Zaire case was recorded in 1976, in Yambuku, a town in northern Zaire. The man's name was Mabalo Lokela. He was a forty-four-year-old schoolteacher whose high fever had initially been diagnosed and treated as malaria. A week later, his symptoms had included uncontrolled vomiting, bloody diarrhea, headache, dizziness, and labored breathing. Soon after, he had begun bleeding from his nose and mouth.

Fourteen days later, Mabalo Lokela was dead.

Bennett had seen firsthand the carnage wrought by Ebola-Zaire. So had Erin. Dozens had died these slow, cruel deaths in this camp alone. In southern Lebanon and in parts of Damascus, the virus was taking the lives of untold thousands. Neither Jon nor Erin was directly involved in any care or treatment for such victims. Rather, they served on a team that cooked and distributed the meals the refugees were given each day—at eight o'clock every morning, at one in the afternoon, and at six in the evening.

They had been briefed by the medical staff on the risks they were taking. They knew what to look for and what to avoid. They had taken every precaution. They had been given every possible vaccine. They wore plastic gloves and surgical masks and ate only the food flown in from Europe every week for them and the rest of the camp staff.

But anything was possible in such an environment, and as he remembered those grim warnings from their first day in the camp, Bennett's fears began to grow again and a flood of emotions forced its way to the surface.

"Name?" the administrator demanded. "I need full name."

7

★ ★
★

On approach to Staples Center, Corsetti's phone rang.

He checked the caller ID on his secure satellite phone and found it was Secretary James from the Department of Homeland Security. His stomach tightened. "Hello?"

"Bob, it's Lee. I know you're extremely busy but Ken Costello and I need a minute," James said from his penthouse suite at the Hilton Boston, where he was staying the night. The national security advisor was patched in from the White House.

"Of course, Mr. Secretary," Corsetti replied. "What is it?"

"Ken, you start," James said.

"Sure," Costello said. "Look, Bob, I just got off the phone with the Canadian prime minister. His intelligence services have informed him that three so-called security officers at the Chinese embassy in Ottawa have been missing for a week."

"And?" Corsetti asked, checking his watch.

"And our border patrol just picked up one of them trying to cross from Niagara Falls into Buffalo. During his interrogation, he said his colleagues left for Los Angeles several days ago. They were supposedly coming in on a flight from Montreal to Seattle, using fake passports. He claims he doesn't know if they got in or not and says they weren't supposed to have any contact until they were 'in place.'"

"In place?" Corsetti repeated. "What does that mean?"

"That's just it; we don't know, Bob," Secretary James interjected. "Nor does the Canadian PM. But given what's going on, Ken and I just called Jackie Sanchez, and then Scott Harris at the Bureau and Danny Tracker over at Langley. They all thought you and the president would want to know. And there's something else, as well."

"What's that?" Corsetti asked.

"We're not entirely sure what to make of it," the secretary explained, "but our embassy in Caracas says *Radio Nacional de Venezuela* has been running a series of talk shows for the last several days discussing the topic 'Preparing for a world without MacPherson.' Our political officers had initially written it off as election year hyperventilating. But today they reviewed the full transcripts. The talk was pretty violent, and one guest—a former Venezuelan interior minister under Chávez—suggested that those who hated the United States should just be patient. Quote: *'You'll be hearing good news out of Washington and Los Angeles soon enough.'* Might be nothing. But given the rest of the chatter coming in, I thought I should pass it on."

Marine One was now on the ground, the Secret Service detail was in place, and President MacPherson—code-named "Gambit"—was already out the door.

Corsetti grabbed his suit jacket and briefcase and stepped off the chopper. "Gentlemen, I'm afraid I've got to go," he shouted over the roar of the rotors. "But I appreciate this, and I'll pass it along to the president when he's got a moment. Tell your teams the president is incredibly grateful for their service. Especially tonight. He's got every confidence in you all. Let's not let him down."

Corsetti hung up the phone and clipped it back on his belt. Then he put on his security badge and stepped into a side door of the convention center. But as hard has he tried, he couldn't shake the feeling that maybe Sanchez was right. Maybe he should be worried. Maybe this was the real thing.

☆　☆　☆

"Age?"

"Forty-four," he said, then corrected himself. "No, forty-five."

"And your wife?"

Bennett had to hold his hands together to keep them from shaking. "Thirty-six."

"Nationality?"

"American."

"Both of you?"

"Yes."

Bennett thought he saw the woman roll her eyes, and it made him angry. It wasn't the first time he'd seen it happen. Despite the fact that the U.S. was pouring billions upon billions of dollars into the U.N. humanitarian relief effort—into these refugee camps in particular—and into the overall recovery and reconstruction effort, it was clear that anti-American sentiment was on the rise. It wasn't just here in this refugee camp. It was happening throughout the region. You could see it in the new graffiti on the walls and sides of buses. You could see it on news shows and hear it in more and more comments on the radio. You could read it in the editorials, and occasionally you'd see or hear about an anti-American protest that broke out on some university campus, often in Beirut or Cairo but sometimes even in Amman and what was left of Istanbul.

It made Bennett's blood boil, for it wasn't just their treasures that Americans were donating to care for millions of wounded and displaced families throughout the region. Tens of thousands of Americans had come to the region to volunteer their time and talents as well. They brought expertise as doctors, nurses, pilots, truck drivers, general contractors, and so forth to help where they could. Many who had come to help were young people, in their teens and twenties. They formed a rapidly growing team of evangelical Christians and Catholics known as the "Passion for Compassion" movement.

It wasn't only Americans coming to help, of course. Thousands of South Korean and Australian believers had come as well, as had many Chinese, Indonesians, Filipinos, Indians, and others, many of whom had come to faith in Christ since Ezekiel's War. But thus far, the simple fact was that the vast majority of dollars and volunteers came from the U.S., and more often than not, Bennett couldn't resist getting into an argument with whoever thought his country wasn't doing enough.

But not tonight. This was neither the time nor the place. Besides, he knew he hadn't the emotional bandwidth to argue with anyone, least of all a U.N. hospital administrator. All he wanted to know was, how soon could he go into the examination room? How soon could he see his wife? How soon could he touch her face and hold her hand? Nothing else mattered to Bennett. Certainly not this woman's political beliefs and prejudices.

Yet rather than answers, all he got were more questions. The woman droned on and on. Bennett answered the best he could. Yes, he and Erin had gotten all their vaccinations before coming. No, they had no allergies they were aware of. Yes, Erin was on a prescription medication—Percocet, to manage the pain from a gunshot wound in her leg. No, Bennett wasn't going to explain further; it was all on their volunteer applications. Yes, they'd signed the releases upon arrival. Yes, they only ate food served in the camp's mess tents. No, they had not left the camp since they'd arrived. Well, one time, for the Fourth of July weekend. They'd visited friends at a church in Amman. No, he couldn't remember precisely how long they'd been in Jordan. "Six, seven months," Bennett said. "Something like that."

"Well, which?" the administrator pressed, her voice thick with derision. "Six or seven?"

Bennett told himself to stay calm. It was all he could do not to push this overweight monstrosity out of the way, kick in the door of the examination room, and demand to know what was going on with his wife. But the last thing he needed was to get tossed out by security. So he took a deep breath, looked her square in the eye, and said, "Actually, come to think of it, we've been here seven months. We came in February, soon after we got married. . . ." His voice trailed off.

He was tempted to add, ". . . *and discovered the Temple treasures and the Ark of the Covenant and received a medal of honor from the prime minister of Israel* . . ." But again, he let it go. This woman didn't care. Why prolong the discussion?

"So why did you come here?" the woman asked, matter-of-factly.

Bennett looked up. That one surprised him. *Was that an official question, or a personal one?* he wondered. He noticed the woman was no longer staring at her clipboard. She was actually staring into his eyes. She seemed genuinely curious, even bewildered. For her, this was a job. He noticed that the ID hanging around her neck said she had worked for UNRWA—the United Nations Relief and Works Agency—since 1987.

But why was he here?

It was a good question. What *had* compelled him and Erin to come here of all places, and now of all times in their lives? What *had* compelled them to invest twenty-one of the twenty-two million dollars he'd made on Wall Street caring for those Syrian and Lebanese and Iranian refugees, many of whom had long been enemies of America and Israel and the West, certainly for as long as he could remember?

The woman deserved an honest answer. Bennett knew he should say something. But the words would not come. He wasn't proud of it, but he simply had no desire to talk. Not here. Not now. All he wanted to do was be with Erin. That was it. That was all. And he was fast running out of patience.

Instead of replying, he asked, "Are we done here?"

The woman stared at him in disbelief, then got up quickly and left.

A wave of guilt washed over Bennett. And then, all of a sudden, it was followed by a fresh wave of fear. Something terrible was about to happen. He could sense it. He could feel it. And there didn't seem to be anything he could do about it.

8
★ ★
★

It was almost time.

The president had been reviewing the latest draft of his speech, but now Bob Corsetti slipped him a handwritten note that read, "Nine minutes."

MacPherson nodded, scribbled down a few last changes, handed the speech to an aide, and asked her to make sure the corrections were quickly entered into the teleprompter. Then he took the phone Corsetti handed him and joined a hastily arranged conference call of his National Security Council. More troubling intel was coming in, and the NSC was insisting on a quick conversation with the president.

As the president picked up, Corsetti slipped another sheet of White House stationery into his hands, listing the names of everyone on the call. These included Vice President William Oaks, from his summer home in Jacksonville, Florida; Homeland Security Secretary Lee James, from his hotel room in Boston; CIA Director Danny Tracker, from his office at Langley; FBI Director Scott Harris, from his car en route to Washington from Quantico; National Security Advisor Ken Costello, from the White House Situation Room; Secretary of State Marsha Kirkpatrick, from her office at Foggy Bottom; and Secret Service Director Jackie Sanchez, who was sitting with the president in the secure holding room underneath the main convention hall.

Corsetti picked up a second line and moderated the call. "Ladies and gentlemen, we don't have much time, as you know. But over the past hour or so, we've had some fast-moving developments, and I know several of you wanted to brief the president before his speech—"

"Excuse me, Bob," MacPherson cut in. "Where's Burt Trainor?"

"The SecDef is flying back from Japan," Corsetti explained. "They're having some communications problems on his plane at the moment. The air force is certain they'll have the issue resolved shortly, and he'll join us as soon as he can."

"Fine," the president said. "Let's just make this quick."

"Yes, sir," Corsetti continued. "Ken, why don't you start—just keep it tight."

"Thanks, Bob," Costello said. "Mr. President, at present we believe there are at least four, possibly five, high-value targets converging on the Los Angeles area. These are men suspected of being involved with terrorist organizations—some in Asia, some in Latin America. We believe each of them poses a clear and present danger to U.S. national security."

"Do you have any idea what they're planning?" the president asked.

"No, sir," Costello said. "Nor are we certain that their movements are necessarily connected, much less coordinated, but it seems likely that they are."

"And you're certain they are in or near Los Angeles?"

"It would appear that way, Mr. President," Costello confirmed, "though we don't have a specific location on any of them."

"How solid is the intelligence?" MacPherson pressed. "Is it all from Yemen?"

"No, sir," Costello explained. "In the last few hours, intelligence directors from three friendly countries—Canada, Mexico, and Great Britain—have contacted us to share specific, credible information gleaned from a variety of human sources and telephonic and electronic intercepts."

"Mr. President, this is Scott Harris at FBI."

"Yes, Scott?"

"None of the intel directors knew the others were calling us. Yet all of their leads point to L.A., and all three calls came in today."

"And you think someone's trying to take me out," MacPherson clarified.

"That's a real possibility, sir," Harris confirmed. "You or Governor Jackson."

"What else?" the president asked, glancing at his watch.

"Mr. President, it's Marsha at State."

"Go ahead, Marsha."

"It's unrelated to this developing terrorist threat, but there's something else you need to know about," Kirkpatrick explained.

"Make it quick."

"Well, Mr. President," the secretary of state continued, "it appears, in the wake of all the devastation that has taken place in Turkey, Iran, and the Caucasus, that Kurdish leaders in southern Turkey are planning to declare independence tomorrow and announce the formation of their own sovereign state."

MacPherson turned to Corsetti, who looked as shocked as he was. "Madame Secretary, please tell me you're kidding."

"I'm afraid not, sir," Kirkpatrick explained. "I just got word a few minutes ago. What's more, we're also hearing that the Kurdish province in northern Iraq is apparently planning to secede and join the new Kurdish state."

"What will that do to the upcoming state visit?" the president asked.

"President Al-Hassani is absolutely livid, as you can imagine," the SecState replied. "I just got off the phone with Khalid Tariq, his chief of staff. He's threatening to call the whole trip off if we don't intervene. Tariq says Al-Hassani is mobilizing his military and threatening to send 150,000 troops into Kurdistan in the next forty-eight hours. What's more, he even hinted at a possible oil embargo against us if we were to recognize the new Kurdish state."

MacPherson winced. That was all he needed in an election—oil prices spiking yet again, and gas and airline fuel prices with them.

"So what does the esteemed leader of Iraq want from me?" he asked, realizing his whole night was about to be consumed with another Mideast crisis.

"Tariq says they want you to send an unambiguous message to the Kurds that any attempt to create their own state or secede from Iraq will be met with an international economic embargo," Secretary Kirkpatrick explained. "They want you to vow not to recognize an independent

Kurdistan in any way, shape, or form, and they want you to call Secretary-General Lucente personally and demand a U.N. Security Council resolution condemning any such move by the Kurds under the terms of Chapter Seven."

MacPherson glanced at Corsetti again. "The Iraqi president wants the world to go to war to stop the Kurds from declaring independence?"

"Either that or Iraq will," Kirkpatrick said. "Tariq put it this way, sir: 'Don't make us take matters into our own hands.'"

The White House operator now beeped onto the line to announce the arrival of Defense Secretary Burt Trainor.

"Welcome, Mr. Secretary," MacPherson said. "Please tell me you have some good news."

"I'm afraid not, Mr. President," the SecDef replied. "As you know, I've been meeting with senior defense and intelligence officials in Tokyo and Seoul. They tell me in the past few weeks they've been picking up disturbing signs that the North Koreans might be preparing for an invasion of the south."

"Has the DPRK begun moving troops?" MacPherson asked.

"No, no, not yet," Trainor was quick to clarify. "But they have canceled all military leaves. They're pre-positioning additional fuel, food, medicine, and other supplies to forward areas. We're seeing increased activity around missile sites and air bases. I'm transmitting a memo to *Air Force One*, laying out many of the specifics and suggesting several possible reasons for all this heightened activity."

"Does Pyongyang have any planned military exercises coming up?" the president wondered aloud.

"Nothing official, not until early next year," Trainor responded. "But two days ago NSA intercepted a telephone call from a North Korean general to the Chinese ministry of defense saying there might be 'new activity' soon near the DMZ."

"'New activity'?" the president asked. "As in war?"

"War games, we're hoping, but honestly, sir, we don't really know."

"What's your best guess, Mr. Secretary?"

Trainor paused for a moment. Corsetti, meanwhile, slipped the president another note: "Two minutes."

"To be perfectly candid, Mr. President," Trainor now answered, "I'm worried because the Japanese and South Koreans are worried. And make no mistake, Mr. President, these guys are very worried."

"What do they want?"

"They want you to order a carrier battle group to steam through the Sea of Japan immediately—this week, tomorrow, if you can," Trainor replied. "They want more Patriot missile batteries. They want you, or Secretary Kirkpatrick, to make a strong public statement in the next twenty-four hours reaffirming the U.S.'s commitment to a free and secure Pacific Rim. And during your summit with Al-Hassani next week—if there is still a summit, if the Kurds haven't just blown up that summit—they want you to press the Iraqi leader to get oil prices under $100 a barrel as quickly as possible, even if that means putting pressure on Israel to slow down on the Temple. They say their economies simply can't survive for long the way we're going, and they're looking for you to bail them out."

MacPherson took a deep breath. He wasn't going to miss this job. He really had no idea who was going to replace him—California governor Paul Jackson, the Republican whom he had recently and enthusiastically endorsed, or Illinois senator Elena Martinez, who seemed to hate his guts and loved to say essentially as much as often as she had the chance. The race couldn't be tighter. Both desperately wanted the job and were pulling no punches to get it. But on days like this he wondered if Jackson and Martinez really had any idea what they were getting themselves into.

A new terror threat in Los Angeles. The rapidly rising China threat in the Pacific. Rumors of another war brewing in the Middle East. A possible nuclear showdown on the Korean peninsula. A global economic recession teetering on the brink of an outright depression. A world still trying to recover from the Day of Devastation. The Jews rebuilding their Temple. The Arabs rebuilding Babylon. And an American people deeply divided over how to handle all of it. MacPherson found himself glad he was constitutionally barred from running again. He had done his job. He was proud of what he had accomplished. But now he was exhausted and ready to hand over the baton.

"Look, I need to go," he said, standing up and preparing to head to the convention floor. "Let's reconvene at 9 p.m., my time. I'll be back on *Air Force One* by then. We'll do a videoconference. I want a briefing from each of you, including specific recommendations for handling Al-Hassani and the North Koreans. And, Bill, you still there?"

"Yes, sir," Vice President Oaks said. "How can I help?"

"When are you speaking here?" MacPherson asked.

"Wednesday night, Mr. President."

"Doing the network morning shows on Thursday, as well?"

"Yes, sir, and some radio, too."

"Fine," MacPherson said, "then make plans to meet me at Camp David Thursday night. We should have some more solid intel on all this by then. We can watch Governor Jackson's speech together and review the polls. And we can talk about Al-Hassani's upcoming visit and where Salvador Lucente fits into this whole picture. I don't have a good feeling about where this is headed, and I'd like your input."

"Absolutely, Mr. President," the VP agreed. "I'll see you then."

MacPherson thanked everyone, signed off the call, stood slowly, moved to the door, and then paused. He tried to shake off the gloom of the call, but it wasn't going to be easy. Twenty thousand delegates on the floor above screamed, *Four more years! Four more years! Four more years!*

They had no idea what even the next four weeks held. Neither did MacPherson, and it chilled him to his core.

9

★ ★
★

The desert sun wouldn't rise for another hour.

Yet somehow it remained unseasonably hot. The air was unusually thick with humidity. Storm clouds were rolling in, and Bennett could hear thunder rumbling in the distance. He could feel his shirt drenched in sweat. He could smell his fear, rising by the minute. He half assumed the nurse or guard could hear his heart, pounding relentlessly in his chest. One thing was for sure: he couldn't take much more of this.

In less than four hours he was supposed to be back at his post, unloading newly arrived U.N. trucks filled with food supplies and then helping to make, serve, and clean up after breakfast for five thousand desperate souls. Would he have any answers by then? He had to. But what if they were not the answers he wanted?

Bennett walked over to the head nurse on duty.

"Sorry to bother you again," he said as politely as he could. "I'm just wondering if you could check with the doctor and see how much longer it's going to be?"

He could see a bit of empathy in her eyes this time, but the answer was the same.

"I'm sorry, Mr. Bennett. I really am. But there's nothing I can do right now."

Bennett gritted his teeth and turned away.

☆ ☆ ☆

The president was about to take the stage.

Jackie Sanchez paced the Secret Service command center, desperately hoping she and her team hadn't missed a thing. All the data suggested a hit was coming. *But how? From where? And from whom?*

As far as she could tell, they had every angle covered. She was confident that the only firearms in the convention center were those held by her special agents and counterassault teams and by the local police providing crowd control—all of whose credentials, fingerprints, and retinal scans had been double- and triple-checked just hours before. And her bomb squads had scanned every inch of the premises and found nothing.

More than one hundred electronic air-quality monitors had been strategically positioned throughout the building and on the grounds, continuously checking for any whiff of a dangerous radiological, biological, or chemical substance. Plainclothes agents with handheld monitors were roaming the crowds and the corridors. Thus far, nothing troublesome had been detected, but the Energy Department's elite Nuclear Emergency Support Team was on hand just in case, and members of the army's NBC fast-reaction team—specialists in handling nuclear, biological, and chemical attacks—were on standby, as were all local emergency first responders.

No food was being served on the premises, and the president wasn't going to be eating anything anyway. His bottled water had been specially flown in on *Air Force One*, tested by Secret Service technicians in Washington and again on-site. The president was not staying overnight, but a backup hotel twenty miles away had been fully secured, just in case. The president's blood type had been stocked at three local hospitals. All air traffic over the Los Angeles area had been shut down until a full hour after *Air Force One* lifted off later that evening, and F-16s fully armed with Sidewinder air-to-air missiles not only were flying combat air patrols over the city but would be escorting the president all the way back to Andrews Air Force Base in Maryland.

Sanchez now carefully examined the images on each of the three dozen video monitors in front of her, showing live feeds from surveillance cameras trained on every key checkpoint in and around Staples Center and the surrounding parking lots, as well as from reconnaissance helicopters circling overhead. She reviewed the latest flash traffic reports from USSS headquarters in Washington and the latest threat condition intel from the FBI, CIA, and Homeland Security.

Suddenly the convention stage manager reported in over his Nextel two-way phone. "Sixty seconds, ma'am."

☆ ☆ ☆

Bennett had been tempted.

He could still picture Erin and himself dining by candlelight back on January 14 in La Regence, the five-star restaurant in the King David Hotel in Jerusalem. Their host was E.U. foreign minister Salvador Lucente. They had already left their posts with the CIA and White House, respectively. Now Lucente was offering them both a chance to work for him when he moved over to the U.N. They would not be junior players. They would be senior advisors to the secretary-general, helping hammer out a treaty of historic proportions. It would not, Lucente insisted, simply be an accord between the Israelis and Palestinians—that was almost finished already—but a full and comprehensive peace agreement between Israel and Iraq.

Should he do it? Despite the danger, Bennett had loved his role as "point man for peace" in the MacPherson administration. His favorite verse of Scripture was Matthew 5:9, "Blessed are the peacemakers, for they shall be called sons of God."

It was Erin who had insisted they stay off the political bullet train. She wanted to serve in a refugee camp somewhere in the epicenter. As far away from Wall Street as possible. As far away from the White House as possible. Far even from the horse country of rural Virginia that Erin loved so dearly, where they'd been married and hoped to settle down. It was she who had suggested that they spend the first year of their married life here in northern Jordan. To feed the hungry. To comfort the sick. To make a difference. To be a blessing in the time they had left, however brief that might be.

When that simple truth finally dawned on him, Bennett resolved in his heart to stop second-guessing what they'd done. Erin had long ago decided she was willing to die for what she believed in. It wasn't that she wanted to die, but she was willing to, if that's what God asked of her. That was what gave her the courage to join the CIA. It was what gave her the courage to serve the president in the line of fire. It was also what gave her the courage to come here, to this place, at this time. If she was willing to sacrifice everything to love her neighbors, and her enemies, Bennett didn't want to do anything to get in her way. He just wished he'd had the spiritual maturity to come up with the idea in the first place.

Bennett's phone suddenly rang.

His heart leaped. Perhaps it was good news about Erin. But no one needed to call him. He was standing less than ten feet from Erin's room. He pulled the phone from his pocket and glanced at the caller ID.

Odd, he thought. There was no name, no incoming number. Then again, his own number was unlisted too. He'd given it out to only a handful of close friends and family members, so he wasn't worried. He should have been.

★   ★   ★

This was it, Sanchez thought as she readied her team.

She pressed her wrist-mounted microphone and relayed the word over secure channels to every agent on the president's detail.

"Heads up, everyone. We're sixty seconds out. I want a final sector check. Recon One?"

"Recon One, clear."

"Recon Two?"

"Recon Two is clear."

"NEST?"

"NEST is all clear."

"Snapshot One?"

"We're good."

"Sector Two?"

"Sector Two—we're good to go, Home Plate."

And so it went until Sanchez was satisfied that every *i* had been dotted and every *t* had been crossed. There was nothing more she could do but trust her team and her instincts and say a prayer that they all got through the night alive and in one piece.

*   *   *

"Hello?" Bennett said, pressing the phone to his ear.

"Is this Jonathan Bennett?" said the electronically altered voice at the other end of the line.

"Who is this?" Bennett replied, refusing to confirm anything until the caller identified himself.

"Listen carefully," the voice said. "Something terrible is about to happen. I had nothing to do with it. I cannot stop it. But I know it is coming, and I can assure you it is only the beginning. Much worse is coming as well. But those I can stop . . . if you'll help me."

Bennett knew instantly that this was not a game. Something in the voice convinced him this was deadly serious, though when he asked for details, he was refused.

"You will see what I am speaking about soon enough," he was told. "I will call you back within twenty-four hours. Then you'll have a decision to make. Help me stop what's coming next, or suffer the consequences."

Click.

That was it. The call went dead.

Just then, before Bennett could process any of it, he heard the door of the examining room open. He glanced up to see two doctors—both looking weary and war-torn—emerge from his wife's room and catch his eye. One nodded, then quickly headed off down a side hallway. Bennett held his breath as the other physician, the older of the two, made his way over and sat down at his side.

"Mr. Bennett?"

"Yes, sir," Bennett replied, his mind reeling. "How is she? Will she be okay?"

10

★ ★
★

"Ladies and gentlemen, the president of the United States."

MacPherson stood just offstage and listened as "Hail to the Chief" began to play and the capacity crowd of 22,197 leaped to their feet and began cheering and applauding with a passion and intensity that brought a lump to his throat.

These had been the toughest eight years of his life. Growing up, he had never imagined running for president, much less winning not once but twice. He had certainly never imagined being president through such trying times. His decisions hadn't always been right. He had often had to work with imperfect and incomplete information. But he had done his best. He had tried to protect the American people from a global jihadist threat his parents and grandparents could not have comprehended. He had second-guessed himself many times. He knew in the end he had no one to blame for his mistakes but himself. But now the atmosphere in this room was electric. The base of his party, at least, loved him, and MacPherson couldn't help himself. He closed his eyes for a moment and drank it all in.

The pause only heightened the drama, and with it the intensity of the crowd's reaction. The longer he remained out of view, the more they wanted him. The more they wanted him, the longer he stayed out of view. He waited, and waited a bit longer, and paused still a bit longer until the roar built to a crescendo. And then, when he—and they—could stand it no longer, James "Mac" MacPherson stepped out from behind the presidential blue curtains into the glare of the TV lights and a roar more deafening than anything he had ever experienced before.

It was showtime. And for him, it was the last time. And he had something burning in his soul to tell his supporters, his nation, and the world.

Something that simply couldn't wait.

☆　☆　☆

"Mr. Bennett, my name is Dr. Kwamee. I'm from Ghana."

Bennett nodded impatiently as the man reviewed a folder of notes and charts in his hands.

"I've been caring for your wife, as you know, for the past several hours," the doctor continued. "We've been having a particularly difficult time getting her fever down. Even now, it's still 103. She's very dehydrated. I see from the nurse's notes that you said she hadn't been eating or drinking much over the past week or so. Is that right?"

"No—I mean, yes—that's right," Bennett stammered. "She's had trouble keeping anything down."

"You should have brought her in earlier," the doctor admonished. "We're always stressing around the camp the critical importance of drinking enough fluids. This is why. It's difficult enough to fight off a disease when you're otherwise perfectly healthy. But if your body doesn't have the fluids and nutrients it needs, then I'm afraid everything becomes much more complicated."

Was this his fault? He had urged Erin to visit the clinic several days ago. She'd waved him off. *Should he have insisted?*

"We've got her on an IV at the moment," the doctor continued. "We've given her various medications to combat pain and fight off infection."

Bennett couldn't take it any longer. He had to know. "Dr. Kwamee, what *exactly* does my wife have? Do you know for sure?"

"Not entirely," the doctor replied. "We're still running blood tests. For the moment, we've identified two issues, and one is compounding and complicating the other. But I want to be clear with you, Mr. Bennett. We're living in a petri dish here in this camp and in this region. We're dealing with challenges we've never seen before, on a scale never before imagined by the medical community. All I'm saying is that there could be more issues than what we've identified so far. We won't know for certain for another few days, until all the blood work is completed."

For crying out loud, Bennett screamed inwardly, *get on with it*. It was all he could do not to grab Dr. Kwamee by the lapels and shake him until he cut to the chase.

The man now took a deep breath and set down his notes. "To begin with, your wife has a severe case of bacterial meningitis," he said quietly. "The truth is, she's lucky to be alive."

Bennett tried to stay calm. He had a flood of questions but no idea where to start. His expression apparently conveyed as much, and Dr. Kwamee continued.

"*Streptococcus pneumoniae*—or pneumococcus—is a bacteria that can cause meningitis, a very serious medical condition," he explained. "If not treated quickly and properly, the condition can be fatal. I will be frank with you, Mr. Bennett. For the first few hours, I had my doubts. It was touch and go for quite a while. It would have made all the difference in the world if you had brought her in a day or two earlier, but even so we may have caught this thing in time."

Another wave of guilt washed over Bennett. Could he have done more? Should he have rushed her to the clinic right from the beginning? Erin had begged him not to. She'd insisted she'd be fine. Should he have forced her to see a doctor?

"We have your wife on some aggressive antibiotics right now," the doctor went on. "I feel fairly confident we're going to see her fever come down over the next twenty-four hours, especially as we get her fluid levels back up. We'll know more then, but she will probably be fine, barring some unforeseen complication."

Bennett didn't like what he was hearing. *Fairly confident? Probably be fine? Unforeseen complications?* Those were hedges, not ringing votes of confidence.

"But you're sure she's going to be okay?" he pressed.

"I think so," Dr. Kwamee replied. "Almost definitely."

Bennett's stomach tightened. Language like that wasn't helping. "How long until she's back on her feet?" he asked.

"Assuming all goes well, I'd say the symptoms should last for about seven to ten days," Dr. Kwamee explained. "She's going to need a lot of bed rest. A lot of fluids. I'll give her something to manage the headaches and fight off the fever. But I'd say within two weeks she should pull out of this."

Two weeks? Bennett felt a lump forming in his throat. "What's the second issue?" he asked, not entirely sure he wanted to know.

"I have to be honest with you, Mr. Bennett," the doctor explained. "Given your wife's medical condition, it's not what I would have suspected."

"What?" Bennett asked. "Is it serious?"

"Yes, I'd have to say it is pretty serious," Dr. Kwamee replied.

"Just say it," Bennett insisted. "I have a right to know."

"That is true," the doctor said. "You do."

There was another long, unbearable pause, and then the doctor said, "Mr. Bennett, you and your wife are going to be parents."

Bennett froze. *What?* Had he heard the man right?

"You mean, Erin's . . ."

He was so stunned he couldn't finish the sentence, but Dr. Kwamee nodded anyway.

"She and I . . ."

The doctor nodded again.

"You're sure?" Bennett asked, incredulous.

"Positive," Dr. Kwamee assured him.

"But how? . . . When?"

"The how I'll leave to your own imagination," the doctor laughed. "As for when, sometime next May, it would seem."

Bennett did the math. Eight months. He and Erin were going to have a baby in eight months. He stared at the man in utter disbelief.

What he wanted to ask was, *"Does the world even have eight months?"*

What he actually asked was, "What about the meningitis?"

"I'm not sure about that quite yet. I suspect everything will be fine. I have no evidence that your baby won't be completely healthy. But I don't know for certain at the moment. We're going to have to monitor that, run some more tests. Like I said, I think we caught the problem in time. But the first trimester of any pregnancy, as I'm sure you are aware, is a very sensitive time, and the fact is we just won't know the impact that your wife's illness has had—or is going to have—on the baby for some time."

"Are we talking days or weeks?"

"One day at a time, Mr. Bennett," Dr. Kwamee said, looking him straight in the eye. "But we might not really know for certain until next spring when she delivers."

"Does she know yet?" Bennett asked.

"No, not yet," Dr. Kwamee said. "She's still sleeping."

Bennett took a deep breath. "May I see her?"

"Soon," the doctor replied, glancing at his watch. "Let's give her a few more hours. She's had a rough night."

Bennett thanked the doctor and then stepped away to collect his thoughts. His hands suddenly felt cold. His entire body began to shake. A torrent of emotions was forcing its way to the surface, and now a dam burst within him. He backed into a corner and in the shadows began to sob. He pleaded with God to forgive his lack of faith. He pleaded with Him to forgive his cynicism and fear. And he kept saying *thank you*, overwhelmed by grace he didn't deserve, favor he didn't merit, blessings he hadn't earned, love he had no idea how to reciprocate.

He felt so deeply unworthy. *Why him? Why now? Why had he been blessed with such an amazing woman of God? Why had they been chosen to serve together, in the eye of the storm, in history's last days?* None of it made any sense. It was too much, too fast, and Bennett suddenly found himself petrified at the thought of doing something or thinking something or saying something that would somehow bring shame and dishonor to the holy and precious name of Jesus, to the God who had rescued him from the small and worthless dreams he had once held so dear.

Lieutenant General Charlie Briggs was winding up a very long day.

A three-star with nearly three decades of service defending his country, Briggs had been the commander of NORAD—the North American Aerospace Defense Command—and U.S. Northern Command—more commonly known as USNORTHCOM—at Peterson Air Force Base in Colorado Springs for nearly three and a half years. No one on active duty had more experience in defending the American homeland than Charlie Briggs. But even as he heard the sirens go off in the Cheyenne Mountain Operations Center, all he could think was, Why had some knucklehead scheduled an exercise and not informed him?

Then came the words over the loudspeaker that stunned Briggs to his core.

"*Launch detection,*" the senior watch officer yelled. "*I have a launch detection just off the coast of Baltimore. This is not a drill. I repeat—this is not a drill.*"

Briggs jumped to his feet, bolted from his office, and reached the side of the watch officer just as the lieutenant colonel yelled, "*Strike that—I have two launch detections. I repeat, two launch detections—no, make that three—two off the coast of Baltimore, another off the coast of Vancouver, Canada.*"

All eyes were now fixed on the large-screen video monitors in front of them, showing the high-speed radar track of three unknown projectiles.

Briggs let out a string of expletives and then asked, "Are those from subs?"

"They can't be," the watch officer replied. "SUBLANT hasn't reported anything that close to the East Coast, and SUBPAC has been quiet for days," he noted, referring to the navy's submarine tracking systems in the Atlantic and Pacific, respectively.

"Then what the—?"

Briggs's naval liaison suddenly burst into the CMOC from a side room. "Container ships," he said breathlessly. "Someone's firing missiles—probably Scuds—off the back of commercial container ships."

"You're absolutely sure these aren't sub-launched?" Briggs pressed.

"Positive, sir," Briggs's deputy confirmed. "The speed, the trajectories—they're all wrong for a sub launch, sir. Those appear to be Scud C ballistic missiles, and I agree, sir—they do seem to be coming off the back of commercial container ships or frigates, sir."

It seemed impossible, Briggs thought, but unfortunately it wasn't. As far back as the Rumsfeld Commission report to Congress in the 1990s on the emerging ballistic missile threat to the United States, the possibility of an attack like this had been growing. Years before, Iran had tested firing high-speed, short-range, single-stage, tactical ballistic missiles off of ships. So had the North Koreans. But after the Day of Devastation, the prospect of such an attack seemed so implausible that Briggs could barely believe what his top advisors—and his own eyes—were telling him.

"Look there," his deputy insisted, pointing to the latest telemetry pouring into his computer monitor. "No question—those are Scuds."

"Range?" Briggs demanded.

"About six hundred kilometers, sir," the senior watch officer replied.

"Probable targets?"

"The computers are saying D.C. and Seattle, sir."

"How long until impact?" Briggs asked, realizing how long it had been since the first Gulf War, the last time he'd been Scud hunting. "Five, six minutes?"

"No, sir," said the watch officer, twenty years his junior. "Scud Cs only carry enough fuel for an eighty- to ninety-second burn. They're going to hit in less than two minutes. Guaranteed."

Briggs cursed again. This could not be happening. Not on his watch.

It had been a while since he had brushed up on the specifications of a Scud C ballistic missile. But one thing he knew for sure: they could carry quite a payload. So what were these two carrying—conventional high explosives or eighty-kiloton nuclear warheads? They were about to find out, and fast.

He immediately ordered his staff to alert the Pentagon, Homeland Security, and the Coast Guard and to get him an open line with the Secret Service. They were going to DefCon One. They were going to war, but with whom? He had no idea.

And then it happened again.

"Sir, we have another launch detection," the watch officer shouted.

"Where?"

"Just off the Port of Newark, sir."

"Probable target?"

"Manhattan."

"Time to impact?"

"Sixty seconds, if that."

Briggs and his team were in a state of shock. All of them knew the terrible truth, but none of them dared say it aloud. They could alert anyone and everyone, as many as they had time for. But that was all they could do. They had no ability to stop the missiles. The U.S. had no defenses against short-range ballistic missiles fired so close to her coastlines. They certainly didn't have the capacity to evacuate Washington, New York, or Seattle, even if they'd had days, not seconds. These missiles were going to strike. Millions were going to die. And all they could do was watch.

"We have another launch detection," the senior watch officer yelled. *"I repeat, we have a fifth missile launch."*

Not again, Briggs thought. *How was it possible? How many more were coming? And who was launching them in the first place?*

"Where's this one coming from?" Briggs demanded.

"About a hundred kilometers west-southwest of Long Beach, sir."

"Probable target?"

"Everything in Southern California is probably in range, sir," the officer replied.

It was a true statement, as far as it went. But Briggs knew instantly what NORAD's supercomputers were going to tell him in another few seconds. The point of impact was going to be Staples Center. The Republican National Convention. Someone was gunning for the president of the United States.

And then Briggs noticed that the flight path of this fifth missile was radically different from the others. Rather than gaining altitude over Los Angeles in a classic ballistic arc, the missile was rapidly descending toward the water.

"That's not a Scud," he said as the missile leveled off.

As he stared, mesmerized, at the radar track, he could see the incoming projectile skimming the water, just eight to ten feet off the ocean's surface and racing inland at twice the speed of sound.

"Then what is it?" the senior watch officer asked, looking on in horror.

"A death sentence," Briggs said quietly.

The cold, hard truth was becoming clearer with each passing second. They were watching a highly coordinated decapitation strike, aimed at taking out the entire American government in a matter of minutes.

Sure enough, an instant later, the computers had it pegged. They were tracking a land attack cruise missile, most likely a Chinese- or North Korean–built model known as the "Sunburn." The most lethal cruise missile in the world, the Sunburn was capable of carrying a two-hundred-kiloton nuclear warhead. And it was accurate to within ten feet.

Now there was no doubt for anyone in the room. Someone was targeting the president of the United States. And they didn't just want to kill him. They wanted to annihilate him and his government.

12

★ ★
★

"Mayday, Mayday. Vessel in distress. Over."

Telecommunications Specialist of the Watch Carrie Sanders had been having a very quiet night. She was in her third year with the U.S. Coast Guard, serving in the tradition of her father and grandfather. It was her job to listen for distress calls and issue safety bulletins to boaters over the VHF radios from the Communications Center in the Guard's mid-Atlantic regional headquarters. But it had been business as usual all evening, and she certainly hadn't heard anything about what was transpiring at NORAD. In fact, she'd been so bored up to that moment, she had her feet up, was sipping her umpteenth Diet Coke of the night, was reading *The Hunt for Red October* yet again, and had been counting the hours until her shift was over and she could see her boyfriend, Tomas.

But now Sanders sat bolt upright at her console and pressed her headphones tightly against her ears to get all of the incoming transmission.

"Vessel in distress, this is the U.S. Coast Guard Sector Baltimore, channel one-six," Sanders said calmly and professionally into her radio, though her heart was racing. "Vessel in distress, I repeat, this is Coast Guard Sector Baltimore, channel one-six. What is your position and nature of distress?"

"U.S. Coast Guard, this is the captain of the Panamanian container ship *Double Dolphin*. . . . GPS system not working . . . other electronics have failed. . . . Last known position was twenty-three miles east-southeast of Port Baltimore . . . inbound for Seagirt Marine Terminal. . . . Over."

"Vessel in distress. Coast Guard Sector Baltimore. Roger that, Captain. Understand you are twenty-three miles east-southeast of Port Baltimore, on approach to SMT. Over."

"Affirm, that's affirmative, Coast Guard. . . . We've got . . . strange . . . here. Over."

"Request you say again your last, Captain. What is the nature of your distress? Over."

The next transmission from the Panamanian freighter was even more garbled and virtually indecipherable. Sanders ran a diagnostics check of her equipment, but all her systems were working well.

"Vessel in distress, this is Coast Guard Sector Baltimore. You are broken and unreadable. Need you to speak more clearly. Over."

But again the transmission was clouded by static.

"Vessel in distress, this is Coast Guard Sector Baltimore on channel one-six—please repeat last transmission."

"Roger that, Coast Guard. . . . I repeat, this is the captain of the *Double Dolphin*. We've got something really strange going on out here."

"Roger that, Captain," Sanders said. "Please explain."

"Yeah, well, Coast Guard . . . I'm not sure. . . . The thing is . . ."

Sanders took a deep breath. She couldn't let herself sound flustered. But she needed more information and she needed it quickly.

"What is the nature of your distress, Captain?" she asked again.

"I'm looking at a Liberian-flagged container ship. . . . It's about a half mile off my port side, and I think . . ."

"You think what, Captain?"

"I think some kind of rocket just fired off its bow—and not just one, but two—one after the other."

Sanders was speechless. Had she heard the man right? How could she have?

"*Double Dolphin*, this is Coast Guard Sector Baltimore; come again?"

"I'm telling you, Coast Guard, I think these guys have just fired some kind of rocket. . . . My crew and I saw a flash of light—like an explosion—on the bow. . . . Then we saw something explode off the deck and shoot up into the sky. It had a long flame beneath it, like when you see the space shuttle take off, but not that big. . . . I can still see the contrail—we all can. A few minutes later, it happened again. What's going on?"

Sanders had no idea.

"*Double Dolphin*, this is Coast Guard Sector Baltimore, can you describe the ship in question?"

As the captain replied, Sanders scribbled notes as fast as she could. It was a commercial container ship, at least a thousand feet long, with Liberian registration, a black hull, and massive white letters *LSC* painted on the side. For the last twenty minutes or so, it had been dead in the water, the captain said. That's how the *Double Dolphin* had come upon it out of nowhere. But now the freighter was reengaging its engines and seemed to be preparing to head back out to sea.

"What do you want me to do?" the captain asked, his voice betraying his fear.

"Nothing; just sit tight, shut down your engines, and stay close to your radio," Sanders instructed. "I'll be right back to you. Over."

Sanders quickly reviewed her notes and tried to process what she was hearing. She hadn't been alerted of any rocket or missile tests in the area. To her knowledge, there had *never* been any rocket or missile test in the area. And even if some secret test had been planned—a missile defense test, for example—how could it possibly involve a container ship flagged from Liberia? It made no sense, and that's what worried her. All she knew for certain was that she had to pass this up the chain of command immediately.

She picked up the red phone on her console and speed-dialed the command duty officer at the operations center on the other side of the building. The CDO also served as the search-and-rescue mission controller for the area. He could not only dispatch Coast Guard choppers and cutters but pull in resources from the Patuxent Naval Air Station and the Maryland State Police if need be.

The CDO picked up the call on the first ring.

"Ops, this is the Comm Center," Sanders said, trying desperately to keep her voice steady and her facts in order. "I just got a distress call you need to hear."

But it was already too late.

13

★ ★
★

Without warning, the capital of the United States was obliterated.

At precisely 9:12 p.m. Eastern, in a millisecond of time, in a blinding flash of light, the White House simply ceased to exist, as did everything and everyone else for miles in every direction.

No sooner had the first missile detonated in Lafayette Park than temperatures soared into the millions of degrees. The firestorm and blast wave that followed consumed everything in its path. Gone was the Treasury building, and with it the headquarters of the United States Secret Service. Gone was the FBI building, and the National Archives, and the Supreme Court, and the U.S. Capitol and all of its surrounding buildings. Wiped away was every monument, every museum, every restaurant, every hotel, every hospital, every library and landmark of any kind, every sign of civilization. Every building was just gone, and every soul as well.

Across the Potomac River, the Pentagon shuddered violently from the blast wave and then began to partially collapse. What remained standing was utterly ablaze, as was every structure not flattened for as far as the eye could see.

Howling, scorching winds soon began sweeping lethal radioactivity through the city's northeast quadrant and into Maryland, surging through Prince George's County and Anne Arundel County, as if they were following 295 to the north and Routes 50 and 214 to the east, through Capitol

Heights and Lanham and Bowie toward Crofton and Annapolis. Soon more than five thousand square miles of Virginia, Maryland, and the District of Columbia were contaminated with deadly levels of radioactivity. And the nightmare had only just begun.

Moments after the first missile hit D.C., a second missile struck the CIA building at Langley directly, its superheated fireball and cataclysmic blast wave obliterating the nation's premier intelligence headquarters in the tree-lined suburbs of northern Virginia and vaporizing every home and office building, every church and mall for mile after mile in every direction. Those poor, unfortunate souls who didn't die instantly suddenly found themselves blinded and burning and unable to move. Some would hang on for hours. Some would endure for days or even weeks. But there was no hope of survival. Nor was there any hope of rescue or evacuation.

The vast majority of those who didn't die immediately sustained third-degree burns over most if not all of their bodies. People's eardrums were blown out. Their hands and feet were blistered and bleeding. And they would continue to suffer horribly, until they eventually succumbed to the most excruciatingly painful deaths imaginable; there was absolutely nothing they or anyone else could do about it.

Manhattan took the next hit.

The Scud C hit the heart of Times Square, and it, too, carried a nuclear warhead. The effect was as ghastly as it was instantaneous. The detonation eradicated every life-form in a half-mile radius within a fraction of a second. Every building from the theater district and the New York Times Building to Grand Central station and beyond was vaporized in the blink of an eye, just as experts had long predicted and military commanders had long feared. Even buildings miles away from the epicenter were flattened by the blast wave. The firestorm ignited by the detonation spread at speeds upwards of six hundred miles an hour, and every borough was suddenly a raging, radioactive inferno that would blaze for weeks, if not months.

Apartments and office buildings began collapsing from the shock waves and the intense heat. All but one hospital was incinerated or destroyed beyond recognition. And then the Lincoln Tunnel imploded. A billion gallons of the Hudson River—now superheated by the thermonuclear blast—surged into Chelsea, annihilated Penn Station, and boiled everything and everyone south of Broadway.

Seattle was next in line, mere seconds after Manhattan.

The missile seemed to emerge out of nowhere. Launched from a ship several hundred miles off the Canadian coastline, it quickly arced over Victoria, over Port Angeles and Olympic National Park, on a direct trajectory into the center of the city.

Ground zero was Pike Place Market, and when the fifty-kiloton nuclear warhead detonated, it instantly and completely vaporized anything and everything for miles in all directions. The Space Needle. The aquarium and the science center. Amazon.com's headquarters. Safeco Field. And every Starbucks in between. All of it was gone in the snap of a finger.

None of the city's twenty-one state-of-the-art air raid sirens went off. They had originally been installed in the early 1950s during the Cold War. They'd been cosmetically upgraded in 2006 at a cost of $91,000. But they'd been useless. No one in the mayor's office or the police department or the fire department knew the missile was coming. No one knew the threat that was inbound. Thus no one had activated the sirens. But even if someone had, would anyone in Seattle have known what to do or where to go? Would there have been any time to seek shelter? No one was left to ask the questions, for now the air raid sirens and the city they were designed to protect were gone entirely.

Untold thousands lay dead and dying. More would join them soon. Indeed, the death toll in Seattle alone would soar into the hundreds of thousands within hours. An enormous mushroom cloud, crackling with toxic radioactive dust, now formed over the city. Those not blinded by the initial blast could see the lethal, glowing plume from miles away. It was certainly seen on the Microsoft campus in Redmond, just ten miles away, and as the killer winds began to blow, death and destruction soon followed. It was only a matter of time. There would be no escape, and no place to hide.

Surely first responders would emerge from surrounding states and communities, eager to help in any way they possibly could. But how would they get into the hot zones? How would they communicate? Where would they take the dead? Where would they take the dying? The power grid went down instantly. All communications went dark. The electromagnetic pulse set off by the warhead's detonation had fried all electronic circuitry for miles. The electrical systems of most motor vehicles in Seattle—from fire trucks and ambulances to police cars and military Humvees, not to mention most helicopters and fixed-wing aircraft—were immobilized completely or, at the very least, severely damaged. Most cell phones, pagers, PDAs, TVs, and radios were rendered useless as well, as were even the backup power systems in hospitals and other emergency facilities throughout the blast radius.

The same was true in Washington, D.C., and New York. No amount of emergency planning had prepared anyone for something of this scale. Raging fires and radioactive winds were killing everyone in their paths, yet fleeing for safety was difficult if not impossible. Shock paralyzed millions. The lack of electricity paralyzed millions more, as did the inability to communicate. *What had just happened? What was coming next? Where could one go to be safe? And how in the world should one get there?*

And then the City of Angels became the City of Demons.

☆　☆　☆

Jackie Sanchez picked up the secure phone on the console in front of her and took the priority-one call from General Briggs at NORAD. She could barely believe what he was telling her, but she had no time to argue. They had a minute, if that, to get the president to safety.

She slammed down the phone and quickly shouted a series of coded commands into her wrist-mounted microphone. Her team reacted instantly, just as they'd been trained. She wasn't sure if it really mattered. Perhaps all their efforts would be in vain. Maybe they wouldn't save any lives. But they had to do it anyway. They had to try. They had taken an oath, and they would be faithful to the end.

On the bank of surveillance monitors in front of her, she saw a dozen of her best agents—guns drawn—suddenly rush the convention stage, surround the president, grab him by the arms, and literally carry him away, his feet barely touching the ground. Sanchez then bolted out of the command post and met the president's protective detail backstage and ordered them downstairs, into the makeshift bunker.

"*Go, go, go,*" she yelled as they raced the president down one corridor after another, into a heavily guarded stairwell, and down five flights, eventually bursting into the basement, where all the convention center's HVAC systems were housed. They turned one corner and then another, ducking pipes and ducts along the way. A moment later, they raced the president into a large storage freezer, slammed the door shut behind them, and worked feverishly to put him in a protective suit, gloves, and mask, pre-positioned there by the army's nuclear, biological, and chemical fast-reaction team.

That done, Sanchez and her agents began to suit up themselves. But just then, Sanchez felt the ground shake violently beneath her feet. She could hear the deafening blast. She could suddenly feel the scorching heat. She had enough time to realize that her best efforts to protect the president had failed, that it was over, and then, sure enough, it was.

14

★ ★
★

The waves lapped gently, rhythmically, upon the shore.

A full, majestic moon hung over the Atlantic and a balmy breeze swept in off the water, carrying with it the distant cries of seagulls and the horn of a freighter veering a bit too close to the shore. The mood was festive, and everyone was drinking champagne and eating chilled shrimp as the vice president's small but loyal staff huddled in the living room of the gorgeous summerhouse on a six-million-dollar stretch of exquisite beachfront property, just outside of Jacksonville in a community called Ponte Vedra.

They had gathered to watch the president's third, final, and most important address to a Republican convention. They had gathered to see how James MacPherson's daring new policy would play before the country, and the world. But suddenly, they saw nothing on the vice president's new plasma screen but snow.

Bobby Caulfield, the VP's twenty-three-year-old personal aide, quickly grabbed the remote and switched from FOX to CNN. The picture was out there as well. His fellow staffers groaned. Caulfield switched to MSNBC. Nothing. Next he flipped through each of the broadcast networks, but they, too, all seemed to be knocked off the air.

"*What in the world . . . ,*" he muttered to himself as he clicked his way through nearly two hundred cable channels in the next sixty seconds.

He found some still functioning. A food channel here. A travel channel there. An exercise show or two. But none of the networks carrying the president's address at the Republican convention was working, and he could feel the small crowd of senior staffers turning on him, as though somehow this were his fault.

Caulfield didn't dare look at his boss. He just stayed focused on trying to figure out what was wrong, checking the batteries in the remote and playing with the wires in the back of the console to see if any of them were loose. None of them was. It didn't make sense.

Without warning, six Secret Service agents—including the head of the detail—burst into the room, grabbed the VP, and hauled him out, shouting back for Bobby to join them—fast.

Caulfield grabbed his BlackBerry and raced to catch up, leaving the rest of the staffers with their jaws open, as bewildered as he. But as he ran through the kitchen, he stopped suddenly and turned back.

"Caulfield, let's go; move!" an agent shouted.

"One minute," he shouted back.

"No, now!"

Caulfield scanned every counter, the table, the floor. *Where was it? It had to be here somewhere.* His heart was racing. Then an air raid siren went off and he could hear the sound of *Marine Two* powering up. *He couldn't leave it behind. Where was it?*

He raced back into the living room in a panic, running headlong into the vice president's executive assistant, her face drained of all color.

"Looking for this?" she asked, holding Caulfield's briefcase.

"Last chance, Caulfield," another agent shouted over the roar of the rotors. *"Let's go. Let's go."*

They were about to close the chopper door and lift off.

"Thanks," Caulfield told his colleague.

He grabbed the bag, gave her a kiss on the cheek, and bolted out a side door toward the VP's green and white Lockheed Martin VH-71. Even as he did, Caulfield became more confused. *Marine Two* was surrounded now by at least thirty or forty heavily armed agents. *What in the world was going on?* he wondered as he jumped into the helicopter, climbed into the seat behind the vice president, and buckled up as quickly as he could.

Two Black Hawks suddenly roared into view. Caulfield could see two

Apache helicopter gunships racing up the coast. Marines toting machine guns were taking up positions around the VP's compound. Whatever this was, it had to be bad. It couldn't be a drill. He'd been through several of those, but the Secret Service wouldn't be stupid enough to hold one in the middle of the president's speech.

Then Bobby Caulfield heard words that made the hair on the back of his neck stand on end. As soon as the doors of the chopper slammed shut, the lead pilot said into his radio, *"Checkmate is secure. I repeat, Checkmate is secure. All airborne support, move into formation. Marine One is lifting off."*

Caulfield repeated the words in his mind. Had he heard the pilot correctly? *Marine One?* It had to be a mistake. But Marine pilots didn't make mistakes. Not that one, at least. *So what was going on? Why was everyone acting as though the president were on board?*

☆   ☆   ☆

The vice president took the call on a secure line.

"Sir, this is Lieutenant General Charlie Briggs at NORAD. Can you hear me?"

"I can, General, and you had better have a good explanation for this," Oaks replied, having no idea why he'd been dragged away from his family, friends, and staff at such a time as this.

"Sir, I don't exactly know how to say this," Briggs began.

"I'm in no mood for games or exercises," Oaks shot back. "The president of the United States is giving a major address, General. I'm not exactly supposed to be missing it. Hear what I'm saying?"

"Yes, sir," Briggs said. "I understand that, sir."

"Then what in the world is going on here, General?" Oaks insisted.

"Sir, I'm afraid it's my duty to inform you . . ." Briggs hesitated again.

Oaks was rapidly losing patience. *"What?"* he demanded.

"Sir, the United States is under attack."

"Under attack?" Oaks asked in disbelief. "What are you talking about?"

"Sir, in the last few minutes, four American cities have been hit by ballistic missiles—Washington, New York, Los Angeles, and Seattle."

"My God . . . ," Oaks gasped.

"Each of those missiles was equipped with a nuclear warhead," the general continued. "I can't tell you what kind. I can't tell you what size. Not yet. But casualties in each city are extensive. Damage in each city is extensive."

"How extensive?" Oaks pressed as a chill shuddered through his body.

"Sir, the White House and Capitol are gone," Briggs explained. "The Supreme Court, the FBI building, and all of the Cabinet agencies are gone. The Pentagon is badly damaged. Langley has been completely wiped out as well. The entire city is a hot zone, sir. Nobody's going to be able to get in there for . . . well, a long, long time. And . . . well . . . I regret to inform you, sir, but USNORTHCOM is operating under the belief that the president is dead."

Oaks couldn't say anything.

"Hello?" Briggs asked. "Sir, are you still there?"

Oaks tried to process the magnitude of what he'd just heard. But how could he? How could this actually be happening?

"Tell me this is some kind of drill, General."

"It's not, sir."

"Did you just tell me that the president of the United States is dead?"

"Yes, sir," Briggs replied. "I'm afraid so. Staples Center received a direct hit. There's nothing left."

"Four *nuclear* attacks?" Oaks repeated, still not able to believe what he'd been told.

"Actually, *five*, sir," Briggs corrected. "Washington was hit twice— once downtown and once in northern Virginia. Langley, to be precise."

"It can't be," the vice president said. "It must be some kind of mistake."

"I wish it were, sir, but it's not," Briggs said, his voice now surprisingly calm and professional under the circumstances. "It will take days to as- sess the damage, sir, but there are a few critical things you need to know right now."

Oaks loosened his tie. "Start with my family. Is someone getting Marie?"

"We have another chopper picking her up and bringing her to you," Briggs explained.

"What about my boys?"

"We have agents picking up David and his wife in Phoenix and Tom in Atlanta," Briggs said. "They'll both be taken to secure facilities until we figure out exactly what's happening."

"You sure they're okay?"

"I don't have any word on them yet, but I will get you an update as soon as I can."

"I want them all brought to me."

"Yes, sir," Briggs said. "Now there are a few things I need to go over."

"Go ahead."

"First of all, sir, I need to inform you that under the Twenty-fifth Amendment to the Constitution, you are now the president of the United States."

Again Oaks couldn't think of anything to say. He sat in shocked silence.

"Mr. President, are you there?" Briggs asked. "Sir?"

"No," Oaks suddenly shot back. "Don't call me that, General. Not unless you have absolute proof that President MacPherson didn't survive the initial blast."

"He couldn't have, sir," Briggs replied.

"Why not?" Oaks demanded. "How do you know?"

"No one could have survived that blast," Briggs explained. "Our initial assessment is that Los Angeles was hit with a warhead between one hundred fifty and two hundred kilotons in size. It will take us time to know for sure. But one thing I can tell you for certain, sir—the casualties will be in the millions, sir, starting with President MacPherson. I know it's hard to hear, sir, but there's no question about it. The president is dead, God rest his soul."

15

★ ★
★

Oaks felt nauseated.

He heard the words but they didn't compute. It wasn't possible. How could it be? He had known Jim MacPherson most of his adult life. They had been through so much together. They had served side by side through perhaps the most difficult eight years of any American administration, at least since FDR's tenure during World War II or Lincoln's term during the Civil War. Terrorists had tried to take them both out multiple times, and nearly succeeded. But MacPherson couldn't really be dead. Not now. Not at the pinnacle of his career.

Hadn't they just turned a corner in the global War on Terror? Weren't things starting to get better? With Russia neutralized, along with Iran and Syria, the world was getting quiet. Or quieter, at least. Wasn't it?

And then it suddenly struck him. It wasn't just MacPherson who had been killed in the blast. The First Lady must be dead too, and the MacPhersons' daughters. Bob Corsetti. Jackie Sanchez. The entire leadership of the Republican party.

Oaks unfastened the top button of his dress shirt. He was having trouble breathing. His pulse was racing. He could barely grasp the magnitude of what was happening to his country. But the death of so many of his friends made it personal. If Washington was gone, so was Marsha Kirkpatrick at State. Scott Harris at FBI. Ken Costello at the NSC. Danny

Tracker at CIA. All their staff. The entire White House staff. They were gone. All of them. He would never see them again. It was more than he could bear, but General Briggs didn't give him time to mourn.

"Sir, I know it's a lot to deal with," the three-star said, empathy in his voice. "But there's more I need to tell you."

"Lieutenant, could you give me some air back here?" Oaks asked the lead pilot. He took a few deep breaths and tried to steel himself for what more was coming.

"Continue, General," he said after a few moments. "I'm listening."

Or trying to, he said to himself.

"Sir, once you're on board *Air Force One*, we'll feed you live satellite images of each of the affected cities, beginning with Los Angeles. I'll put my experts on a videoconference to walk you through the specifics and answer every question you have. After you board, you're going to be met by the chief U.S. district judge out of Jacksonville. I don't have her name in front of me, but you'll have a full dossier on her in a few minutes. She is going to administer the oath of office. We need a commander in chief immediately, sir. We're going to war."

"With whom, General?" Oaks demanded. "Who's behind all this?"

"I don't know, sir," Briggs conceded. "Not yet. But I will soon. And when I do, I'll give you a package of possible response options. For now, though, that's getting ahead of ourselves. First things first. I'm so sorry to have to say this, but as best as we can tell at the moment, you have virtually no Cabinet to speak of, sir, and most of the National Security Council is dead as well."

Oaks gasped. It wasn't possible.

"You're absolutely certain, General?" he asked. "Couldn't any of them have survived?"

"No, sir, I'm afraid not," Briggs said. "All but two members of the Cabinet were in D.C. at the moment of impact, and D.C. is gone. The White House has been completely destroyed. So have the Capitol, all of the Cabinet agencies, the Supreme Court, the FBI building. They're gone. All of them. And Washington's going to be uninhabitable for a century, sir, maybe longer."

Oaks was certain he was going to be ill. He motioned to Caulfield— horrified by the bits and pieces of news he was overhearing—to get him a bottle of water as quickly as possible; then Oaks peered out the window and noticed that they were on approach not to the Jacksonville International Airport as he had expected but to the Naval Air Station, a few miles away.

All nonessential air and ground traffic had been shut down. A detachment of heavily armed marines was moving rapidly to boost base security, and Oaks noticed that *Air Force One* and an unmarked Gulfstream jet were already out on one of the runways, flanked by two F/A-18 Hornets, armed with air-to-air missiles and ready for emergency takeoff. He wasn't sure why the Gulfstream was there, but he didn't have much time to think about it either.

He took the bottle from Caulfield's hands, drank a third of it in a matter of seconds, and then asked, "Who's left?"

"As far as we know, sir, only Secretaries James and Trainor are left," the three-star continued. "Secretary James is in Boston. The SecDef is still inbound from Tokyo."

"We need to move Lee James out of Boston—*fast*," Oaks said. "I want him in a secure military facility ASAP."

"I'm already on it, sir," Briggs assured him, then quickly explained that in accordance with the administration's top secret "continuity of government" plan, he had ordered Secretary James to be evacuated immediately and taken to Mount Weather, the classified underground emergency operations center in the Blue Ridge Mountains of western Virginia, about seventy-five miles from Washington, D.C.

Mount Weather had been built in the 1950s for government leaders to run the country from in case of a nuclear war with the Soviets. Oaks had actually been there through numerous crises, including the Day of Devastation. He'd also run countless COG drills from there, as had Secretary James, and both knew its layout and capabilities well.

Briggs also reminded Oaks that as per the continuity of government plan, the secretary of defense was being routed to Site R, or Raven Rock, the site of the Alternate National Military Command Center, located along the Pennsylvania-Maryland border, not far from Waynesboro and about ten miles from Camp David. From there, Secretary Trainor and his team would be able to run the Defense Department's state-of-the-art underground war room as they ramped up for a nuclear revenge scenario Briggs had already dubbed "Operation Reciprocity."

"What's the status of the primary war room?" Oaks asked.

"The Pentagon was badly damaged, sir," Briggs noted. "The only survivors we know of were those who were actually in the NMCC when the missile hit. I'm in contact with them but their communications systems aren't working well. They're understaffed. Shell-shocked. They've got serious radiation leakages, and it's not clear if they're going to be able to contain—"

"General Briggs," Oaks suddenly interrupted, "are you telling me the Pentagon's billion-dollar, nuclear-blast-proof war room isn't functional?"

"Not the way it was designed to be, no; I'm afraid not, sir," Briggs replied. "That's why I'm sending the SecDef to Raven Rock."

Oaks shook his head and rubbed his eyes. "How long until Trainor's in place?"

"Another few hours, sir," Briggs said. "But Secretary James's plane should be wheels up in a few minutes. He'll be secure at Mount Weather in an hour."

"I want them both to have fighter escorts," Oaks ordered.

"Done."

"Good," Oaks said. "And I want a full ground stop—no planes in the air unless they're military or are authorized by you or Secretary Trainor. Got that?"

"We're on it, sir," Briggs said. "It's going to take some time to implement. We currently have more than three thousand flights in the sky and FAA headquarters is gone. So is the Transportation Department. We're having to contact each airport and regional air traffic control center individually. We're telling everyone to get their planes on the ground within thirty minutes."

"Good. What else?" Oaks asked.

"I've scrambled combat air patrols over each border and every major city. I also ordered the full fleet to sea."

"You sure that's the best move, General?" Oaks asked skeptically. "Shouldn't we hold back some assets in reserve, at least until we figure out what's happening and who our enemy is?"

"I considered that, sir, but we have to safeguard against another Pearl Harbor," Briggs quickly replied. "We don't know what else is coming, and we don't want our naval assets concentrated and vulnerable. With your permission, sir, I'd also like to order two carrier battle groups off both coasts and order a series of navy ships armed with the Aegis ballistic missile defense system off both coastlines, as well as in the Gulf of Mexico. But we need to do this fast."

"You have my authorization," Oaks said without hesitation. "Now, where do you want me?"

"I'd like to bring you here, Mr. President," Briggs replied, reminding Oaks that Peterson Air Force Base was not only home of USNORTHCOM but also the NORAD command center buried deep inside Cheyenne Mountain. "You'll be safe here. We've got everything you'll need on hand, or close by. My staff and I can help you begin to reassemble a government. And I think it's better that you and I are in the same room, not separated by two thousand miles and a communications system that could still get knocked out. Is that okay, sir?"

"It is, General—I trust your judgment," Oaks said. "Now, what about Congress?"

"Too soon to say, sir," Briggs admitted. "We're still trying to piece together that picture. At this point, I can tell you that we are operating under the assumption that all of the Republican leadership and more than two hundred GOP members of Congress are dead. They were all at the convention. At the moment, we're simply not sure about the Democratic leadership or other members of the Democratic caucus. Many of them were converging on Manhattan to begin their convention in a few days. The rest are scattered all over the country and I assume were preparing to head to New York in the next few days. We're trying to contact everyone, but much of the civilian communications grid is down, as are major segments of the national power grid."

"Where's the Speaker of the House?" Oaks asked.

"I don't know," Briggs conceded.

"How about the president *pro tempore* of the Senate?"

The general didn't know that either.

"We're looking for him," he said, his tone betraying his lack of hope that they were going to find him any time soon.

"Are you expecting more attacks?" Oaks pressed.

Briggs said that was the most difficult question of all to answer. The

CIA was gone. So was the Defense Intelligence Agency. As such, America's intelligence-gathering systems had been badly disrupted. No one knew what was coming next or from where, much less when. They had no idea who was hitting them or where to strike back. All U.S. forces world-wide were now at DefCon One. But without a clearly defined enemy and clearly defined targets to strike, there wasn't much the military could do. At least for now.

What's more, they had a very serious succession crisis on their hands.

"So what happens if my plane's taken down on the way to NORAD?" the new president asked his senior surviving military commander. "If I'm killed, who exactly is supposed to run the country?"

16

★ ★
★

It was painful even to open her eyes.

And when she did, Erin Bennett had no idea where she was. It didn't seem like the tent that had been her home for the past seven months. Then again, it didn't smell as bad either. There was a distinct odor to the room, but she couldn't place it.

Her temples throbbed. It hurt too much to think, too much to figure out where she was or why. So she began to drift away . . . back . . . back . . . to a simpler time than this.

Suddenly she found herself standing behind her desk in her penthouse office, high atop London, overlooking the Thames. In the window, she could see a reflection of herself in her black suit and black pumps, her hair back, her nails done. She turned and saw her team gathered around her in that high-tech financial war room she had once designed and run for Global Strategix. The satellite boxes. The shortwave radios. The bank of television monitors. The high-speed Internet access and fiber optic cables, streaming thirty million phone calls across the Atlantic and back in a single second. The little ceramic plaque sitting on her desk, the one that read, "Know well the condition of thy flocks." And there was that smell again. Perfume? Cleaning supplies?

Whatever it was, it was stinging her throat, making her eyes water, and forcing her against her will back to some semblance of reality. She wasn't in London, she realized, and the disappointment spread over her like a cloud.

Erin struggled to open her eyes again, and when she did, she noticed a clock on the wall. It was four thirty, though whether it was morning or night she had no idea. She tried to recall the past few hours, but it was all a blur. Slowly, and with great difficulty, she turned her head to the right, then to the left. Every muscle in her body ached. Her throat was on fire.

At first she felt like she was burning up. After a few moments, she found herself chilled. Her arms were covered with goose bumps. An IV needle was jammed in one of them, covered in tubing and tape. Even her eyes ached in their sockets. But the mental fog was lifting a bit. She was in the hospital. Jon had brought her here. But why? What was happening to her?

She groped around for a while and finally found a call button, which she pressed repeatedly. A few moments later, a tall, gentle-looking black man—probably in his late fifties or early sixties, she figured—opened the door. He had a warm, friendly smile and a cup of water and some pills in his hands. Erin squinted and tried to read his ID tag: "Francis P. Kwamee, MD." It said he was from Accra, Ghana. It said he worked for the World Health Organization. All well and good, but where was Jon?

Erin tried to ask, but the pain was too much. The doctor spoke instead.

"How are you feeling, ma'am?"

Not well enough to answer. She just shook her head.

"Don't you worry, Mrs. Bennett," the doctor said. "We're going to take care of you right. But first, I must say, you have a pretty eager visitor out there in the lobby. May I let him in? I don't think he can wait much longer."

Erin's heart leaped and she smiled weakly.

"Very well," Dr. Kwamee said. "But I do need you to take your medicine first."

She nodded slowly and with his help took the pills, despite the pain of swallowing. When Dr. Kwamee stepped out of the room and she was alone again, Erin closed her eyes and took a deep breath. She thanked the Lord for being merciful to her, for keeping her safe, and she asked Him to bless Jon and hold him close to His heart. As she said amen, the door swung open and she quickly found herself in the arms of the man she loved, and all was well.

"Hey, how are you feeling?" Bennett asked as he sat beside her on the bed and gently stroked her hands.

Erin desperately wanted to tell him. She desperately wanted to talk to him, to catch up with him and find out how he was doing, but she winced as she tried.

"That's okay; just rest," he assured her with a soothing bedside manner that she sensed she was going to need a lot of over the next few days.

She was privately grateful there wasn't a mirror to be found. She knew she must look horrible, but Jon didn't seem to care, and it made her love him all the more.

"By the way," he said, as if reading her thoughts, "has anyone told you how beautiful you look today?"

She tried to shake her head.

"Good." He smiled. "I'd have to punch them in the nose."

Her smile broadened, and as it did she finally felt the new pain relievers coursing through her veins. Could the pills really be working so quickly? Maybe it was something in the IV instead. At any rate, her eyelids were getting heavy, though she was determined not to lose this moment.

"So, did the doc say anything? Besides, of course, how desperate I was to see you?" he asked.

She shook her head ever so slightly.

"Dr. Kwamee didn't give you your diagnosis yet?"

Again she shook her head just enough to make the point.

"He didn't give you your prognosis?"

"No," she managed to whisper.

"Then perhaps I should fill you in."

Erin felt herself drifting, but she did everything she could to focus as Jon explained that she had bacterial meningitis, explained how it was affecting her, how she would be treated, and how long it would probably take to recover. Erin was relieved to hear it wasn't something worse, and she squeezed his hand when he was finished to thank him for being the bearer of such good news. After all, God only knew what other diseases she could have contracted in this place. She had made out like a bandit, she thought, and hoped now she could let herself drift away in a long and peaceful nap. She could see Jon soon enough. But she really needed to sleep, perchance to dream. . . .

But Jon wasn't finished.

"Actually, sweetheart, there's a little bit more," he said.

He had a curious look, she thought—as if he was hiding something, though something not altogether bad. It almost looked like he was *trying* to look grim.

"What?" she whispered.

"You sure you want to know?" Jon asked.

The drugs were making her feel so groggy, so dreamy. But yes—she nodded; she wanted to know, and soon, before she slipped away for another few hours.

"You're sure?" he teased. "It's been a long night, after all, and you really need your rest."

Her eyes pleaded with him to tell her, and as always, it didn't take much to win him over.

"Very well, Erin Christina Bennett," he began, leaning in close and kissing her softly on the forehead. "I have the pleasure of suggesting that you not make any plans for May third of next year . . . plans that don't include being in a hospital, that is."

She had no idea what he was talking about. She wanted to, but it didn't compute, and Jon's face was already beginning to blur. Her eyes were closing. She tried to hold on, tried to think of what she might possibly have planned for May of next year. She blinked hard and tried to refocus, but it was a battle she was quickly losing.

He leaned close to her face and put his finger to her lips. "Finally, a little good news, sweetheart," he whispered at last.

"What?" she managed to ask.

Bennett paused for a moment, then whispered, "You're pregnant."

Erin's eyes suddenly opened wide. Her heart felt as if it skipped a beat. *Had she heard him right? Or had she fallen asleep and dreamed it?* But the look in his eyes told her all she wanted to know. She hadn't dreamed a thing. She was going to have a baby, with the man she had longed to marry since the day she had met him. *How could she be so lucky? Why had she been so blessed?*

The room began to spin. She was dizzy with joy. The drugs probably had something to do with it too, but it wasn't only the drugs. She began to giggle a little. Her face ached from smiling, but she couldn't help it. Every minute with Jon Bennett had been an adventure, and she had loved each moment of their lives together.

Erin suddenly realized that she had never felt as safe as she did at this moment. Somehow, in a way she loved but couldn't explain, a soothing, comforting peace seemed to wash over her disease-ravaged body like the cool waters of a gentle mountain stream. And as hard as she had fought to stay awake, she surrendered to the narcotics and slipped into a sound and dreamless sleep, with a smile on her lips and her best friend at her side.

She never heard Dr. Kwamee burst in a minute later and say, *"Mr. Bennett, come quickly; something terrible has happened."*

17

★ ★
★

Carrie Sanders waited for instructions from her superiors.

But they weren't coming. Sanders and her colleagues were horrified. They were tracking a flood of fast-breaking intel reports on the missile attacks around the country. They now knew for certain that the mysterious reports of rockets being fired off container ships near the ports of Baltimore, Newark, Seattle, and Long Beach were all true. They knew more missiles might be out there on more ships, preparing to launch at any moment. They knew the president was dead. They just didn't know what to do next.

Sanders's supervisor was frantically calling his way up the chain of command, but without success. Most calls didn't even go through. Those that did either weren't answered or were rerouted to other Coast Guard command posts around the country that had even less information than Sector Baltimore. Chaos and confusion were everywhere, and for the first time in Sanders's tour of duty, she began to experience real fear.

This *was* real. This was the nightmare scenario. This was the grand finale the analysts at Langley and DIA had been warning about for years. A terrorist network or terrorist regime had actually hit the American homeland with nuclear weapons. They had apparently decapitated the American government. They had clearly crippled the American military's command and control system, or at least so disrupted it as to render it ineffective in the most important early stages of the war. *Now what?*

Rear Admiral Scott Conklin was commander of the Fifth Coast Guard District, based in Portsmouth. He was responsible for the mid-Atlantic region, stretching from New Jersey to North Carolina. A gruff, chain-smoking, fourth-generation admiral, Conklin had previously served with distinction at Coast Guard headquarters in D.C. as director of port security. In fact, Sanders knew that in Washington, Conklin had been largely responsible for making sure a scenario like this—a sea-based attack on the capital—never happened. He had helped draft the new maritime security regime covering all U.S. ports and vessels and operational security protocols covering all eight thousand foreign vessels coming in and out of U.S. ports every year. If anyone knew how to handle a crisis like this, Sanders thought, it would be Conklin.

But no one at the ops center in Annapolis could find the rear admiral or any of his five senior deputies. All of them were scheduled to be in Manhattan the next morning for a U.N. conference on maritime security. *Were all of them now dead? Were they alive but severely wounded? Were they alive but unable to communicate back to the ops center? What did that mean? Who was in charge?*

The face in the picture on the wall of her Communications Center—in the frame next to President MacPherson and Vice President Oaks—was that of Admiral Jack Allenby, the commandant of the U.S. Coast Guard. The only four-star admiral of the Coast Guard, Allenby, fifty-eight, had been appointed to a four-year term by President MacPherson and confirmed unanimously by the Senate. But he was stationed at Coast Guard headquarters in Washington, D.C. So were his vice commandant, his two area commanders, and his chief of staff, all of whom were three-star vice admirals. Now the Coast Guard's central command center had been obliterated. *Did that mean all of the Guard's senior officers were gone too? Who, then, was authorized to make decisions?*

Before 9/11, Sanders had been taught, the Coast Guard had served under the direction of the secretary of transportation. After 9/11, a sweeping federal reorganization put the Guard under the secretary of Homeland Security. Everyone in the Guard knew the revamped mission. Sanders certainly did. It had been drilled into her from day one.

"As part of Operation Noble Eagle, the Coast Guard is at a heightened state of alert protecting more than 361 ports and 95,000 miles of coastline, America's longest border. The Coast Guard continues to play an integral role in maintaining the operations of our ports and waterways by providing a secure environment in which mariners and the American people can safely go about the business of living and working freely. In the wake of the September 11 terrorist attacks, the Coast Guard immediately mobilized more than 2,000 Reservists in the largest homeland defense and port security operation since World War II."

Clearly this was no longer peacetime. America had been attacked. America was at war. That meant the Coast Guard now served under the command of the secretary of the navy. But Sanders had already heard that the secretary, who lived with his wife and three kids in D.C., was missing and presumed dead. Sanders had also heard that all of the Joint Chiefs were missing and presumed dead. Ultimately, of course, the chain of command led to the secretary of defense and the president of the United States. But with the Pentagon virtually destroyed and the National Military Command Center barely functional, it wasn't yet clear to Sanders or anyone around her who was making operational decisions. And one decision had to be made immediately.

Sanders picked up the phone and speed-dialed the command duty officer.

"I'm sorry to bother you again, sir, but it just hit me," she began. "Has anyone ordered a strike against the Liberian container ship?"

"That *just* hit you?" the CDO snapped. "What do you think I'm doing on the phone? I'm trying to get authorization for a strike, but I still can't get anyone on the line that can pull the trigger."

"Sorry, sir. But what if the enemy is preparing to launch another missile? Can't you just authorize a strike yourself, before it's too late?"

"Sanders, you're out of line."

"I am serious, sir," Sanders insisted. "Can't you order a cutter out there to intercept the ship and send in a boarding party?"

"I've already done that," the CDO said. "But the closest cutter is an hour away."

"What about choppers?" Sanders asked.

"What about them?" the CDO asked.

"Sir, you launch choppers for search and rescue out of Atlantic City and Virginia Beach all the time. Why not now?"

"You want me to send a Seahawk out there with a couple of rescue swimmers? Forget it, Specialist. You're wasting my time."

But Sanders wouldn't let it go.

"No, not Seahawks. I'm saying, order a couple of MH-68s out there to take this ship out. They've got night vision. They've got the firepower."

"Not to sink a container ship."

"Well, at least to disable its engines."

"That's not enough," the CDO said. "Not if the ship is preparing to fire another missile. We need to sink it, and sink it fast. Look, I'm with you. I get it. But I've got a protocol I've got to follow. Now let me get back to it."

"*No!*" Sanders shouted, shocked at her chutzpah but not nearly as shocked as her CDO.

"What did you just say?" he demanded.

"Sir, there's no time for the protocol," she insisted.

"Watch it, Sanders. You're about to cross a line you really don't want to cross. Now get back to work and call me only if you get more intel."

Still Sanders wouldn't give up.

"With all due respect, sir, this *is* my work—guarding the coast and the people of the mid-Atlantic. And, sir, I'm telling you, we've got a ship out there that has fired two ballistic missiles armed with nuclear warheads, and we have to assume they're preparing to fire again. Now the chain of command has been compromised. The rear admiral is gone. The commandant is gone. You've got to go to the navy."

"Are you out of your mind?"

"No, sir. You've got to skip the Guard protocol, get a naval base commander on the line, give him the coordinates of the Liberian container ship, and tell him to scramble some jets and blow that ship out of the water—*now*."

"Specialist Sanders, that's enough," the CDO shouted back. "You are hereby relieved of duty. Report to my office immediately."

18

★ ★
★

Was he ready?

He had always thought so. Suddenly he wasn't so certain. Bill Oaks knew he had to start thinking differently. He knew he had to start thinking as a president, and a wartime president at that. It wasn't going to be easy.

Oaks had never really aspired to the presidency. He had never had any intention of running to succeed James "Mac" MacPherson. Eight years earlier, he and Marie had agreed to help a lifelong friend run the country. Ever since, it seemed, they had wondered if they had done the right thing. The hours. The stress. The travel. The time away from their sons. It was all too much. With the second term winding down, they'd been eagerly looking forward to retiring and spending time with their children and grandchildren.

And now this.

Two terms as the nation's vice president and a lifetime of government service certainly made him better prepared than most. But there was something different about actually becoming the leader of the free world that changed a man and demanded that he summon something more.

Marine One touched down at the third largest naval installation in the United States, home of twenty-three thousand military and civilian personnel, all of whose jobs were to keep him safe. But to his shock, the Secret Service didn't move him to the gleaming blue and white 747 emblazoned with the great seal, as he had fully expected. Instead, with a coat covering his head and face, they rushed him onto the Gulfstream V that was idling on the tarmac not far from the 747, sealed the doors, and prepared to take off with an urgency that suggested they might be expecting an imminent attack.

"What's going on here?" he asked the head of his new protective detail.

"Good evening, Mr. President," the agent-in-charge said.

"There's nothing good about it, young man," the president-to-be shot back. "Now why are we on this G5, and where's my regular detail?"

"I'll explain everything in a moment, sir," the agent replied. "Right now I need you to take a seat and buckle up fast. We need to get you in the air and out of harm's way as quickly as we can, Mr. President."

Oaks wasn't happy, but he could see the anxiety in the agent's eyes. There wasn't time to get a full briefing on the threats to this base, this plane, just yet. So he did as he was told and ordered Bobby Caulfield to do the same.

"Mr. Caulfield, you're going to want to tighten that seat belt a bit more," the agent said as they moved into the first position for takeoff.

"Why's that?" the young man asked, still somewhat dazed and confused by the rapid pace of events.

"You'll see," the agent said, tightening his own belt and then giving the pilot the thumbs-up sign and saying, "Get this thing off the ground, Lieutenant—*now*."

★   ★   ★

The Gulfstream hurtled down the runway.

It was racing to catch up with the 747 that had taken off before it, and from the moment the Gulfstream lifted off the ground, Caulfield knew why his seat belt had to be as tight as possible. This wasn't going to be a normal ascent. They weren't going to climb gently into the night.

Sure enough, the pilot pulled back on the stick and took the G5 nearly straight up, as if it were the space shuttle. They all felt themselves snapped violently against the backs of their seats by g-forces rarely, if ever, experienced by civilians.

Seconds later, they were already racing past ten thousand feet. Then twenty thousand. Then thirty. Then forty. Only when they approached fifty thousand feet did the G5 begin to level off. Only then did an air force officer get up from his seat and bring the president a stack of briefing papers that someone at USNORTHCOM had faxed to the plane. And only then did the Secret Service agent-in-charge speak again.

The agent quickly briefed everyone on the plane on the nuclear attacks, the death of President MacPherson, and the emergency game plan they were now executing. A few years before, he explained, this military-owned Gulfstream had been retrofitted with rocketlike engines, similar to the ones on board *Air Force One*. The purpose, he said, was to make it possible for any plane carrying the president to get off the ground and out of range of shoulder-mounted rockets and Stinger missiles as rapidly as possible. Such tactics were rarely used in peacetime, of course, unless the president was flying in and out of a war zone. But with America at war and much of the federal government wiped out in the past hour, every precaution possible was being taken.

Caulfield's mouth was dry. His hands were perspiring. He felt confused and disoriented. With every moment that passed, he feared for his divorced mother and his four younger brothers back in the Bronx. Were they alive? Were they safe? He had to track them down. He had to know and get word to his older brother, Derek, a staff sergeant with the Eighth Army along the DMZ in South Korea.

"I still don't understand—why aren't we taking *Air Force One*?" Caulfield asked finally. "Wouldn't that be a whole lot more secure?"

"Usually, yes," the agent said, "but right now we need something more."

"What's that?" the young aide pressed.

"The element of surprise."

"Meaning what?" Caulfield asked.

"Given all that's going on," the lead agent continued, "we have to assume that someone's trying to target *Air Force One*. If that's the case, they are most likely to target that 747 in front of us. So I decided to run the 747 as a decoy and put the president on this G5. Technically, of course, any plane that carries the president is *Air Force One*. But on the radios, we're letting the 747 use the AF1 call sign, not us."

"What's our call sign?" Caulfield asked.

"I'm afraid that's classified," the agent replied.

"With all due respect, sir, I've got the highest possible security clearance," Caulfield explained. His clearance was a necessity in working so close to the top.

"Not that high, son," the agent replied. "This isn't just a war. It's a nuclear war."

Every muscle in Caulfield's body tensed. Everything was different. The world had changed forever, and these guys weren't taking chances.

"How many people know we're on this plane instead of the Boeing?" Caulfield didn't want to think about the horrors unfolding all around him. To the extent he could, he preferred to think only about the bubble around him, and just how secure that bubble was.

"Just us," the agent said, "and three of the agents on the other plane. Most of the crew up ahead doesn't even realize the president isn't aboard. Two of my agents put a coat over the head of a fellow agent, rushed him on board the Boeing, and locked him in the president's private quarters. As far as most of the crew knows—even the pilots, for that matter—POTUS is on their aircraft. And right now, that's exactly how we want it."

"Where's the vice president's regular security detail?" Caulfield pressed, knowing that if he didn't ask, his boss certainly would.

"With all due respect, young man, he is not the vice president anymore," the agent explained. "Under the Twenty-fifth Amendment, he is currently acting as the president of the United States. He's about to be formally sworn in as such."

A different designation meant a different detail. Caulfield was scared. He'd been rattled from the moment he and the vice president had been rushed out of Ponte Vedra on *Marine One*. But it was worse now. All hell was breaking loose, and he was powerless to do anything about it.

He swallowed hard and stuck out his hand. "Bobby Caulfield, sir," he said quietly.

"Curt Coelho," the man replied, shaking Caulfield's trembling hand with firmness meant to inspire confidence. "Don't worry, son. We'll be fine."

Caulfield wasn't so sure.

Agent Coelho then turned to the acting president and vowed to do everything in his power to keep him safe. Oaks unbuckled his seat belt, stood, thanked Coelho, and asked him to get word back to the agents who had served on his VP detail how grateful he was for their service.

"That's very thoughtful, Mr. President," the agent replied. "But you'll be able to thank them yourself soon. They're all on *Air Force One*. Once we get on the ground in the Springs, I'll figure out a way to integrate them onto my own team. They know you well and have served you faithfully for years. And to be honest, Mr. President, we're going to need all the help we can get."

19

★ ★
★

Sanders was stunned.

Her hands were shaking. She closed her eyes and tried to think. *She had to do something. Somebody had to do something. But what?*

She picked up the phone again and tried to speed-dial colleagues at Coast Guard stations throughout the Fifth District, but all the landlines were down. She was getting busy signals, recordings, or static. She tried calling the Eleventh District, covering California. Nothing. She tried calling numbers in the Guard's Thirteenth District, covering Seattle. Again, nothing. *Had everyone been taken out? Or was it just the communications systems that had been destroyed or compromised?*

She glanced at her watch. She was supposed to report to the CDO immediately. *How much longer could she stall before he sent someone to arrest her?* A few more minutes, she figured. She might as well make the most of them.

She tried to log on to the secure military intranet system, but a message kept popping up saying the main system was temporarily down, and she didn't have clearance for the top secret channels. *Should she try a satellite line? Whom should she call? What would she say?*

Desperate, she pulled out her own private cell phone and speed-dialed her boyfriend, Tomas Ramirez, a plebe at the Naval Academy in Annapolis. She wanted to make sure he was safe, of course. But she also wanted the phone number of Tomas's brother, Carlos, a fighter pilot based out of Naval Air Station Oceana in Virginia Beach. Carlos's squadron was known as the "Gunslingers." They flew F/A-18E Super Hornets, the fastest and deadliest fighter jets in the navy.

Maybe, just maybe . . .

The phone began to ring. That was a good sign. But it kept ringing, and Sanders started to worry.

Finally, on the fifth ring, Tomas answered, in a whisper. "Babe, it's me—you okay?"

"I'm fine," she whispered back. "And you?"

"Okay for now, but they're evacuating us."

Sanders gasped. *"What? Why?"*

"They say the winds are bringing the radioactivity from D.C. toward us," he explained.

"Where are you now?"

"I'm on a bus," Ramirez said. "I have no idea where they're taking us. I'm not even supposed to be using my phone. That's why I'm whispering. Can I call you back later?"

"No. Listen—I'm right in the middle of this thing and I don't know what to do. I'm in contact with the captain of a ship who actually saw the missiles launch from a container ship near him. He knows exactly which ship attacked D.C. We've got them, Tomas. I know where they are."

"Really? That's incredible. Have we sunk it yet?"

"No, not yet," Sanders said. "That's just it. I can't get anyone to do anything."

"Why not? What's the problem?"

"Nearly all our communications have been knocked out. Power is out over much of the country. Most of the Guard's ranking officers are dead. And my supervisor doesn't know what to do. He's panicking. But we've got to move fast."

"I'll say," Ramirez said. "What if that ship fires again?"

"Exactly," Sanders responded, relieved not just to hear her boyfriend's voice but to find someone who shared the urgency she felt. "That's what I've been saying. But no one's listening."

"Fog of war," Ramirez said. "Textbook case."

"So what do I do?" Sanders asked.

"What do you need?"

"I need a pair of fighter jets—fast."

Ramirez suddenly got it. *"Carlos."*

"Would you call him?"

"Absolutely—just hold on, and pray I can get through to him."

"Will do, Tomas, and thanks. I love you."

"Love you too, babe. Now stay safe, and I'll see you soon."

Sanders hung up the phone and bowed her head. Then she radioed the captain of the *Double Dolphin*. If they had any chance of success, she needed to have the latest intel and be able to pass it up the chain of command at a moment's notice.

Had the Liberian ship moved? she asked the captain.

No, he said. Its engines were running but it didn't appear to be going anywhere. Not yet, anyway.

Could he see any movement on deck?

Yes, he said. There were lots of people scrambling about. They seemed to be opening one of the containers on the bow. They seemed to be constructing something, though he couldn't tell what and much of his view, he admitted, was obstructed by stacks of containers.

Could the crew be preparing to fire a third missile? Sanders pressed.

The captain said again that he couldn't be certain. But something was happening, and he was worried.

Did he have his GPS system working yet?

No, not yet, he conceded, though he insisted his crew was working feverishly to get it fixed as quickly as possible.

The phone on Sanders's desk rang. It had to be the CDO, or one of his deputies, but she wasn't ready to answer. Not yet. She had one more question for the captain of the Panamanian frigate, and she knew it might be her last.

"Are you and your crew armed?"

"No, should we be?" the captain replied, the anxiety in his voice suddenly rising another notch.

"I think that would be prudent," Sanders said, fearing for all their lives if the Liberian crew was listening in on their transmissions, which she now considered an increasingly likely scenario.

☆ ☆ ☆

A priority-one call came into NORAD at 9:58 p.m.

It was handled initially by a desk officer, then by a senior naval officer, who immediately raced over to Lt. General Briggs with the news.

"Sir, you've got an urgent call."

Briggs looked up from his computer screen, where he and two colleagues were frantically scanning the latest satellite imagery from the Atlantic and Pacific coastlines.

"From who?" Briggs asked, growing impatient with one interruption after another.

"Captain John Curry, sir."

"Oceana?"

"Yes, sir."

"Fine; put him on line six," Briggs ordered.

He didn't need to be reminded that Naval Air Station Oceana in Virginia Beach, Virginia, was the East Coast's only master jet base running 24-7-365 and a critical component to the NORAD air defense strategy for the Atlantic seaboard. Home to seventeen strike-fighter units, NAS Oceana was a six-thousand-acre complex employing eleven-thousand-plus navy personnel and handling a quarter of a million takeoffs and landings a year. If its base commander called on a day like today and said it was urgent, it had to be. Besides, Briggs had known Curry for nearly a decade and trusted him implicitly.

Briggs grabbed the receiver and hit line six. "Jack, it's Charlie. I'm swamped here—what've you got?"

"A Christmas present, Charlie. I just need permission to open it."

"What are you talking about?" Briggs asked, glancing at his watch.

Curry quickly explained that he had in his possession the approximate coordinates of the ship that had launched the Scud missiles against Washington, D.C. He briefly summarized how he had received the information—from one of his fighter pilots whose brother was dating a Coast Guard communications specialist who was in direct contact with the captain of a Panamanian ship who saw the whole thing go down.

"Can you verify this guy's story?" Briggs demanded, his pulse racing.

"We're doing that now, sir," Curry replied, informing the NORAD commander that he had already scrambled two F/A-18E Super Hornets on the hope that he would be able to give them authorization to fire en route. Both jets were inbound to the coordinates. Both were heavily armed. Both had orders to do a flyby over the deck of the Liberian container ship and report back immediately.

"If this thing checks out, General, do my men have permission to take this ship down?" Curry asked.

"Absolutely," Briggs replied without hesitation. "I just wish I could do it myself."

Briggs hung up and closed his eyes. He desperately wanted to get the U.S. on offense against somebody, anybody. But for that he needed a target. Was this the break he'd been waiting for, or the first of many false alarms?

20

★ ★
★

Caulfield stared at himself in the bathroom mirror.

His eyes were bloodshot. His hands were trembling. His head was pounding, and now a Secret Service agent was pounding on the door.

"Mr. Caulfield, you need to take your seat, sir."

"Just a moment," he replied, fumbling with the lock on his briefcase.

"Now, Mr. Caulfield," the agent said. "The pilot says we're approaching some serious turbulence. We need everyone in their seats."

"I said just a minute," Caulfield snapped back.

He frantically worked the combination, knowing he hadn't much time. The first time it failed to work. He had to slow down. He had to calm down. He tried again. This time the briefcase opened like a charm.

Caulfield fished past the briefing books marked TOP SECRET and folders crammed with policy papers. He reached past his digital camera and the yellow legal pads and his binder with the home, cell, pager, and e-mail information of every key figure in the American government. *There it was.* He carefully opened up the leather bag's false bottom and quickly found the glass bottle, a small mirror, and a razor blade. Next he pulled out his wallet and rolled up a twenty-dollar bill.

The plane began to shake, mildly at first; then it began to shudder violently.

"*Now, Mr. Caulfield,*" the agent said again. "*I really have to insist.*"

The aide tried to breathe deeply, then wiped off his nose, carefully put away everything in his briefcase, and washed his face and hands. A moment later he was sitting again, his seat belt fastened, his eyes closed, his mind reeling, terrified about his mother, his brothers, and his friends.

✭ ✭ ✭

Twenty minutes later, the turbulence had passed.

Special Agent-in-Charge Curt Coelho unbuckled his seat belt, stood, and straightened his tie. "Sir, it's time," he said.

He then introduced Oaks to the Honorable Sharon Summers, the sixty-three-year-old chief United States district judge for the Middle District of Florida, who thus far had been sitting unnoticed in the back of the executive jet.

"I appreciate you joining us on such short notice, Your Honor," Oaks said as he shook the judge's hand and offered her a seat at the small conference table.

"I'm horrified, sir," Judge Summers replied. "But be assured, Mr. President, I'll do whatever you need to get our government up and running again, consistent with the Constitution."

"Thank you, Judge Summers—I'm going to hold you to that. How long have you been serving on the bench?"

"President Bush 43 nominated me to serve just after 9/11, sir," she explained. "Senate confirmation went quite quickly, compared to most of my colleagues. I was confirmed on March 27, 2002, and received my commission three days later."

"Thank you for serving your country," Oaks said.

"It is my honor, sir."

"Do you have a copy of the Constitution?" Oaks asked.

"Yes, sir," she said. "I always keep a copy in my purse." She held up a small, leather-bound edition.

"Does someone have a Bible?" Oaks asked a few moments later.

"I have my personal Bible with me, sir," the judge said. "Will that do?"

"It will," he said. "Are you a woman of faith, Judge Summers?"

"Not growing up, I'm afraid," she replied. "But I have to admit, Mr. President, the Ezekiel War changed everything for me. So, yes, I am now, you could say."

"Very well," Oaks said, thankful that someone with faith he himself didn't possess could be with him at this terrible moment. "Then I'd very much appreciate your most earnest prayers in the hours and days ahead, Judge Summers."

"You have not only my prayers but those of a grateful nation, Mr. President," she said, her voice thick with emotion.

Oaks appreciated the sentiment and deep down hoped it was true, but he wasn't so certain that it was. He had been an agnostic for as long as he could remember. He wasn't hostile to people of faith, not by any means. His own wife had found herself drawn back to the church in the months since the war. But he simply couldn't seem to put himself in their shoes. He'd always been a Frank "I Did It My Way" Sinatra kind of guy, and he had no idea how to change, even if he had wanted to.

"Well, we had better not wait," he said, taking a deep breath. "Let's get this done, and then we'll talk about the line of succession and the chain of command."

"Yes, sir," Judge Summers replied.

She stood, as did everyone else on the plane, aside from the pilots themselves. Bobby Caulfield pulled out his digital camera to record the event for the nation, for the world, and for generations yet unborn.

"Mr. President, is there a particular passage you would like me to open to before I administer the oath of office?" the judge asked.

Oaks found himself embarrassed by the question. MacPherson had been the religious man on the ticket, not him, and at this moment, his mind was blank.

"Whatever you think would be appropriate would be fine with me, Your Honor," he said, hoping to sound gracious rather than ignorant.

"Well, sir, ever since the Secret Service picked me up at my home and told me what was happening, I just keep thinking of 2 Chronicles 7:14," she explained, opening up to the passage, clearing her throat, and reading it softly. "The Lord says, 'If My people who are called by My name humble themselves and pray and seek My face and turn from their wicked ways, then I will hear from heaven, will forgive their sin and will heal their land.' We need a whole lot of healing right now, sir. Which means we need a whole lot of prayer and a whole lot of humility."

Oaks nodded. "I couldn't agree more, Your Honor. That will do nicely."

"Thank you, sir. Are you ready?"

Oaks looked around a plane full of strangers. The only person he recognized was Caulfield. Marie wasn't with him. Nor was his chief of staff or any of his military or political advisors. He felt alone and overcome by the magnitude of the task ahead of him. He couldn't let it show, of course. He had to project strength, particularly here, particularly now. But the truth was he was scared, and he knew he wasn't the only one. He could see the fear in all of their eyes, no matter how brave and professional they acted or sounded. It was up to him to set the tone and to rally a nation paralyzed with shock.

"Yes, ma'am, I'm ready," he said at last.

"Very well, sir, please place your left hand on the Bible. Thank you. Now, please raise your right hand, and repeat after me as I administer the oath of office, from Article II, Section 1, Clause 8 of the U.S. Constitution."

Oaks did as he was told. So the judge began.

"I, William Harvard Oaks, do solemnly swear . . ."

"I, William Harvard Oaks, do solemnly swear . . ."

". . . that I will faithfully execute the Office of President of the United States . . ."

". . . that I will faithfully execute the Office of President of the United States . . ."

". . . and will to the best of my ability . . ."

". . . and will to the best of my ability . . ."

". . . preserve, protect, and defend . . ."

". . . preserve, protect, and defend . . ."

". . . the Constitution of the United States."

". . . the Constitution of the United States."

Judge Summers lowered her right hand and held it out to the man who now legally held the fate of the nation—and perhaps the world—in his hands.

"Congratulations, Mr. President," she said as Caulfield continued to snap pictures. "Please lead us well."

Everyone applauded.

"I'll do my best, Judge Summers," the president replied. "May God have mercy on us all."

21

★ ★
★

The bloodred sun rose quickly over the desert.

It was already nearly a hundred degrees, and it wasn't even six in the morning. The camp was stirring back to life, thus far unaware of the horror unfolding in the United States.

But Bennett and Dr. Kwamee knew. They huddled with a few other night shift doctors and nurses around a small television the camp's chief physician kept in his office. Not a single American broadcast television network was on the air, but Dr. Kwamee kept switching back and forth between the BBC, Sky News, and CNN International. None of them could believe what they were hearing or seeing.

". . . and to recap for those of you just tuning in, the BBC has now confirmed that four American cities—Washington, D.C., New York, Los Angeles, and Seattle—have been hit by nuclear bombs. Sources at Whitehall have confirmed for the BBC that killed in the attack on Los Angeles was American president James MacPherson. I repeat, the BBC can now confirm from senior British government sources that the American president is dead. He was killed in a nuclear explosion just as he was beginning to deliver his address to the Republican National Convention at Staples Center in Los Angeles. No word from 10 Downing Street yet, though we expect the prime minister to make a statement shortly.

"We can report that casualties in the United States are expected to be in the millions. Damages, we are told, are utterly beyond comprehension. Wall Street has been completely annihilated, we understand, and all trading across Asia has been halted after the markets began collapsing—the Nikkei alone dropped 36 percent before officials were able to shut it down. European markets are not expected to open this morning.

"At the moment, it is not clear whether these bombs were smuggled into the country by terrorists or launched into American cities by missiles. Defence Minister Allister Morgan says he has no indication that intercontinental ballistic missiles were used. Nor does he have any . . ."

So this was it, Bennett thought, his mind suddenly reverting back to the phone call he had received earlier. Whoever had called him had known these attacks were coming. He'd been telling the truth, which meant he probably knew what was coming next. So who was he? How much did he know? Bennett still couldn't figure out how anyone could have obtained his unlisted satellite phone number. But he began wondering how to seize the initiative and find out who this person was. This was a lead—a lead the authorities back in the States needed. But whom should he call? Almost everyone in the administration—many of whom he knew personally—was likely dead.

Bennett shook off the horrible thought. First things first, he decided. He took out his satellite phone and dialed his mother's home number in Orlando. All he got was a recording.

"I'm sorry, your call could not go through as dialed. Please recheck the number or hang up and dial again."

He tried several more times, without success. He tried his mother's cell phone number. Again, no luck. He tried the neighbors but was told repeatedly that all circuits were busy. This did not bode well, Bennett thought, though he quickly tried to drive the notion from his mind.

Dr. Kwamee switched stations again.

"This is CNN Breaking News . . ."

The distinctive music and imagery drew Bennett's attention.

". . . from the CNN Center in Atlanta, here's Terry Cameron."

"As a nuclear crisis of unimaginable proportions unfolds across the American homeland, CNN can now report that Vice President Bill Oaks has not only survived the four nuclear blasts but has just been sworn in as the new U.S. commander in chief. Moments ago, William Harvard Oaks became the forty-fifth president of the United States. What you are seeing on your screens is a digital photograph taken by a White House staffer on board *Air Force One* as the oath of office was being administered to the vice president by the Honorable Sharon Summers, who we understand is a federal judge from somewhere in Florida. . . ."

Cameron paused for a moment, perhaps, Bennett thought, to let the enormity of what he was saying to the country and the world begin to sink in. Or perhaps just to steady his emotions. News anchors typically weren't supposed to show their feelings on air. CNN International anchors in particular—at least in Bennett's experience—rarely showed flashes of any kind of patriotism or special affection for the United States. But Cameron was having trouble remaining emotionally detached from this story. *And thank God*, thought Bennett, who was having trouble keeping his own emotions in check. The woman on the BBC was acting as if this were simply an earthquake or a hurricane of some sort. Did she not get how serious this was, or was she secretly happy about it?

Maybe that wasn't fair. She was a professional. She had a job to do. But didn't this mean anything to her? Why was she so calm, so unmoved by the enormity of the carnage? Then again, wasn't he fighting to keep control? Had he been alone, Bennett might have lost it. But as the only American in the room, and as the only person Erin had in the world at the moment, he had already decided he had to keep his emotions in check.

What's more, he knew he had to keep this all from Erin. She was too weak to take any of it right at the moment, and perhaps for days. After all, every friend she had at the White House was dead. So were all her friends at the CIA, where she had worked for nearly a decade, and where her father had worked for a quarter of a century before his death in Afghanistan during the war with the Soviets.

And how would he ever tell her that the entire MacPherson family had been killed? Bennett wondered. The MacPhersons had practically adopted Erin when her mother had died of ovarian cancer in the early nineties. The MacPherson girls were the only sisters she had in the world, and they had always treated her as part of their family. And now they were gone. All of them. The truth was, nearly everyone he and Erin had ever known was dead, and the feeling of helplessness that had gripped him for most of the night began to come over him once more.

The clinic's air-conditioning had broken down, Bennett noticed. Perspiration soaked the collar of his shirt. Bennett's eyes were growing heavy. He didn't know if it was denial or depression, but something was telling him none of it mattered and lulling him to sleep. He could hear the CNN anchor remark on how quickly the American government was moving to reconstitute itself, but Bennett found that he didn't really care. He could hear some expert commenting on how important it was for the rest of the world—and particularly the enemies of the U.S.—to see that someone was in charge, but little of it registered.

At the same time, Bennett could hear the doctors around him arguing over who might be behind the attacks and what the new president should do about it. *But what did any of that really matter?* he asked himself. The world was going up in flames. Evil was being unleashed. What were another few nuclear missiles lobbed at innocent civilians? All he wanted to do was sleep.

Erin, he decided, was the fortunate one at the moment. She was so drugged up she had no idea what was happening. The last thing she had heard was that she was having a baby in eight months, and now she was savoring the sweetness of that moment with no idea it might be her last. *Why not join her?* Bennett mused. *Why not just curl up for a few hours or a few days and dream about a life that could have been?*

He leaned back in his chair and closed his eyes. His thoughts drifted, away from the news, away from the camp, away from the nightmare unfolding around him. He could suddenly see Erin again, as he had the first time he'd ever laid eyes on her. He could still remember the physical sensation he had felt as she'd stepped into his thirty-sixth-floor conference room in Manhattan with that brown skirt, silk blouse, and pearls. She'd been there to interview for a stock analyst job or investment strategist or something, but he could still remember thinking that if this beautiful girl had half a brain in her head, he would never forgive himself if he didn't hire her for something and figure out the details later.

He could still picture her handing him a résumé and smiling. He could still smell the scent of her perfume that seemed to linger in the air. He could feel the law bond cotton stationery in his hands, and he could feel his heart accelerate as he scanned the text while she sat at the conference table across from him.

Summa cum laude from UNC Chapel Hill with a bachelor's in economics. An MBA from Wharton. World traveler—London, Paris, Berlin, Hong Kong, and Cairo. A great-grandfather who had once been the U.S. secretary of state. And no rings on either hand. *How could a girl this beautiful still be single?* he had wondered then. *How in the world did she ever fall in love with me?* he wondered now.

22

★ ★
★

They came fast, hard, and without warning.

One after the other, the two F-18s swooped down from the night sky and buzzed the deck of the Liberian freighter at Mach 1.8, nearly twice the speed of sound. They shattered the windows of the bridge and knocked everyone on deck off their feet, sending them scrambling for safety. Seconds later, the fighter pilots were radioing back to NORAD.

"Crystal Palace, this is Canyon One-Niner. We have a visual on the target; do you copy? Over."

"Canyon One-Niner, this is Crystal Palace. What do you see, son?"

The pilot of the lead Super Hornet from the 105th Strike Fighter Squadron quickly confirmed all the details Coast Guard Specialist Carrie Sanders had sent up the system. It was a massive ship—at least three football fields in length—with a black hull marked with large white letters, a Liberian flag, and plenty of containers, several of them open. He saw no evidence of missile contrails. The winds had probably erased them. But what really terrified him was what was happening at the stern.

"Crystal Palace, this is Canyon One-Niner. The crew has set up another mobile launcher. I repeat, they have set up another mobile launcher. They've got a missile in place. It looks ready to go. It looks like they'll be ready to fire again any moment."

✦ ✦ ✦

Briggs gasped.

He had dozens of fighter jets, navy destroyers, fast attack subs, and Coast Guard cutters heading into the air and waters off New York, New Jersey, Maryland, California, Oregon, and Washington State in the frantic hunt for the ships that had fired upon American cities. But suddenly he had a live target and only seconds to act.

Two large-screen monitors mounted on the far wall of the NORAD Operations Center showed him live streaming video from each of the F-18s. A third screen displayed a newly acquired live satellite feed of the Liberian frigate, just coming into view. Sure enough, Briggs thought, he was staring down the barrel of a Scud C ballistic missile, armed and ready for launch. He could see the billows of smoke pouring out from its engines, and every muscle in his body tightened.

"Canyon One-Niner, Canyon Two-Zero, this is Lieutenant General Charles Briggs, commander of NORAD. *I order you to take that missile out and sink that ship immediately. Take that ship down immediately. Do you copy?*"

There was a flash of static.

"Canyon One-Niner, Canyon Two-Zero, this is Crystal Palace. Do you copy?"

But all he heard was more static.

"Canyon One-Niner and Canyon Two-Zero, this is Lieutenant General Briggs at NORAD. Do you copy? I repeat, do you copy?"

A transmission came in, but garbled. Briggs's mouth went dry. His face was covered with sweat. From the satellite image he could see the crew on the deck of the Liberian ship scrambling for cover. The launch was imminent. They were out of time.

Every eye in the ops center was riveted to the video screens. Several staffers clasped their hands to pray. They all knew what Briggs knew. A few seconds more and it would be too late. Another American city could be obliterated.

Briggs blinked hard. He ordered a glass of water and wiped his brow. This couldn't be happening again. But it was. His vision was blurring. He felt light-headed and dizzy. Just like he had before, on a day seared into his memory forever.

Instead of a Liberian frigate, Briggs suddenly found himself staring at a live video feed of a Russian jumbo jet, thirty-five miles from Washington and coming in red-hot. He found himself listening to the voice of Bob Corsetti, the White House chief of staff, pleading with the president to make a decision.

"Sir, you don't have a choice. You need to take this guy out fast."

Briggs could feel his pulse skyrocketing as he waited for the president to speak, to act, and quickly. Corsetti was right. MacPherson had been out of options, out of time. It was his constitutional duty to defend the country. What was taking so long? Why was he hesitating? Didn't he understand the stakes?

Seconds passed, though they felt like an eternity. Then MacPherson had finally come to his senses. He gave the order and it was quickly passed down the chain of command. Briggs could still see images like they were yesterday. He could still hear the audio. How could he ever forget?

"Devil One-One, POTUS declares the target is hostile. You are cleared to engage."

"CONR Command, do I understand you right? Target is hostile? You want me to engage? You want me to fire on an unarmed civilian jetliner?"

He could still hear the tremor in the flight leader's voice. It wasn't just nerves. It was something else—hesitation, resistance. But why? It wasn't a pilot's job to wrestle through the moral justification of a call like this. It was the president's. It was the commander in chief's. And now that commander had just issued an order. *Why wasn't it being executed?*

The Aeroflot jet was now twenty-five miles out. They were out of time.

As though he were hovering outside his own body, Briggs could see himself lunge forward, grab the radio, and scream at the lead pilot.

"Devil One-One, this is Lieutenant General Charles Briggs at NORAD. Son, you are ordered to take this Russian jet down. Repeat, take the target down—now."

For the longest moment, there was nothing but silence.

Then the lead pilot said, *"I can't, sir. . . . I'm sorry, sir. I . . . I just can't do it. . . . It's not right."*

With the Russian aircraft closing in on Washington, Briggs had grabbed the radio. All this time later, he could once again feel his heart pounding in his chest as it had on that day. He had already had three heart attacks. He couldn't afford a fourth. Certainly not now.

MacPherson had spoken before Briggs could. *"General Briggs, this is the president of the United States. The capital of the country is under attack. I am ordering you to take that plane down—now."*

Briggs had never heard the president so angry. Nor would he ever again.

Aeroflot 6617 was just fourteen miles out and picking up speed. Briggs could still feel the cold radio receiver in his hand.

"Devil One-One, this is General Briggs at NORAD. Peel off immediately. Devil One-Two, do you have a shot?"

There was nothing but silence.

"Devil One-Two, do you have a shot?"

Suddenly a flash of static, a garbled transmission, and then, finally, *"Roger that, General—I have a shot."*

"Then take it, son—before ten thousand people die."

Until the day he died, Briggs would never forget the image of that Russian jumbo jet, screaming down the Potomac River, on a suicide mission into the heart of the capital, an American F-16 flown by a twenty-five-year-old kid hot on his tail.

"Sir, I have radar lock. . . ."

The Russian plane was just eight miles from the White House.

"I have tone. . . ."

It was now or never. *Take the shot,* Briggs screamed inwardly. *Take the shot.*

"Fox two!"

But now the memory—painful though it was—faded, replaced by the reality of an ongoing operation somewhere over the Atlantic, just off the coast of Maryland. Briggs winced as he watched an air-to-ground missile explode from the right side of one of the F-18s, and then another, and a third. And a fourth. The second jet fired as well—again and again.

Briggs was mesmerized as he watched the barrage of missiles streak through the sky, homing in on their prey. Pain shot through his stomach, and then his chest. He winced again, opening his eyes just in time to witness the impact. But it wasn't a Russian jetliner he was watching explode. This time it was an African freighter, erupting in a massive fireball, sinking to the bottom of the frigid Atlantic, with an unfired Scud sinking with it. The ops center erupted in applause. But Briggs collapsed to the floor.

23

★ ★
★

Only a handful of people knew of the drama in the Atlantic.

The rest of the world was riveted on a new drama unfolding in China. Bennett certainly was. He shook off the fatigue that had been lulling him into inaction and asked Dr. Kwamee to turn up the volume as several more doctors and a few off-duty orderlies crowded into the physician's cramped office. Kwamee quickly complied as the anchor—looking shaken and pale—began to speak.

"This is Terry Cameron at CNN Center in Atlanta. We will continue, of course, to bring you the latest on the horrific events unfolding in four American cities at this hour, but we now have word of breaking news in Beijing. We're going to take you live to a press conference that is about to begin at the Great Hall of the People. . . . CNN correspondent Wang Li Peng is standing by. Wang Li, can you hear me?"

"Yes, Terry, I can hear you."

"I understand you have some serious developments there. What can you tell us?"

"Terry, just a few moments ago, Foreign Minister Zeng Zou gave an off-camera briefing to a hastily assembled group of Western reporters," the correspondent said, his voice quick and agitated. "He expressed sorrow for the attacks on the United States. He condemned those attacks in no uncertain terms. He insisted that China had absolutely no role in the attacks whatsoever. But what he said next struck my colleagues and me as quite ominous, to say the least. The foreign minister said that Chinese satellites have observed U.S. strategic nuclear forces going to DefCon One—or Defense Condition One. That's military lingo for America preparing for all-out war. The question is, against whom? The foreign minister also claimed that two U.S. nuclear aircraft carriers have just been ordered into the East China Sea, which in the next few hours would put them right off the western coast of China, not far from Shanghai, one of China's most important cities. The foreign minister called these—let me make sure I quote him precisely. . . ."

Peng flipped through his notepad to find the exact quote. "Yes, here it is—the foreign minister called these 'highly provocative military moves' that are 'tantamount to a declaration of war' and could push China and the United States into what he called 'an apocalyptic moment.'"

Was China behind these attacks? Bennett wondered. *Did the president know it? Was he considering a nuclear retaliation against the most populous country on the planet?*

The CNN correspondent in Beijing said that they were awaiting a hastily called press conference with the Chinese premier himself. He said that based on his conversations with high-ranking officials in Beijing, he believed there was a real and growing fear in the Chinese government that the U.S. may believe China was somehow behind the attacks and might be planning to retaliate. What's more, the correspondent noted that one of the problems the Chinese government was having was that its own ambassador to the United States—as well as all of its embassy staff in Washington—had been killed in the nuclear attacks. The same was true of its consulate staff in New York and Los Angeles.

"The government here is finding it difficult to get precise information on what is happening in the U.S.," Wang Li Peng explained. "Government officials here are not exactly sure who to speak with in the U.S. or how to establish direct contact. So far as we can tell, that's why the premier himself is about to come out and make a statement. We're not sure if he will take questions. I can tell you, Terry, that the PLA—the People's Liberation Army—has gone into a state of emergency. Mobile antiaircraft batteries are being positioned around the capital. We've seen numerous fighter aircraft scrambled to protect the capital, and we assume this is happening in other cities as well. According to state radio, all military leaves have been canceled, and the mood here is darkening very quickly."

Terry Cameron in Atlanta asked, "Has the U.S. Embassy in Beijing had any comment yet?"

"Not officially, not on the record," his correspondent replied. "But one senior American Embassy official told me by phone just a few minutes ago—on the condition of anonymity—that he himself is not sure who to talk to back in the U.S. As he understands it, the State Department has been destroyed. Secretary of State Marsha Kirkpatrick is believed to be dead. The president—President Oaks, that is—has apparently been sworn in aboard *Air Force One*, as you've reported, but no one seems to know where *Air Force One* is or how to reach it."

Events were about to spiral out of control, Bennett realized. *Why in the world would the Chinese have attacked the U.S.?* It made no sense. They had to know the U.S. would launch an all-out retaliation that could leave a billion Chinese dead in less than an hour. *Had they calculated that taking out the American president and his Cabinet would prevent a response?* The notion was as insane as it was suicidal.

Then again, Bennett thought, *what if the Chinese weren't involved? What if the president and whatever staff he still had around him were misreading the intelligence? Or what if they were ramping up for retaliation against someone else, and it was the Chinese government that was misreading the signals?* He had to call someone. He had to do something. But what?

Now a CNN military analyst—a former two-star U.S. Air Force general—was on the air from a studio in Berlin explaining just what military assets Beijing could bring to bear in a war with the U.S.

"Red China has 1,525 fighter jets," the general said. "At least 425 of these jets are typically pre-positioned within range of Taiwan. Beijing also has almost eight hundred bombers, some of them very sophisticated. About a quarter of those—about two hundred bombers—are also typically stationed within range of Taiwan. By contrast, Taiwan has barely three hundred fighter jets and no bombers to speak of."

"Is it possible that China could be using the attacks on the U.S.— whether Beijing was responsible for them or not—to prepare for an invasion of Taiwan?" Cameron asked.

"It's certainly possible," the American general said. "When I served in the Pentagon, one of my responsibilities was to plan for a Chinese move on Taiwan. Beijing has wanted to do it for as long as any of us can remember. They've been building up military assets for years. They've been planning, preparing, biding their time. Now let me be clear: I'm not saying the Chinese had anything to do with the sickening attacks. I have no access to classified intelligence. It's all moving too fast anyway, and I've heard that the CIA and DIA were completely destroyed in the attacks on Washington. But I am saying we'd better watch the PLA closely because they could take advantage of a terrible situation."

"That's a very chilling picture you're painting, General," Cameron said. "Hard to imagine, even."

"It would have been yesterday, maybe," the general replied. "But not anymore. Everything has changed. We're not living in the same world we were in even a few hours ago. And let me also be clear that while I am not accusing Beijing of being behind these nuclear attacks against the U.S., we cannot rule out that they could be involved in some way, shape, or form."

"Why do you say that?" Cameron asked.

"Well, don't forget that back in the 1990s, a Chinese general—I think he was the second or third guy in command of the PLA—actually threatened to vaporize Los Angeles."

"Wasn't that just a bit of saber rattling?" Cameron asked.

"I thought so," the general said. "But now? Who knows what Beijing is thinking, or what some rogue faction within the PLA is thinking?"

Bennett watched Cameron swallow hard. He could see the fear in the man's eyes, and the anchor didn't seem to know where to take the interview from there.

"What about the Chinese navy?" Cameron asked, clearly scrambling for something—anything—concrete, not theoretical. "How formidable are they?"

"They're no match against the American navy," the general explained. "But believe me, aside from us—and with Russia out of the picture— they're the most dangerous fleet on or under the seas."

"Can you give us a sense of their specific capabilities?"

"I can try," the general said. "As I recall, the Chinese have at least twenty-five destroyers. They've got about fifty frigates, about two dozen tank landing ships. More importantly, they've got fifty diesel submarines and at least five nuclear submarines. That's a whole lot of firepower, and nearly all of it could be thrown against Taiwan with devastating effect."

"What do the Taiwanese have to defend themselves?" Cameron asked.

"The Taiwanese have a small but impressive navy, much of it built by us," the American general said. "And they have one simple objective: to deter an invasion by the PRC. But a critical element of Taiwan's strategic doctrine is that the U.S. Navy and Air Force would be there to help them in the case of an attack. Will we be, under the circumstances? Honestly, given what's unfolding at the moment, I'm not so sure."

"The Chinese say the U.S. is moving two aircraft carriers into the East China Sea," the CNN anchor noted.

"Maybe, and that would help," the general replied. "But the brutal truth is that if the Chinese are really behind these attacks on the U.S., then they're willing to annihilate anyone or anything that gets in the way of their objective."

Missiles, Bennett thought.

"Might Beijing resort to nuclear missiles against Taiwan?" Cameron asked, as if on cue.

"That's the X factor," the two-star said. "That's the real worry. The Chinese have at least twenty silo-based ICBMs. Each is armed with a nuclear warhead. Each is capable of reaching the United States—the West Coast, at least. Plus, they've got a bunch of sub-launched nuclear missiles; I'm not sure how many. I'm not sure if anybody knows how many. They've got nearly fifty missile boats. What's more, they've got literally hundreds—maybe thousands—of medium-range missiles, many of which were also equipped with nuclear warheads. And all of them can reach Taiwan—or our aircraft carrier battle groups—before you and I go to a commercial break."

Bennett couldn't take any more. He couldn't just sit around and watch TV. But what difference could he make? And even if there was something he could do, he couldn't leave Erin, could he?

He suddenly remembered his satellite phone. He pulled it out and prepared to call back whoever had called him. *But that was odd,* he thought. *There was no call-back number.* There was, to his surprise, no evidence that such a call had ever come in.

24

★ ★
★

Mustafa Al-Hassani lit his pipe and turned to Khalid Tariq.

"Events are moving rapidly now, Khalid," he said with an air of calm assurance.

"You have your empire," Tariq replied. "But can you keep it? Can you expand it? Today might determine that once and for all."

"Yes, Khalid, it might."

In the wake of the Day of Devastation, Arab and Persian leaders—what was left of them, anyway—had literally begged Al-Hassani to help them, protect them, rebuild them, restore them, lest they be swallowed up by American and European imperialists or by the incompetents at the U.N. Iraq was the only Arab country left standing after the so-called War of Gog and Magog. With oil prices soaring through the roof, trillions of petrodollars were flowing into his coffers, and with them unprecedented leverage to shape events in a way that his predecessors could not have imagined in their wildest dreams.

Al-Hassani had agreed. He would help his brothers and sisters in their desperate hour of need. But only on one condition. They had to agree to unification under his command.

The only way the peoples of the Middle East could truly compete and succeed against the U.S. and the European Union—and against the increasingly powerful trade alliance between China and the ASEAN economic community (the Association of South East Asian Nations, which included Indonesia, Singapore, the Philippines, Thailand, and Cambodia, among others)—was to come together as one, and fast, he had argued. They needed one leader, one legislature, one court system, one tax system, one currency, and one capital—Babylon. The faster they agreed, the faster they could tap into Iraq's enormous oil wealth. The faster they could rebuild their own oil industries. The faster they could become players again on the world stage.

Everyone in the region could see Al-Hassani's offer for what it was: a power grab, pure and simple. But what choice did they really have? They could unify under Babylon or risk being carved up by Washington and Brussels.

And thus was born the United States of Eurasia.

From the provinces of Mauretania in the west to the provinces of Kazakhstan, Kyrgyzstan, Tajikistan, and Afghanistan in the east, nearly a half billion people now lived and moved and had their being at Al-Hassani's pleasure. The unification process was going faster than even he or his most trusted advisors had expected. Reconstruction efforts, especially in the Gulf states, were well ahead of schedule. New oil wells were coming on line at the rate of between six and ten a day. Four brand-new, state-of-the-art petroleum refineries were already up and running. Five more would be operational by the end of the month, with another five slated to be completed by year's end.

It was all good, but not good enough, which was why he had summoned Salvador Lucente to Babylon.

Al-Hassani savored the sweet, mellow aroma of his golden Virginia tobacco, laced with buttered Jamaican rum, the one sinful pleasure he allowed himself from the Americas. He stared out over the city of his dreams, blazing in the late-summer sun and teeming with cranes and construction equipment as far as his eye could see.

So, what exactly was Salvador Lucente going to say now? he wondered, though he said nothing to Tariq. *What excuse was the U.N. secretary-general going to bring this time?*

Al-Hassani vividly remembered their meeting eight months earlier, right here in his private suite, on his private balcony, actually. Lucente had explained very carefully what he needed, and Al-Hassani had explained very carefully what it would cost him.

"Our economies are choking," Lucente had begun. "Oil is topping 175 euros a barrel. Unemployment in Europe is soaring. We can't operate with prices this high. We've got to get oil flowing out of the Middle East again, and we need you to take the lead. We need you to get oil prices under a hundred euros by summer"—and this Al-Hassani would never forget—"or I am afraid we will have to consider some unpleasant scenarios."

"Did you just threaten me?" Al-Hassani had asked.

"Of course not, Mr. President," Lucente lied. "You know how much we have done to rebuild your country. I have no doubt you will now help us in our time of need."

"Or else?"

"Well, I wouldn't put it that way," Lucente replied.

Al-Hassani wasn't convinced. "But didn't you just?"

Al-Hassani could still recall Lucente pausing, processing, and then leaning forward and saying in no uncertain terms, "Look, Mr. President, there is no question you have a formidable military. You now have two hundred thousand troops, armed with the latest weaponry. I know this full well. After all, NATO and the Americans recruited them, trained them, equipped them, and helped them gain valuable combat experience in crushing the insurgency, did we not? But do not deceive yourself, Mr. President. Your forces are not yet ready to face the combined forces of a unified Western alliance that is determined to achieve energy security at all costs. I urge you, my friend, do not miscalculate, as Iraqi leaders historically are wont to do. Your country cannot afford a misstep, not in this current global environment."

To which Al-Hassani had countered, "We want Russia's seat at the U.N. Security Council."

"So does Israel," Lucente replied.

"Nevertheless," the Iraqi leader explained, "if you want our oil, we want a permanent seat on the Security Council. It can be Russia's. It can be new. It does not matter to me, but it is nonnegotiable. And we want assurances that neither the E.U. nor the U.S. nor the U.N. will interfere with our efforts to unify the region's political and economic structures."

"You mean you want carte blanche to rebuild the Babylonian Empire?" Lucente had asked. The man had a penchant for stating the obvious.

"My dear friend," Al-Hassani explained, "my people have the same right to reorganize our part of the world as you had to reorganize Europe in a fashion that suited your interests. But let me be clear. We are not asking for permission. We are looking for assurances that no one will interfere."

"Assurances?" Lucente asked. "What kind of assurances?"

"Withdrawal of foreign troops from the region," Al-Hassani said. "Coordination of all relief and reconstruction efforts through my office, not through the U.N. Guaranteed accession to the WTO. And a guarantee on Jerusalem."

Al-Hassani recalled most clearly the feigned look of surprise on Lucente's face at that moment. It was all an act. Lucente was a congenital liar, the Iraqi had concluded. But it didn't really matter. For the moment, at least, Al-Hassani had all the leverage he needed to get what he wanted. And he had no hesitation to use it.

"And just what kind of guarantee on Jerusalem are you looking for?" Lucente had asked.

"The U.N. must internationalize the holy sites," Al-Hassani replied. "They must seize control of the Temple Mount in particular. The Jews must not be allowed to build anything there—not a Temple, not a visitor center, not a falafel stand. Nothing. Ever. Period. End of story."

"*Or else?*" Lucente asked.

"Oh, my friend, I wouldn't put it *that* way," Al-Hassani had replied, a twinkle in his eye.

Lucente forced a smile. "But didn't you just?"

At that moment, the deal seemed done. Or so Al-Hassani had thought. Since that day, he had, in fact, been granted the permanent seat on the U.N. Security Council, instead of Israel. He now had his WTO membership, and nearly all foreign troops had been removed from the region, except those assisting humanitarian relief and reconstruction efforts, all of which were now being coordinated through his office, just as he had demanded.

On Jerusalem, however, Lucente had balked, saying he simply couldn't get it done. Lucente claimed the U.S. had too much leverage, that while the MacPherson administration was not formally backing Israeli prime minister David Doron's decision to build the Third Jewish Temple, the

White House wasn't opposing it either. Doron was taking this as a green light and was proceeding with all haste.

Al-Hassani's provincial governors were furious, as was Tariq. They insisted that Al-Hassani force Lucente—who was now the U.N. secretary-general, after all—to stop the Israelis or each of them would break away from the Eurasian empire and declare their own independence. The Kurds were already making good on their threats. The rest of the Eurasian governors were calculating that Al-Hassani couldn't risk a further breakup of the alliance he had so carefully constructed over the past year.

Unfortunately, they were right. Al-Hassani had to find a way to force Lucente's hand. He had to find a way to stop the Temple from being built. He had tried Operation Black Box, but that had failed disastrously. He had been able to seize the treasures of neither the Copper Scroll nor the Ark of the Covenant. Now the Jews had both, and with them an unprecedented zeal to finish the Temple as quickly as possible.

But now, it seemed, fate had handed the Iraqi leader a gift.

25

★ ★
★

Prime Minister Liu Xing Zhao stepped to the podium.

Only forty-nine, he was the seventh premier of the modern People's Republic of China and by far the youngest. Widely perceived by his countrymen to be the most physically and intellectually vigorous of the nation's recent leaders, he had a well-known passion for afternoon tennis and a legendary photographic memory. He had a penchant for finely tailored black silk suits, like the one he was wearing today, and a great command of China's rapidly growing economy, carefully cultivated during his tenure as finance minister before rising to foreign minister and then being confirmed by the National People's Congress to be prime minister just three years earlier.

Amid a dizzying array of flashbulbs and the sounds of hundreds of autoadvancers, Premier Zhao cleared his throat and addressed not only the throng of reporters but a worldwide television audience to whom he was now speaking live.

"Ladies and gentlemen, it with a deep sense of concern that I have asked you to gather on such short notice. As you know, there are more than two thousand journalists from China and abroad covering the current session of the National People's Congress. Allow me to say to all of you here that on behalf of my entire nation, I unequivocally condemn these dastardly terrorist attacks on the United States. I offer the American people any and all assistance they will need in the coming days and months. And my government and I stand ready to work with the American people and their government to hunt down those responsible for these atrocities and bring them to justice."

The premier paused for a moment to let his translators catch up.

"Furthermore, I want to say in no uncertain terms that the People's Republic of China was not in any way responsible for these attacks. Let me repeat: the People's Republic of China played absolutely no role in these attacks, nor would we."

A murmur spread through the press corps.

"Based on the latest available information, my generals tell me that these were not attacks from intercontinental ballistic missiles. Nor were these attacks launched from submarines. They appear to be the work of short-range missiles launched from container ships operating near the Atlantic and Pacific coastlines of the United States, and I can assure you that not a single ship owned or operated by the PRC is currently— or has been in the last twenty-four hours—within eight hundred miles of the American homeland. What's more, the container ships that we do currently have on the high seas, headed for the U.S., have all been ordered to turn around and come back to Chinese ports to be reinspected. We have also ordered all Chinese submarines and other naval vessels to return to our ports to make absolutely clear to the American authorities that we have no hostile intent toward the American people whatsoever."

Again, Premier Zhao paused to let his translators keep pace. Then he said, "I have just spoken personally with the U.S. ambassador here in Beijing to extend my condolences and to give him the same message I am delivering here. Foreign Minister Zeng Zou is doing everything he can to contact the American government for the same purpose. This is a very dark day in the history of the world. What has happened is unimaginable. We must all take care that this crisis does not lead us into the abyss."

The premier now took questions.

"Mr. Prime Minister," the Associated Press bureau chief asked, "have all Chinese intercontinental ballistic missiles been accounted for?"

"I just told you, these were not ICBM attacks," the premier said. "But yes, all of our missiles are present and accounted for. None of them were fired at the United States. Nor would we ever consider a sneak attack like this."

"Is it true, Mr. Prime Minister, that you are concerned that the Americans might be considering a retaliatory strike against China?" asked the editor of the *People's Daily*.

The premier shook his head. "There is no reason to fear that the Americans would retaliate against us," he tried to assure the reporter. "We have done nothing against the Americans. Indeed, we are offering to help the Americans in any and every way we can, including helping to retaliate against any country that is responsible. Two more questions—yes, you, in the second row."

A woman with Reuters stood up and asked, "Is it true that the United States is moving two aircraft carriers into the East China Sea?"

"I have heard these reports in the media, but I cannot confirm them independently at this time," Zhao said.

"A follow-up, sir?"

"Yes."

"If this turns out to be true, how would your government react?"

"You are asking a hypothetical," Zhao demurred. "This is a sad enough day without responding to hypotheticals. Yes, you in the back row."

"Mr. Prime Minister, the wire services are reporting that President Al-Hassani has mobilized nearly 150,000 troops to stop the Kurds in the northern parts of Iraq from seceding and joining a new, independent state of Kurdistan."

"I am hearing similar reports, yes," Zhao said. "But that's not our topic right now."

"I understand," the reporter said. "But given that China and Iraq signed a series of strategic alliance agreements just a few months ago, are you considering sending Chinese military forces to the Middle East to put down an independence movement by the Kurds?"

Zhao replied, "We are in discussions with the Iraqis and U.N. Secretary-General Lucente on the possibility of sending peacekeepers to the Gulf region. We have no plans at present to join forces with the Iraqis against the Kurds."

"At present?" the reporter asked. "Does that mean you haven't ruled out the possibility of joint action?"

"The Kurdish issue is very sensitive. I'm very concerned that this could be the spark that blows up the Middle East again. The last thing the world needs is another war in Iraq. We will do everything we can to bring a new era of peace to the region, not more war."

Everyone noted that the premier hadn't really answered the question, and that he quickly moved on.

"Yes," he said, pointing to a correspondent for the BBC in the third row.

"Mr. Prime Minister, you say you won't respond to hypotheticals," she began. "But you have clearly put the Red Army on full alert. The streets of Beijing are flooded with troops and missile batteries. Fighter jets are circling the capital. The BBC is reporting that the Chinese navy is being ordered to sea, your statement about Chinese vessels near the U.S. coasts notwithstanding. Who are you worried about, if not the Americans?"

At this, the premier took his time, carefully considering the stakes, and carefully weighing his words.

"You must understand the present situation," he said slowly. "A great power has been viciously attacked today. The American president has been killed. Untold millions of Americans have been killed. I am hearing that as many as half of the members of Congress have been killed. The White House and Pentagon have been destroyed. Who knows the state of mind of the American leaders right now? Do you? Has the newly sworn-in president given a press conference? Have you seen any live images of him, or his advisors? No, not yet, so we are left to guess. And what shall we guess? We are operating in the fog of a very serious crisis. We can only imagine that the American leadership is angry and eager to strike back at someone. So we must exercise great caution."

Zhao paused a moment, looking around the room before continuing. "I know, as do you, that there are some in the U.S. who say China is the great evil in the world today. There are some who would wish to trigger a conflict between the U.S. and the PRC. They are agitating for it today, as they have been for many years. Perhaps this will be tempting for the Americans in this present hour, to see China as the enemy and to see this as the moment to attack us. Well, we are not the enemy. And let there be no misunderstanding; any attempt to treat us like an enemy will be dealt with in the most decisive manner possible."

26

★ ★
★

Bennett watched Premier Zhao leave the podium.

It had been a useful press conference right up to the end, he thought. But then it had taken an ominous turn. CNN's Terry Cameron seemed to agree.

"The Chinese premier seems to be offering both condolences to the American people and what could only be seen as a threat to the American government; wouldn't you say, Wang Li?" Cameron asked.

"I'm afraid so," the Beijing correspondent agreed. "The premier's words were particularly sharp, especially given the fact that no one—least of all the American government—has actually accused the Chinese of attacking the U.S. Nor have we heard any speculation from official sources in the U.S. that they even suspect China was involved in these attacks at any level whatsoever."

"Is it possible that the U.S. has been communicating threats to Beijing through back channels of some kind?" Cameron asked.

"Possible, but doubtful, in my view," the correspondent replied. "Surely the U.S. Embassy here would be aware of this and interested in letting the international press corps know of such warnings. But at the moment, I'm not aware of anything like that."

"So from your vantage point, Wang Li, where does that leave us?"

"It's a tough question, Terry—there aren't many countries capable of causing this kind of apocalyptic destruction inside the United States, but Red China is certainly one of them," the correspondent explained. "The PRC is clearly very worried that what's left of the American government may point the finger of blame at Beijing and retaliate, and the premier is obviously taking preemptive action to head off such a dangerous confrontation between themselves and the U.S."

"It's a situation we'll be watching closely over the coming hours," Cameron said. "But one more thing before we leave you. I understand that U.N. Secretary-General Salvador Lucente was in Beijing overnight and then left this morning for Babylon. What can you tell us about his meetings there?"

"That's true, Terry," the reporter confirmed. "Secretary-General Lucente was originally scheduled to be in New York all this week, hosting a human rights conference. But at the last minute, something apparently came up that persuaded him to leave Manhattan and to come to Beijing. It's a move, of course, that now seems almost miraculous. Had he remained in New York, he most certainly would have been among the casualties. According to senior officials who spoke with me on the condition of anonymity, the secretary-general came here to negotiate the possible introduction of Chinese peacekeeping forces into the Persian Gulf region. Mr. Lucente has been pressing China to play a critical role in speeding up the economic reconstruction and recovery in the Middle East, and to help increase the rate of oil production, which of course is vital to bringing down the international price of oil and stabilizing the global economy. Chinese leaders have been reluctant to get heavily involved, but something seemed to change over the weekend, something that apparently convinced the secretary-general to change his plans and come here for a series of high-level negotiations. But neither side made any public comment when talks ended this morning."

"Thanks, Wang Li," Cameron said. "We understand the secretary-general will be holding a press conference later today in Babylon to discuss the destruction of the U.N. headquarters in New York and where the international community goes from here. CNN will bring that to you live when it happens. For now, we go to London to bring the latest international reaction to . . ."

Bennett excused himself, took a bottle of water from the small refrigerator in Dr. Kwamee's office, and stepped outside the clinic.

The temperature was now soaring. There was little shade and no breeze. But he couldn't watch any more television. He couldn't listen to the doctors arguing over whether China was behind the attacks or what the U.S. should do if they were. Erin was still asleep. He couldn't reach his mom or anyone else he knew in the States. He needed to be alone. He needed time to think, time to pray, time to figure out what in the world he was supposed to do in light of the events unfolding around him.

He walked past the guards at the main gate, who expressed their shock and their condolences and asked if there was anything they could do. Bennett thanked them and moved on. The answer was no, there was nothing they could do, but he greatly appreciated the concern.

Bennett now walked toward his and Erin's tent, baking in the morning heat. Perhaps he could take a shower and change his clothes before Erin awoke and needed him again, he decided. But first he headed to the mess tent and apologized to his supervisor for missing the breakfast shift. It wasn't necessary, she assured him. She had heard what had happened to Erin and about the attacks in the U.S. She urged him to take as much time as he needed. She and her team of volunteers would get by. She didn't know how exactly, but somehow they would get by.

Bennett thanked this kindly older woman from Bangladesh and began heading back to his tent when a thought hit him: they were leaving. He wasn't sure when. It couldn't be soon. But something within Bennett told him he and Erin weren't going to be in Jordan much longer.

If Erin were healthy, of course, there would be no question. They would head home immediately. What they would do when they got there, he had no idea. How they would even get back into the country—he had no idea about that either. All flights in and out of the continental United States were shut down. Canada, too, for the moment.

Mexico? The Caribbean? Were any of these options? He really didn't know, and there was no point thinking about it. He couldn't move Erin. Not for another week or two, at least. Perhaps by then things would be clearer. But something made Bennett wonder if they had another week.

Bennett took a sip of water and kept walking. As he did, he found himself mulling over the photo he had seen on CNN of Vice President

Oaks taking the oath of office from the federal judge from Jacksonville. To Bennett, it was eerily reminiscent of the famous November 22, 1963, photo of Vice President Lyndon Johnson being sworn in aboard *Air Force One* after the assassination of President John F. Kennedy in Dallas. Johnson, Bennett recalled, had also been sworn in by a woman. Bennett had even met the woman once—Judge Sarah T. Hughes—at some party in Washington his parents had dragged him to as kid. He hadn't been even the slightest bit interested back then. Now he couldn't help but wonder what it had been like on that plane at Love Field as the nation mourned the tragic death of Camelot and tried to adjust to a new president, with a vastly different style and temperament, in a vastly different America than had existed just a few hours before.

William H. Oaks was a good man, Bennett reminded himself as he made his way through the dusty alleyways of the camp. He had been one of the most effective vice presidents in the country's history, and Bennett respected him enormously.

For one thing, Oaks had far more government experience—particularly federal experience and national security experience—than MacPherson had had when the two were elected eight years earlier. That seemed to give Oaks a confidence Bennett found reassuring. He could always be trusted to be calm, cool, and collected in a crisis. Bennett had seen it firsthand after the kamikaze attack in Denver had nearly killed MacPherson five years earlier. He had seen it again when suicide bombers had taken out the Palestinian leadership and triggered a civil war in the West Bank and Gaza.

What had really impressed Bennett about Oaks was that, at heart, the man was a strategist. In the 1980s, he had been a key Senate ally to President Reagan in helping outflank and outfox the Evil Empire. In the 1990s, he'd been a staunch and unwavering voice for expanding the CIA's HUMINT—or human intelligence—capacity, as well as for modernizing U.S. nuclear forces and special operations capabilities.

Oaks had also applied his impressive intellectual heft to the rethinking of the U.S. role in a post-Soviet world. He was one of the first leaders in Washington to warn that radical Islam would replace Communism as the most serious threat to U.S. national security, and he had seen the Iranian threat long before most others in the American political system had.

The man had an uncanny ability to play three-dimensional chess, the ability to calculate and assess each possible move and countermove and counter-countermove when it came to domestic politics and global affairs. And more often than not, he was right. It was no wonder to Bennett that the Secret Service had code-named Oaks "Checkmate." But now Checkmate was no longer a deputy. He was the president of the United States at a moment of tremendous peril. What was he seeing? Bennett wondered. What was he thinking? What was he getting ready to do?

Bennett's satellite phone rang again. He checked the caller ID again. No name. No number. It was him. It had to be. He wasn't entirely sure what he was going to say, or do, but he answered the call, and silently prayed for the wisdom to do the right thing.

"Mr. Bennett?" said the voice at the other end.

"Yes, this is he," Bennett said, steeling himself for what was coming.

But the words that came next caught him completely off guard.

"Mr. Bennett, this is the *Air Force One* operator; please hold for the president of the United States."

27

★ ★
★

Salvador Lucente looked pale and exhausted.

Al-Hassani greeted him warmly with the traditional Arab kiss on both cheeks, but Lucente was distant and largely unresponsive. Then again, with all that he was going through, Al-Hassani was surprised he had not canceled the meeting altogether.

"Salvador," Al-Hassani began somberly, "on behalf of my people, please accept our condolences for the terrible tragedy that has befallen the entire United Nations family."

Lucente nodded but said nothing. The two men stepped out onto the Iraqi president's private balcony and took seats in their usual places. Khalid Tariq followed them and sat to one side. Lucente, for once, had left his entourage back at the hotel.

"We are hearing conflicting reports on the extent of the damage in New York," Al-Hassani said. "What can you tell me?"

Lucente turned and stared out over the cityscape. "Manhattan no longer exists," he said softly. "Turtle Bay was completely destroyed, and the U.N. building with it. All of our New York staff is dead. All of our records were destroyed. Our computer backup facility was destroyed. Every diplomatic mission has been wiped out. The magnitude is simply incalculable."

"I don't know what to say," Al-Hassani said.

The two men sat in silence for several minutes.

"Can Khalid get you anything?" the Iraqi leader finally asked quietly.

"No, nothing," Lucente said.

A few minutes later, Lucente changed his mind and asked for some hot tea. Tariq signaled a steward, and a pot of tea and two china cups were promptly brought over to their table.

"We have to rebuild—to show the world there is still hope of a peaceful future—but we will have to start over from scratch," Lucente said.

Al-Hassani added some honey to his tea and asked, "Will you rebuild in the U.S.?"

The secretary-general shook his head. "Honestly, I haven't had time to give it much thought," he replied. "Brussels, perhaps. Maybe Rome. I was just in China, as you know. I'm sure there will be a great deal of pressure to relocate to Asia, though—between you and me—I don't picture us being in Beijing. Indeed, based on the rumors I'm hearing out of the U.S., there may not be a Beijing by week's end. I'm afraid this whole thing could go from bad to worse."

Al-Hassani nodded but said nothing for a little while. He wasn't sure he was ready to discuss a nuclear war between the U.S. and China. *One step at a time*, he told himself. He needed to control this conversation, guide it where he needed it to go, and he needed to do it carefully, precisely.

"You are certainly welcome to come here, Salvador," he said at last. "We would count it a great honor. We would even build you a headquarters at our own expense."

"Thank you," Lucente said. "That is most generous. It really is. But I'm not sure if I can afford your price, Mustafa."

Al-Hassani sat quietly, careful not to smile.

"Jerusalem, right?" Lucente asked.

It was actually more of a statement than a question, but it was right on the mark.

Al-Hassani shrugged. "The attack on the United States—the situation, shall we say—has changed everything, has it not?" he asked.

"How do you mean?" Lucente asked.

"Well, perhaps this is not the best time to be discussing this—I certainly don't want to appear insensitive—but it was President MacPherson, of course, who was supporting Prime Minister Doron in his efforts to build the Jewish Temple."

"That's not entirely accurate, Mr. President, and you know it," Lucente said.

"Fine," Al-Hassani conceded. "Perhaps MacPherson didn't support the Temple, but he didn't oppose it either, and that has had the same effect. But now, tragically, everything has changed. The new American president, President Oaks, will surely have other issues to wrestle with than the future of the Temple Mount, will he not?"

"Just what are you trying to say, Mustafa?" Lucente pressed.

"I'm saying that perhaps in the current environment, new pressures could be brought to bear to stop the Israelis from completing the Temple."

"Nothing can stop the Israelis," Lucente said bluntly. "I'm told construction will be done by fall, perhaps by Yom Kippur."

"I hear the same rumors you do," Al-Hassani assured the secretary-general.

"Then you know this isn't a project Prime Minister Doron is about to abandon," Lucente said.

Al-Hassani shook his head. "Don't be so sure," he countered. "With America neutralized—and thus with the might of the American military no longer backing the Israelis—I suspect Mr. Doron could be forced to think twice about defying the will of the international community."

Lucente set down his teacup and looked Al-Hassani straight in the eye. "Mustafa, tell me you were not behind these attacks."

Al-Hassani affected a stunned expression. "*What?* How could you even think such a thing?"

"Tell me I'm wrong," Lucente said.

"I won't even dignify that with a response," the Iraqi leader sniffed, not daring to look at Tariq.

"I will ask you again," Lucente pressed. "Did you or did you not have anything whatsoever to do with these attacks on the United States?"

"I'm insulted by the very premise," Al-Hassani snapped back. "We don't even have any nuclear weapons. You should know that better than anyone."

"Maybe yes, maybe no," Lucente said. "I have seen intelligence reports that several Russian tactical nuclear weapons that were known to be in the region, or on the way, were unaccounted for after the Day of Devastation."

"I have heard such reports myself," Al-Hassani agreed.

"And?"

"And what?"

"And I have heard rumors that those tactical nukes were found by Iraqi forces and brought back to Babylon for safekeeping," Lucente said.

"*Lies,*" Al-Hassani shot back. "Who told you that? the Kurds? the ones who now want to pressure you and the rest of the world into letting them illegally secede from the United States of Eurasia to form their own pathetic little country? *Liars.* They are all liars! We have no nuclear weapons. We've never had nuclear weapons. We never will have nuclear weapons. And I for one am deeply offended that you would come here, to my home, and accuse me of seeking to annihilate the very country that liberated me and my people from the tyranny of Saddam and his sons."

"I am not accusing," Lucente repeated calmly. "I am simply asking questions—questions the whole world will soon be asking me. Do you not agree that the secretary-general of the United Nations should have answers to such questions?"

But the Iraqi leader made it clear with his expression that the answer was an adamant no.

28

7:14 A.M.—A REFUGEE CAMP IN NORTHERN JORDAN

Bennett was stunned.

It wasn't *him*. It was Oaks. But why would the new president call him? Why now?

"Jon, is that you?"

"Yes, sir, Mr. President," he replied, swallowing hard.

"I understand you're in the Middle East right now—is that right?"

"Yes, sir—Jordan, sir."

"In a refugee camp of some kind?"

"That's correct, sir. Erin and I have been here since just after our honeymoon."

"What's that, about six months now?"

"Closer to seven, sir."

"Well, good for you—both of you. It must be rewarding to do something good while all hell breaks out, no?"

"It was until today," Bennett said, grateful for the kind words but uncomfortable with the focus on him and Erin under the circumstances.

"Indeed," the president replied so quietly that Bennett could barely hear him. "That's why I'm calling."

"I don't even know what to say, Mr. President," Bennett said. "I'm so sorry to hear about President MacPherson and his family, and about everything that's happened, of course. Words cannot even begin . . ."

Bennett's voiced trailed off. Powerful emotions were again forcing their way to the surface, and he had to fight to keep them back.

"What's happened today is incomprehensible," Oaks agreed, his own voice wavering a bit.

"Are Marie and the boys safe?" Bennett asked.

"They are. Thanks for asking. They're not with me, but I just spoke to them by phone. We were all very lucky."

"I'm afraid I don't believe in luck, Mr. President."

Oaks seemed startled. "What do you mean?"

"Luck is random," Bennett explained. "But God isn't random. He has a plan."

"You think America getting attacked by nuclear bombs is God's plan?"

"No, sir, that's not what I meant."

"Then, forgive me, but what did you mean?"

"Men make evil plans, not God," Bennett replied. "But the Bible says what man plans for evil, God can turn for good."

"So God knew this was all going to happen?"

"Yes, sir."

"Why didn't He stop it?"

"I don't know, sir."

"He could have."

"Yes, He could have."

"But He didn't."

"I can't explain it all, Mr. President. All I know for certain is that in your case, He has chosen to keep you safe and to make you the next leader of the free world. That's not luck, sir. That's not random. That's the grace of God. That's His supernatural hand on you, guiding you, positioning you just where He wants you. And to be honest, sir, there are only two relevant questions now."

There was no point beating around the bush, Bennett thought. Too much was at stake. If he had the president's ear, he might as well speak his mind.

"What are they?" Oaks asked.

"The first is the question every one of us must face before it's too late: if, God forbid, you were to die tonight, do you know beyond the shadow of a doubt that you'd spend eternity with God in heaven?"

There was a long, uncomfortable silence.

"And the second?" Oaks asked.

"The second is a question only you must face: what are you going to do with this enormous responsibility God has just handed you?"

There was another long pause. Bennett wondered if he had gone too far. Yet, again, under the circumstances, he knew he didn't have a choice. This wasn't a political moment. Bennett wasn't a political advisor. The president's soul hung in the balance. The man was an agnostic in the earth's final days, days that would lead straight to the ultimate Day of Judgment. Oaks needed to get right with God before it was too late.

"Actually, Jon," the president stammered, uncharacteristically, "this is . . ."

"Yes, sir?"

"This really is why I called."

Bennett wasn't sure what to say next, so he just listened.

"I never thought anything like this was possible, not after the last war," Oaks continued. "I thought such horrors were behind us. But in the last few hours, I keep recalling your old friend Dr. Mordechai saying that the whole Gog and Magog thing wasn't the end, just the beginning of the end."

"He did, sir; that's true," Bennett acknowledged, surprised that Oaks had paid attention, much less remembered the line.

"I'm beginning to think that you and he might have been right about a lot of things," the president continued. "I'll admit, I was a skeptic until now—a cynic, perhaps. But after this . . . I don't know. . . . That's why I'm calling. I'd . . . well, I'd be grateful for your counsel, Jon."

"I beg your pardon, sir?" Bennett asked, not sure he'd heard the man correctly.

"I'd like to see you as soon as possible—you and Erin," the president explained. "Most of our top people are dead. Nearly all the White House and NSC staff are gone. State is gone. Most of the team at the Pentagon. And I'm sure you've heard about Langley."

"Yes, sir, I'm afraid I did."

"I need people around me I know, people I can trust," Oaks said plainly. "I need to assemble a team of people who can give me wise counsel through some very dark days, people who are willing to speak their minds even if it's not popular. I haven't had much time to process all this yet or form a plan of action going forward. But I immediately thought of you and insisted my staff track you down."

"You're very kind, sir, but I—"

"It's not kindness, Jon," the president interrupted. "It's desperation. Look, I'll be honest with you. I thought you'd completely lost your mind when you gave Mac and me that 'Ezekiel Option' memo. And when you quit the White House staff after the U.N. vote and headed into Russia to find Erin, I seriously thought you had become delusional or suicidal or both. I've never been a religious person. I always thought religion and politics were a bad combination. I thought only weak people needed to believe in God, you know, as a crutch. And again, to be completely candid with you, I really lost respect for you when you put your religious views ahead of what I thought were our country's national security interests. But . . ."

The president paused.

"Yes, sir?"

"Well, I have to say, while I still don't understand anything about the Bible or prophecy or any of that . . . well, whatever . . . Anyway, it's obvious that you've been downright prescient—eerily so—about some major events. . . . You seemed to know they were coming, and maybe all those prophecies have something to do with that."

Oaks paused again. Bennett still wasn't certain how to respond.

"What I'm saying," the president finally continued, "is that I need you to come back to the U.S. and spend some time with Marie and me—as soon as humanly possible."

"Doing what exactly, Mr. President?"

"I'm sure we both would like to hear more about your own spiritual journey, how you and Erin, you know, found God, or whatever. But look, Jon, the bottom line is, I need to know what you know. I need to know what's coming next. I need to understand where the U.S. fits into Bible prophecy. Like, are we going to be hit again?"

"I honestly don't know, sir."

"Does the Bible say anything about us, about America?"

"Not really, sir, no; it doesn't."

"What about China? Are there any prophecies about China in the End Times or the last days or whatever you call it?"

So there it was, Bennett thought. The president really was considering action against the PRC.

"Mr. President, I'm not sure I'm the right person to advise you on this," Bennett demurred.

"There isn't anybody else," the president replied, "and there isn't much time. I need you here by tomorrow. How far are you from Amman?"

Tomorrow? A shudder ran through Bennett's system. He wanted to help the president. He wanted to do something for his country, and if this was it, it was a tremendous and unexpected honor. But it was impossible, wasn't it? He couldn't move Erin so quickly, and he certainly wasn't going to leave her in Jordan.

He quickly explained Erin's condition. Oaks was sympathetic, but he was equally adamant that time was of the essence. There was only one conclusion Bennett could draw. The president must be seriously considering a massive retaliatory strike against China and wanted to know as quickly as possible if there was a prophetic angle to such a nightmare scenario. It wasn't something they could talk about over the phone. Indeed, Bennett was surprised the president wanted to talk about it at all. He had never shown any interest in prophecy before. But clearly events were now forcing the issue. Nancy Reagan had turned to astrology in her darkest hours after her husband was nearly assassinated. At least Oaks wanted to turn to the Bible. But still . . .

The president knew full well that the Bennetts were both loath to reenter government service. Then again, he wasn't asking for Jon's assistance on any normal day. He was asking on the very day four American cities had been obliterated by nuclear weapons. A full-blown global thermonuclear war was just hours or days away, and with it, perhaps, the Rapture and the beginning of the Tribulation. Still, the last thing Bennett wanted to do was force a long, difficult, and premature move on Erin.

"Don't worry about a thing," the president insisted, accurately sensing the depths of Bennett's hesitation. "I'll have my staff arrange for one of the camp's ambulances to take you and Erin to Amman. From there, we'll figure out a way to get you both back to the U.S. But look, I've got NORAD on the other line. I'll see you tomorrow. Be safe. Take care of that sweet wife of yours. And pray for me, Jon. Whatever you do, don't stop praying for me."

"You have my word on that, Mr. President," Bennett replied.

"I know I do," the president said, "and I appreciate that very much. I promise to be thinking about the questions you posed."

"Thank you, sir."

"And you'll let me know if there is anything I can do for you?"

"Actually, Mr. President," Bennett said without hesitation, "there is."

"What's that?"

"Would you help me track down my mother and see that she's safe?"

29

★ ★
★

Bennett couldn't believe what had just happened.

He felt honored that the president had reached out to him at such a moment and was eager to help. He was also deeply grateful that the president had agreed to assign Bobby Caulfield, his personal aide, to do everything he possibly could to track down Bennett's mother. But he suddenly realized that in his shock at hearing the president's voice, he had said nothing about the mysterious caller. Nor had he gotten a number to call the president back, and a quick glance at the caller ID on his satphone confirmed Oaks had been calling on an unlisted and most likely scrambled line.

Now what? Bennett wondered. America had been attacked. Millions lay dead or dying. Prophetic events were moving quickly. The leader of the free world—what was left of it, anyway—was asking for his help.

Bennett finally reached his tent and grabbed his toiletries, a clean pair of khakis, a fresh shirt, and a towel before heading to the showers. He needed to clear his mind. He needed to figure out how to proceed. His instincts had been right after all. He and Erin were leaving—quickly, and for good.

News of the attacks in the U.S. was just starting to spread through the general population of the camp. He noticed small groups of people huddled around shortwave radios, listening to the latest developments.

Some were crying. Many looked shell-shocked. But there were also gangs of young boys laughing and cheering the attacks on the U.S.

Bennett's first instinct was to grab several of them and knock their heads together. But it was a temptation he would have to resist. He and Erin had come to Jordan, after all, to love their neighbors and their enemies, not to punch their lights out. It wasn't easy for Bennett to stay calm in such circumstances. But he had to be faithful to the mission for which he'd been called. People were watching his every move, especially now. As one of the few Americans in the camp, he couldn't betray his country. More importantly, though, as one of the few followers of Christ there, he couldn't betray the God who had sent him there to be His hands and feet, to bless the poor and needy in the name of Jesus. He had to stay focused.

Hearing young boys mock his country suddenly put in sharp relief the question on so many people's minds—the same question that until yesterday had been front and center in his own. Ever since Ezekiel's War, people had been asking him where the United States fit into End Times prophecy and what else was going to happen before Jesus returned. He hadn't been certain what to tell them. He'd never claimed to be a prophecy expert, as Dr. Mordechai had been.

But people kept asking, and the question kept gnawing at Bennett's soul. So for the last few months, he'd been devoting his spare time to finding the answer. Amid all their responsibilities in the camp, of course, there was precious little "spare" time. At first, he and Erin would get up ten or fifteen minutes early to read the Bible and have some quick prayer together before heading to their post for work. But that quickly proved insufficient. The spiritual warfare was too intense. Bennett's hunger for God's presence and His Word was too deep, too desperate.

Soon he found himself waking up at two or three in the morning to study the Scriptures by flashlight. He was taking detailed notes in the leather journal Erin had given him. He was often on his knees until daybreak, asking the Lord for wisdom and insight and the ability to explain what he was learning to others. He prayed for his mother. He prayed hour upon hour for every friend he could think of, asking that Christ would open their eyes to His love, draw them into His Kingdom, and build them up strong in the faith.

Occasionally, when he had a few hours off, he would use his laptop's satellite connection and jump on the Internet. Then he would scour the Web site and weblog that Dr. Mordechai had left behind, trying to glean every tidbit on End Times prophecy he could. He would often e-mail Mordechai's friends, as well as various pastors and seminary professors around the world, asking for their wisdom and insight as well. It was a crash course in biblical eschatology, to be sure. But he had no choice. People wanted to know the truth. Increasingly, they were turning to him for answers. And the clock was ticking.

Bennett reached the showers and let the cool water wash over him as he processed a flood of new emotions and new questions. Was he ready? Ready to talk about where China fit into the last days? Ready to discuss the future of Israel and the Third Temple? Ready to explain the future of Babylon? Ready to explain why there were no biblical references to America in all of Bible prophecy—none at all?

This last one was the toughest of all, he mused, for it raised a deeper question: if they were really living in the last days, then how was it possible that the United States, the wealthiest and most powerful nation on the face of the earth in the history of mankind, didn't seem to have a role?

30

★ ★
★

Bennett forced himself to be analytical, not emotional.

For the moment, there was nothing he could do about whatever attacks lay ahead. But he could get prepared for his meeting with the president, and this, he decided, had to be his focus. He tried to clear his head and concentrate on what he had learned so far.

Ezekiel 36 and 37 had been his starting point, and initially the clearest prophecy of all. It plainly described Israel being reborn as a nation at the end of history, the Jews pouring back into the Holy Land after centuries of exile, and the Jews of this resurrected Israel then rebuilding the ancient ruins, making the deserts bloom, becoming wealthy, and creating "an exceedingly great army." To Bennett's astonishment, all of this had come to pass in his lifetime, even though the Hebrew prophet had written it twenty-five hundred years earlier.

What's more, the next two chapters of the book of Ezekiel had come true as well. Ezekiel 38 and 39 clearly described the rise of a future dictator in Russia who would build a military alliance with Iran and a host of Middle Eastern countries to attack Israel in something that would become known as the "War of Gog and Magog." The prophecy also indicated that just when it would appear as if all hope for Israel was lost and a holocaust was about to occur, the God of Abraham, Isaac, and Jacob would supernaturally intervene and come to Israel's rescue. Ezekiel described fire and hailstones falling from heaven on the enemies of the revived Jewish state. He wrote of a massive earthquake that would be unleashed, the chaos and carnage that would ensue, and he wrote that when the smoke cleared, Israel would be physically saved from destruction and the Lord would pour out His Spirit on "the whole house of Israel," bringing about a spiritual salvation as well. Ezekiel 38:16 specifically described the event as happening in "the last days." And to Bennett's amazement, he had seen it all happen over the past year. There was no question that he was now in what the Bible called the last days.

If that weren't enough, Ezekiel stated categorically that as such events unfolded, the entire world would perceive Israel and Jerusalem as God Himself did, as the center of history. Ezekiel chapter 5, verse 5, put it this way: "This is what the Sovereign Lord says: This is Jerusalem, which I have set in the center of the nations, with countries all around her." And sure enough, it was all coming true. All eyes were now riveted on Israel, the epicenter of all the major events that were shaking the world and shaping its future.

As for Europe, Dr. Mordechai and most of the Bible scholars Bennett had been studying since the older man's death strongly believed that it had a starring role in the End Times drama as well. In Daniel chapter 2 and chapter 7, for example, the Hebrew prophet foretold not only the rise of a ferocious and powerful Roman Empire emerging after the empires of Babylon, Media-Persia, and Greece—something that happened just as Daniel said it would, hundreds of years after he wrote those prophecies—but also of a revived and all-powerful Roman Empire at the end of history.

Daniel 8:8-9 seemed to indicate that the Antichrist would be a ruler who emerged from the ashes of the Greco-Roman Empire and would gather enormous powers as his military forces moved south and east toward the land of Israel, to surround and eventually conquer it.

Daniel 9:26-27 indicated that the Antichrist—whom the Bible described as a horrifically evil, all-powerful future world dictator—would emerge from the people who would destroy the Temple and the Holy City of Jerusalem after the Messiah was "cut off." It was the Romans, of course, who had destroyed the Temple and Jerusalem in AD 70, not long after they crucified Jesus, the King of the Jews and the Savior of the Gentiles.

It seemed obvious to Bennett, therefore, that the Antichrist was going to rise out of a revived Roman Empire.

Of course, the very notion of a revived Roman Empire had seemed absolutely impossible during the twentieth century. With the onslaught of World Wars I and II and the deaths of tens of millions of people, no continent on earth was more divided, more destroyed, more enfeebled, more soaked with blood and steeped in hatred for one another than Europe. But then, lo and behold, Israel was reborn in 1948, just as the Scriptures foretold, and Europe began to rise as well. The European Economic Community—the forerunner of the European Union—was created on March 25, 1957, upon the signing of the now-famous Treaty of Rome. Sixteen hundred years after the Roman Empire had faded into the night, it was suddenly rising again, like a phoenix from the ashes. *And look at it now*, Bennett thought. The EU comprised more than two dozen member states, nearly half a billion people, one tightly integrated economic system, one currency, one increasingly integrated political system, one foreign policy czar, one passport for all its people, borderless crossings, and all of it right on schedule according to Bible prophecy.

Iraq, too, had a role in the last days. The Hebrew prophets Isaiah and Jeremiah had made that clear, as had Ezekiel and the apostle John in the book of Revelation. And amazingly, Babylon really had risen from the dead and was now the center of power and commerce in the postwar Middle East. People had said it could never happen, but it had. Bennett had seen it with his own eyes.

Remarkably, Asia seemed to have a powerful presence in history's last chapter, Bennett had discovered. Revelation 16:12 explicitly stated the "kings from the east" would come marching through Iraq, up the Euphrates River valley, onward to Babylon, and eventually on to Armageddon, in Israel's oil-rich Jezreel Valley. Who exactly were these kings? Bennett wasn't yet sure. The leaders of China seemed to be waiting in the bull pen, as it were, for their moment on the field. Perhaps North Korea and Indonesia would join them. India and Pakistan might too. Time would tell, but based on what he had witnessed so far, it wasn't hard for Bennett to imagine a new coalition of Asian military machines banding together to attack Israel in the not-too-distant future.

But no matter how hard he looked, he couldn't find any specific reference in the Scriptures to the United States playing an End Times role, and it bothered him greatly. Was he missing an obvious reference? Or was it true that none were there? And if America wasn't in the Bible, Bennett had wondered for months, then what was going to happen to his country?

Several months earlier, he and Erin had had dinner with a Jordanian pastor friend who suggested the answer to his question was the Rapture. At some point soon, the pastor had argued, hundreds of millions—possibly even billions—of born-again followers of Jesus Christ were suddenly going to disappear around the world in the blink of an eye, caught up in the heavens with Jesus Himself. When that happened, the pastor had asked, wouldn't America essentially implode?

That was probably true, Bennett realized. He remembered how devastated the American people had been after losing nearly three thousand souls on 9/11. How would they react when twenty or thirty or fifty million people or more were suddenly gone? What would happen when some of the highest-ranking officials in the government suddenly disappeared? What if tens of thousands of military commanders and police officers and firefighters and doctors simply vanished, from the Carolinas to California? Could any country recover from such an event? Not quickly, Bennett concluded. That would certainly explain how the U.S. could effectively be neutralized in the last days.

But what Bennett had never really considered carefully until now was the possibility that something else might devastate the American people, rendering them ineffective heading into the last of the last days. A financial downturn on Wall Street. The sudden collapse of the dollar. The beginning of another Great Depression. A series of devastating earthquakes. Or hurricanes. Or other natural disasters, like a tsunami. Now America had been hit by the most cataclysmic terrorist attack of all time—five nuclear warheads. And there might be more to come. None of it was clearly prophesied in the Scriptures. Not that he could find. But perhaps he should have foreseen the neutralization of America by reading more carefully between the lines.

If so, what else was he missing? What exactly was coming next? What would he tell the president when they stood face-to-face—a meeting that was less than twenty-four hours away?

31

***

"Perhaps it is time for you to leave," Al-Hassani said coldly.

The seventy-six-year-old Iraqi leader had no intention of being accused of genocide by the secretary-general of the United Nations, especially one who was all but threatening him with invasion if the United States of Eurasia didn't start shipping his pals more oil and lowering prices for them more quickly. But Lucente clearly wasn't ready to go.

"I'm not leaving here until you and I come to an understanding," the secretary-general replied.

"There is nothing more to discuss," Al-Hassani shot back. "I am telling you point-blank that neither I nor anyone employed by, paid by, or associated with the USE had anything to do with these evil attacks against the U.S. Period. End of sentence. End of discussion."

Tariq sipped his tea and said nothing.

"On the record," Al-Hassani continued, "I tell you what I have already said publicly. I condemn these attacks and anyone who was involved. But between you and me, Salvador, while this is a very dark day, it has—albeit unexpectedly—created a historic opening, and you know it. Sitting before you and me is an opportunity to reshape the world in a way not seen since the collapse of the Roman Empire. Are you going to just let it slip away? Or are you going to seize the moment and fulfill your destiny?"

"What exactly are you saying, Mustafa?"

Al-Hassani leaned forward and lowered his voice. "I am saying that a world without the United States—or at least a world in which the U.S. is, for all intents and purposes, militarily and financially neutralized—creates an enormous global leadership vacuum that you and I could battle to fill, or . . ."

"Or what?"

"Or a vacuum you and I could work together to fill."

"Toward what end?" Lucente asked.

"Toward whatever end we wish," Al-Hassani whispered in reply. "But as for me, I don't dream in black and white."

"You apparently have given this some thought," Lucente said.

"Tell me you haven't, Salvador," Al-Hassani challenged. "Look me in the eye and tell me you haven't thought about a world without America, a world without a superpower, a world where the United Nations secretary-general is the king of kings and the lord of lords?"

Lucente refused to take the bait.

"Perhaps we should spend some time brainstorming this together, Mr. Secretary-General," Al-Hassani continued. "I have a feeling you and I could be very creative in crafting a new world order, and very effective in bringing it about. But make no mistake: if you try to pin these attacks on me, you'll be facing five-hundred-dollar-a-barrel oil by Christmas. I don't care how many troops you send to stop us. My people would rather set our oil wells on fire than give away our national treasures while you let the bloody Jews build a Temple and emerge as a financial and military superpower unchecked and unhindered."

Lucente sat back in his chair and sipped his tea. "Mustafa, you are telling me without qualification that you had absolutely nothing to do with these attacks?"

"That is exactly what I am telling you," Al-Hassani said.

"But you are also telling me that you don't mind taking advantage of the moment to further your own expansionist ambitions?"

"I'm telling you everything has just changed, Salvador," Al-Hassani said. "I'm saying the whole world is in our hands. For better or for worse, we have been handed a gift. I have no earthly idea who is responsible for what has happened and honestly, I don't very much care. My interest is not the past. It's the future, and 'the future belongs to those who prepare for it today.'"

Lucente raised his eyebrows. "Malcolm X?"

Al-Hassani nodded.

"Odd," the secretary-general observed, "you don't strike me as being prone to quoting African-American revolutionaries, Mustafa."

Al-Hassani smiled. "A little revolution is a good thing every now and then; don't you think?"

"It depends," Lucente said.

"On what?" the Iraqi asked.

Lucente took his last sip of tea. "On who's being revolted against, and who's doing the revolting."

The two men sat in silence for a few minutes, each contemplating the enormity of what the other was proposing, as Khalid Tariq wrote quietly in his notebook. They had come at last to the moment of truth, Al-Hassani believed. It was time for Lucente to decide just what kind of world leader he was destined to be: caretaker or game changer?

With James MacPherson dead and the American people reeling from the loss of four major cities—including their political, financial, technological, and entertainment capitals—Al-Hassani was convinced that a charismatic European like Salvador Lucente and an intellectual Arab like himself could emerge as historic figures. Al-Hassani, after all, had the vision, the oil, and half a billion sheep eager to follow his lead. Lucente had decades of experience uniting a deeply divided continent into one political entity, one military command, and the strongest currency on the planet. *Imagine*, Al-Hassani thought, *if they worked together. Imagine if as one voice they moved quickly and decisively to offer a chaotic and confused world the way forward into a new era of peace and prosperity.* The leadership of the entire globe was ripe for the picking. It was time for the harvest. The question was, could they work together?

For his part, Al-Hassani was still furious at Lucente for a host of reasons—for barely lifting a finger to stop the Zionists from building the Temple in Jerusalem, for threatening to send E.U. forces to seize his oil fields, for all but accusing him of attacking the U.S. with nuclear weapons, to name just a few. Lucente surely had his own list. The secretary-general, Al-Hassani knew firsthand, was a deeply ambitious man. Moreover, he was short-tempered and—how to put this?—an occasional stranger to the truth. Theirs would not be an easy partnership.

But Al-Hassani had no doubt this was the moment, and he had the leverage. A new world order could not be fashioned without Babylon and her oil. Nor could a new world order emerge if there was continued chaos and bloodshed in the Middle East. If Lucente truly wanted the unprecedented global power of which Al-Hassani spoke—and of which Al-Hassani was sure he privately fantasized—he would have to strike a grand bargain, and he would have to strike it fast.

32

★ ★
★

President Oaks was surprised to see Briggs alive.

The last he had heard, the NORAD commander had been rushed to the medical unit after collapsing from an apparent heart attack. Fortunately for both men, it was not a heart attack, just a sudden decrease in blood pressure, brought on by stress and the fact that in all the chaos, Briggs had forgotten to take his pills.

When Oaks asked about his condition, Briggs waved off his concern and said he was under careful medical supervision. He was back on his feet now and insisting he felt fine. The president was in no mood to argue. He needed the general's expertise, and he was grateful the man was still functioning. So that was that. There was too much more to be done, and too little time to do it.

The two men moved immediately into a secure conference room known as "the Tank," which was quickly sealed off by an entourage of Secret Service agents. Joining Oaks and Briggs by secure videoconference was Secretary of Defense Burt Trainor, who had arrived at Site R, and Homeland Security Secretary Lee James, now at Mount Weather in a hardened communications bunker eighty feet underground.

"Where are the Joint Chiefs?" the president asked as they began.

"I'm sorry to report to you that they are all dead, sir," Trainor said bluntly.

"All of them?" Oaks asked in shock.

"Yes, sir, I'm afraid so."

The president felt shell-shocked. "What about Congress?"

"We've confirmed that the Speaker of the House was in Manhattan at the time of the attacks," James said. "We're listing him as missing and presumed dead. The Senate majority leader was at his daughter's wedding in D.C. and was killed in the attack. So far, we've only been able to track down a dozen members of the House and five members of the Senate. But we're still looking."

"And the ones you've found?" the president asked.

"All Democrats, mostly from the Midwest, sir," James said. "I wired you the names."

The president picked up a piece of paper marked "EYES ONLY" and glanced down the list. Nearly all were relatively junior members. None were committee chairs. None were on the Foreign Relations or Armed Services committee. How exactly was he supposed to rebuild the American government with this?

"Where are they all right now?" he asked.

"All of these have been found and secured by local law enforcement or National Guard MPs," Briggs assured him. "They're being transported by Guard units to Mount Weather as we speak. We'll continue to bring as many as we find there until we can figure out more comfortable accommodations for them."

"Their comfort is not my concern, General," the president snapped. "Their safety is, and their access to secure communications."

"Yes, sir—we're on it, sir," Briggs said.

"Good," the president said. "Now, where are we with hunting down the ships that fired these missiles?"

"The navy and the air force have sunk three container ships so far, Mr. President," the SecDef said. "I'm told we have just identified a fourth ship off the coast of Long Island. We're convinced it's the one that launched the attack on Manhattan. It should be at the bottom of the Atlantic by the time we're finished with this call, sir."

"What are you doing to recover any missiles and nuclear warheads that may have still been on those four ships?" the president asked.

"We've got search-and-rescue teams heading to all four locations, sir," Trainor said. "I'll get you updated reports as I get them myself."

Oaks nodded and asked Secretary James, "How many dead and wounded so far?"

"It's impossible to say at this point, Mr. President."

"How soon will we know?"

"Honestly, sir, it could be days—maybe weeks."

Oaks couldn't say so, of course, but the truth was that he didn't want to know. It was too horrible, too depressing. But as the leader of the nation, he felt it was his duty to ask, and he gave James forty-eight hours to compile a preliminary estimate.

The biggest questions he addressed to Secretary Trainor.

"Who did this, Burt, and how quickly can we strike back?"

He noticed Trainor hesitate. "Mr. President, I'm not ready to give you an answer on that."

Oaks had anticipated this, but unlike the casualty numbers, this was one he had to have. "How soon will you know?" he pressed.

"It could be a while, sir," Trainor stalled. "We're sifting through the intel, but it's slow going. As you know, DIA was destroyed. Langley was destroyed. NSA headquarters at Fort Meade has been evacuated because of high winds bringing massive amounts of radiation their way. We're shifting a lot of the satellite imagery and electronic intercepts to other facilities around the country. But the fact is, our top analysts are all dead, and most of our best linguists as well."

"That's not good enough, Mr. Secretary," the president countered. "I have a constitutional obligation to defend this country, and I can't do that if I have no idea who attacked us."

"Believe me, Mr. President, I understand the gravity of the situation," Trainor said. "But I don't want to speculate without hard information, and that's going to take time to compile, process, verify, and get to you."

"You must have something," the president insisted. "Start with China."

Trainor quickly scanned a stack of the latest intelligence reports in front of him but apparently found little to go on. "Zhao is worried, no question about it," he improvised. "His press conference was unprecedented but his message was certainly clear enough. They think we think they did it, and as a result, Beijing is mobilizing every military asset they have."

"Even their strategic missile forces?"

"I'm afraid so, sir."

"All this aggressive military activity just makes them look guilty," Oaks noted.

"They would say they're being prudent," Trainor cautioned.

"Unless they *are* guilty," the president said. "So are they?"

"I don't know yet, Mr. President. It's simply too soon to say."

Trainor explained that for the last several days, the navy had been tracking five Chinese nuclear submarines approaching unusually close to the Pacific coast of the U.S. Three more Chinese submarines had been operating suspiciously close to Maine, New York, and Florida. Another was lurking on the edge of U.S. territorial waters in the Gulf of Mexico.

"Any evidence these subs were used in the attacks?" the president asked.

"No, sir," Trainor said.

"Then what's China up to?"

"I don't know, sir—they may simply have been testing our sub-tracking capabilities. At the time of the attacks, we were moving more than a dozen Los Angeles–class fast attack subs to counter them."

"And where are the Chinese subs now?" Oaks asked.

"All but two have retreated into deeper waters in the Atlantic and the Pacific," the SecDef said.

"And the other two?"

"They've pulled back several hundred miles, but they're essentially still patrolling, albeit slowly, up and down the coasts—one in the east and one in the west."

"Are they armed with missiles?"

"We believe they are, sir."

"Nuclear?"

"Yes, sir," Trainor said. "What worries me in particular is that these are all Russian-built Kilo subs, type 636, very fast, very stealthy, tough— not impossible, but very tough—for us to track if they really decide to go dark on us."

The president mulled that over. "You're saying Beijing wants us to know they're out there?"

"Yes, sir," Trainor confirmed. "They seem to want us to know that they're waiting, ready to act if provoked."

"So how big is the danger of a miscalculation by either side?"

This time, Trainor didn't hesitate for a moment. "It's growing by the hour, sir."

33

9:12 A.M.—OFFICE OF THE PRESIDENT, BABYLON, IRAQ

"What you are proposing is very risky," Lucente said.

"Perhaps," Al-Hassani said. "But without risk, where are the rewards?"

Lucente did not reply immediately, but this was a positive sign, Al-Hassani thought. It meant the secretary-general was not ruling out his scenario after all. Indeed, he was listening carefully. He was considering. He was tempted.

Finally Lucente asked, "Theoretically speaking, where would you propose we start?"

"You know where, Salvador," Al-Hassani said softly.

"Jerusalem?" Lucente asked, obviously knowing the answer already.

"Where else?" the Iraqi said.

Lucente sighed. "Mustafa, how many ways can I make this clear? My hands are tied. I've done everything in my power to stop the Temple from being constructed, short of building an international coalition to invade Israel. There's nothing more I can do."

"Would that really be so wrong?" Khalid Tariq, Al-Hassani's chief political strategist, suddenly interjected.

"Would what be so wrong?" Lucente asked.

"Building an international coalition to invade Israel," Tariq clarified.

"Tell me he's kidding," Lucente said, turning back to Al-Hassani.

"He's not," the Iraqi leader said.

"Then he's crazy," the secretary-general laughed. "You both are. Didn't you two see with your own eyes what happened to the last coalition that tried to destroy Israel? Nobody but you would be brazen enough to try that again."

Tariq cursed as Al-Hassani looked on. "Then what?" the aide snapped. "You're just going to give the Zionists a free pass to do whatever they want, whenever they want, with no consequences?"

"Mustafa, Khalid, have you forgotten the fire falling from heaven on Israel's enemies?" Lucente asked, incredulous. "Have you forgotten the hailstones, the massive earthquake, the torrential storms? Didn't you see it all—live—on Al-Jazeera and CNN and in *Al-Hayat*? Haven't you noticed it's been nearly eleven months and still the Israelis are burying the bodies of their enemies? And you know as well as I do it would have taken a lot longer but for all the birds and beasts that came along and ate most of the bodies. Can you really watch all that and think for a moment that you can persuade the world to take on Israel again in such a short amount of time? People will think you're insane."

"Salvador, Salvador, you don't really believe all that was an act of God, do you?" Al-Hassani demanded to know. "You're not going to tell me you think a bunch of superstitious prophecies came true, are you? Come, come; tell me you are smarter than that."

"I don't know what happened out there, and neither do you," Lucente said carefully, weighing every word. "And frankly, I don't care. I know only one thing: nobody in his right mind is going to try to invade Israel again anytime soon. I certainly wouldn't."

Tariq was disgusted. "So the Jews just get what they want; is that it?"

"No," Lucente said, more forcefully than Al-Hassani had expected. "But we need to be wise, gentlemen. We need to be shrewd."

"Meaning what?" Tariq demanded.

"Meaning we need to bide our time, take things one step at a time," Lucente said. "Don't forget, the world desperately needs Israel's oil every bit as much as it needs yours. And the world needs oil prices to stabilize and start coming down, not continue spiking ever upward. That means the world wants peace in the Middle East, not another war. Not yet. Not now. So don't fool yourselves, my friends. You think a war with Israel would help you, and maybe it *would* help the USE in the short run. You are raking in hundreds of billions of petrodollars, and this city you've built is quickly becoming the world's commercial nerve center. But for the rest of us, another war in this region would be a disaster. The U.S. economy is finished. Wall Street has been obliterated. Most of the world's major banks based in Manhattan have been wiped out as well. The world is about to plunge into a global depression. You and I have the power to stabilize things and to consolidate power in the process. But we must cooperate with the Israelis, not confront them."

"We have absolutely no intention of cooperating with the Jews," Tariq insisted. "We're trying to build a new nation, and believe me, Salvador, nobody wants me to make nice with the Zionists. We've been humiliated by them for too long. Now they build a Temple on the site that has been holy ground to us for the ages, and no one dares lift a finger to stop them, not even you?"

"Mustafa, Khalid, please," Lucente countered, "you're not listening to me. We don't have a choice. Not yet, anyway. Look, you know I am with you both in spirit. Between you and me, I don't like the Jews any more than you do. Mark my words, as soon as I can do something about them, I will. On that you have my word. But if we're going to do it right, it's going to take time."

"How much time?" Tariq pressed. "Our people cannot wait forever."

"They won't have to," Lucente assured him. "But first we need to win the Israelis' confidence. We need them to lower their guard. Look at how weak they are. Their political leaders are feckless. Their Zionist ideology is exhausted. Their military leaders are corrupt. Their diplomatic leaders are so desperate to be loved, to be accepted by the rest of the world, they're willing to give away almost anything. But we must not make the ridiculous mistakes of the past. We must not threaten Israel with war. We must invite them to make peace. We must not turn our backs to them. We must offer them an open hand. We must not boycott them. We must take you and your top leadership there to Jerusalem. We must shock them. We must offer them a comprehensive peace treaty, the likes of which the world has never seen before. We must lure them into feeling safe and secure. We must lull them into trusting us, into trusting me, and all the while consolidate our power and build a military coalition far greater than what the Russians and the Iranians ever had. And then, when all this has been accomplished, when the time is right, you and I will make our move. We will seize Jerusalem. We will raze the Temple. Perhaps we will even build the new U.N. headquarters there, right on the Temple Mount. But not now. We're not ready . . . yet."

34

★ ★
★

"Mr. President, may I ask you a question?"

It was Homeland Security Secretary Lee James.

The president nodded. "Absolutely."

"Mr. President, on a scale from one to ten, with ten being absolute certitude that China is behind these attacks, where would you say you are at the moment?"

Oaks pondered that for a few moments. "I'm not sure yet—six or seven. Why do you ask?"

"Well, sir," James continued, "I'm just thinking—what would possibly be Zhao's intent? I mean, he has to know that if we find proof it's them, we'll launch a massive counterattack and wipe them off the face of the planet. But then they'd retaliate in kind before our missiles landed and launch all of their nuclear missiles at us, wouldn't they?"

"Probably," the president said. "So what's your point?"

"My point, Mr. President, is, do we really believe Zhao and his cronies are suicidal? Power hungry, yes. Tyrannical, absolutely. But are they suicidal?"

"What if they didn't see this sort of attack as suicidal?" the president asked. "What if they were counting on us being completely decapitated and thus unable—or unwilling—to launch a full retaliation?"

"You really think they'd try that, completely unprovoked?" James responded.

"Look," the president said, "China desperately wants to be a super-power, don't they?"

Secretaries James and Trainor and General Briggs all agreed.

"So what if they concluded this was their moment?" Oaks asked. "Russia's gone. If we were gone too, they'd be the only ones left standing, right?"

"Of course," Trainor said. "But, Mr. President, I find myself leaning in Lee's direction here. I mean, the Chinese have had a very clearly stated no-first-strike policy since they did their first nuclear test back in '64. It just doesn't seem plausible to me that they suddenly changed their minds today."

"Come on, Burt," the president shot back. "You know as well as I do that several high-ranking Chinese generals through the years have threat-ened the use of nukes over the Taiwan conflict, right?"

Unfortunately, the president was correct on that. Back in July of 2005, for example, Major General Zhu Chenghu, the head of China's National Defense University, was discussing the possibility of an armed conflict with Taiwan and warned, "If the Americans draw their missiles and position-guided weapons on to the target zone on Chinese territory, I think we will have to respond with nuclear weapons. We Chinese will prepare ourselves for the destruction of all the cities east of Xian. Of course, the Americans will have to be prepared that hundreds of cities will be destroyed by the Chinese."

China's first-strike military capabilities had increased significantly since 2005. What's more, even tougher threats had been voiced by other high-ranking Chinese military officials in recent months. One of the most strident anti-American voices was now China's defense minister, and a close personal friend of Premier Zhao.

Still, was it really possible that China's first-strike policy had changed without anyone in the U.S. government realizing it? Then again, why would Beijing announce such a change in policy, if one had, in fact, occurred?

☆　☆　☆

The rush was fading.

Fear was quickly replacing the high he'd felt for the last few hours, and Caulfield could sense that the demons were back. They were haunting him again, telling him he was no good, telling him he had no place working for the president of the United States, telling him it was better to sleep, forever, and put all the horrors of the world behind him.

Caulfield excused himself from a staff meeting and wandered past the conference room where the president was meeting with his war cabinet.

"Can I help you, Mr. Caulfield?" Special Agent Coehlo asked, standing post outside the conference room door.

"Just checking to see if the president needs me," Caulfield lied.

"He hasn't said anything to me," Coelho replied.

"Fine," Caulfield said. "I'm going to the men's room if he needs me."

Coelho nodded and Caulfield headed around the corner and glanced down a side hallway. No one was there. He had a clear shot. He grabbed his briefcase, moved as quickly as he could without drawing attention to himself, and slipped into the bathroom. He could hear the voice of his older brother, Derek, telling him no, begging him not to. But it didn't matter. He wasn't listening. He desperately needed another hit. He needed it now. His brother didn't understand. He never had. He never would.

Secretary Trainor tried to refocus the conversation.

"Mr. President," he began, "with all due respect, most of these generals have been talking about a scenario in which there was already a shooting war over Taiwan under way and we intervened militarily. It's saber rattling, sir, not a serious threat to annihilate four American cities, much less hundreds of them."

"Yesterday, honestly, I might have agreed with you," the president said. "Today I'm not so sure. How many countries could have pulled off an operation like this? India, Pakistan, North Korea, and China, right?"

Trainor agreed, as did James and Briggs.

"Is there any evidence to suggest the Indians are involved?"

"No, sir," Trainor said.

"Islamabad?"

"No."

"What about Pyongyang?" the president asked, referring to the capital of North Korea, a country once described by one of his predecessors as a member of the "Axis of Evil."

"Not to my knowledge, sir."

"Then we're running out of suspects, aren't we?" the president noted. "Lee, isn't it true that Homeland Security has been concerned for years about the Chinese using their shipping companies to aid and abet terrorist groups?"

James reluctantly agreed, and when the president asked for specifics, he noted that the Chinese Ocean Shipping Company (COSCO), as just one example, had once been singled out by the U.S. House Task Force on Terrorism for presenting itself "as a commercial entity" when it was "actually an arm of the Chinese military establishment," providing "services to the logistics and transportation arms of the PLA's navy and air force." In 1996, James recalled, citing the task force's report, "U.S. Customs agents confiscated over 2,000 assault weapons that were being smuggled into the United States aboard COSCO ships." More recently, he added, COSCO ships had been caught smuggling other weapons, drugs, and even illegal aliens.

What's more, James noted, the task force found that "COSCO ships serve as a vehicle for the transportation of strategic material to allies of the PRC in support of their strategic programs—development of ballistic missiles, nuclear weapons, chemical and biological weapons." Just as troubling, "COSCO not only carries military and strategic cargoes from the PRC and North Korea to such countries as Pakistan, Iran, and Syria—but also carries strategic items and materials illegally purchased in Western Europe to these countries while concealing the ultimate destination."

"The Chinese even tried to buy the port at Long Beach back in the nineties, right?" the president noted.

"Actually they were trying to lease it, sir, but yes."

"When was that?"

"Around 1996 and '97, Mr. President."

"And Clinton supported that deal at the time, did he not?"

"At first, he did, sir," James explained. "But to be fair, once more facts became known about how China was using its shipping companies for military and terrorist purposes, Congress passed a law preventing the lease from going through."

"Did Clinton sign it?"

"Yes, sir."

Oaks paused briefly, then said, "Look, you and I both know in the past several decades, China has become a clear and present danger to the United States. They're working feverishly to become a world military power. They've stolen classified designs for at least seven of our latest thermonuclear warheads. They've stolen the design of our neutron bomb. They've been caught stealing other classified information on American nuclear weapons systems from all our top research labs—Los Alamos, Sandia, Lawrence Livermore, Oak Ridge—you name it. They've used their container ships in the past to smuggle weapons targeted at the U.S. They've been ratcheting up their rhetoric against us. And then last summer, of course, I agreed to that arms deal with Taiwan. The CIA warned me at the time the deal could backfire. As I recall, you were a little concerned yourself, Burt."

Trainor nodded.

"Then, just three months ago," the president continued, "Danny Tracker over at CIA warned me of a growing clique of generals inside the Chinese air force arguing Beijing had to move against Taipei before those weapons systems were delivered and installed. When is the first shipment scheduled to arrive in Taipei?"

"Next month, Mr. President," Trainor admitted.

"My point exactly," Oaks said. "Which raises the question, what if the Chinese leadership in Beijing concluded that they were running out of time, that they had to strike now or lose Taiwan forever?"

The room went completely silent as everyone realized the magnitude of what the new commander in chief was contemplating.

"Burt, how many nuclear weapons does China currently possess?"

"Our latest assessment says about four hundred, Mr. President," Trainor said. "Roughly 250 are strategic warheads for intercontinental ballistic missiles. Another 150 or so are tactical nukes—battlefield nukes—typically mounted on short- to medium-range missiles."

"Like the ones someone just fired at us?" Oaks asked.

"Theoretically, yes, Mr. President," Trainor confirmed. "The last CIA assessment about six months ago put the number of Chinese nukes aimed at the U.S. at between 150 and 200."

"About half of all the nukes they have?" the president asked.

"Yes, sir," Trainor said, "give or take."

The president looked up from his notes. "What did Mao once say? 'Every Communist must grasp the truth: political power grows out of the barrel of a gun.'"

Again there was silence.

"You've got twenty-four hours, gentlemen," the president concluded. "By this time tomorrow, I want a detailed plan for a full-scale nuclear retaliation against China. I can't tell you if I'm going to use it, but I'll tell you one thing: *somebody's* going to pay for this, and soon."

35

★ ★
★

Bennett's satellite phone began to ring again.

This time, he had no doubt who it was. He took a deep breath and, after four rings, finally picked up.

"Hello? This is Jon."

"You've been expecting my call," said the voice at the other end, once again electronically disguised.

"You told me something terrible was about to happen," Bennett said.

"Now you know I'm telling the truth."

"The only way you could have know those attacks were coming was if you were complicit in them," Bennett charged.

"I had nothing to do with it," the voice countered. "Not directly."

"You really expect me to believe that?" Bennett said. "You obviously know the players. You knew what they were planning. You knew how serious it was going to be. You knew when it was going to happen. You knew where it was going to happen. You knew how to track me down. And you gave me no time to warn anyone. In my book, that makes you part of the conspiracy to commit genocide."

"I do know the people responsible," the voice conceded. "And yes, I know what they're capable of. But they have gone too far. This wasn't what we had agreed to when I first signed on. What they're planning is unimaginable. Millions will die. Tens of millions. Believe me, Mr. Bennett, these were merely the appetizers. You don't want to taste the main course."

"What is it?"

"Cooperate and I'll tell you," the voice said. "But not yet."

"Why should I cooperate with you?" Bennett demanded. "You've just annihilated millions of people. Maybe more."

"How many more do you want to see killed?" the voice asked.

"If you really want to stop the next attacks, then do it," Bennett shot back. "Call the U.S. military. Tell them everything. But why get me involved? I'm out of the game. That's not my world anymore, and you've killed everyone I know inside the American government."

"Not all of them," the voice said.

"All of them," Bennett repeated.

"That's not true, Mr. Bennett, and you know it. You know the new president. You've known him for years."

Bennett immediately tensed. He spun around, scanning the faces in the crowded alleyway by his tent. Was someone watching him? Could this person know that he had just spoken to the president? How? It wasn't possible. Was it?

"We were never close," Bennett replied, trying not to lie but walking the line.

"Close enough for my purposes."

"Which are what?" Bennett asked, his blood pressure rising. "You never answered my question. If you're really serious, why didn't you stop these attacks? And why don't you stop the next ones? Why get me involved?"

"I couldn't stop these attacks," the voice insisted, betraying the first trace of emotion thus far. "And the truth is, I can't stop the next ones either—not by myself, anyway. I need help, which is why I'm talking to you."

The two were silent for a moment as each sized up the other.

"You believe I'm telling the truth?" the voice finally asked.

"I believe you knew the attacks were coming," Bennett said cautiously. "Beyond that, the jury's still out."

"That's not what I asked."

"How do I know you'll tell me the truth going forward?" Bennett asked.

"You don't," he was told. "You'll have to trust me."

"I don't know that I can do that."

"It's your only hope to save millions of lives."

"You've given me no proof you can deliver."

"Look, Mr. Bennett," the voice said sharply, "you're either in or out. You're in no position to negotiate."

"I'm not trying to negotiate," Bennett said. "But I need to know what I'm being asked to do and whether I can deliver."

"If you couldn't deliver, I wouldn't waste my time calling you," he was told.

"Then what do you need?" Bennett asked.

"Five million dollars and seventy-two hours of your life."

"What? What are you talking about?"

"It's very simple, Mr. Bennett," the voice said. "I will e-mail you a Swiss bank account number. You will wire the money today. Then you'll get on a plane to Bangkok. Alone. If the money clears and I'm convinced you're alone, my people will meet you at the airport. They'll bring you to me, and I'll explain what I need you to do. If you're not alone, or if I think you're working with someone . . ."

"Then what?" Bennett asked.

"Then I'll keep your money and people will die," the voice said.

Bennett was incredulous. "You want me to pay for the privilege of risking my life to help you?"

"Mr. Bennett, five million dollars is a small price to pay to save the lives of fifty million; is it not?"

Bennett gasped. Fifty million people? It seemed unimaginable. Or it would have, before all this.

"Pay me the five million and I'll tell you everything I know," the voice said.

"If it's so urgent, why not just tell me now?" Bennett asked.

"We will do this my way, or we won't do it at all. Look, I will give you everything—a list of everyone involved, what their motives are, where they are based, and what their plans are. But I'm not going to do it over the phone. You and your wife must meet with me face-to-face. You come to Bangkok. My people will find you. They will bring you both to me. And then we will talk. That's it. That's the deal. It's not open for discussion.

It's a simple proposition, Mr. Bennett: save the world or suffer the consequences. Are you in or out?"

Bennett took a deep breath. "There's been a slight complication since you last called," he said cautiously.

There was a long pause at the other end of the line.

"What kind of complication?" the voice asked.

"I got a call from the president."

"Which one?"

"The president of the United States."

"*Oaks?*" the voice asked, clearly caught off guard.

"Yes," Bennett said, trying to figure out how to explain this without making a bad situation worse.

"Why? What did he want?" the voice demanded.

"He's trying to rebuild his government, and he wants my help."

"I thought you were out of the game," the voice said. "You just said so."

"I had been."

"But now?"

"Everything's changed—you changed it," Bennett said. "I'm supposed to leave in two hours for the U.S. to meet with the president."

"Where?"

"I have no idea."

"How are you getting there?" the voice asked. "All flights in and out of the U.S. have been canceled."

"I don't know—it's being arranged," Bennett said. "That's all I can say. But look, if you really want to help stop these attacks, forget the money. Tell me what you know. I can talk to the president. I can persuade him to take action. Maybe I could get a deal for you as well. Immunity from prosecution. Witness protection. What do you say?"

The voice laughed. "Forget it, Mr. Bennett. Now I want fifty million."

"What?" Bennett asked. "Why?"

"Fifty million dollars, Bennett, wired to my account today," the voice replied. "And you and Erin on a plane to Bangkok—or you get nothing."

36

★ ★
★

For almost a full minute, Bennett said nothing.

"I will talk to the president about the money," he said at last. "I doubt he will give you that much. But Bangkok isn't going to happen."

"I told you, Bennett, this isn't a negotiation. You and Erin are coming to Bangkok, and that's final."

"I'm not coming to Bangkok," Bennett repeated. "Neither is Erin. It's out of the question."

"Are you insane?" the voice shot back. "Do you understand what's going to happen if you two don't come?"

"We can't," Bennett said firmly. He explained that he had an ailing wife, a baby on the way, a nation in mourning, and a president who had asked for his help. "I'll do my best to get you the money, but only if you e-mail me everything you know. If you're really sorry about what's happened, if you're really serious about saving lives, then that's it. That's the deal. I'm sorry. It's the best I can do."

The voice was seething. "I'm not interested in your troubles, Mr. Bennett. I've got troubles of my own. I will call you in precisely twenty-four hours. Either you've wired the fifty million, are standing with your wife at the airport in Bangkok of your own free will, and have thus earned the chance to save the world, or the deal is off. You'll have just sentenced fifty million people to die. And you'll have no one to blame but yourself. It's your choice, Mr. Bennett. Choose wisely."

The line suddenly went dead.

Bennett's heart was racing. He had no doubt whoever he'd been speaking with was deadly serious. He wiped his brow, took a swig of water, and prayed the plan had worked as it was supposed to.

He stepped into his tent and quickly dialed a phone number in Europe that cross-linked him via secure fiber optic cables into the Communications Center at Site R, the Pentagon's top secret war room in the Catoctin Mountains near the border between Maryland and Pennsylvania. Once in, he got a stutter tone. He then punched in the nine-digit code that immediately patched him through to a colonel working directly for Defense Secretary Burt Trainor.

"Mr. Bennett, we've been waiting for your call," the colonel said.

"Did it work?" Bennett asked immediately. *"Could you trace it?"*

"Hold on, sir," the colonel said. "I should know in a moment."

Bennett paced his tent.

He knew it was a huge risk. But he was sure he'd done the right thing. A few minutes after President Oaks had hung up from his phone call with Bennett, a senior aide to the secretary of defense had followed up the president's call to arrange the details of their extraction from Jordan. With mushroom clouds rising over four American cities, Bennett hadn't hesitated to tell the aide what had happened. After all, if he was agreeing to advise the commander in chief, he could do no less than be fully candid with those around him.

The colonel had been instantly intrigued. He'd offered to trace every call that came into Bennett's satellite phone. Until then, Bennett had thought all satphone calls were untraceable. Apparently that wasn't exactly true. Bennett hadn't the foggiest idea of all the technology involved. All he knew was what the colonel told him to do: as soon as contact was reestablished with the mystery caller, Bennett was supposed to dial into the military's top secret command post and await further instructions.

Bennett stopped pacing.

He was still on hold, but he knew he had to start packing his and Erin's things as quickly as possible, for it was clear now that one way or the other, they'd be leaving soon. He pulled their two large suitcases out from under the army cots they had been using and began loading them with clothes and their toiletries. Then he gathered their Bibles, journals, iPods, and chargers and packed them in his large leather briefcase.

Next he powered up his laptop, pointed his antenna toward the southern sky, and connected to the Internet via satellite. A moment later, he was downloading e-mails for the first time in several weeks—319 and counting.

Bennett scrolled through the list. There were at least a dozen from his mom, but none of them were within the last few days. None of them would help him find her. All of them, therefore, would have to wait. Two e-mails were from Chuck Murray, President MacPherson's former press secretary. Bennett scanned them quickly. Murray was working on a book about the administration and was trying to track him down to confirm various details, as well as to catch up. All that was no doubt irrelevant, he realized. He wondered if Murray had even survived the attacks and said a prayer for his safety, and his soul, just in case.

An e-mail from Dmitri Galishnikov now caught Bennett's eye. The Medexco gazillionaire wanted to know where in the world Jon and Erin were, and when could they come to Jerusalem and have dinner with him. Bennett made a mental note to give Galishnikov a call on the flight back to the States. They hadn't seen each other or spoken since January. It was time to reconnect.

The Russian Jewish petroleum engineer had become one of Bennett's dearest friends since his days on Wall Street. But the blunt truth was that Galishnikov was a man on his way to hell unless something changed radically, and soon. He was rich. He was powerful. He had everything he wanted. But he hadn't nearly everything he needed. He needed *Yeshua HaMashiach*, Jesus the Messiah.

Bennett had been heading to hell as well. But now, by God's grace, he had found a personal relationship with Jesus. More than a million Israelis had found Him too, and had planted more than ten thousand messianic Jewish congregations just since the firestorm. Why couldn't Dmitri find that hope and forgiveness and a peace that defied understanding through *Yeshua* as well?

Bennett immediately thought of the words of Jesus in Matthew chapter 16: "If anyone wishes to come after Me, he must deny himself, and take up his cross and follow Me. For whoever wishes to save his life will lose it; but whoever loses his life for My sake will find it. For what will it profit a man if he gains the whole world and forfeits his soul?"

Not many on the planet had gained the whole world faster than Dmitri Galishnikov. But his soul was in danger. He was running out of time. And Bennett's heart suddenly cried out in prayer for him and his beautiful family. He prayed that the Lord would have mercy on them. He prayed the God of Abraham, Isaac, and Jacob would pour out His love on them and open their eyes that they might see and understand and fall in love with *Yeshua* the way Bennett himself had done. Yes, it had cost him dearly. Yes, it might cost him more. But what a treasure he had gained, and what a treasure now awaited the Galishnikovs.

As Bennett opened his eyes, he noticed an e-mail from Natasha Barak. The subject line read, "GOOD NEWS!" Still on hold with Site R, he clicked on the message and read it quickly.

> "Jon, Erin—hey, it's me. Hope you're well! I'm praying for you every day. Several times a day. Wish I knew where you were. Would love to call you. Miss you both terribly. But I have good news! Remember my cousin? Miriam Gozol. VP at Medexco. We stayed at her house in Tiberias when we were hunting for the Copper Scroll treasures. Last night, she prayed with me! She became a follower of Yeshua! She's had so many questions. We've been studying the Bible together. The Lord has given me answers right from His Word. It's been so exciting. Please call me. I hope you get this. I want to thank you for blessing me and my family. I can never repay you! Love in Yeshua, Natasha."

Bennett felt a lump form in his throat. Erin had been praying so much for Natasha Barak and e-mailing her regularly, though never disclosing where she and Jon were. He couldn't wait to read this to her. He couldn't wait for Erin to see just how much her young disciple was growing.

But he was startled when the SecDef's top aide suddenly came back on the line.

"Mr. Bennett, we have some news. Some good. Some not so good."

"Cut to the chase, Colonel," Bennett pressed. "Did we get him or not?"

37

★ ★
★

"Secretary James?"

"Speaking."

"This is Crystal Palace. Please hold for POTUS."

"Yes, ma'am."

There was a long pause, then a hiss of static; then the president turned off the mute button on the speakerphone on the conference table in front of him.

"Lee, that you?" he asked with a sense of urgency.

"Yes, sir," the Homeland Security secretary said. "How can I help you, sir?"

The president paced the conference room of the NORAD ops center as Bobby Caulfield prepared to take notes, and Judge Sharon Summers, who had sworn him in just hours before, worked on a laptop, tapping out a memorandum to the president about how to rebuild and possibly restructure the Supreme Court. The president, in his anxiety, barely noticed Caulfield's bloodshot eyes or the jitters in Caulfield's left leg.

"Lee, I'm sensing you're quite uncomfortable about where I may be going with China."

There was a brief pause, and then the secretary replied, "Honestly, Mr. President, I'm not sure your analysis is wrong. But I'm not sure it's right, either, and I shudder to think of the consequences of a full-scale nuclear war with Beijing."

"As do I," Oaks said. "And I appreciated the questions you raised. They're important and they have to be asked."

"I've got more where that came from," James said.

"I'm sure you do, and that's why I'm calling," Oaks said. "The country needs a vice president, Lee, and so do I. I need someone I know. Someone I trust. Someone I can count on to give me wise counsel, even when it's uncomfortable. And God forbid something should happen to me . . . Let me read you something."

The president turned to Judge Summers, who slid over a copy of the U.S. Constitution. Oaks began to read a passage Summers had highlighted.

"'In case of the removal of the president from office, or of his death, resignation, or inability to discharge the powers and duties of the said office, the same shall devolve on the vice president,'" Oaks noted, reading from Article II, Section 1, Clause 6, "'and the Congress may by law provide for the case of removal, death, resignation, or inability, both of the president and vice president, declaring what officer shall then act as president, and such officer shall act accordingly, until the disability be removed, or a president shall be elected.'"

Oaks paused.

"One way or the other," he continued, "the United States is going to war in the next few days. We're at war already, of course. We just don't know with whom. But regardless, we need a vice president. We need a clear chain of command, a clear line of succession, and I'm trying to figure out exactly how we do that on such short notice."

The president asked James to pull up a copy of the Twenty-fifth Amendment on his laptop, which Judge Summers had e-mailed over to him. A moment later, James had the full text—ratified on February 10, 1967—in front of him. The two men then reviewed it carefully, line by line, as Summers and Caulfield looked on.

SECTION 1. *In case of the removal of the President from office or of his death or resignation, the Vice President shall become President.*

"Right now," Oaks said, "Judge Summers says we're operating in a kind of constitutional limbo."

"That's a dangerous place to be, Mr. President," James said. "At any time, but especially now."

"My thoughts exactly, Lee," the president concurred.

He proceeded with another section of the amendment.

SECTION 2. *Whenever there is a vacancy in the office of the Vice President, the President shall nominate a Vice President who shall take office upon confirmation by a majority vote of both Houses of Congress.*

"That's pretty straightforward language, sir," James said.

"It is indeed, Lee," Oaks agreed. "And it's the real reason I'm calling. I want to nominate you to be my vice president. But my problem is, we don't have a Congress, so who's going to confirm your nomination?"

"My goodness," James replied. "I'm deeply honored, Mr. President. But . . ."

There was a long, uncomfortable pause.

"But what?" the president finally asked, in no mood for a debate.

"Well, sir, with all due respect," James explained, "aside from the constitutional issues you raise—which are formidable, I agree—I don't know if the nation needs a failed Homeland Security secretary getting a major job promotion right now."

"And who would you suggest I ask instead? the failed Defense secretary?" the president replied. "Or perhaps should I reach back into the grave and nominate the failed director of Central Intelligence? or the failed director of the FBI? or the failed secretary of state? or maybe the failed director of the Secret Service?"

"Sir," James replied, "I'm just saying—"

But the president cut him off. "I know what you're saying, Lee. But I need a vice president—*today*. Not tomorrow. Not next week. Not next month. Too much is at stake. The way it looks now, it could literally take weeks before we find out who in Congress is still alive and healthy enough to reconvene the House and the Senate. That's crazy. We simply don't have that kind of time. And what if I'm incapacitated somehow? What if I have a heart attack or a stroke or whatever in the next few days or weeks?

Given my history, anything's possible, right? But look at sections 3 and 4 and tell me how that's going to work."

They continued to pore over the text.

"Mr. President," James finally noted, "if I'm reading this correctly, and I think I am, all of these 'line of succession' provisions hinge on the presence of a constitutionally valid vice president, which we don't have, and we can't get because we don't have a Congress."

"Exactly, Lee," Oaks said, "but I'm moving forward anyway."

"What do you mean, sir?"

"Judge Summers and I have been discussing this in detail," Oaks explained. "She agrees we have to move quickly and decisively to protect the chain of command and the line of succession. Thus, I hereby nominate you as vice president of the United States. I'm transmitting a letter to that effect to Congress in absentia, and I'm going to have you sworn in as acting vice president by a federal judge from Philly. He's on his way to Mount Weather even as we speak. He should be there within the hour. Then I'm going to give you the portfolios of State, Treasury, and Homeland Security. We've got a lot to do, and I can't do it alone. Can I count on your help?"

"Absolutely, Mr. President; but again I have to ask you: under the circumstances, are you really sure that all this is legal?" James asked.

"To be perfectly honest, Lee," Oaks replied, "at this point, I'm not really sure of anything."

★　★　★

Hell hath no fury like a woman scorned.

And Indira Rajiv was angrier than she had ever been. She had taken an enormous risk. She had reached out to the only two people in the world she thought she could confide in—Jon and Erin Bennett—and they had turned her down.

They didn't know it was her, of course. That would have been too much, at least for now, and thus she had electronically altered her voice in both of her calls to Bennett. But she literally had no one else to talk to. She wasn't about to call the president herself. She barely knew him and she was, after all, on the FBI's Most Wanted List. Why would they believe her? What deal could she possibly cut? She was guilty of treason. She was facing the death penalty.

The Bennetts, she knew, were her only option. If she could get to them, they could get to the president. They could make him listen. They could make this right. But she had to see them in person. She had to tell them what she'd done, and why, and how sorry she was, face-to-face. They had to look in her eyes, and she needed to look in theirs. They had to know the remorse she felt, or they would never believe her.

Maybe she shouldn't have asked for the money, she thought as she paced her tiny, anonymous, windowless office, chain-smoking cigarettes and mumbling to herself. Maybe that was too much. Maybe she'd gone too far. But no, Bennett hadn't balked at the money, had he? He had promised to get it for her. The only point he had actually refused was the trip to Bangkok.

Rajiv suddenly felt a pang of sympathy for Erin, and for the tiny baby growing inside her womb. She couldn't really blame Jon for not wanting to drag his sick, pregnant wife all the way to Asia. Yet the more she thought about it, the more adamant Rajiv became. There was no other way to do this. It had to be in person.

She picked up her phone, scrolled through her contact list, and dialed a contact in Amman. It took six rings, but he finally picked up.

"Hello, Jamal?"

"Who is this?" said a suspicious voice at the other end.

Rajiv gave him her alias, the one she'd used for years at Langley, and he relaxed.

"What do you need, my old friend?" he asked.

"How'd you like to make some fast money?" Rajiv said.

"How much?"

"A million," she said.

"Dinars?"

"No, dollars."

"You must be joking?"

"I'm not," Rajiv said. "I'll wire you half now, half on delivery."

"What am I delivering?"

"People."

"What kind of people?"

Rajiv explained who Jon and Erin Bennett were. She told him they would soon be traveling to Amman.

"They cannot be allowed to get to the airport," Rajiv insisted. "You must intercept them; take them to the old landing strip we used to use."

"The one near Madaba?"

"Yes, that's the one. Bring them here to me. I will have people meet you at the private airfield. You'll get the rest of your money then."

Rajiv had just one stipulation: the Bennetts could not be harmed in any way.

38

★ ★
★

Bennett had no time to argue.

He needed to be at the airport in Amman by noon, and it was already rapidly approaching eleven. But Dr. Kwamee didn't like the situation one bit.

"I'm telling you as plainly as I can, Mr. Bennett," he insisted. "I don't think it's wise to move your wife yet. I understand you have an urgent appointment overseas. That's fine. Go on without her. But don't put her life in jeopardy. I'll take care of Miss Erin for a few more days—no more than a week. When she's ready, I promise, I'll send her to you by medevac, wherever you are. In the meantime, I will personally see to it that she is safe and well cared for. You have my word."

Bennett wouldn't hear of it. He wasn't going to leave Erin behind. Transporting her now was a risk, he knew, but he had no choice. Erin was still sleeping. He didn't want to wake her or tell her what was happening. Not yet. It would devastate her, and she needed all the rest she could get. So he was moving forward by faith, if not by sight.

"Erin's coming with me," he said firmly, worried he was about to lose his patience. "With all due respect, Dr. Kwamee—and I appreciate all you've done for her, and for me; I really do—I'm not asking for your permission. I'm asking for your help."

"I understand," the doctor said. "I just think it's a terrible risk."

"I fully understand the risk."

"I don't think you do," the doctor replied.

"Nevertheless," Bennett said, his impatience growing, "I need to move quickly."

Bennett stared into the doctor's eyes, and the man finally relented.

"You need to get her to Amman?" Dr. Kwamee asked.

"Right."

"And you'll have transportation waiting for you there?"

"Yes," Bennett said. "It's all being taken care of."

"Will there be a doctor on board that flight?"

"Absolutely," Bennett replied. "I've explained her situation to my contacts. I've been assured they're making all the arrangements."

"You realize we have no helicopters here at the camp right now."

Bennett nodded.

"We'll have to drive her by ambulance," Dr. Kwamee explained.

"Of course."

"It's about eighty kilometers—almost fifty miles—and, as you know, the roads are very bad. They were bad before all this destruction. They're much worse now."

"I understand," Bennett said. "Now please, we need to move fast."

There was no way he was going to tell this man what he was really up to, not even a man who had saved his wife's life. But the plan that was now in motion had very specific time elements built in, and Bennett knew there was no time to spare.

The NSA had, in fact, been able to trace the satphone call to an office building in the center of Bangkok. U.S. special forces were being sent to the Thai capital at that very moment to raid the office building and hunt down the caller and his cronies. To buy time, the secretary of defense had personally authorized a wire transfer of $25 million into the account of Bennett's mystery caller. What's more, he had sent a message through the bank to the recipient that the other $25 million would be paid as soon as Bennett received an e-mail detailing the conspiracy, the players, and the details of the forthcoming attacks, and the information could be "verified" and "canceled."

But Trainor's message via Bennett to "the voice" had also made clear that the U.S. government wasn't offering a blank check. It wouldn't keep paying for more information. This was one-stop shopping. Trainor had a list of precise questions that he needed answered before the rest of the payment was wired.

On reflection, Bennett had told the SecDef that he was now willing to go to Bangkok, despite Erin's condition, if they needed him. He didn't want to, of course, but if the president needed him, he wouldn't say no. Trainor wouldn't hear of it. The president needed Bennett's counsel, not his sacrifice, and Trainor dared not put him in harm's way. The last thing he wanted was a repeat of the disaster in Moscow when Jon and Erin had been held by Yuri Gogolov and his thugs, and Erin had been tortured to within an inch of her life.

So the Bennetts were ordered back to the United States, to Crystal Palace deep inside Cheyenne Mountain. That's where the president wanted them. That's where Secretary Trainor wanted them. And that's the way it was going to be.

Meanwhile, to continue buying time and keep anyone connected with "the voice" off guard, a first-class ticket from Jordan to Rome to Bangkok was purchased in Jon Bennett's name with Jon Bennett's American Express number. A CIA field agent working out of Europe and fitting Bennett's basic description would be given Bennett's passport and would take the flight from Rome to Bangkok, in case anyone was watching or tracking Bennett's movements. Hopefully, by the time the flight landed in the Thai capital, several Delta teams would have already converged on the location the satphone calls had originated from, and the U.S. military would be that much closer to stopping all future attacks.

It was a long shot, they all knew, but it appeared to be their only shot.

Every part of the operation was highly classified. Bennett couldn't breathe a word of it to anyone, least of all to a U.N. doctor he barely knew. All Dr. Kwamee needed to know was how urgently the Bennetts needed to get to the Jordanian capital. What he and Erin did from there was their own business, not his.

"Very well," the doctor said finally. "I will go along with you, and I will bring two of my best nurses, to make sure she has proper treatment."

"No," Bennett said. "I couldn't ask you to do that."

"Please, Mr. Bennett, I feel an obligation to help you," Dr. Kwamee insisted. "Your country has suffered so much. So have you and your dear wife. If I can do anything to ease your suffering, even a little, then I must. Please, just to Amman, then I will say my good-byes."

Bennett protested again, but it was becoming clear Dr. Kwamee had made up his mind. He was not going to be swayed. Bennett was touched, but worried. The man was not only an excellent physician. He had a heart of mercy. But that's not what he and Erin needed at the moment. They needed privacy. They needed secrecy. They needed to get themselves into the protective custody of the U.S. government as rapidly as possible, before anyone connected to "the voice" figured out which choice they were making.

Still, Bennett couldn't very well refuse this man's kindness. Erin certainly needed excellent medical care on the way, and they couldn't afford to make Dr. Kwamee suspicious. So Bennett tried to act as normal as the situation would allow.

"That's very kind," he replied, shaking the man's hand vigorously. "Thank you so much."

"It is my pleasure," the doctor said. "Now, go finish packing. I will get the nurses, get Mrs. Bennett into the ambulance, and meet you at the south gate in ten minutes."

Bennett nodded and thanked the doctor again, but the man wouldn't hear of it.

"Go quickly, my friend," Dr. Kwamee said. "You said it yourself—we haven't a moment to spare."

39

★ ★
★

11:06 A.M.—A REFUGEE CAMP IN NORTHERN JORDAN

Bennett, bags in hand, finally saw the ambulance approaching.

But as it came to a stop, he also heard Dr. Kwamee shouting, *"Mr. Bennett, Mr. Bennett, get in quick; you have a phone call."*

"Let me just throw these in the back," Bennett replied, but the doctor jumped out of the driver's side and scooped up the bags away from him.

"Please, my friend, it's a very important call," he insisted, pointing to the satellite phone sitting on the passenger's seat.

"What about my wife?" Bennett asked.

"She'll be fine," Dr. Kwamee insisted, pulling Bennett to him and whispering in his ear. "Please, my friend, it's Prime Minister Doron's office on the line. They say it's urgent. I will take the bags. I will take care of everything. But please, you must hurry."

Bennett was stunned. "David Doron?" he asked, nearly in shock.

"Yes," the doctor said. "He's waiting."

"I'll be right there," Bennett said. He had to see Erin, give her a kiss, let her know everything was going to be all right.

Despite the doctor's protests, he opened the back of the ambulance and greeted the two nurses caring for his wife.

"She's sleeping right now, Mr. Bennett," one said.

She looked so peaceful. There was no point waking her up. They'd talk later. There was so much to catch up on, so much to tell her. But they had a long flight home.

Bennett closed the doors, ran around the front of the ambulance, got in, picked up the phone, and stared at the caller ID.

"PMO—secure," it read.

It was, in fact, directly from the prime minister's office. Doron was the last person he wanted to talk to at the moment. He was in the early stages of a highly sensitive operation. It was no time for making idle chitchat with the head of the best intelligence agency in the world.

"Hello?" Bennett said tentatively.

"Who is this?" asked a brusque Israeli woman at the other end of the line.

"Jon Bennett," he replied. "Who's this?"

"Jonathan Meyers Bennett?" the woman asked, ignoring his question.

"Yes, that's me," he confirmed. "Who am I speaking with?"

"Please hold for the prime minister," the woman replied simply. "He's just finishing up a call with Secretary-General Lucente. Then he'll be right to you."

"Thank you," Bennett said. "I'll wait."

The woman parked him on hold, and he was soon listening to an instrumental version of "HaTikva," the Israeli national anthem. Bennett tried to compute how Doron could have tracked him down. He and Erin had left the U.S. in February and intentionally slipped into this U.N. camp without telling anyone besides his mother where they were going. They didn't want publicity. They didn't want pen pals. They didn't want communication of any kind with the outside world, least of all the political world. They just wanted to disappear and do some good, and yet somehow it seemed everyone knew where they were. *How? Why? It didn't make any sense.*

Dr. Kwamee slammed the back doors of the ambulance and jumped into the driver's seat. He flipped on the flashing lights, mercifully chose not to use the siren, threw the specially equipped vehicle into four-wheel drive, and pulled out of the refugee camp's heavily guarded south gate. A moment later, they were driving through the town of Umm Qais, also known as Gadara, headed to Route 15—the main north-south artery— which would take them straight to Amman.

As they maneuvered around numerous and often enormous potholes, and the occasional charred wreckage of military vehicles that had been destroyed in the war, Bennett feared it was going to take them a lot longer than an hour to reach the airport. At this rate, he thought they'd be lucky to make it there in two. And the truth was he had no idea exactly what he and Erin were doing next.

Bennett's military liaison, the colonel working for Secretary Trainor, had assured him someone would meet them at the CENTCOM regional operations facility set up in one of the hangars at the edge of the airfield. But he hadn't said what kind of aircraft they'd be using to leave the country. There was, after all, very little commercial traffic coming in and out of Amman these days. Mostly the runways were jammed night and day with enormous military transport planes—C-5 Galaxies, C-17 Globemasters, and C-141 Starlifters chief among them—bringing in humanitarian relief supplies for refugee camps in Jordan, as well as for those in Syria and the Bekaa Valley of Lebanon. None of them would be appropriate for their flight back to the States. None of them had the medical facilities aboard to care for Erin. Nevertheless, the colonel insisted they be in the Jordanian capital and at the airfield by noon, and every detail would be worked out by then. Bennett just prayed it was true.

"HaTikva" was starting again. Bennett was still on hold. He stared out his window at the passing scenery. He and Erin had never had any time for sightseeing over the past six or seven months. They'd had no time for tour guides or history books or even much time to rest and relax. They had been working themselves to the bone. Moved by all the suffering around them that had come in the wake of the war, they had never felt right about taking time for themselves to explore or to learn much about the area they'd been living in, but now Bennett wished they had at least carved out a weekend or two.

Gadara, after all, had been one of the ten cities built by the Romans that made up the Decapolis. Jesus had spent time here, on the eastern banks of the Jordan River, preaching a message of repentance, teaching the love of an almighty God for sinful men, and demonstrating that love with power and authority. And it was here, of course, that Jesus had done some of His most dramatic miracles.

He remembered Erin poking him in the ribs one night in late March or early April. He had already fallen fast asleep after a particularly intense day. She was exhausted too but was still up reading the Scriptures, and as so often happened, she had just found a passage she simply couldn't resist sharing with him. This time it was from Matthew chapter 4.

> *Jesus went throughout Galilee,*
> *teaching in their synagogues,*
> *preaching the good news of the kingdom,*
> *and healing every disease and*
> *sickness among the people.*
> *News about Him spread all over Syria,*
> *and people brought to Him*
> *all who were ill with various diseases,*
> *those suffering severe pain,*
> *the demon-possessed, those having seizures,*
> *and the paralyzed, and He healed them.*
> *Large crowds from Galilee,*
> *the Decapolis, Jerusalem, Judea and*
> *the region across the Jordan followed Him.*

Bennett could still hear every word as she said it, as if she were reading to him right now. He could still see her underlining the passage with her bright yellow highlighter, reading by flashlight under the stars. He could still hear her asking, *"The Decapolis—did you catch that, Jon? That's right here! That's right where we are!"*

Honestly, he didn't remember answering her the first time. He had probably drifted off, but a few minutes later, she was nudging him again. This time she was reading to him from Matthew chapter 8.

> *When He [Jesus] came to the other side*
> *into the country of the Gadarenes,*
> *two men who were demon-possessed*
> *met Him as they were coming out of the tombs.*
> *They were so extremely violent*
> *that no one could pass by that way.*
> *And they cried out, saying, "What business*

do we have with each other, Son of God?
Have you come here to torment us before the time?"
Now there was a herd of many swine
feeding at a distance from them.
The demons began to entreat Him, saying,
"If you are going to cast us out,
send us into the herd of swine."
And He said to them, "Go!"
And they came out and went into the swine,
and the whole herd rushed down the steep bank
into the sea and perished in the waters.
The herdsmen ran away, and went to the city
and reported everything, including what had happened
to the demoniacs. And behold, the whole city came out
to meet Jesus; and when they saw Him,
they implored Him to leave their region.

"*Gadarenes, Jon—that's Gadara. That's right here,*" she had whispered again with an almost childlike sense of awe and excitement that gave him goose bumps even now, so many months later. He loved this woman. He loved everything about her, but especially her love for Jesus and her heart of compassion for lost and suffering people.

And then a thought suddenly struck him from out of the blue, as if it had been whispered into his ear by God Himself: had there ever been a time when this part of the world was *not* a battleground between Jesus and the demons?

40

★ ★
★

"Jonathan, is that you?"

Bennett suddenly straightened in his seat. He hadn't heard that voice since January, but just doing so brought back a flood of memories and immense respect.

"*Shalom*, Mr. Prime Minister; *boker tov*. What an honor."

"*Shalom*, Jonathan—but please, the honor is all mine," Doron said, his familiar voice kind but urgent. "I'm so sorry to hear about Erin's illness, but I've also heard the good news. *Mazel tov*, young man. You're going to be a wonderful papa."

Bennett was startled. No one knew Erin was pregnant. How could Doron?

"That's very kind," he said, "but how did you know?"

"You cannot keep secrets from a man who possesses the Ark of the Covenant." Doron laughed. "Look, Jonathan, this is a terrible day, your own personal blessing notwithstanding. I cannot even begin to tell you how terrible I feel for you, for your entire country, and for my dear friend Jim MacPherson and his beautiful family."

"Thank you, sir," Bennett replied. "That means a great deal to me."

"Jim MacPherson and I had many disagreements, as you know," the prime minister continued. "But I truly did count him my friend, and my wife loved Julie as one of her dearest friends. We absolutely cannot believe they are gone."

"I can't believe it myself, Mr. Prime Minister," Bennett said. "I keep telling myself it's a nightmare I'll soon wake up from."

"I wish that were so. The whole thing sickens us, and I am afraid it's about to get worse. I am sorry to say that I am calling you with more bad news."

"What do you mean, sir?" Bennett asked, wondering how in the world this could all get worse. "What now?"

"Well, first of all, you and Erin are in grave danger."

"We are? Why?"

"I know you spoke earlier with President Oaks," Doron said. "And I know all about the operation under way in Bangkok."

Bennett was stunned, but his surprise quickly turned to anger. Israeli intelligence was monitoring his satellite phone? They were listening in on his calls? But why? And for how long?

"Yes, Jonathan, we've been watching you," Doron said, before Bennett could ask. "We've been doing so since you arrived in Jordan."

"But why, sir?" Bennett asked, trying to keep his emotions in check.

"Because you found the Temple treasures," Doron said.

"So?"

"So I owe you."

"Owe me what?" Bennett asked.

"Anything I can do to keep you alive, my friend," Doron replied.

"But I don't get it—why would Erin and I be in danger?"

"Don't be so naive, my friend. The Mossad captured and killed a lot of Legion operatives involved in the hunt for the Temple treasures, and those involved in killing my team of archeologists and advisors. And the U.S. just killed Umberto Milano, the Legion's number two. But you know very well that neither we nor the U.S. has this group under control. There are more out there—too many more."

"I'm not following," Bennett admitted.

"Whoever wants to prevent me from building the Third Temple is still out there; he's not going to stop until I stop, and I'm not going to stop," Doron explained. "Tactically, the operation to halt the Temple construction is being run by the Legion. This much we know. What we don't know is who is running them from a strategic standpoint. Who's paying them? Who's feeding them intelligence? Who's giving them orders? And what's their endgame? Is stopping the Temple all they want? Or is there something larger at work here? We've been hunting down leads ever since you decoded the secret of the Copper Scroll, but one thing I've always been sure of is this: whoever came after you before, Jonathan, is coming after you again. You can count on it."

"But why me?" Bennett asked. "I'm out of the game, off the grid. I'm irrelevant."

"*Au contraire*, Monsieur Bennett," Doron insisted. "You, my friend, are the missing link."

"What's that supposed to mean?"

"Whoever is running the Legion thinks you're the link to the treasures," Doron continued. "You're the link to me. You were the link to President MacPherson. Now you're the link to President Oaks. If someone wants to get to me, or to Oaks, all he has to do is kidnap you and Erin, torture you both mercilessly, send a message to me or the president demanding whatever he wants, and what are we supposed to do? Disavow our friendship to you? Abandon our loyalty to you? Cut you loose? The State of Israel can't afford to have you fall into the hands of the enemy, Jonathan. You and Erin have become too valuable. Maybe the Americans don't see it that way. But we certainly do."

"Well, I certainly appreciate that," Bennett said. "But with all due respect, Mr. Prime Minister, I really think you might be overstating the threat."

"I'm not. If anything I'm understating it. That's why after you and Erin found the Ark and the Temple treasures, I ordered the Mossad to put a team in Jordan to keep an eye on you 24-7. Look behind you."

Bennett glanced in the ambulance's side mirror and saw a black Ford Expedition about half a kilometer behind them.

"That's one of yours?" he asked.

"It is," Doron confirmed.

"How many men?"

"In that vehicle?" Doron asked.

"Yes."

"Four."

"All armed?"

"Heavily."

"And is that all?" Bennett wanted to know.

"Hardly."

"Did you have Mossad agents inside the camp?"

"Of course."

"Where?"

"On the loading docks, in the mess hall, in the infirmary—you name it," Doron explained. "At the end of every day, Avi Zadok personally sends me a report assuring me that you both are okay."

"I had no idea," Bennett said.

"That was the point," Doron said. "We didn't want to interfere with your humanitarian work. We just wanted to keep you safe. But I must say, Jonathan, I am more impressed with the depth of your and Erin's faith than ever before."

"We thought no one was watching," Bennett said.

"That's what impressed me so much," Doron said.

Bennett, still trying to process all this, ran his hand through his hair and glanced back again at the SUV trailing them. "You actually had agents inside the medical clinic?"

"Of course."

"Like who?"

"For starters, the man who's sitting beside you," Doron replied.

Bennett turned to Dr. Kwamee. "You?" he asked in disbelief.

The man nodded.

"You're not really from Ghana?"

"Ethiopia, actually," Kwamee explained.

"Falasha?" Bennett asked.

Dr. Kwamee nodded again, saying, "My wife and I escaped to Israel on November 21, 1984."

"Operation Moses?" Bennett asked.

"Yes," Kwamee said. "We were part of the first airlift, and because I was a doctor and spoke English and French and several African dialects, I was quickly recruited by . . . well . . . you know who. The rest is history, as they say. We've been working for them—mostly undercover—ever since."

"But you really *are* a doctor, aren't you?" Bennett asked, suddenly wondering about the medical care Erin had been receiving.

"Yes, yes, of course," Kwamee assured him as he continued driving southward, trying to get to Amman by noon. "Board certified, trained originally in Paris, worked in a number of refugee camps in Africa in the early eighties, then was assigned to work for a while at Hadassah when I first got to Israel as I learned Hebrew."

Relieved that his wife had been treated by a professional medic, not merely a spy, Bennett exhaled and then turned back to the satphone.

"Well, Mr. Prime Minister, I'm afraid saying thank you doesn't seem to suffice, but I need to say it anyway. Thank you. For both of us. Thank you."

"You're welcome," Doron said. "I'm just sorry that our men weren't able to help you faster when Erin became so sick. They were about to change shifts and were all on a conference call with the director of the Mossad. But I'm grateful everything seems to have turned out okay."

"As am I," Bennett said. "But I must ask you something."

"What's that?" Doron asked.

"You said you're aware of the operation I'm involved in now?" Bennett asked.

"Absolutely. In fact, we helped the NSA track the call and are assisting the DOD in putting together a strike team in Bangkok even as we speak."

"So you think whoever's calling me is telling the truth and is really involved in the attacks?"

"Honestly, Jonathan, I couldn't say yet," Doron conceded. "He clearly knew the attacks were coming. That suggests to me he's deeply involved. But whether he can actually stop the next attacks, I don't know. It's just too early to say."

Bennett felt a wave of guilt come over him. "I should have called the White House or Langley or the FBI or somebody the minute I got that first call."

"That's okay," Doron said. "My team did it for you."

"Did what?" Bennett asked.

"As soon as we intercepted the call and heard the threat, Avi Zadok immediately tried to contact Danny Tracker at Langley, may he rest in peace. Unfortunately, by the time they connected, it was too late. The missiles were inbound."

Bennett leaned back in the passenger seat and stared out the window, emotionally drained and feeling exhausted.

"Mr. Prime Minister?" he asked finally.

"Yes, Jonathan?"

"How much danger do you really think Erin and I are in?"

"You don't want to know," Doron said.

41

"Orlando Police Department, how may I help you?"

"I need to speak to Chief Williams, please."

"Now? It's the middle of the night."

"I'm aware of that, ma'am. My name is Bobby Caulfield. I'm a special assistant to the president. It's quite urgent."

"The president of what?"

"The president of the United States, ma'am."

"Oh, my . . . well, I suppose I could connect you to his cell phone."

"Thank you."

"One moment, please."

As Caulfield went on hold, he closed his eyes and rubbed his temples. He felt awful—physically, emotionally. He was having to force himself not to watch any of the umpteen TV monitors throughout the NORAD complex. The news was too grisly. And all he was hearing from the president and the commanders around him suggested the world was about to go from bad to worse. He didn't know if he could make it through the day. Perhaps the end of the world really was at hand. What future did any of them have? He was trying to stay focused on small, measurable tasks. Things he could have control over. Ways of putting one foot in front of the other. But it wasn't working. He'd had no luck tracking down any of his own family. He didn't have much hope of finding Bennett's. He didn't have much hope at all.

A sleepy voice finally came on at the other end of the line. "Hello?"

"Chief Williams, please."

"Speaking. Who's this?"

"Sir, my name is Bobby Caulfield. I work for the president of the United States. I'm calling you from NORAD Operations Center in Colorado Springs on behalf of the president."

"What can I do for you?"

Caulfield's eyes were blurring. His head was pounding. His mouth was dry. It was all he could do to stay focused, but he tried desperately to sound professional and get this task done, if for no other reason than to keep his mind off the millions who lay dead and dying on both coasts.

"The president has asked me to track down a woman who lives in the Orlando area. I have phone numbers for her—home and cell—but no one is answering. I'm wondering if you could send a patrol car over to her home, see if she's there, talk to the neighbors. We need to find her. It's very important."

☆   ☆   ☆

Mustafa Al-Hassani's entire demeanor had changed.

After starting out so poorly—indeed, almost disastrously—his meeting with the U.N. secretary-general had actually turned out far better than he had ever expected. Salvador Lucente not only seemed to be on board with his vision to work together to craft a new world order in their own image, he had all but committed himself to invading Israel and seizing control of Jerusalem and the Temple itself, albeit, "when the timing was right."

When Kalid Tariq, Al-Hassani's chief of staff and senior political strategist, had pressed him on the details of that timing, Lucente suggested that if a comprehensive peace treaty between Israel and the United States of Eurasia could be signed, sealed, and delivered within the next six months or so, he could foresee "dealing" with the Zionists in the next three to four years, perhaps even sooner. That would seem like an eternity to Al-Hassani's governors and chief advisors.

But Lucente had a point, Al-Hassani realized: first things first. Their top priority had to be consolidating global political, economic, and military power into their own hands and making sure they had strong but loyal allies all around them. That would take some time. But once accomplished, they could exterminate the Jews and seize the Holy Land and the Holy City, and who would dare stop them?

Al-Hassani led Lucente into his sumptuous presidential dining hall for a lavish afternoon banquet that had been planned by Tariq.

"So, my friend, where would you propose we start?" the Iraqi leader asked as they took their seats on the dais.

"*China*," Lucente whispered back without hesitation.

Al-Hassani was taken aback. "What do you mean?"

"I mean we absolutely cannot—under any conditions—let the U.S. declare war on the PRC," Lucente insisted. "We need China too badly. Her consumers, her military, her influence in Asia—we need them all."

"That's not going to be easy," Al-Hassani said. "My sources tell me the U.S. is increasingly convinced Beijing is to blame."

"Do you think they are?" Lucente asked.

"No, I don't, actually," the Iraqi replied.

"Neither do I," the secretary-general agreed. "As you know, I was just in Beijing. As far as I could tell, they were completely caught off guard by this. But it was also clear that they are deeply worried the Americans are going to single them out."

"Do you still think I'm responsible?"

Lucente smiled. "I take you at your word, Mustafa."

"Good," Al-Hassani said. "Then who's your lead suspect?"

The two men looked out at the room from their places of honor at the head table as hundreds of USE legislators, Cabinet officials, and senior military commanders filed into the hall and found their assigned seats.

"I don't know," Lucente conceded, still talking only barely above a whisper to keep from being overheard. "And that's the problem. I'm afraid if the Americans don't get some solid proof—and fast—that someone besides the Chinese did this, they're going to feel they have no choice but to do the unthinkable."

"How far do you think the Americans will go?"

"All the way," Lucente said.

Al-Hassani was startled. "A full-scale retaliatory strike?"

Lucente nodded.

"ICBMs?"

Lucente nodded again.

"With nuclear warheads?" Al-Hassani asked.

"Of course," Lucente said without hesitation. "Don't forget, Mustafa—Bill Oaks was the hawk-in-chief in the MacPherson administration, far more so than Marsha Kirkpatrick or Burt Trainor or even President MacPherson himself. Oaks has been warning about the Chinese threat for years. Indeed, if you read his speeches over the past twenty years or so, you'll find he's been far more worried about the Chinese than the Russians."

"Look how wrong he was about that one," Al-Hassani said.

"That's not how he sees it," Lucente countered.

"What do you mean?"

"I guarantee you if Bill Oaks were sitting with us right here, right now, he'd be telling us that as dangerous as the Russians were, they never attacked the U.S. with nuclear weapons. He'd also be telling us that his fears about the Chinese were spot-on. And I suspect he'd be telling us it was time to destroy them once and for all."

"Sounds like you've had that conversation with him already," Al-Hassani said.

"Not today, if that's what you mean," Lucente demurred. "But I've spent enough time with him to know how he thinks."

"And you really think he'll go all the way."

"I absolutely do," Lucente replied. "Unless we give him another suspect."

42

★ ★
★

"The U.S. is going to attack somebody."

Al-Hassani leaned forward in his chair and listened as Lucente continued.

"You can count on it. Oaks will feel it is his moral and constitutional obligation to strike back fast and hard. It's not a matter of if, but when, and whom. And if we don't want it to be China—and I'm sure you'll agree, Mustafa, that it's certainly not in our interests for the Americans to turn Beijing into a parking lot—then we've got to give the Americans another target, a convincing target, and quickly."

The speaker of the parliament came over to the head table, greeted Al-Hassani and the secretary-general with a traditional Arab kiss on both cheeks, and expressed his condolences to Lucente for the tragic loss of U.N. life and property in Manhattan. Then, with Lucente's permission, the speaker called everyone to order and asked for a moment of silence "to honor all the innocent souls who have perished in today's unspeakable events in New York, Washington, Los Angeles, and Seattle" and to ask "the unseen hand of light that guides us all to bring the perpetrators of such crimes to justice swiftly and without mercy."

Each man bowed his head and closed his eyes, and the room grew still and quiet. Then the speaker introduced President Al-Hassani, who, in turn, would introduce Lucente. As these were about to be the secretary-general's first public remarks since the attacks, dozens of television cameras and still photographers were on hand to capture the scene, and several international networks—including CNN, Sky News, and the BBC—were carrying the event live.

It took all of Al-Hassani's years of discipline and willpower, much of it forged in the gulag during the reign of Saddam Hussein, to keep from smiling as he introduced Lucente. He could hear himself saying things to the august assembly like "this is a great day of sadness" and "we join the world in mourning for the American people."

But the truth was, Al-Hassani felt no sadness. He had not mourned, nor did he plan to. The American people, in his view, had gotten what they deserved. Yes, they had "liberated" his country, but so had they occupied it. So had they desecrated it. So had they looted its people and its natural resources.

What irony, he mused, as his lips uttered one banality after another about the suffering of a "wise and great people to whom the world owes a deep debt of gratitude." American Christians loved to quote the book of Revelation about the coming destruction of Babylon, about the merchants of the earth "crying out as they saw the smoke of her burning." Yet who was burning now?

Ever since he had taken office and started rebuilding the ancient city of Babylon into the wealthiest and most powerful city in the modern age, Al-Hassani had heard pompous prophecy gurus go on their glitzy TV programs and raise millions of dollars from hapless morons in the audience by saying idiotic things like "Babylon, the great city, will be thrown down with violence and will not be found any longer" and "Woe, woe, the great city, Babylon, the strong city! For in one hour your judgment has come. And the merchants of the earth weep and mourn over her, because no one buys their cargoes any more—cargoes of gold and silver and precious stones. . . . In one hour such great wealth has been laid waste!" and "In one day, her plagues will come, pestilence and mourning and famine, and she will be burned up with fire; for the Lord God who judges her is strong."

Yet who was being judged today—Babylon or Washington? Baghdad or New York? Fallujah or Los Angeles? Mosul or Seattle?

He could not speak such things in public, of course. Only to Tariq. The last thing he could afford was to redirect the wrath of the American government—or what was left of it—from the People's Republic of China to the United States of Eurasia. Moreover, there were many world leaders who did feel a pang of sympathy for the Americans. If he and Lucente were to win them over, they would have to play upon such sympathies, not offend them. But just because he could not say such things did not mean he could not feel them. And feel them he did, with an intensity that was building by the hour.

America was finished. The Great Satan was being consumed by fire. A new world order was emerging. And it was all going according to plan, Al-Hassani realized. He had literally had a dream about these very events when he was a six-year-old boy growing up in the outskirts of Baghdad. He had woken up in a cold sweat, terrified by all that he had seen and heard—terrified, yet strangely comforted as well. He had had the same stunningly vivid dream two more times over the years—once days before he had been released from prison and once just before the Day of Devastation. None of it had made any sense at the time. Yet now, incredibly, it was all coming to pass.

Al-Hassani suddenly heard the roar of applause. He blinked hard and realized he had finished introducing Lucente, who was now standing at his side, feigning humility and drinking in the adulation. He gave Lucente a gentle hug—hoping somehow to convey in visual terms to a worldwide audience the "sorrow of a sympathetic nation" of which he had just spoken—and then took his seat.

Lucente cleared his throat, wiped the tears from his eyes, then looked out over a sea of friendly faces and began spouting similar banalities about the Americans and their great losses and how the community of nations must rally together to stand with their brothers and sisters in North America on such a dark day. But after saying all the things Al-Hassani had expected to hear, Lucente said something he had not expected at all.

"On behalf of the entire family of nations that I am honored to represent, I thank you for your heartfelt condolences, I thank your president for his generous offer to rebuild the U.N. headquarters, and I hereby accept."

Al-Hassani gasped. He glanced at Tariq, standing against the back wall, surveying the crowd. Then he turned from the audience to look up at the secretary-general. Had he heard the man correctly?

"We will count our losses and mourn our dead," Lucente continued. "But we will not be discouraged. We will not be depressed. We will not be delayed in doing the work for which we have been called. We shall not be overcome with evil but overcome evil with good. We will press on to build a newer and stronger and more unified global community; we will start by building a newer, and stronger, and more glorious United Nations headquarters, and we will do so here in Babylon, this glorious symbol of the death and resurrection of a great and glorious city, state, and spirit."

43

★ ★
★

Dark clouds were gathering overhead.

The winds were shifting. They were coming from the west now, from the Mediterranean, not the desert. A rare summer storm was brewing. Bennett just hoped it wouldn't slow down their journey.

A storm was building inside him as well. He was grateful, of course, that Erin's medical problems were only temporary, not life threatening, and even more so that he and the woman he loved so dearly were expecting their first child. He was grateful, too, for Prime Minister Doron's friendship and moved by how the Israeli leader, unbeknownst to him, had been looking out for his safety and Erin's nearly since the day they had arrived in Jordan.

At the same time, he was devastated by the unspeakable horrors unfolding back home, by the rapidly mounting death toll in the U.S., by the loss of his dearest friends—the MacPhersons, Ken Costello, and Bob Corsetti chief among them—by his inability to track down and talk to his mom, and by the steadily intensifying fear that more attacks were coming soon if this plan he'd concocted with Secretary Trainor didn't work.

What's more, Bennett felt sick to his stomach at the thought that untold millions of Americans who had died in the attacks might not be in a better place. The MacPhersons had been strong believers. He'd get to see them again. But so far as he knew, many of his closest friends had never gotten right with God. Ken Costello, for example, had been perhaps his closest friend in government. Yet to the best of his knowledge, Costello had never made the decision to accept Jesus Christ as his personal Savior and Lord, unless he'd done so since his last e-mail ten days earlier, which Bennett highly doubted.

Bennett had shared the gospel with him countless times. He had pleaded with Costello to examine the evidence of Jesus' miracles, His death, and His resurrection. He had implored his colleague to consider the fact that they were watching with their own eyes the literal, dramatic fulfillment of major End Times prophecies—the rebirth of Israel, the War of Gog and Magog, the rebuilding of the Temple in Jerusalem, the rise of Babylon—and to realize that their time on this planet was very, very short.

Costello had been fascinated by all the End Times prophecies in the Scriptures. He and his wife, Tracy—both long-time agnostics and self-described lapsed Catholics—had studied them carefully and had long talks with Dr. Mordechai about them before he'd been murdered. They had admitted being fascinated with Mordechai's "theory," as they put it, but they weren't yet convinced by his conclusions. They'd begun attending a Bible church in Bethesda, Maryland, a few months before their twins were born.

Tracy had seemed the most open to spiritual things, but it was Ken who asked Bennett on more than one occasion, "How much time do we have left?" Bennett admitted he had no idea. Jesus, he had explained to Costello, had refused to throw the game. When asked by the disciples in Matthew 24 about what to look for, Jesus had explained the general signs that would foreshadow His return: wars, rumors of wars, revolutions, earthquakes, persecution, the spread of the gospel to every nation on earth. But He had refused to tell His disciples the exact time He was coming back to them.

"But of that day and hour no one knows," Jesus told His closest followers, "not even the angels of heaven, nor the Son, but the Father alone. For the coming of the Son of Man will be just like the days of Noah. For as in those days before the flood they were eating and drinking, marrying and giving in marriage, until the day that Noah entered the ark, and they did not understand until the flood came and took them all away; so will the coming of the Son of Man be. Then there will be two men in the field; one will be taken and one will be left. Two women will be grinding at the mill; one will be taken and one will be left. Therefore be on the alert, for you do not know which day your Lord is coming."

Bennett had all but begged Costello to be ready, to realize that the signs were in place, that time was running out. He had urged Costello to get on his knees and ask Christ to come into his heart and forgive him his sins and give him a new life. But Costello kept hemming and hawing and saying he wasn't quite ready. And now it was too late.

Bennett could not bear the thought of where his friend was now.

"Jonathan? Can you hear me? Hello?"

Bennett realized Doron was still on the line. He felt embarrassed. How long had he zoned out on the prime minister? Bennett suddenly noticed the temperature was dropping and the winds were picking up strength. He quickly apologized and tried to refocus.

"Where are you now?" Doron asked.

Bennett realized he didn't know. "Good question, sir; one moment." He turned to Dr. Kwamee. "Where are we?"

"Jerash," came the reply.

The very name of the ancient city stirred another clash of emotions. Bennett knew the name Jerash from one of the guidebooks or tourist Web sites Erin had read to him. He remembered phrases like "nestled in a quiet valley among the mountains of Gilead" and "one of the largest and most well-preserved sites of Roman architecture in the world outside Italy." Like Erin, he had hoped to someday visit Jerash and stroll down its "paved and colonnaded streets, soaring hilltop temples, handsome theaters, and spacious public squares and plazas." But now, he knew, that would never happen—not in this lifetime, anyway—and that only fueled his growing depression.

"How far is that from Amman?" Bennett asked, getting more to the point.

"Maybe forty kilometers, give or take," Kwamee said.

Bennett nodded and told the prime minister, "We're about twenty-five, thirty minutes out, sir. Why do you ask?"

"I'm asking because I know you're in direct contact with President Oaks," Doron said, "and I need you to get him an urgent message."

"Of course," Bennett said. "Whatever you need."

"I need you to tell the president that I'm accelerating construction of the Temple."

"Whatever for?" Bennett asked.

"The Levite priests are trained and ready to go," Doron said. "I want them to place the Ark of the Covenant in the Holy of Holies by Yom Kippur. And I'm hoping that the entire structure can be complete by Hanukkah at the very latest."

Bennett tensed. *Yom Kippur? That was only three weeks away.*

"Mr. Prime Minister, are you sure that's such a good idea?" Bennett asked, thinking through the implications, none of which struck him as good.

"The Jewish people have waited nearly two thousand years to rebuild the Temple; why should we wait any longer?" Doron said.

Bennett could think of a host of reasons. "For one, most of the world is going to see this as a highly provocative act at a moment when the peace of the world hangs in the balance."

"You don't think we have a historic right to rebuild the ancient ruins of our holy places?"

"Of course I do," Bennett said. "I'm just saying that perhaps now would be a better time to announce a suspension—perhaps a temporary one—of the construction of the Temple until a regional peace treaty can be hammered out, or at least until the international climate can cool a bit."

"No, I'm sorry, Jonathan. I can't do that," Doron replied bluntly.

"Of course you can," Bennett insisted. "You're a leader, Mr. Prime Minister. You're a statesman. The world is about to go up in flames. You have the chance to pour cold water on the flames, not gasoline."

"Jonathan, the reason I'm accelerating the completion of the Temple is precisely because the world is going up in flames. Don't you see? There won't be world peace until the Messiah comes. And the Messiah won't come until there's a Temple. Now is not the time to apply the brakes. Now is the time to hit the accelerator and get this thing done. The world needs the Messiah now more than ever. You should know that better than anyone. As to whether it's His first visit or His Second Coming, well, we'll ask Him when He gets here."

"That's it? That's the message you want me to pass to the president?" Bennett asked, stunned by the prime minister's chutzpah, given the events of the past twenty-four hours. "You don't think the American people are paying a high enough price for standing with Israel as you defy international opinion and build the Temple before a comprehensive peace treaty is signed? Have you completely lost your mind?"

Remarkably, Doron stayed calmer than Bennett would have expected. "Jonathan, with all due respect, your analysis is backward."

"How so?" Bennett asked.

"The United States wasn't attacked because she stood valiantly by the Israeli people," Doron replied. "She was attacked because she has abandoned us in our time of need."

"*What?*" Bennett asked, incredulous.

"Where was the United States when the Russians and the Iranians formed an alliance to wipe us off the map?" Doron retorted, an edge of anger now in his voice. "Where were your president and the leaders in Congress when my people faced an imminent holocaust? Where? Nowhere to be found, were they? Your government abandoned us, Jonathan, and you know it. That vote in the United Nations condemning us to obliteration? Did the U.S. defend us? No. Did the U.S. veto that cursed resolution, as we asked them to, as we begged them to? No. No. No. You abstained. You *abstained!*"

"I had no part of that, Mr. Prime Minister," Bennett reminded his friend. "You know that."

"I'm not saying *you* personally abandoned us," Doron agreed. "But your country did. America did. You know it's true. That's why you resigned—because you couldn't work for a president, for a government, that would cut us loose. And what have you and Eli told me time after time, year after year? Haven't you always quoted me Genesis chapter 12 verse 3? 'He who blesses Israel, the Lord will bless, and those who curse Israel, the Lord will curse.' Right? Well, it seems to me the Lord may very well have removed His blessing from America the moment America stopped blessing us."

Bennett sat in stunned silence as he stared out at the Jordanian countryside passing him by and the first drops of rain beginning to hit his window. It was the first time, Bennett noted to himself, in the many years he had known David Doron, a largely unreligious man, that Doron had quoted Scripture *to him*. His words stung bitterly, but the fact was, Bennett wasn't entirely sure Doron was wrong.

"I'm not saying I'm happy about what has happened, because I'm not, and you know that," Doron said after a long, awkward pause. "But I am saying you have your national interests, and we have ours. And one of ours is finishing this Temple. The Bible says it's going to be built. We Jews have been praying for it to be built for the past two millennia. And now we have the unprecedented opportunity to finish the job and clear the way for the coming of the Messiah, and I'm going to seize that opportunity. If the world wants to go to war with Israel to stop the Temple and wipe us off the map, then I say bring them on. We have the Ark. We have the God of the Ark. So let's just say, we like our chances."

44

★ ★
★

The rain was falling harder now.

Dr. Kwamee turned on the windshield wipers. Bennett hoped like crazy the NSA was getting all of this. They had to be. Within the hour, Secretary Trainor would be reading the transcripts or listening to the recording. Soon the president would be. Doron had to know it as well. That was, after all, the whole point of the exercise, wasn't it? To communicate directly with the president of the United States?

Bennett tried to process what the Israeli prime minister was saying, but it wasn't easy. It cut too close to home. He felt guilty for entertaining the question, even for a moment. But was Doron right? Had God removed His favor on the United States because the U.S. had turned her back on Israel in her moment of need?

Bennett knew many Christians felt America had long been living on borrowed time. After all, they said, why should God keep blessing a nation that celebrated its sin? More than forty million abortions since 1973. Pornography sales topping $13 billion annually, more than annual NFL, NBA, and Major League Baseball revenues combined. The most toxic cultural pollution imaginable pouring out of Hollywood and the music industry every day. Nearly seventeen thousand murders a year, more than double that of the 1950s. The list could go on and on.

Bennett had always tried to avoid the debate. He loved his country. He loved being an American. He loved America's freedom and her generosity. Americans had done so much good. They had been such a blessing to people all over the globe for so long. But while all that was true, as much as he hated to admit it—and he really did—he knew it wasn't the whole truth. America had a dark side, and as the apostle Paul put it to the Galatians: "God cannot be mocked. A man reaps what he sows." So does a nation.

Bennett felt a gloom descending upon him that he couldn't shake. He grieved for everyone suffering back home. He grieved, too, at the very thought that the worst was yet to come. But he had no time to grieve alone. Doron had more to say.

"Please tell President Oaks that the Temple project notwithstanding, I will help the American people in every way I can," the prime minister continued.

All Bennett wanted to do was hang up, get in the back of the ambulance, and take care of his wife—to love her, to comfort her, and to hold her as the darkness began to overwhelm them both. But it didn't matter. He knew he couldn't. Not yet, anyway.

He asked Doron for an example.

"With Dmitri Galishnikov's help, I'd be willing to sell Israeli oil to the U.S. at a significant discount below global market prices, and we can start this immediately."

"I'm sure that would be very helpful," Bennett replied, though his heart wasn't in it. "I'm sure the president would be very grateful, as would the entire country."

"Good, and there's more," Doron said.

Bennett waited, trying to stay focused.

Doron lowered his voice. "Mossad has a mole deep inside the North Korean military command structure."

Bennett was suddenly alert again. "What do you mean?" he asked.

"We've been working with him for nearly a decade," Doron explained. "He's the one who told us about the North Korean nuclear tests a few years ago and the one who tipped us off to how closely Pyongyang was working with Iran on long-range ballistic missiles, back before the Day of Devastation."

"And?"

"And he's giving us incredibly valuable information on the most sensitive military thinking inside the country. He says it looks as though the DPRK is gearing up for a strike against Seoul. He says the leadership believes that with the U.S. government in chaos, this may be the best chance they've ever had. They think they can win, and he says he wouldn't be surprised if the war starts in the next seventy-two hours or so."

"Wait a minute," Bennett said, trying to process yet another bombshell from the Israeli prime minister. "You're saying North Korea is about to invade South Korea?"

"In the next two to three days, yes," Doron confirmed. "What's more, he's convinced the DPRK was responsible for the nuclear attacks against the U.S."

"Does he have proof?" Bennett asked.

"He's gathering what he can. But he says the Legion has been using the country to create terror training camps. They've been running operations through North Korean embassies around the world. He even says Indira Rajiv has been through Pyongyang several times in the last few months."

Bennett was stunned. Was Doron sure? Indira Rajiv?

Doron related what he knew about her, but it wasn't much. She seemed to have formed some kind of partnership with the DPRK and the Legion. She was receiving payments from someone outside the country, though he didn't know who.

"Can you find out?" Bennett asked.

"About the payments?" Doron asked.

"Anything you can," Bennett stressed. "She's a high-priority target, as you know."

"Fine. I will ask him to get us more on her," Doron agreed. "In the meantime, he made two points."

"What are they?"

"First, he said your people at DOE should test the radioactivity at each of the blast sites. When they do, they should be able to determine that the plutonium used in each of the bombs came from the reactors at the Yongbyon Nuclear Scientific Research Center, a hundred kilometers or so north of Pyongyang."

"DOE?" Bennett asked, referring to the U.S. Department of Energy. "There is no DOE—it's been obliterated."

"I realize that, and so does he," Doron said. "But the research couldn't have all been kept in Washington, right? Don't you keep stuff like that out at Sandia Labs or Los Alamos?"

"I don't know," Bennett said. "I really don't. What's the second thing?"

"He said that the speed with which the DPRK's military is mobilizing suggests to him that they knew all along that the attacks against the U.S. were coming," Doron replied. "He says he believes the leadership is executing a very carefully developed plan of attack, and if the U.S. has any hope of saving Seoul and the rest of the peninsula, they'd better start airlifting troops and moving naval assets in immediately."

Thunder boomed overhead. Bennett felt nauseated. He was operating on no sleep, no food, and pure adrenaline.

"You believe this guy?" he asked.

"He hasn't steered us wrong yet," Doron said.

"How high up is he?"

"I can't say, Jonathan. I'm sorry."

"Mr. Prime Minister, you're asking my president to base war decisions on this information," Bennett noted. "We have to know. How close to the top is he?"

"Believe me, Jonathan, I understand," Doron said. "But it's very sensitive. This man is terrified. He wants out. He wants us to extract him. Honestly, I don't know if we can—not in the next two or three days—not without everyone at the top of the food chain over there missing him."

"But it's fair to say he's a very senior official?" Bennett pressed.

"I really can't say any more than I have," Doron said.

"I know," Bennett sighed. "We have our national interests, and you have yours."

"I'm giving you as much as I can—advance warning of a war your government doesn't know is coming," Doron responded. "The president is fixated on China. But with all due respect, I think he's wrong. China's leaders don't have anything to gain by nuking you. But the North Koreans? Well, that's a different story. Their president is a lunatic—an absolute psychopath."

"You think he'd really try to decapitate the American government just to get the South back?" Bennett asked.

"Frankly, Jonathan, I think he's capable of anything," Doron said. "I will share all the intel this source gives us before we pull him out—if we can pull him out—and believe me, he's a treasure trove. He can provide detailed targeting info on every sensitive military and industrial site in his country. And that could come in very handy for Secretary Trainor and his staff, especially if the president chooses a fast strike."

"What do you want in return?" Bennett asked.

"You know very well what we want," Doron replied without hesitation. "The president gets Salvador Lucente and the U.N. to back off. We're not giving up the Temple project. I don't care what Lucente offers us, or how much of a stink he makes. I'm not compromising on the Temple, and that's final. That said, however, everything else is on the table."

"What do you mean, *everything*?" Bennett asked.

"I mean *everything*," Doron repeated.

"Even the peace proposal Lucente has been shopping around?"

"Even that," Doron said.

Yet again, Doron had caught Bennett off guard. Breathing life into the Arab-Israeli peace process seemed laughable, after all. Bennett had all but given up hope, especially since work on the Temple had begun. Perhaps his tactical pessimism had gotten the better of him.

"You would really consider Lucente's plan?" Bennett inquired, still not believing he had heard the prime minister correctly.

"Between you and me, it's the best plan I've seen so far," Doron said.

"And you're ready to make real compromises?" Bennett pressed further.

"Yes," Doron said.

"The West Bank? The Golan Heights? Water? The right of return? East Jerusalem?"

"Maybe not the right of return, but everything else, yes," Doron said. "We're ready to agree to nearly all of his suggested compromises. What's more, we're ready to begin full diplomatic relations with *all* of our neighbors—including Iraq—*immediately*. We are ready to sign a comprehensive peace treaty *immediately*. You tell me when. You tell me where—Brussels, Rome, Babylon, wherever; it doesn't matter. I'll be there. I'll sign on the dotted line. And Lucente can have the grand ceremony he's been long-ing for. So long as he and everyone else in the U.N. understands that the Third Temple is absolutely nonnegotiable. Period. Is that clear enough for you?"

45

★ ★
★

Khalid Tariq was enraged.

His face red and his temples throbbing, he had already popped a pill for his high blood pressure that morning. It wasn't working. He popped another.

"How much longer?" he barked, feeling beads of perspiration form on his upper lip and around his collar.

"We're almost there, sir," the pilot said. "We should be on the ground in less than ten minutes."

Tariq didn't think he could wait that long. Within the past hour, Kurdish leaders in southern Turkey and northwestern Iran had held a joint press conference in what was left of Ankara, formally declaring their independence. They had already cabled word to U.N. Secretary-General Salvador Lucente, requesting recognition of their new "Democratic Republic of Kurdistan." Reuters and the Turkish news services were reporting what had been rumored for days: that Kurdish leaders in the Iraqi province of Arbîl would soon be declaring their secession from Iraq to join the new Kurdish state.

On Tariq's phone was a text message from the Iraqi intelligence station chief in Arbîl. He reported at least two dozen Kurdish leaders were holed up in the governor's palace and had been meeting for the past several hours. Electronic surveillance indicated the topic was how quickly to make their announcement and how seriously they should take Al-Hassani's threat to use force to stop them from seceding.

At Tariq's command, nearly two hundred tanks and some 150,000 Iraqi ground forces were now mobilizing in Mosul and moving slowly but steadily toward Arbîl, the provincial capital, Kirkuk, and Sulaymaniyah. For the moment, it was merely a show of force, designed to convince the Kurdish leaders that they were making a fatal mistake. But Tariq was not a man of hesitation. If the Kurds wanted to commit suicide, so be it. He for one wouldn't lose any sleep over invading their oil-rich province and crushing their insolence once and for all.

Tariq speed-dialed the senior military commander in Mosul.

"Get me General Qassim," he demanded when a subordinate answered.

"Yes, sir; right away, sir," came the reply.

A moment later, he was patched through.

"If they were moving at full speed, General, how soon can your lead mechanized units be rolling down the streets of Kirkuk?"

"Within the hour," the general replied. "Why?"

"Then get them moving at full speed."

"Yes, sir," the general replied. "But, if you don't mind my asking, sir—are you sure this is the wisest course of action?"

"I do mind you asking, General," Tariq retorted. "Just do your job. Let me worry about the political strategy. I'll see you in ten."

"Yes, sir, Mr. Tariq," the general said. "Consider it done."

☆ ☆ ☆

"Mr. President, it's Chuck Murray. Thanks for taking my call."

Oaks hadn't talked to MacPherson's former press secretary since Murray had left the White House to join a big-ticket PR firm in New York and write a book.

"It's good to hear your voice, Chuck," he replied. "Are Tammy and the kids okay? Where are you right now?"

"I'm in Chicago, Mr. President," Murray explained, noting he had planned to attend the GOP convention but had skipped it at the last minute because his wife and daughters weren't feeling well. "We were lucky," he said somberly, "not that we feel like it."

Murray offered his condolences and his help if the president needed anything.

"As a matter of fact, I could use your help, Chuck," the president replied. "Are Tammy and the girls well enough for you to be away for a few days?"

"They are mostly frightened at the moment, sir."

"I imagine they're terrified."

"But Tammy's mom is in town. She's been here helping the last few days anyway. Why? What do you need, sir?"

"Head to the airport," Oaks said. "I'm sending a jet for you. We're going to need a lot of help shaping a message and getting it out over the next few days. Longer, really, but let's just take things a few days at a time."

"Actually, sir, that's why I'm calling," Murray said.

"What do you mean?" Oaks asked.

"I'd be honored to come and help, Mr. President," Murray explained. "But you need to go on television quickly—as soon as possible—and talk to the American people."

"I'll do that later this morning," the president demurred. "I've got a staffer working on some remarks as we speak."

"With all due respect, Mr. President, it can't wait for later. You have to do something now, in the next few minutes."

"It's the middle of the night."

"Sir, do you really think anyone is sleeping?" Murray said. "Everyone is up. All over the country. All over the world. They're up. They're watching TV, if they have power. They're surfing the Internet, if they can. They're consuming every morsel of news they possibly can. And now they need the president of the United States to come out and reassure them, tell them exactly what's happening—no holds barred—and let them know that you'll be giving them regular updates over the next few days."

"Chuck, really, I'm in the middle of—"

But Murray interrupted him. "Mr. President, forgive me, but please— everyone knows we're on the brink of nuking someone. People are terrified. They don't know what's happened, not for sure. They don't know what's coming next. They know MacPherson is dead. They've seen one picture of you being sworn in on some dinky little executive plane, not

Air Force One. They need a leader. They need to hear from you. And they need it now."

Oaks pondered that for a few moments. "Perhaps you're right. What do you recommend?"

For the next ten minutes, Murray walked the president through some suggested remarks. He didn't have access to classified data, of course, but he urged the president to be as candid as possible. Only the truth—as hard as it was going to be to hear—would bond him to the American people and give him the credibility to rally the nation for the war that was coming. Ten minutes weren't nearly enough, but they were all Oaks had.

When they hung up, the president ordered General Briggs to set up a briefing room and a satellite feed. There could be no mention or visual hint of where he was. But Murray was right. He couldn't hide, much less appear to. Too much was at stake.

46

★ ★
★

Events were moving too fast, but Oaks had no choice.

He made some brief televised remarks, then got back to business, joining just-sworn-in Vice President Lee Alexander James, Defense Secretary Burt Trainor, and Lieutenant General Charlie Briggs for another secure videoconference. Together, they listened to a replay of the NSA intercept of Bennett's call with the Israeli prime minister.

"What do you make of it, gentlemen?" Oaks asked his war council.

"I'd like to get my hands on that source," Briggs said.

"Me too," Trainor said, "but that's not going to happen. The Israelis will never give up a mole inside a hostile government, and it doesn't really matter. The question is, do we believe Doron? Do we trust him? Because if we do, we're about to go to war with North Korea instead of China."

"That's a big assumption to make based on the reporting of one source," James said. "What are we hearing from the ROK?"

"South Korea has nothing conclusive as of yet, but there is no doubt President Woo believes the North is about to attack," the SecDef responded. "But think about it, sir. We really don't have any proof that China's involved in this thing. And Doron makes an important point: why would Beijing attack us? It doesn't compute. They have everything to lose and nothing to gain. But Pyongyang is just crazy enough to try to pull off something like this. And I must remind you, Mr. President, that what Doron's source is saying is consistent with everything I heard at the meeting of Asian-Pacific defense ministers I met with in Tokyo. The DPRK has canceled all military leaves. In recent weeks, they've been pre-positioning additional fuel, food, medicine, and other supplies to forward areas. We've been seeing increased activity around missile sites and air bases. That's what President Woo is so worried about. Just before Mac's speech at the convention—God rest his soul—you'll recall that I sent a memo to *Air Force One*, laying out many of the specifics and suggesting several possible reasons for all this heightened activity."

"Burt, how certain are you that North Korea is the enemy here, not China?"

The SecDef thought about that for a few moments and then said, "We obviously need to gather more evidence, Mr. President, but yes, I am beginning to think there is a credible case here that Pyongyang and not Beijing was responsible for these attacks and may very well be preparing to move against one of our most important Asian allies."

"What about the source's claim that the warheads that hit us used plutonium from Yongbyon?" the president asked. "How quickly can we verify or discredit that?"

"Mr. President, I've already dispatched four WC-135W Constant Phoenix jets, one over each city," Briggs reported.

"English, General; I need English," Oaks insisted.

"Sorry, sir," Briggs said. "The Constant Phoenix is an atmospheric collection aircraft, a modified C-135. They operate out of the 45th Reconnaissance Squadron at Offutt Air Force Base in Nebraska, sir. Each plane has external devices that collect particulates from the atmosphere. A compressor system analyzes the air samples collected in holding spheres. They can detect radioactive clouds in real time. Bottom line, Mr. President, these guys are high-tech 'sniffers.'"

"Like the ones we used over North Korea in '06?"

"Yes, sir, Mr. President," Briggs said. "The very same."

Bobby Caulfield quietly entered the conference room and slipped the president a note: "Your wife just landed at Peterson. Will be here shortly."

The president nodded and continued with Briggs.

"How soon will you have results?" he asked, the urgency in his voice unmistakable.

"Well, sir . . ." Briggs paused as he made some fast calculations. "It's going to take a few days to collect everything. I'd say another week or so to analyze the data, at least, maybe two weeks. It depends on a lot of variables, sir."

"Forget it, General," the president said. "We don't have two weeks. Tell the air force they've got two days. I need to know if the bombs that were used against us were plutonium, and if they were, did the plutonium come from either of the reactors at Yongbyon, North Korea? If not, then I need to know where it did come from. You got that?"

"Well, yes, sir, Mr. President," Briggs stammered, "but I—"

"Two days, General," the president said again. "Not a second more."

47

★ ★
★

Flashes of lightning lit up the rapidly darkening sky.

Bennett glanced at his watch. It was already noon. They still had at least another fifteen or twenty minutes to go. But there was nothing he could do. He reached into a cooler beside him, finding an icy bottle of water for himself and one for the man who had saved Erin's life.

Dr. Kwamee gratefully accepted the bottle, took a long sip, and then turned up the air-conditioning another notch. As the rain increased, the windows were beginning to fog.

"So," Bennett said after a long silence, "the Mossad?"

Dr. Kwamee shrugged. "I was grateful for all they did to extract my wife and me from Addis Ababa," he replied. "Not just us, of course. There were more than eight thousand of us they came to rescue."

There was a long pause.

"That was a long time ago," Bennett said after a while.

"It was," Kwamee agreed.

"Why stay with the Mossad? Why not do something else?"

The doctor shrugged again and increased the speed of the windshield wipers. The rain was coming down in torrents now. The roads were getting muddy.

"I'd grown up in Ethiopia, Mr. Bennett—Ethiopia and Sudan, really. Spent a few years in Eritrea, in grade school, as well. I knew what the radical Muslims were up to. I could see they were preparing for a jihad against Israel. I couldn't just sit by. I wanted to do something . . . something to help."

Bennett nodded and glanced back at the black SUV behind them. "How many men are on your team—total, that is?"

"Sorry, Mr. Bennett. I cannot say."

Bennett turned, wiped the fog off his window, and peered into the storm. "This was a really beautiful country once."

Looking back, he wished he and Erin had taken some time off, poked around a little, and gotten to learn more about this fascinating land and its warm, hospitable people. By remaining neutral—or trying to, anyway— during the lead-up to the War of Gog and Magog, Jordan had largely been spared the level of destruction that Lebanon and Syria had experienced. Still, the firestorm had consumed every mosque, every Islamic school, every military base, and most military vehicles. The collateral damage had not been insignificant, and it was going to take a long time to recover.

"Ever been here before?" Bennett asked.

"No," Dr. Kwamee replied. "Before my training in Paris, I had never been outside of Africa before this—except to Mecca when I was a child."

"Mecca?"

"Yes, when I was very young, my parents refused to admit they were Jews, except to each other. They pretended to be Muslims when I was growing up."

"Did they come out of Ethiopia with you back in '84?"

"No," Dr. Kwamee said softly. "They were killed by a bomb in Dangila, on the border with Sudan."

"Oh," Bennett said. "I'm so sorry."

"Can you imagine?" the doctor said, slowing the ambulance as he weaved through the increasingly water-filled potholes on Route 15. "Two Jews, killed by jihadists not because they were Jews but because they were pretending to be Muslims. They thought they'd be safer that way. They thought I'd be safer."

"How old were you when they died?" Bennett asked as gently as he could.

"Fifteen."

"Were you with them at the time?"

"I was," he said, tears filling his eyes. "We were in a little hole-in-the-wall restaurant. I went to the bathroom. It was in the back. I was washing my hands when the bomb went off. I was covered with plaster and shards of glass. My arm was broken. My head was bleeding. I finally crawled out of the rubble and found the entire front section of the restaurant blown to pieces."

"It must have been awful," Bennett said.

Dr. Kwamee nodded. "I'd never seen anything like it. Blood everywhere. Broken glass. I searched desperately for my parents. They'd been sitting at a table near the front. It took a few minutes to climb through all the bodies and pieces of the collapsed ceiling, but I finally got to them."

"Were they already dead?"

"My father was. My mother was still breathing. She was bleeding profusely. There was a big blade—a cooking knife of some kind—stuck in her chest. I just stood there. I could see she was dying. But I didn't know what to do. I froze. Eventually, I held her in my arms. I was sobbing and screaming for help, but no one came. No one could hear me. And then just like that, she was gone."

The two men drove in silence for a few miles. Then Bennett asked, "Is that why you became a doctor?"

The man nodded. They drove another few miles in silence before he said, "I never went back to the mosque. I couldn't. I couldn't understand why Muslims were killing Muslims. And then I found my birth certificate, in with some of my parents' papers. It said I was a Jew. I couldn't believe it. I didn't know what that meant or how it could be. But something inside me told me it was true, and it was time to learn about my heritage."

"So what did you do?" Bennett asked.

"I wasn't sure what to do," Dr. Kwamee replied. "I was all alone. My older brother had died of malaria. My younger brother died during childbirth. Most of my aunts and uncles were killed in the civil war. My one surviving uncle was still pretending to be a devout Muslim. He had taken me on the *hajj*, for crying out loud. There was no one to teach me what it meant to be Jewish. I finally decided to be an atheist, or at least an agnostic. I didn't know what I believed. I just knew I couldn't be a Muslim and I had no idea what it meant to be a Jew. But I did have a cousin in Nairobi. He was ten years older than me, but he was always very nice to me when I was growing up. He left for university when I eight, but he came back in the summers to visit, and he'd take me swimming and rock climbing and what have you. He even taught me to drive one summer. So I called him. I begged him to let me come live with him, and he finally relented."

"Was he a Muslim, or at least pretending to be one?" Bennett asked.

"No, no," Dr. Kwamee said. "Well, I assumed so. I'd never thought to ask. But when I got there, I found that he had become a follower of Jesus."

48

★ ★
★

Bennett hadn't seen that one coming.

"How'd you feel about that?" he asked.

"Honestly, Mr. Bennett, I didn't understand it at all, and at that age, I wasn't much interested. I just needed a stable, safe place to live. My cousin was an emergency room physician at a large hospital in Nairobi. He wasn't making a lot of money—not by American or Israeli standards, of course—but he told me if I got good grades, he would help me pay for college. I'd never been real focused in high school. But I was so grateful, I studied harder than I'd ever imagined. I wanted to make my cousin proud."

"I'm sure he's very proud of you," Bennett said. "Is he still in Nairobi?"

"No, sir."

"Where is he now?"

Kwamee didn't answer for several minutes. The tension in the vehicle was suddenly palpable. Bennett was sorry he had asked. But after a while, Kwamee said at last, "He died in the firestorm."

Bennett listened in silence.

"He'd gone back to Ethiopia last summer for a few months to help start an orphanage for children whose parents had died of AIDS. I got an e-mail from him in October. He said he felt something terrible was about to happen. He wanted to stay and help. And then . . ."

A flash of lightning lit up the car. Thunder boomed directly overhead.

"It was the last I ever heard from him. I cabled the Mossad station chief in Addis Ababa, asked him to check on my cousin. It took a few months, but I finally got confirmation recently that he didn't make it."

"I'm so sorry, Dr. Kwamee," Bennett said.

They drove in silence for another few minutes. Bennett took another sip of water and watched the driving rain pelt the windshield in front of him as he tried to process this man's story. And then, almost before he realized what he was doing, he asked, "Dr. Kwamee?"

"Yes, sir, Mr. Bennett."

"May I ask you a question?"

"Of course, please."

Bennett hesitated. He knew it was a very personal question. But the man was baring his soul. He clearly wanted to talk. And how much time did they have left anyhow?

"Are you really convinced there is no God?"

Dr. Kwamee cleared his throat and said, "I didn't think so. Not after my parents died. How could there be?"

There was another long pause.

"And now?" Bennett asked.

Dr. Kwamee didn't turn to look at him. He kept his eyes fixed on the road and swallowed hard. "After the Day of Devastation, you mean?"

"Yes," Bennett said.

"It is very difficult," Kwamee confessed.

"Why is that?" Bennett asked.

"Because I don't want to believe in God," the man replied. "I am very angry with Him."

"Because of your parents."

"Because of my parents. Because of my brothers. My cousin. My whole family. There has been so much death, so much killing, so much sadness. It makes no sense. If God is love and joy and peace and happiness, why am I not experiencing any of it? And yet, what am I supposed to do now?"

"What do you mean?" Bennett asked.

"I mean, I felt the earthquake. I saw the hailstorm. I saw the fire fall from heaven. I saw it with my own eyes. I saw what it hit, and what it didn't."

"And?"

"And it's very clear to me now that there is a God," Kwamee said, staring straight ahead at the road as more lightning flashed and more rain fell. "It's clear to everyone, isn't it? And He is not the god of the Koran. He is not the god of the Buddhists or the Hindus. He is most definitely the God of the Bible. Now it's not a matter of whether I believe He exists. I do."

"Then what *is* it a matter of?"

"It's a matter of whether I want to be His follower."

"What holds you back?"

"Fear."

"Fear?" Bennett asked, not sure if he had heard correctly.

"Yes," Dr. Kwamee said.

"Of what?" Bennett asked.

"Fear that Jesus—*Yeshua*—might actually be the Messiah."

"Why does that frighten you?"

Kwamee said nothing.

"It's okay," Bennett assured him. "You can be honest with me."

Kwamee seemed to think about that for a moment, and then said, quite bluntly, "The truth is, Mr. Bennett, I don't want to believe."

That was honest, Bennett thought—dangerous, but honest. "Why not?" he asked.

Kwamee shrugged. "It's many things. Partly, I just don't want to change who I am, you know? Following Jesus means giving up a lot of stuff . . . stuff I like . . . stuff I don't like to be told not to do; you know what I mean?"

Bennett nodded. He knew all too well.

"And . . ."

"And what?" Bennett asked, even more curious now.

"I don't know," Kwamee conceded. "Believing in Jesus feels like . . ."

"Like what?" Bennett pressed.

"Like . . . betrayal."

"Betrayal?"

"Yes," Kwamee confessed. "It's like betraying my people, my country. I mean, I know all the facts. Jesus was Jewish. His disciples were Jewish. The apostle Paul was a rabbi—a Pharisee, for crying out loud—before his experience on the road to Damascus. As best I can tell from reading the New Testament, almost all of Jesus' early followers were Jewish, but . . ."

"But what?"

"But that was two thousand years ago—before the Romans burned down Jerusalem and destroyed the Temple, before the Crusades, before the Inquisition, before the Holocaust."

"None of that was the fault of Jesus," Bennett said. "Jesus said, 'Love your neighbor. . . . Love your enemies and pray for those who persecute you.'"

"But, Mr. Bennett, please—you can't deny an awful lot of terrible things were done in the name of Jesus," Kwamee insisted.

"But Dr. Kwamee, none of those horrible things were done by people who were truly following Jesus," Bennett replied. "They were done by people who were denying *everything* He taught, *everything* He modeled, *everything* He stood for. Look, I don't deny horrible things have happened to the Jews, and a great deal of it by those who said they were Christians. But were they really Christians? How could they have been true followers of the Jewish Messiah and done such horrible things to the Jews? And why would Jesus—who you rightly noted was a Jew—why would He have set into motion a movement to do such horrible things to Jews? He wouldn't have. He didn't.

"The truth is," Bennett continued, "the more people love Jesus, the more they're going to love the Jewish people and want to bless them. And look what's happening all around us: more Jews are coming to faith in *Yeshua*, in Jesus, as the Messiah today than at any other time in human history. Millions of Jews around the world. Upward of a million Israelis—maybe more—just in the last eight months. They're not betraying their Jewishness. They're discovering it in a whole new way."

"I know; I know," Kwamee said, shaking his head.

"So what's the problem?" Bennett asked. "The time is now, my friend. Jesus is coming back, and soon. There's not a lot of time to decide, and believe me, you don't want to be here when the Antichrist arises and the four horsemen of the apocalypse are unleashed. You really don't."

"But I can't, Mr. Bennett. I just can't."

"Can't?" Bennett asked. "Or won't?"

"Is there a difference?" Kwamee asked.

Bennett couldn't believe the question. But before he could answer, a gunshot rang out. The windshield in front of them shattered. Dr. Kwamee slumped forward, his foot still on the gas. The ambulance accelerated rapidly. It glanced off a guardrail, then swerved into oncoming traffic.

Bennett's heart froze. His eyes went wide. An oil tanker was bearing down on them, and they were heading straight into it.

49

★ ★
★

Bennett instinctively grabbed the wheel and pulled it right.

Again the ambulance swerved violently, hydroplaning on the slick pavement. Bennett heard the shrill blast of the tanker's horn. He could see the giant rig fishtailing, but there was nothing more he could do. He couldn't reach the brake. He didn't have a free hand to pull Dr. Kwamee away from the wheel, and the gap between the two vehicles was narrowing fast.

Bennett heard another blast of the horn. The oil tanker rushed by, barely missing them, but before he could catch his breath, he realized they weren't out of danger yet. They were now racing for an embankment and about to go plunging over the edge.

Bennett knew he had only seconds to react. He had to hit the brakes and slow this thing down or they were going to hit the guardrail with full force and they were all going to die. But he couldn't do it. He wanted to. Desperately. But he couldn't reach. He was pinned by his seat belt, and there was no time to hit the release, slide over, shove the doctor's lifeless body out of the way, and reach the brakes before it was too late.

He could hear the nurses in the back screaming but heard nothing from Erin. Was she conscious? Was she alive? He had to do something. He couldn't lose her. He lunged for the emergency brake, pulled it hard, threw the gearshift into park, and prayed for a miracle. He knew the risks.

But they didn't really matter. There was no other choice. He took his chances and hoped they could live with the consequences.

The wheels suddenly locked—the front ones anyway. Black smoke poured from the squealing tires. The ambulance began to spin out, but at the velocity it was traveling, it didn't stop. It couldn't. Instead, it lurched forward and flipped over not once but twice. Bennett was thrown hard against his seat belt, then back against the seat and then forward again.

Broken glass and razor-sharp pieces of metal were flying everywhere. The screaming in the back was gone now, replaced by the deafening roar of crunching metal. The ambulance skidded across the pavement. It slammed into the guardrail, spun nearly 180 degrees, and rocked back and forth—teetering on the edge but stopping just short of plunging into the abyss.

Unfortunately, they had come to a standstill upside-down and in the wrong lane. The entire vehicle was soon engulfed in flames. The cab was rapidly filling with smoke. Bennett's eyes stung. His mouth was filled with blood. He had to get out. He had to get Erin and the nurses out. The whole thing could blow in a matter of seconds, but he could barely move. Searing pains shot through his right leg. He couldn't feel his left leg at all. Panic was overtaking him.

And then, as he looked through the gaping hole that had been the windshield, he saw a cement truck heading straight for them.

It was at most a few hundred yards away and coming fast. The driver laid on the horn. Bennett could see the truck's brakes lock. He could see the smoke. He could hear the squealing tires. But the truck wasn't turning. It wasn't fishtailing. It was still coming straight at him.

Despite the intense pain—now in his arms as well as his legs—Bennett felt a sudden rush of adrenaline course through his body. As if an external force was grabbing him and forcing him through the motions, he found himself up on his knees, diving through the front windshield, and rolling through broken glass to escape the oncoming truck. He was just in time. A millisecond later, he felt the rush of wind blow past his face and watched in horror as the cement truck careened into the ambulance and smashed through the guardrail, and both disappeared over the edge.

Bennett gasped. An instant later, he heard the crash of glass and steel. He knew it was the ambulance hitting the ground first. He heard the second crash, the cement truck coming down on top of it. Oblivious to his own injuries, he jumped up and raced toward the edge of the embankment. As he did, he heard the first explosion. He saw the second and felt the fireball erupting from the valley below.

"*No!*" he screamed with a cry of desperation that echoed through the valley.

His heart pounding, his mind racing, he scrambled down the embankment and rushed into the flaming wreckage. This couldn't be happening. God wouldn't let it.

"*Erin!*" he screamed. "*Erin!*"

He kept shouting her name. Again and again he called her name, that name he loved so dearly, the name that had captured his heart from the first time he'd ever heard it, though he'd never dreamed at the time she could be his. But amid the fire and the smoke, he suddenly realized he was calling in vain. She wasn't answering. He couldn't even find the ambulance, only the roaring remains of the cement truck.

He was sobbing now—sobbing and coughing and circling the truck, weaving through the flames, trying to find an access point to the ambulance. But there was none. It was gone, crushed, yet Bennett refused to believe it. The sobs deepened. He doubled over, heaving, gasping for air, but in the process he was sucking in huge amounts of smoke. The more he searched, the more he wept, but the more he wept, the more he choked on the acrid smoke and noxious fumes around him. He gagged and began throwing up. Again and again he vomited until there was nothing left. But the vomiting didn't stop.

As if the poison of death itself had entered his system and his body was trying to force it out, the innermost parts of his being convulsed again and again. Such dry heaves, however, only forced more smoke and fumes into his lungs and he began to panic all the more. He was suffocating— emotionally, physically—but he wouldn't leave the wreckage. He couldn't, not without the woman he loved.

His skin was blistering from the intense heat. His feet were shredded by glass and shrapnel. And then he heard what sounded like automatic gunfire. It didn't make sense. But even if it was, so what? He wasn't going anywhere without her. He wasn't going anywhere without his Erin.

Bennett stumbled about in the acrid fog, circling the blazing wreckage, still calling Erin's name, distantly cognizant of the danger to his own life but disinterested in his own fate just the same. He refused to believe she was dead. It was all a mistake—a nightmare perhaps, a wicked hallucination—but it certainly wasn't true. He would find her. He had to. He would find her, and he would rescue her, and he would take her to a safe place, a place where he could nurse her back to health, a place where no one could find them—not the president, not his staff, not Doron, not this mystery caller or the monsters for whom he worked.

But suddenly he heard another burst of automatic gunfire and felt a sharp blow to the back of his head. His knees buckled. He hit the ground hard. The force of the impact knocked the wind out of him. He struggled to breathe. He struggled to get up. He was choking. He was gagging again. Someone hog-tied his hands and feet, stuffed a bandanna in his mouth, and forced a hood over his head.

Bennett couldn't breathe, couldn't think. He was slipping into shock, about to black out, and then he heard the sound of footsteps. Many footsteps, running hard and approaching fast. He heard the pump action of several shotguns and of magazines being ejected and replaced in automatic assault weapons and sidearms as well. The Mossad team was getting mowed down, he realized. He heard voices, shouting something he couldn't understand; then he felt a boot in his groin and everything went black.

50

★ ★
★

"Ladies and gentlemen, may I have your attention please?"

Claire Devreaux, Salvador Lucente's press secretary, cleared her throat and waited for the commotion to settle down. She looked out at the bank of at least fifty or sixty television cameras, several dozen photographers, and several dozen reporters and network news producers from around the globe. The press pool seemed to be growing week by week. Coverage of the U.N. secretary-general was approaching that of the American president, and the logistics of handling such a massive international media operation were becoming overwhelming to their small staff, she realized. They had to hire some more experienced hands, and they had to do it fast.

A junior aide signaled Devreaux that everyone was now in place. Several networks, including BBC and CNN, were carrying the press conference live. It was time.

"Very well," Devreaux continued, "thank you for assembling on such short notice. The secretary-general is going to make a brief statement and then take a few questions. I need to inform you, however, that we will not be flying to Brussels as planned. Rather, I have just been informed that we are returning to Beijing for emergency talks. What's more, the secretary-general has a phone call scheduled with U.S. president Oaks exactly one hour from now. So we need to make this fast, get everyone on the plane, and get airborne. That said, ladies and gentlemen, the secretary-general."

A less experienced man might have been blinded by all the camera flashes and distracted by the buzz and whir of autoadvancers. But Lucente didn't seem fazed.

"You and I stand at a very precarious moment in human history," he began, dispensing with all preliminaries. "The forces of evil have attacked us when we least expected. We will strike back when they least expect. Let there be no doubt. I am a man of peace and diplomacy; this is true. What's more, I represent an international community that seeks peace and prosperity for every man, woman, and child on this great, green earth. But there is 'a time to plant and a time to uproot, a time to heal and a time to kill, a time to tear down and a time to build . . . a time to love and a time to hate, a time for war and a time for peace.' This, I am afraid, is a time for war."

Devreaux looked at the faces of those in the press pool. They were clearly as taken aback as she was.

"I will be talking to the American president by phone in a short while," Lucente continued. "I will brief him on the many conversations I have had with world leaders over the past several hours, including with President Al-Hassani. I will be telling President Oaks that sixty-three countries have pledged to me the full use of their military forces, intelligence services, and any other resources they have to help track down those responsible for this barbaric act of genocide and to impose the justice that is needed and rightly demanded."

As Lucente continued speaking, Devreaux could barely believe what she was hearing. Curiosity was killing her. How was the international media playing this? She pulled up CNN's Web site on her iPhone and a few moments later found headlines she had never expected to read in her lifetime.

TIME FOR WAR, NOT PEACE, U.N. CHIEF SAYS
LUCENTE CALLS ATTACK ON U.S. 'GENOCIDE'
ASSEMBLES 63-NATION COALITION TO RESPOND MILITARILY

But Lucente was not yet finished.

"That said, I am pleased to report that I have just spoken with Chinese prime minister Liu Xing Zhao. He told me that in the interest of world peace, he is ready to negotiate a full peace treaty with the United States and the United Nations. He said everything is on the table, including a dramatic reduction of Beijing's nuclear warheads and long-range ballistic missiles, if the U.S. will reciprocate. What's more, the People's Republic of China is prepared to send 100,000 peacekeeping forces—to serve under U.N. command—and $100 billion worth of reconstruction aid to the Gulf region to help stabilize the Middle East and intensify our efforts to rebuild the oil and gas industry and thus sharply bring down the price of oil worldwide."

The press corps was buzzing now. They had been expecting a pro forma press conference. But Lucente was dropping media bombshells one after another. And there was still more.

"I am also pleased to report that President Al-Hassani told me earlier that he is ready to make some news of his own," Lucente explained, waiting a few beats until the press corps settled again and were hanging on his every word. "The president tells me that the United States of Eurasia is now prepared to forge a historic, comprehensive peace agreement with the State of Israel. Mr. Al-Hassani says that after much deliberation—and after seeing how close the world is to even further disaster—he is prepared to fly to Israel, address the Knesset, and share his vision for peace with the people of the Jewish state. He said that will include full recognition of Israel as a state, full diplomatic relations, and access to the Middle East Free Trade Area. What's more, President Al-Hassani said he has no preconditions. In light of unfolding events, he simply wants to sit down with the Israelis and begin their discussions as quickly as possible."

Devreaux again scanned the stunned faces of her colleagues. They were all scribbling furiously and trying to make sense of this unexpected turn of events. Was the world at the brink of war or peace? How could it possibly be both?

"There is much more to this story," Lucente noted, referring to the possibility of a peace agreement between Israel and the USE. "But these are the broad outlines that he has authorized me to share with you at this point. I can tell you that I plan to speak with Israeli prime minister Doron later today, en route to Beijing, and I am hopeful that we can begin working out a date for President Al-Hassani to travel to Jerusalem."

51

★ ★
★

Secret Service Agent Coelho stuck his head in the door.

"Mr. President, General Briggs needs a word."

"Send him in," Oaks said, having just finished an emergency video-conference with the National Governors Association and the mayors of the fifty largest American cities thus far unscathed by the nuclear attacks.

The death toll was continuing to spiral. Millions of Americans were dead. Tens of millions more were on the move, fleeing for safety to cities, towns, and villages far from the blast sites and far from the projected radioactive hot zones.

State and local officials were panicking, unequipped for such a disaster and looking to the president for guidance, and funding. Oaks had little of either. He barely had a constitutionally functioning government. He certainly had no treasury, much less the mechanisms with which to distribute financial aid. He was urging the governors and mayors to mobilize their national guards to keep law and order; to protect food, water, and fuel supplies at all costs, and begin rationing those as quickly as possible; and then to work together to pool their expertise and their resources.

"The federal government is going to war," the president had bluntly told those patched in by satellite. "It's your job to care for people on the home front. I trust you will do your jobs, and do them well."

Oaks hadn't had the heart to tell them more nuclear attacks might be coming. After all, he still hoped Bennett's source could stop them.

The videoconference now over, Briggs entered the president's personal office, a hastily converted conference room right off NORAD's top secret ops center. He stood at attention and set an unmarked DVD onto the conference table.

"Is my wife here yet?" the president asked.

"She is, Mr. President," Briggs said. "She's not feeling well—had some heart palpitations on the plane. She's in the infirmary right now. They're running some tests, but they're not worried at all, sir."

"I want to see her," Oaks said, starting toward the door.

"Actually, Mr. President," Briggs continued, "there's something I need to tell you first."

"About Marie?"

"No, sir."

"About my boys? Are they okay?"

"They're fine, sir. They'll be here tomorrow."

"Then what, General?"

"I really don't how to tell you this, sir."

Oaks braced himself. "What is it, General?"

"Well, sir . . ."

"Just tell it to me straight, Charlie," the president insisted.

"It's about Jon and Erin Bennett's convoy."

"In Jordan?"

"Yes, sir."

"What about it?"

"It's been attacked, Mr. President."

"What?" Oaks gasped. *"When? By whom?"*

"It happened about an hour ago. We're not sure by whom."

"An hour? Why wasn't I notified?"

"I just learned about it myself, sir."

"Where did it happen?"

"On a highway north of Amman," Briggs said. "They were en route to the airport from the refugee camp where they had been working."

"I thought Doron had his people watching them."

"They're all dead, sir."

"*All* of them?"

"I'm afraid so, sir."

The president cursed and began pacing the room. "What about Jon and Erin?"

"We're still trying to nail down all the details, sir. It's going to take several hours at least before we can reconstruct precisely what happened."

"That's not what I asked, General," the president insisted. "I want to know if Jon and Erin Bennett are safe."

Briggs paused and took a deep breath. "No, Mr. President, not exactly."

"What are you saying, General?"

Briggs shook his head slowly.

"Jon Bennett?" the president asked. "Is Jon alive?"

Briggs hesitated. "I don't know, sir."

"What about Erin?"

"It's too early to say, Mr. President. We're just beginning to assess the damage. Jon Bennett is missing. That much I can tell you. There are many casualties on scene. It was a terrible car accident. Multiple vehicles. Huge pileup. One of the worst wrecks in Jordanian history. I've got this video uplinked from the scene from Amman Station."

Briggs gestured to the DVD sitting in front of the president. "It's unspeakable, sir. And, not to be too graphic, Mr. President, but it's going to be tough to piece through. Most of the bodies are unrecognizable— crushed by other vehicles or burned beyond recognition. We're doing DNA tests as fast as we can."

The president stopped pacing. "And?"

"And as best as we can tell, Jon Bennett is not one of the KIAs."

"So what's his status?"

"We're listing him MIA at the moment, Mr. President."

"Missing in action?"

"Yes, sir."

"And Erin?"

Briggs hesitated again, but the president insisted.

"The initial assessment on the scene is that she was killed instantly, sir. She was strapped down in the back of the ambulance. The ambulance was pushed off a bridge by a cement truck, which then landed on the ambulance. It appears to have crushed everyone inside."

Oaks staggered back into his seat. He loosened his collar as beads of perspiration formed across his forehead. "Wasn't Jon in that same ambulance?"

"Yes, sir, he was. But the CIA station chief in Amman reports that there is reason to believe he may have escaped at the last second."

"Escaped?"

"There are a few eyewitness reports that someone crawled out of the wreckage just before the cement truck hit. But there are also reports of about a half dozen men firing automatic machine guns."

"You think it was an ambush?" the president asked.

"It certainly doesn't seem like a normal car accident," Briggs said. "And it's too much of a coincidence."

Oaks sat there, shaking his head. "I spoke to him only a few hours ago," he said. "I ordered him back here." He looked up at Briggs. "I thought we had people taking care of all this."

"We had a team waiting for the Bennetts at the airfield in Amman, Mr. President," Briggs noted. "He would have been in our protective care from that point forward."

"What about on the way to the airport?"

"We didn't anticipate that being a problem, sir."

Oaks buried his face in his hands. He felt sick, and personally responsible. "So what are we talking about here, General—best guess?"

"Mr. President, my guess is that Erin's dead. Jon's either on the run or taken hostage by whoever contacted him."

"The thing in Bangkok?"

Briggs nodded. "We've got a Delta team still en route to Bangkok now."

"We should have sent a Delta team to guard Jon and Erin."

"I guess so, Mr. President. So much has been happening. It's been happening so fast, I guess . . ."

Briggs never finished the sentence, but Oaks wouldn't have wanted him to.

Bobby Caulfield popped his head in the door. "Mr. President?"

"Not now, Bobby," Oaks replied, waving him off.

"I think you need to see this, sir."

The president turned and glared at him. Caulfield stepped into the conference room, set a note down in front of Oaks, and left the room as quickly as he had entered. The president picked up the note, read it, and felt his heart sink.

"Orlando PD called," it read. "Found Ruth Bennett's body. Kitchen floor. Double-tapped to the head. No break-in. No apparent robbery. Seems like a professional hit. FBI now on scene. How would POTUS like to proceed?"

Oaks felt as if he'd been punched in the stomach. A wave of guilt washed over him. He couldn't believe what was happening. It didn't make any sense. He'd just talked to Jon, asked him to come back and help him, advise him, walk him through the prophecies of the last days. Had the Bennetts been targeted because of that? *All* of them? His guilt quickly turned to anger, and finally to thoughts of vengeance.

The president looked up and turned to Briggs.

"Somebody needs to pay for this," he said finally. "Find out who."

52

★ ★
★

Move fast; be invisible.

Those were their orders, and they had come directly from the president. The pilots powered up, ran through their checklist as quickly as possible, then used hand signals to alert the ground crew they were ready. They were at war and radio silence was critical. Moments later, the hognosed Boeing RC-135 "Cobra Ball" spy plane—a high-tech military version of the commercial 707—was being pushed out of the hangar. Captain Victor "Vic" Harris, twenty-six, said a prayer for his wife of only two years and their new baby girl, barely three months old. He, his copilot, and his entire flight crew of thirty-two were fully briefed on what had happened back in the U.S. They had also been briefed on the latest developments with China and North Korea. They knew scores of F-15 Eagles had already been scrambled to protect the base and patrol the Sea of Japan. The 961st Airborne Air Control Squadron had been launched, and now they were being sent into action as well.

Harris proceeded to taxi to runway 23L. Morning traffic was heavy outside Kadena Air Base, he noticed. Highways 58 and 74 were bumper-to-bumper, but that wasn't surprising. Not today. Nearly twenty thousand American servicemen and -women and some four thousand Japanese employees worked on the base, located just outside of Okinawa, Japan, and now all leaves had been canceled. Everyone had been ordered in.

They were at Threat Condition Delta. Security was as tight as he'd ever seen.

As his second-in-command instructed their crew to do a final check on all systems and prepare for takeoff, Harris checked his onboard computer monitor and got a text message from the tower giving him the winds, which doubled as their green light to go when ready. This was it, Harris thought. They were heading into enemy territory. No escort. No cover. And the stakes couldn't be higher. He took a deep breath, got the nod from his copilot, and throttled up.

Ten minutes later, they were at forty-nine thousand feet, cruising at 520 miles an hour.

"Everyone stay sharp," Harris said. "We really need to deliver on this one. As you know, our orders are straight from the top. Move fast; be invisible. The Boss needs our best today. Let's give it to him."

The mood on board was somber. The flight crew from the 45th Reconnaissance Squadron—both pilots and two navigators—knew they had one task today: get their team of a dozen "Ravens" (electronic warfare officers), fourteen intelligence operators and linguists, and four airborne systems engineers from the 97th Intelligence Squadron close enough to get what the president and the SecDef needed, and then get them home without ever being detected.

What they needed was real-time, on-scene intelligence and reconnaissance data on the rapidly intensifying North Korean military buildup near the DMZ and unconfirmed reports of heightened activity at long-range missile silos surrounding the capital of Pyongyang. To help them was some of the best spyware ever developed. Their communication equipment included high frequency, very high frequency, and ultra high frequency radios. Their navigation equipment incorporated ground navigation radar, a solid state Doppler system, and an inertial navigation system that merged celestial observations and Global Positioning System data.

At least that's what the public was told, but that only scratched the surface. On board were the latest high-speed digital cameras, with such remarkable clarity that from five miles up they could look over the shoulder of a man reading a newspaper and actually read the headlines and much of the text. They carried infrared telescopes capable of tracking ballistic-missile tests at long range. They could relay all this and more to intel operators stationed at Kadena, and then back to NORAD, Site R, and any other military or intelligence facility it needed to go to, where it could be analyzed in real time and cross-linked to American bombers and fighter jets, if need be.

"How's Janie?" Harris asked his copilot, trying to lighten the mood.

"She took quite a spill."

"Stitches?"

"Nine, in her arm."

"Ouch," Harris said. "That *was* quite a spill. How's the arm?"

"Not as bad as the bike."

"Poor kid."

"Aw, she'll be fine. Tomboy through and through."

"Quite the firecracker."

"I'll say. Did I tell you she—?"

An alarm suddenly went off, followed almost immediately by their chief navigator saying, "Captain, we have a bogey at two o'clock. Mach 2 and coming in red-hot. No, make that two bogeys."

"How far out?" Harris asked.

"A hundred and fifty miles."

"Where'd they come from?"

"Not sure, sir. A second ago, I had nothing; now I've got two—no—make that four bogeys. I repeat, four bogeys."

"What kind?" Harris asked, scanning his instruments and plotting a possible course change.

"MiG-29s, sir."

"Four of them? You're sure."

"Positive, sir."

"You sure they've seen us?" Harris asked, though he already knew the answer.

"They're coming straight for us, sir."

This wasn't good. They weren't ready. They certainly weren't done. They had barely begun to gather what they needed. They were a full 240 kilometers, or 150 miles, off the coast of the Korean Peninsula. Below them was the Sea of Japan. They were still in international airspace. But Pyongyang was clearly sending a message. What was it they didn't want U.S. intelligence to see? What exactly were they hiding?

Harris alerted the AWACS operators four hundred miles to the north, as well as the air operations center back at Kadena. Sixty seconds later, four F-15s were scrambled and ordered to give the Cobra Ball the cover they needed. But how should they handle things before that help arrived?

There was no place to run, no place to hide. And suddenly the first two MiG-29s roared into view. The first came in above them from the north and made an incredibly dangerous pass, slicing past their window at Mach 2 and coming within fifty feet of their windshield.

No sooner was it gone than Harris spotted the second MiG several miles in front of them, climbing at a rate of sixty-five thousand feet per second. And then its pilot decided to play a game of chicken. Harris could see the MiG coming straight at them. Like the first, it was going supersonic. Harris's heart was pounding in his chest. Should he break right, left, or keep heading straight? He knew he had only a moment to react, but by the time he made his decision it was already too late. At the last second, the North Korean pilot pulled up. The MiG screamed over their heads. And then one alarm after another began buzzing in the cockpit.

"Someone just painted us, Captain," his second-in-command shouted.

"*What?*"

Harris scanned his instrument panel. Sure enough, in all the chaos of dealing with the first two MiGs, the other two had come in behind them. One of them now had a radar lock on them. Harris tried to steady his nerves. Each of the Russian-built jets behind him carried six air-to-air missiles, not to mention a thirty-millimeter cannon with enough rounds of ammunition to blow the Cobra Ball out of the sky.

Harris instinctively took the plane into a dive, but the 275,000-pound bear was not exactly the most agile plane in the world to fly.

Forty-five thousand feet.

Forty.

Thirty-five.

Thirty.

Twenty-five.

They were descending fast and hard. One of the navigators behind Harris began to vomit. The g-forces were killing them all. At twenty thousand feet, Harris leveled out and broke right. But the MiGs were still there. They were still locked on. And the American F-15s were still several minutes away, at best.

"How bad is this, Captain?" asked his copilot, his knuckles white and his shirt soaked in perspiration.

"No problem," Harris replied a bit too quickly. "It'll be fine. Just do your job."

Harris knew that typically when a North Korean fighter pilot intercepted an American spy plane, they'd shadow the American for fifteen, twenty minutes, bring in some colleagues, come in dangerously close—sometimes within forty or fifty feet—and then make it clear it was time for the American to go home. He had seen it happen countless times. But rarely did the NK jets lock on. To do so was an incredibly hostile act, the prelude to actually firing one of their missiles. It had never happened to Harris in the past five years he had been stationed at Kadena and running these recon missions along the North Korean coastline. Indeed, he'd heard of it happening to only one other crew, and that had been years before he had even arrived in the Pacific theater.

But Harris wasn't about to recount any of that. For one thing, his crew probably knew most of it, or ought to have, anyway. For another thing, Harris didn't have the luxury of time to chat. Right now he needed to buy as much time as he possibly could until the good guys arrived. *But how?*

The second two MiGs were now inbound hot. Four on one wasn't going to work, especially when he had no way to defend himself or his crew. Harris put the RC-135 into another dive. Soon they were rapidly descending below fifteen thousand feet, ten, five. The Boeing was shuddering violently as it dropped precipitously. Half his crew were retching their guts out. The other half wished they were.

When they reached two thousand feet, Harris pulled out of the dive, pushed for maximum speed, and began climbing as rapidly as he could. One moment, he was banking right. The next, he'd break left. None of it mattered. They were essentially sitting ducks if the North Koreans were going to blow them out of them sky. But at least they were taking whatever evasive measures they possibly could. And they were eating up the clock, and that was everything.

"Two more minutes, sir."

That was his chief navigator. The cavalry was on their way. That should have felt comforting, but it seemed like an eternity. How was he supposed to outrun four MiG-29s for another 120 seconds?

The answer came fast and without warning. At six minutes after 8 p.m. local time, the lead MiG pilot fired two AA-10 "Alamos." The missiles were armed from the moment they launched. Harris's eyes went wide, but he had no time to react, no time to maneuver. They were too close.

Impact came an instant later. The American RC-135 erupted in a horrendous fireball. Wreckage rained down over several fishing trawlers operating in the Sea of Japan.

NORAD Commander Charlie Briggs received word ten minutes later. Captain Vic Harris and his fellow airmen had died instantly, and with them, Briggs realized, any chance for peace.

53

★ ★
★

Marie Oaks slowly opened her eyes.

Seeing her husband sitting at her side was more comforting than she could express at the moment, but she squeezed his hand and tried to smile.

"Hey," she said softly.

"Hey," he whispered back.

"Are the boys okay?" she asked.

He nodded. "The Secret Service has them tucked away for the moment, safe and sound. If all goes well, they'll bring them here tomorrow."

"Can we call them? I want to talk to them."

"Of course," the president said. "But not right now, sweetheart. You need to rest. How are you feeling?"

It was a good question. She hadn't really had time to think about it. On the flight from Jacksonville to Colorado Springs, she had feared she was having a heart attack. In the rush to leave their house, she'd forgotten to grab her pills. Now she could tell all kinds of medications were coursing through her veins. She felt light-headed, almost dreamy—peaceful and trying for the life of her to remember what had caused all that stress.

"I'll be fine," she assured him. "I just need some more sleep."

"You hungry?" he asked.

She thought about that for a moment. "No, not yet."

"How about we have dinner together later?" the president asked.

She smiled. "It's a date," she sighed, her eyes slowly closing, her mind drifting again.

*   *   *

Word of the attack on the American RC-135 spread quickly through NORAD.

The mood was tense. Voices were quiet. The nation was already at war. But now, some were saying, at least they had a target. Lieutenant General Briggs asked Bobby Caulfield and Judge Summers to clear the conference room. The president would be back from the infirmary any moment for a top secret briefing.

"Is everything all right, Bobby?" Judge Summers asked as the two stepped into the corridor.

"Fine," Caulfield said curtly.

"You sure?" she said kindly, "Because . . ."

"It's really none of your business, ma'am," Caulfield snapped. "I just . . . I don't want to talk about it."

Summers was taken aback. She hadn't known Caulfield for long, but his behavior certainly seemed out of character. She was about to try one more time but just then the president came around the corner, Agent Coelho and a team of Secret Service agents at his side.

"How's the First Lady?" the judge asked as the president passed.

He stopped for a moment. "That's the first time anyone has called her that."

"Will she be okay?"

"She will," Oaks replied. "She's under a lot of stress. I guess we all are. But yes, I think she'll be fine."

"I'm glad," Summers said.

Agent Coelho apologized for interrupting but noted that the war council was waiting.

"Judge Summers, I'd like you to sit in on this meeting," the president said.

"Of course, sir."

Oaks turned to Caulfield, told the aide that he'd be at least an hour, maybe longer, then stepped into the conference room. Summers followed, and the room was immediately sealed off by Coelho and his team.

★ ★ ★

General Briggs called the videoconference to order.

On the line were Vice President Lee James; Defense Secretary Burt Trainor; several of Briggs's senior aides; Admiral Neil Arthurs, commander of USPACOM—the U.S. Pacific Command—based at Camp Smith, Oahu; Brigadier General Jack Bell, commander of the 18th Wing at Kadena Air Base, Japan; and Army General Andy Garrett in Seoul, commander of Combined Forces Command Korea, overseeing some six hundred thousand active duty U.S., Korean, and U.N. ground, air, and naval forces and now another 3.5 million ROK reservists called up over the past few hours.

Briggs immediately turned the meeting over to General Bell at Kadena, who quickly briefed the president on the details of the incident, played the radar track of the entire event with what little audio was available, and showed the latest satellite imagery of the crash site.

"Just to be clear, General," the president asked, "our plane was in international airspace, correct?"

"Our planes don't need to penetrate North Korean airspace, Mr. President," Bell replied. "We can get what we need from a safe, legal distance."

"That's not what I asked, General. I asked if our plane was, in fact, in international airspace."

"It was, Mr. President."

"There's no doubt about that?"

"No, sir."

"None whatsoever?"

"None whatsoever," Bell replied.

"Was our plane doing anything provocative?"

"No, sir."

"Could it have been doing something that may have been misperceived as hostile?"

"No, sir," Bell maintained. "Look, Mr. President, these are routine recon missions. We do them every day, several times a day. We've been doing them for years."

"Were our guys doing anything out of the ordinary, anything at all?" the president pressed.

Bell shook his head. "The only thing different about today was the urgency of your request that we give you real-time updates on the state of DPRK troop and missile deployments."

"Has anything like this ever happened before, General?"

"Mr. President, our planes get intercepted all the time. It's a game of cat and mouse, cheat and retreat. You know the drill. I briefed you in detail on this the last time you came out to visit us."

"I remember it well, General."

"Sir, the last time a North Korean fighter jet shot down an American recon aircraft was 1969. It was an EC-121. Thirty-one American airmen were killed that day, Mr. President."

"I'm well aware of the incident, General," the president replied.

"Well, just for the record, on January 23, 1968—fifteen months before that recon flight was shot down—you'll recall that the North Korean navy attacked and seized the USS *Pueblo*. They killed an American sailor. The captain and the rest of the crew—eighty-two men in all—were held and tortured for eleven months."

"Of course I recall the *Pueblo*," the president said. "What's your point, General?"

"My point, sir, with all due respect, is that President Johnson did nothing to punish Pyongyang for the *Pueblo* incident. That was an act of war. So is this. Is it really any wonder the North Koreans then shot down an American plane a few months later when they realized there was no price to be paid for taking American lives?"

"That's enough, General Bell," Admiral Arthurs at USPACOM said. "I know you and your men are hurting, Jack, but watch your step. And don't forget: Johnson already had a pretty serious war on his hands, General. Perhaps he didn't think it wise to start another one with a million Korean Communists."

"Yes, sir," Bell said. "My apologies sir."

"Look," the SecDef said, stepping in, "the past is past. We're not about to relitigate Vietnam and the *Pueblo* incident. The question is, what should we do now?"

The president turned to General Garrett at Command Post Tango, the high-tech, state-of-the-art American war room in Seoul.

"What are you and your men facing, General? How bad is it?"

"Mr. President, it's a pretty serious situation we've got on our hands over here," Garrett replied. "My heart goes out to General Bell and the families he's having to console. But I would remind everyone that Pyongyang has the fourth largest military in the world—1.2 million active duty forces, seven million more in the reserves, and one of the largest special ops forces on the planet—about 125,000 men—and they're all pointed my way. They've got 170 infantry divisions and brigades, 3,800 tanks, 12,000 pieces of artillery, and on a normal day, 70 percent of it all is pre-positioned within ninety miles of the DMZ, in some four thousand concrete-hardened underground facilities, none of which our satellites can penetrate."

"And today?" the president asked.

"The latest intelligence estimate was 90 percent."

"Then they really are mobilizing for war," the president said.

"That would be my assessment, yes, Mr. President," General Garrett concurred. "And that doesn't take into account their air force, navy, submarines, or long-range ballistic missiles, all of which we are seeing on a heightened state of readiness as well."

"What kind of firepower are we talking about?"

"If they don't go nuclear?"

"Right."

"Using just the artillery pieces already on the front lines, they could hit Seoul and our frontline forces with half a million rounds an hour."

54

★ ★
★

The news hit Caulfield hard.

He hadn't eaten all day. He was surviving—if you could call it that—on coffee and cocaine. Darkness seemed to be closing in around him, hour by hour. And now this. The North Koreans had just shot down an unarmed U.S. plane. Without provocation. In cold blood. Caulfield didn't need to be in the briefings to see what was coming next. He could read the handwriting on the wall.

The president was going to hit back. He had to—hard. And there was Derek, his older brother—the brother who had practically been a father to him since his real father had left home when he was five—sitting on the DMZ. Directly in the line of fire.

Sweat began pouring down his face. His skin felt like it was crawling. He had to get out of here. He needed fresh air and time to think. But none of that was going to happen. Not today. Maybe not for weeks.

★   ★   ★

The president felt every muscle in his body tense.

He had no illusions about what was coming. It was going to be a bloodbath, and the South wouldn't be the only ones to suffer. North Korean *No-dong* and *Taep'o-dong* missiles could reach Tokyo, U.S. bases in Okinawa and Guam, even Beijing. The whole region could be engulfed in war within days. Where would it stop? How would it end?

The president's father had been a young staff assistant in army intelligence in Washington during the Korean War. Oaks still remembered the phone call ordering his father into the Pentagon that Saturday night, June 24, 1950. He remembered gathering around the radio with his mother and younger brothers. He remembered listening to reports of more than 135,000 North Korean infantry troops and hundreds of Soviet-built tanks racing across the 38th parallel in an audacious pre-dawn, Sunday morning raid, local time, backed by unrelenting artillery fire.

Three days later, they had seized Seoul, backed by Communist China and aided by a phalanx of Soviet advisors.

By the time the cease-fire was signed on July 27, 1953, 2.5 to 3 million had been killed, including 36,940 Americans. Millions more were wounded and maimed. The damage up and down the peninsula was incalculable. But this, Oaks suddenly realized, would be much worse.

The very notion of a capital city being hit by half a million artillery rounds per hour was absolutely staggering. He couldn't let it happen. *Then again*, he wondered, *how was he supposed to stop it?*

"How long would it take for the North Korean army to roll across the border, defeat the ROK's forward deployed forces, and take Seoul?" the president finally asked.

"It depends on their strategy, sir."

"What do you mean?"

"It all depends on whether they want Seoul intact or not," Garrett explained.

"Assume they do."

"Assuming all we have is the current twenty-five thousand American boots on the ground, along with the ROK and U.N. forces?"

"Right."

"They could have Seoul in a week, maybe less—probably less. It's only thirty-five miles south of the DMZ, after all."

"Less than a week?" the president asked. "Even with the ROK reserves in place?"

"The reservists won't be fully up and running for another two weeks, at best—if the North moves in the next few days, they'll have the advantage, and they know it."

"And if Pyongyang doesn't want Seoul?"

"Then they use WMDs," Garrett said.

"What do they have, and how much?"

"Mr. President, we estimate the DPRK is producing about three thousand tons of chemical weapons a year. Best we can tell, they've weaponized mustard gas, sarin—you name it, they've got it. As far as biological weapons, we believe they've weaponized anthrax, cholera, smallpox, and typhoid as well, sir. The last time I was at the DMZ—which was maybe six months ago—a top South Korean general told me their intelligence shows that the DPRK has between forty and seventy-five missiles armed with chemical and biological weapons, all deployed on the front lines. They can launch without warning and would kill upward of 40 percent of the population of Seoul in less than an hour."

"And if the North goes nuclear?" Oaks asked.

Garrett was silent.

"General Garrett, I'm asking you a direct question," the president insisted. "How many could the North Koreans kill if they choose to go nuclear?"

"Mr. President, everyone in and around Seoul could be dead in less than four hours."

"How many people is that, General?"

"Twelve million," Garrett said, "including a hundred thousand Americans, sir."

Oaks winced.

"What's more, Mr. President," Garrett continued, "almost half of South Korea's population lives within an hour of the capital. The casualties, sir, would be apocalyptic."

The word jarred Oaks, though he took pains not to show it. Was that what they were seeing—the dawn of the apocalypse?

"How much warning would we have before they attacked?" he asked.

"I suspect they're ready now, Mr. President," Garrett said. "Jack's plane was sent out to confirm that. And based on the North's reaction, and all the other data we're seeing, I believe they could launch at any minute.

That's why the South Koreans and Japanese were asking the SecDef to move so quickly, even before today's attack and the nuclear attacks back home."

Oaks could see it clearly now. Seoul and Tokyo were desperate that he not repeat the mistakes Truman and Acheson had made back in 1950. On January 12 of that year, U.S. Secretary of State Dean Acheson had delivered a major address at the National Press Club in which he had actually excluded South Korea from the "defensive perimeter" of U.S. military strategy in Asia. Five months later, apparently convinced the U.S. would not intervene, the North made their move.

Oaks remembered how infuriated his father had been, believing that Truman and Acheson had effectively invited the war. He remembered General Dwight Eisenhower's famous Cincinnati speech excoriating Acheson, stating, "In January of 1950, our secretary of state declared that America's so-called 'defensive perimeter' excluded areas on the Asiatic mainland such as Korea. He said in part: 'No person can guarantee such areas against military attack. It must be clear that such a guarantee is hardly sensible or necessary. . . . It is a mistake . . . in considering Pacific and Far Eastern problems to become obsessed with military considerations.'"

Compounding matters, Acheson's top Asia expert at the time, Dean Rusk—then U.S. assistant secretary of state for the Far East—had actually briefed Congress on June 20, stating that despite rising tensions, he did not believe an invasion of the South was likely. Five days later, the invasion began, and the U.S. was caught disastrously unprepared to respond quickly and decisively.

There was no question now that South Korea was part of the U.S. security sphere in Asia. But the U.S. had been steadily downsizing the number of American troops on the peninsula. All U.S. tactical nuclear weapons had been removed from South Korea. The danger of miscalculating again was enormous, Oaks realized.

He turned now to Admiral Arthurs. "How do we stop them, Admiral? What's it really going to take?"

The admiral, fast approaching his forty-fifth year in the navy, took a deep breath. "Mr. President, as you know, OPLAN 5027 is our contingency plan for a North Korean invasion," he began, somewhat tentatively. "Secretary Trainor ordered an overhaul of all our war scenarios after the

Day of Devastation, based on the dramatically changed strategic situation. I'm afraid that's not yet complete."

"Just give me an executive summary of what you have," the president insisted.

"Well, sir, the version we developed for President Clinton in 2000 and updated for Presidents Bush and MacPherson called for more than 690,000 U.S. troops to be deployed into South Korea in the event of an invasion by the North."

"Six hundred ninety thousand troops?" the president asked.

"Yes, sir," the admiral said. "We scaled that up from 480,000 in the early 1990s."

"But we've only got 25,000 U.S. troops there at the moment, right?"

"That's true, sir," Briggs said. "The plan is based on the Joint Chiefs' assessment of how many U.S. forces would be needed to drive the North back up past the 38th parallel in the event of an invasion."

"It assumes that the South would be overrun?" Oaks asked.

"Yes, sir, almost immediately," the admiral said.

"And it assumes the entire peninsula would be held by the North until we could mobilize and deploy enough men and weaponry to drive them out?"

"Yes, sir. That's correct."

"How long would that take?"

"My staff is working on that right now, Mr. President," the admiral explained. "But it would take several months, at least; I can tell you that."

"How many troops could we get into Seoul in the next forty-eight hours?"

"Ten thousand, sir," Briggs guessed. "Maybe fifteen."

"How long would it take to get a hundred thousand troops there?"

"A month, maybe longer."

"We don't have a month, do we, Admiral?"

"No, sir, I don't believe we do, Mr. President. Like I said, the DPRK could have Seoul by the end of the week, if that."

"So now we're back to my original question," Oaks said. "How do we stop a full-scale North Korean invasion of South Korea?"

"Mr. President, I'm afraid the answer isn't in OPLAN 5027."

"But you do have a plan for this, right?"

"Yes, sir, but—"

"I want to see it."

"Mr. President, I have to tell you that—"

"I need to see it, Admiral. Now."

55

★ ★
★

Bennett had no idea where he was.

Or where he was going. Or how long he had been unconscious. Minutes? Hours? Days? He had no point of reference. His thoughts were scrambled and foggy. He couldn't see a thing. A black hood had been pulled over his head and was tied tightly around his neck. Even if he had been able to see, his watch was gone. It had been stripped from him, as had his clothes, he now realized. What's more, his hands and feet were shackled, and he was strapped to a cold metal chair.

His head throbbed. Every muscle in his body ached. Perspiration dripped down his face and neck and back. And someone was sitting very close to him.

A plane. He was on a plane, he realized as he became aware of the pressure difference in his ears. That much was certain. Whoever was near him was now dialing an air phone. Bennett could hear the touch-tone and someone mumbling something, though he couldn't make out the words. And then, as quickly as he began, the man stopped talking, and everything grew quiet again.

Bennett strained to listen for any other sound that might give him a clue as to who was with him. *Was it just one, or were there several of them? Were they armed? Were they going to beat him? kill him? If not, where were they taking him?* But for now, he heard nothing save the roar of jet engines.

And then the fog began to lift. Like a flashback in a movie, he could suddenly see the cement truck bearing down on him. He could see himself scrambling through the front window of the ambulance. He could hear the impact and feel the concussion of both explosions. He could feel the heat of the flames and see the fire roaring and crackling and hissing in the storm.

Another tsunami of guilt and grief washed over him. It had been his job to protect this woman he loved so dearly, but he had failed. He desperately wanted to believe it had all been a terrible nightmare. He longed to believe that when he opened his eyes, Erin would be sitting with him, holding his hand, in first class on some British Airways flight from Amman to London and then on to the States. But in his heart he knew it wasn't true.

She was gone. She was dead. And he was a prisoner. A hostage. A man drowning in sorrow. His stomach ached terribly, and so did his heart. Denial was useless. Daydreaming was pointless. He had lost her. He had failed her. And there was absolutely nothing he could do about it.

He began to weep, quietly at first, and then uncontrollably. No one stopped him. No one said anything. No one cared. And then someone jabbed a needle in his arm, and that was the last thing he remembered.

☆　☆　☆

Caulfield's cell phone finally rang.

He'd been pacing the hallways of NORAD for hours. He'd been waiting for this call. But now that it was here, he was too scared to answer it. His vision kept blurring. The intense cramps in his stomach nearly made him double over in pain. *What if . . . ?*

The phone rang again. And again. And a fourth time. He finally picked up.

"Hello?"

"Is this Robert Caulfield?" said a man's voice at the other end.

"Speaking."

"This is Special Agent Karl Miller. I'm with the FBI field office in Dallas. I'm returning your call."

Dallas? Caulfield had called several FBI field offices around the country in the past several hours, but he certainly didn't remember calling Dallas or talking to a Karl Miller. Perhaps this wasn't what he thought.

"Uh, I . . . I'm not sure that I did . . . call you," he replied, his voice raspy, his thoughts sluggish and disjointed.

"You asked for Missing Persons," Miller explained. "All that's being run out of Dallas for the moment."

"Oh," Caulfield said, now even more worried than he'd been earlier. "Okay . . . right . . . well . . ."

His voice trailed off. He was sweating profusely and could barely stay on his feet. He staggered into a nearby men's room, locked himself in a stall, and sat down, his head in his hands.

"Mr. Caulfield," the agent continued, "I understand you work for the president."

Caulfield didn't respond.

"Hello? Hello? Sir?"

He finally snapped to. "Yes? . . . What? . . . How's that?" he mumbled.

"Are you okay, Mr. Caulfield?" the agent asked.

"I'm fine," he lied. "What about my family?"

"You were calling about your mother, Dorothy Caulfield, and your younger brothers, correct?"

"That's right," Caulfield said. "How are they? Are they okay?"

"Your brothers' names are Kevin, James, Lawrence, and—"

"Christopher," Caulfield nearly shouted. *"His name is Christopher. He's the baby. Now talk to me—what's happening with them?"*

The silence at the other end of the line was chilling.

"Mr. Caulfield," the agent finally said, "I hate to say this . . ."

"No."

". . . especially over the phone. But I'm afraid . . ."

"No!"

". . . I'm afraid I have some very bad news."

☆　☆　☆

The voice of a colonel came over the speakerphone.

"Mr. President, we have the secretary-general on the line. You ready for it now?"

"One moment," the president said, turning to Briggs and those on the videoconference. "Can you gentlemen hang on? This will only take a few minutes."

"Of course, Mr. President," Briggs replied. "Take as much time as you need. We'll be fine."

The president thanked his team, then scanned the bank of phones in front of him, picked up a receiver, and hit the one blinking line. "Salvador, is that you?"

"Yes, Mr. President; thank you for taking my call."

"Sorry I wasn't able to call sooner," Oaks replied.

"No, no, it is quite all right," Lucente said. "I can't fully imagine what you are going through, Mr. President. How are you and Marie doing?"

"We're doing reasonably well, under the circumstances," Oaks said, dodging the question about his wife. "Thanks for asking. I appreciate it very much."

"Of course, Mr. President," Lucente said. "I wanted to tell you personally that I am doing everything I possibly can to build an international coalition to punish whoever is responsible for this. I know you've had your hands full just dealing with the immediate crisis, but I went ahead anyway. I hope you don't mind."

"Actually, I am very grateful," Oaks said. "My staff told me about your press conference. It was the first bit of good news we had in hours. But, Salvador, before we go any further, please accept my condolences for the loss of your staff in Manhattan. It was our duty to protect them. I cannot tell you how horrible I feel about our failure to do just that. Please forgive us. Please forgive me personally."

"Thank you, Mr. President," Lucente replied. "You are very thoughtful. But you have nothing for which you must apologize. We have all suffered in this tragedy. Indeed, in talking to leaders all over the world, I can tell you firsthand that the entire international community is grieving for the evil that has been unleashed. What's more, I believe we are more united today than ever before, and perhaps that can be a positive legacy from all of this horror."

"Perhaps it can," Oaks said. "Where are you right now?"

"En route to Beijing, Mr. President," Lucente explained. "I just left Babylon."

"How is my friend Mustafa?" Oaks asked, choosing not to comment on the reference to China.

"Sickened by your losses," Lucente replied. "He wants to know if there is anything he can possibly do to help."

Oaks didn't miss a beat. "He could stand down his 150,000 or so troops headed into Kurdistan."

Lucente seemed caught off guard. "I'm not sure it's quite that many, Mr. President."

"It's at least that many, Salvador, and I won't have it," Oaks said firmly. "Not today. Not right now. The last thing we need is another war in the Middle East."

"I quite agree, Mr. President. But the Kurds' timing couldn't have been worse. They've declared independence at a time that could really provoke a conflict."

"Then why are you flying back to Beijing? You need to get Mustafa to pull troops back—now—before things spin out of control."

"It's a problem, I know," Lucente said, conceding the obvious. "But compared to the situation between you and China, I must say it doesn't even come close. I will see Premier Zhao in a few hours. Perhaps there is a message I could convey for you, Mr. President."

"I will call the premier myself in a few minutes," Oaks said. "But my message to him will be the same message I give to Mustafa: stand down."

"Beijing has mobilized its military because you have, Mr. President," Lucente said. "They mean no harm. They're only taking defensive measures."

"Salvador, have you seen the intelligence?" Oaks countered. "Those aren't defensive measures. The PLA looks like it's getting ready to invade Taiwan, and the Taiwanese are apoplectic."

"The premier insists he has no hostile intent," Lucente reiterated. "But he fears you are about to blame them for the attacks on your cities."

"Should I?" Oaks asked, careful not to tip his hand.

"No, Mr. President," Lucente insisted.

"You sound quite certain, Salvador."

"China is not your enemy, Mr. President. Of this I am sure."

"Then who is?"

Lucente was silent.

"If you know something, Salvador, now is the time to tell me," Oaks said.

"I have spoken with the chiefs of several intelligence agencies within the last few hours," Lucente said.

"And?"

"They have nothing definitive."

"But they have something."

"Pieces. Chatter. Nothing conclusive."

"Where does it point, Salvador?" Oaks pressed. "I have to know."

Lucente paused.

"The world cannot afford a miscalculation, Salvador," Oaks insisted.

"My only reluctance to speak is that my job is supposed to be that of a peacemaker," Lucente protested, "not judge, jury, and executioner."

"You'd be none of the above," Oaks said. "Only a witness."

"Fair enough," Lucente said, "but please don't say anything—publicly or privately—about where you are getting this."

"We're doing an intensive investigation, Salvador," Oaks assured him. "We won't take any action unless we have hard evidence. But I need every lead I can get at the moment."

"Very well," Lucente said. He took a deep breath and then said, "Everything I'm hearing points to Pyongyang."

56

★ ★
★

Bobby Caulfield didn't hang up the phone.

He slammed it onto the men's room floor, where it smashed into pieces. Then he stomped on each piece until it was just bits of plastic that scattered like dust under his feet. He burst out of the stall and grabbed his briefcase off a sink. He tore through it in a rage but didn't find what he wanted. It was gone. All of it. *How was that possible? Where was he going to get more?*

Caulfield grabbed the leather bag and flung it against the bathroom mirror. When all of its contents spilled out and crashed onto the cold tile, his rage only seemed to intensify. He grabbed the nearest object—his digital camera—and heaved it at the mirror again. This time, not only did the camera shatter but so did the mirror.

His breathing heavy, his eyes glassy and dilated, Caulfield stormed out of the men's room and ran to the lounge. There was no one there. He headed next to the senior executive dining room, but it, too, was empty. Then he moved to a small kitchen down the hall and around the corner from the president's makeshift office, and there he found a military police officer pouring himself a cup of coffee.

"Mr. Caulfield, you don't look so good," the MP said. "Everything okay?"

But Caulfield never answered. Instead, he coldcocked the MP in the

face, sending the man crashing to the floor, unconscious and nose bleeding. The man never saw it coming. Caulfield stared down at him, listening
for voices, listening for footsteps. All was quiet. Then he began prying the
MP's gun from his holster.

☆　☆　☆

"I just spoke to the president of Liberia," Lucente said.

"What did he say?" Oaks asked.

"He told me about the Liberian-flagged container ship that your air
force sank."

"That was an act of self-defense," the president noted, sensing a
confrontation.

"I'm sure it was," Lucente assured him. "That wasn't my point."

"What was?"

"The ship, apparently, had been chartered by a company in Bangkok,
but it turns out the company isn't Thai owned."

"So?"

"So the company was bought last year by an outfit called Mercury Star
Holdings, Limited, which Thai intelligence has determined is actually a
front group for the DPRK."

"Interesting," Oaks said. "What else?"

"The head of intelligence for the PLA just told one of my deputies
he's got nineteen hours of telephone intercepts between senior DPRK
officials and known members of the Legion. He's got photos of Umberto
Milano in Pyongyang six weeks ago. He says Vincenzo Milano, Umberto's
younger brother, flew into Pyongyang three days ago."

"Why?"

"He doesn't know."

"What about Aldo Clemenza?" the president asked, referring to the
alleged leader of the shadowy terror faction. "When was he in North
Korea last?"

"He doesn't know."

"You asked?"

"I asked," Lucente said. "He said he doesn't know."

Oaks was skeptical at best. "Forgive me, Salvador, but I'm not certain this is the week I'm going to start relying on intelligence provided to me by the People's Liberation Army."

"They're willing to make the tapes available to the CIA station chief in Beijing."

"I'm sure the PLA would love to know who the CIA station chief is in Beijing," the president replied, then added, "Assuming, that is, we even have a CIA station chief in Beijing."

"Look, Mr. President," Lucente said, "I'm just telling you what I'm hearing. Do you really want a global thermonuclear war with the Chinese? Think about it. They could lose a billion people and still have a bigger population than the United States. But do you really think they won't respond in kind? Of course they will. And how many more Americans are you willing to lose?"

Oaks said nothing.

Lucente continued, "And, really, do you honestly think Beijing would be stupid enough to trigger a war that will force you to go nuclear? They're power-hungry; I grant you that. They want Taiwan back. They want to control the Pacific. Yes. But suicidal? Hardly. The North Koreans, on the other hand—that's an entirely different story. I believe they did this. They had the means, the motive, and the opportunity. And if you hit them—and hit them hard—you can show the entire world America remains the world's only superpower. Right now, isn't that really the point?"

Oaks thanked Lucente for the call, reiterated his request that he persuade Al-Hassani not to launch hostilities against the Kurds, and hung up the phone. His war council was waiting, but his thoughts were racing so fast he needed a moment to refocus.

Was he wrong, and Lucente right? Were the North Koreans, rather than the Chinese, behind everything that had happened in the past twenty-four hours? Where was the proof? He saw hearsay. He saw innuendo. But was that enough to go to war?

He shifted gears and turned to the incident over the Sea of Japan. Had the U.S. jet purposefully or inadvertently strayed into DPRK airspace, or was this a deliberate act of aggression by Pyongyang? And just what would happen if he were to order military strikes against North Korea?

On that, Admiral Arthurs and General Garrett were probably correct. The official OPLAN wouldn't suffice. They didn't have enough men or missiles in place to protect Seoul, much less defeat the North Koreans quickly and decisively with a conventional war. If he was really contemplating war, the only option was a nuclear option. But was he really prepared to launch a preemptive nuclear strike against the DPRK?

The implications were almost too horrible to contemplate. Would China be drawn in? They had been in 1950. They'd signed a defensive alliance with Pyongyang in 1961, requiring them to intervene militarily if North Korea was attacked. They seemed ready, even itching, for war with the U.S. now. Was that worth the enormous price the American people would have to pay?

☆　☆　☆

Caulfield quickly combed his hair.

He tucked in his shirt, stuck the MP's 9 mm pistol in his waistband, then donned his suit coat and buttoned it. After washing and drying his hands and face, he checked the MP's pulse again and picked up his leather binder of notes, briefing papers, and schedules. Convinced he was ready, he straightened his shoulders, took a deep breath, and headed out of the kitchen, racing down the hall, around the corner, and toward the conference room where Oaks was now reviewing nuclear war plans with the head of U.S. Pacific Command.

"I've got an urgent message for the president," he said breathlessly to Agent Coelho, standing post in the hall, and Coelho did what he always did. He nodded and opened the door. They had done this dance dozens of times since arriving at NORAD.

Caulfield knew he wasn't going to be searched. The United States, after all, was at war. Caulfield had top secret clearance. He'd worked for Oaks for more than a year. He'd been thoroughly vetted by the Secret Service. No one suspected him. No one turned to look at him as he entered. Why would they? Everyone in the room knew Caulfield was practically a fixture at the president's side. He'd been in and out all night, and they were consumed with the urgent business at hand.

As Caulfield moved behind the president, presumably to whisper something in his ear, he could see the plans on the table. He could see maps of the peninsula and various bombing scenarios on the flat-screen monitors on the wall. He knew what they were doing. He knew why. And he knew they had to be stopped.

As he closed in behind the president, he unbuttoned his jacket and carefully drew the 9 mm. Quickly now, he drove the pistol into the president's temple with his right hand while putting his left arm around the man's throat.

Stunned, the president began to gag. Everyone turned. Judge Summers, in the room to review the legality of the war plans being contemplated, gasped in horror. General Briggs rose from his seat and reached for the president, but Caulfield shouted him down.

"Nobody move," he yelled. *"Nobody."*

Briggs stopped in his tracks as Agent Coelho burst into the room, gun drawn.

Caulfield took the pistol off the president's temple and fired two rounds at Coelho, hitting him once in the chest and once in the face. Everyone screamed. Coelho dropped to the ground, a pool of blood growing by the second around his head, the acrid stench of gunpowder hanging in the air.

In the confusion, Caufield moved back a few steps, pulling the president in his swivel chair toward the corner of the conference room. Caulfield's back was now covered. He had a clear shot at the door. No one could get in or out of the room without him seeing them. Most importantly, no one could get behind him to take him out.

"Bobby, why?" the president asked, his entire body shaking. "What are you doing?"

"Shut up, Mr. President," Caulfield screamed, pressing the pistol against his temple again. *"Everyone just shut up."*

The room quickly died down but it did not become quiet. Alarms were ringing throughout the complex. Caulfield could hear yelling and boots. Through the clear bulletproof windows of the conference room he saw agents and heavily armed Marines filling the hallway and staring in horror at the slain agent and the gunman holding the president hostage. But for now, he had the upper hand, and he was determined to use it.

"No one is going to war—not against North Korea," Caulfield yelled. *"You want to take someone out? You take out the Chinese. But not Pyongyang. Not the DPRK."*

He could see the fear in everyone's eyes, fear and confusion. No one had any idea what he was talking about or why. But it didn't matter, he decided. They didn't need to know his reasons. Only his demands.

"Bobby, please, everything's going to be okay," said a voice from the back of the room. "Just take it easy, Bobby, and let's talk."

Startled, Caulfield turned and scanned the room. *"Who said that?"* he demanded. *"Who was that?"*

"It was me, Bobby," Judge Summers said softly, and she began standing to her feet. But she didn't get far.

Caulfield squeezed off two rounds. Summers screamed. Both rounds missed her but the plasma screen behind her exploded on impact. Then Briggs made his move. He leaped from his seat a few feet from Caulfield and the president and lunged at the young man. Two more explosions echoed through the NORAD complex and Briggs crashed to the floor, the back of his head gone.

57

★ ★
★

An aide stood by to help Al-Hassani out of the water.

Unless he was seriously ill, the seventy-six-year-old leader never missed his fifty laps a day in the Olympic-size pool just behind the former Saddam palace that had become his home, and today was no exception. Nuclear war. The deaths of millions. An imminent attack on Kurdish rebels. It made no difference. The man had his priorities. He had his routine. And he would not be deterred.

Finally satisfied with his workout, Al-Hassani agreed to take the call. He grabbed one of the metal railings, stepped out of the heated water, and let the aide wrap him in a bathrobe and help him don his slippers. Then he took the satellite phone and retired to a chaise longue on the veranda, peering out over the teeming city of Babylon, his pride and joy, that not so long ago had seemed a godforsaken wasteland.

"Premier Zhao," Al-Hassani said, lighting up his pipe and shooing away his viziers, "to what do I owe the honor?"

"Mustafa, you must call off your operation in Kurdistan," the Chinese premier insisted, the urgency thick in his voice. "It could ruin everything."

"Come, come, Mr. Prime Minister," Al-Hassani demurred. "These are rebels. They are thugs. They are dogs and must be put down. Must I remind you of Tiananmen Square?"

"That was a disaster for us, and you know it," Zhao said.

"Nevertheless, your party is still in power, are you not?" Al-Hassani noted.

"This is different."

"How?"

"The Cold War was ending; tensions were subsiding; peace was breaking out everywhere," Zhao said. "This is no longer the case."

"Why? Because the Americans have a thousand nuclear warheads pointed at your head?" Al-Hassani tut-tutted.

"Were they pointed at yours, perhaps you wouldn't be so cavalier," Zhao countered, his voice measured but his anger clearly rising. "Look, Mustafa, things are getting very dangerous. There is no room for error. The slightest miscalculation at this point could be catastrophic. You must pull back, at least for another day."

"Salvador got to you, didn't he?"

"Salvador has nothing to do with this."

"But you spoke to him."

"Of course I spoke to him," Zhao said. "But that's not the point."

"Of course it's the point," Al-Hassani said, now springing to his feet, his face flushed with anger. "You two are conspiring against me. I just had the man in my home. And now he is willing to turn his back on me without a second thought?"

"Mustafa, please, no one is conspiring against you," Zhao insisted.

"Oh, really? Then why is he making you call me? Why doesn't he have the courtesy to call me himself?"

"He's on the phone with Doron," Zhao said. "He's trying to broker the deal you asked him to make."

"I never asked him to make it," Al-Hassani shot back, pacing the veranda now and discarding his pipe. "He's cut a deal with you, hasn't he?"

"What? What are you talking about, Mustafa?"

"Don't lie to me, Zhao. He cut a deal with you, didn't he? He's trying to turn you against me."

"That's ridiculous, Mustafa. Please, my friend, take a deep breath and listen to what you're saying."

"You offered to send a quarter million troops to my backyard, didn't you?" Al-Hassani charged.

"Peacekeepers," Zhao said, "not combat troops."

"What's the difference?" Al-Hassani asked.

"Intent."

Al-Hassani sniffed in disgust. "They'll be armed, won't they?"

"Of course."

"They'll be combat capable, won't they?"

"They're professional soldiers," Zhao conceded. "Who else would I send, children?"

"Then how will I know they're not a threat?"

"Because you have my word that they won't be."

"Your word?"

"Yes," Zhao said. "And besides, Mustafa, they'll be based in Kuwait, in the Emirates, not anywhere near Babylon or Old Baghdad."

"That's less than a day away by tank and armored car," Al-Hassani said.

"So?"

"So when I least expect it—when my back is turned—how do I know a quarter of a million heavily armed, combat-ready Chinese infantrymen won't march up the Euphrates River valley right into Babylon?"

"Why in the world would I do that?" Zhao asked, his patience evidently wearing thin.

"Oil? Greed? Lust for power? Let me count the ways," Al-Hassani said.

"No one is conspiring to take you out," Zhao said curtly. "Unless you keep talking like this."

"Is that a threat?"

"No."

"Did Salvador tell you to say that?"

"Of course not. Look, Mustafa. I don't have time for your little conspiracy theories. I have enough troubles of my own. I've asked Salvador to come back to Beijing in the hopes that his presence will keep the Americans from launching against us. Perhaps it will buy us some time to turn President Oaks's attention elsewhere. We didn't attack the Americans. Those weren't our bombs."

"Whose were they?" Al-Hassani demanded to know.

"I have no idea."

"I don't believe you."

"Believe what you want."

"I hear you think the North Koreans did it," Al-Hassani said, stirring the pot.

"I told you, I have no idea," Zhao said. "But one thing I know for certain: The Americans are on edge. They're angry. They're ready for revenge. They want justice. They're not thinking clearly, not yet. And if you keep provoking them with this whole Kurdish thing, who knows what could happen? Who knows whether they'll listen to reason? They could start a war, Mustafa, a war that could decimate my country."

58

★ ★
★

Caulfield's hands were trembling.

The conference room was completely silent. No one spoke. No one dared blink, much less move. All activity in the hallway outside the door had ceased. Caulfield could see the phalanx of agents and Marines, guns drawn, ready to storm in if he gave them an opening. But for now, two dead bodies had forced a standoff, and it was his move.

Beads of sweat were streaking down his face and neck, but he didn't dare loosen his grip on the president's neck. With his right hand, he pressed the 9 mm harder against the president's temple and crouched down behind him to lower his profile, in case a Secret Service sniper he might not see took aim.

His eyes were blurring. He winced as the throbbing pain in the back of his head intensified. His body craved a fix he wasn't going to get, and for the first time, thoughts of suicide gripped him. He told himself he didn't want to die. But he couldn't let there be a war. Not with North Korea. Not now. The thought of his older brother, Derek, stationed with the Eighth Army along the DMZ, being mowed down by the DPRK was more than he could bear. If there was something he could do to stop it, he had to, didn't he? Derek was all he had left.

The FBI said his mother and four younger brothers were nowhere to be found. They had very likely been vaporized in the attack on New York.

He hadn't seen his father—a violent, raging alcoholic—in more than a decade. The last he'd heard, the man worked nights fixing subway tracks under the streets of Manhattan. In all likelihood, James Robert Caulfield was dead too. Perhaps that was for the better, but it meant James Robert "Bobby" Caulfield Jr. was all alone in the world.

He looked around the room. No one looked directly back at him. Even here, he was alone, he told himself. He saw fear in the eyes of the men watching him from the videoconference screens. But he also saw a bloodlust for revenge—against him, against Pyongyang, against the Chinese, and against the unseen enemies lurking in the shadows, enemies that had just obliterated four American cities.

He didn't see sympathy. He didn't see compassion. He knew any one of the agents outside this room would kill him in a heartbeat if he showed a moment's weakness. Only in the eyes of Judge Summers did he see what appeared to be a flicker of recognition that there might be a shred of decency somewhere deep inside Bobby Caulfield.

Suddenly his attention turned to the flat-screen monitors and the minicameras built into them. It now dawned on him that everything he was doing was being seen and heard in the ops centers at Mount Weather, Site R, CINCPAC headquarters, Kadena Air Base in Okinawa, and the joint command war room a couple of stories underneath Seoul. The thought of his every action being watched by people he couldn't control repulsed him. He raised his weapon and fired four shots. Each of the four plasma TVs on the far wall exploded, startling everyone and cutting off the live feeds. He was alone again with hostages he could see, hear, and kill.

★ ★ ★

Jack McKittrick huddled with his men.

He'd been commander of a Secret Service Counter Assault Team for less than eighteen months, but he'd been on the president's protective detail for the previous three years. His older brother, Charlie, had been blinded in the line of duty six years earlier protecting President MacPherson in Denver. Now someone had finished the job. MacPherson was dead. His family was dead. Most of the members of his political party and administration were dead. And McKittrick wasn't having any more of it. It was time to make someone pay, and Bobby Caulfield had just volunteered.

"We don't have much time, gentlemen," he began, tucked away in an office down the hall from the conference room so they could talk and plan in privacy. "Caulfield's already killed Agent Coelho and General Briggs. Does anyone have any doubt he'd be willing to kill the president?"

McKittrick, twenty-eight, looked into the eyes of all the men on his team. Only one glanced away. "Agent Thompson?"

"I'm not saying it isn't possible, sir," replied Doug Thompson, the youngest man on the team at the tender age of twenty-five.

"But?"

"But he's worked for the president—well, really for Oaks as vice president—for more than a year. He's got a stellar reputation, a spotless record—"

McKittrick cut him off. "Doug, you really want to tell Agent Coelho's widow and his three fatherless children that the man who killed him has a stellar reputation?"

"I'm just saying I don't think he'd kill the president," Thompson said defensively.

"Anyone else agree with that assessment?" McKittrick asked.

No one did.

"I didn't think so."

They quickly reviewed a floor plan of the conference room, the schematics of the electrical work and the HVAC ducts, and improvised their plan in less than five minutes.

"Let's just hope this works, gentlemen," McKittrick said, almost to himself, as he adjourned their meeting. "The last thing this country needs is another dead president."

★   ★   ★

"Mr. Vice President, I think we should move you."

Lee James stopped pacing the floor of the Mount Weather ops center and turned to Agent Bob Santini, head of his protective detail. "Where?" he asked.

"Off the floor," Santini said quietly.

"But to where?" James pressed.

"Sir, given the situation at Crystal Palace, I'd just feel safer if we had you in a more protected environment. I'm thinking of General Stephens's office upstairs."

"Agent Santini, we're in one of the most secure facilities on the planet."

"So is the president," the agent replied. "Please, sir. Until we figure out exactly what's going on."

James looked around him at the hubbub of activity. Two military aides nearby feverishly worked the phones, trying to track down the whereabouts of Jon Bennett. Some were developing contingency plans for China, others for North Korea, and, of course, new information was constantly pouring in from field teams assessing the damage in New York, D.C., Seattle, and L.A.

"Fine, but I'm not happy about this, Agent," James said, then turned around to find Ginny Harris, his press secretary, standing there with two cell phones in her hands.

"Sir, do you have a moment?" she asked.

"I really don't, Ginny," he said as Santini and the rest of the detail began moving him toward the stairs.

"Sir," Harris continued, "I really think you need to—"

"Not right now, Ginny," James said, cutting her off. "Call me in ten minutes."

He began heading to the second floor but Harris wouldn't take no for an answer.

"Mr. Vice President, with all due respect, CNN has the story."

James stopped in his tracks and turned back. *"What?"*

"Someone's got a source inside NORAD. They know what's happening."

James looked at the cell phones.

"They're on mute, sir," Harris said, seeing his concern.

"They'd better be."

"They are," she assured him.

"Mr. Vice President," Agent Santini said, looking anxious. "Please, sir. We need to keep moving."

"Fine. Walk with me," James told Harris and they picked up the pace. "What does CNN have?"

"They know there's a gunman," Harris said. "They know two people are dead. There are rumors the president has been shot and wounded."

James was stunned. "Is that true?" he asked, turning a corner and stepping inside General Mike Stephens's office with Agent Santini and six other agents at his side.

"I don't know, sir," Harris conceded.

The vice president turned to Santini. "Is that true—has the president been hit?"

"No, sir," Santini said. "I haven't heard anything like that."

"Check it out," James ordered. "And tell the guys at NORAD to get me that video feed again. I want to know exactly what's happening in that room."

"Yes, sir," Santini said. "I'm on it."

Suddenly a military aide rushed to the door, before being stopped by agents. "The president's still alive, sir."

"You're sure?" James asked.

"Absolutely, sir. I've got the head of the Marine security division on the line."

"What's the status inside that room?"

"Caulfield still has the president. But a Counter Assault Team is preparing to move in."

James felt his whole body tense. He'd known Caulfield practically from the day the boy had started working for Oaks. He'd liked him. He'd seen a bright future for him. How was this possible?

"Do they have a clear shot?" he asked, not entirely sure what he wanted the answer to be. *There had to be a way out of this,* he told himself. *There had to be.*

"Not yet, sir," the aide said. "But they expect to have one in the next few moments."

"And then?" he asked, reluctantly.

"They're authorized to use any force necessary, sir."

And James had no doubt they would use it, and soon.

59

★ ★
★

Agent McKittrick carefully moved his men into position.

One set up a small video camera in the hallway, without Caulfield noticing, giving them—and the vice president—a live feed. Another of his agents was now working his way through the heating and air-conditioning ducts. When McKittrick gave the word, he'd release semi-toxic gas that would knock out everyone in the conference room in a matter of seconds.

★　　★　　★

"Does anybody have an idea why Bobby's doing this?"

"Nothing certain, sir," the vice president's senior military aide replied. "But Agent McKittrick is concerned he could be a sleeper agent."

"Bobby Caulfield?" James asked. "That's not possible."

"Maybe yes, maybe no," the aide said. "But it would certainly explain why he's moving now, just as the president is considering war plans against Pyongyang."

"No," the vice president said. "I don't buy it. There's something else going on here."

"I'm only telling you what they're telling me, sir."

"Thanks, that'll be enough for now." The vice president suddenly felt overwhelmed with a sense of sadness and exhaustion. "Call with updates as you get them."

"Yes, sir. I will, sir."

The aide returned to the ops center floor. James sat down in the general's leather swivel chair behind a large oak desk and ordered the agents to shut the door. Santini stayed at his side. Another agent stayed in the room, a few steps from Harris, who took a seat in a chair beside the desk. No longer would he be left alone, even with a longtime trusted aide. The rest of the agents took up positions in the hallway.

"No comment," James said at last.

"Pardon me, sir?" Harris asked.

"Tell CNN no comment."

"You sure, sir?" Harris asked. "We could call it an exercise of some sort."

"Are you kidding, Ginny?" James asked, shaking his head. "The last thing we're going to do is lie to the American people. Especially right now. But we don't need to give them the full truth. Not yet. Let's get this thing resolved, and we'll go from there."

"Yes, sir," Harris said. "Can I get you something, sir? You don't look so good."

"No, I'm fine," James said, not exactly lying but not telling the complete truth either. He took off his glasses and rubbed his eyes. He hadn't slept in more than twenty-four hours. He'd barely eaten. He couldn't remember how many cups of coffee he had consumed. He could see no light at the end of the tunnel.

"To misunderstand the nature and threat of evil is to risk being blindsided by it," the vice president had often heard James MacPherson say. And, "Evil, unchecked, is the prelude to genocide."

As Harris got back on the phone with some producer in Atlanta, James thought about MacPherson's comments. He had given most of the best years of his life trying to protect his country, but what did he have to show for it? He'd certainly thought he understood the nature and threat of evil. He thought he'd been prepared for the worst. But now it seemed he was mistaken. Apparently he hadn't had a clue. And it wasn't over yet.

☆　☆　☆

Caulfield was ranting.

At the top of his lungs, he was decrying the immorality of starting a war with North Korea. Didn't the president know Pyongyang had nuclear weapons? Didn't he know they had chemical and biological weapons?

"The CIA says a war with North Korea could cause a million casualties," Caulfield screamed. *"A million souls. A million people with parents, and brothers, and sisters, and cousins, and friends. And for what? What do we gain? The right to say we won? Who cares? Who cares if there is so much death, so much suffering, so much destruction?"*

Two agents took up positions in the hallway, prepared to throw flash grenades on cue. Six more agents were behind them—three at each end of the hallway, ready to storm the room and take their target out when so ordered.

"Haven't enough people died?" Caulfield continued, his ranting turning to tears, and his tears turning to sobs. *"Haven't enough people suffered? How many more will it take, Mr. President? How many more?"*

McKittrick stared at the monitor and pressed his headphones more tightly to his ears, trying to get every nuance from the audio feed. "He's losing it," he told his team. "All agents stand by."

Tears were streaming down Caulfield's face, but his eyes were still open. Indeed, he was staring at Judge Summers, who was too close to the conference room door for McKittrick's purposes. He kept waiting. A few more seconds. Just a few more. The moment Caulfield looked away, or down, or closed his eyes, even for an instant, McKittrick would call for the attack. He'd pump in the gas, cut the power, send in his men, and hope to God the president made it through in one piece.

But Caulfield kept staring at the judge. His tears were slowing. His breathing was becoming more measured. He wasn't shouting now. He was just mumbling something. But what? McKittrick turned up the volume on the monitor and pressed the headphones still tighter. What in the world was Caulfield saying? Whatever it was, he was saying it over and over again.

McKittrick picked up the remote control on the table in front of him. He started to zoom in to Caulfield's mouth, trying to read his lips. Then all of a sudden he got it. Caulfield was mumbling, "It's over. It's over. It's over. . . ."

NO! McKittrick thought.

He grabbed his wrist-mounted radio. *"Code Red, go now—go, go, go."*

But it was too late.

Caulfield stepped back, closed his eyes, and shot the president in the head. Then he opened his mouth, shoved the 9 mm inside, and pulled the trigger.

60

★ ★
★

Vice President James stared at the TV in shock.

All color instantly drained from his face. His body began shaking. He couldn't believe what he had just seen. His brain refused to process the images, much less the implications. He couldn't hear the screams, the gasps, the commotion moving across the command center floor one flight below. He never heard Ginny Harris scream or saw Agent Santini physically lurch backward—as if someone had punched him in the stomach—at the sight of the president being shot through the right temple.

James just stared at the flickering screen. His eyes began to glaze. The colors around him began to fade. The room began to spin. And then his stomach convulsed and there was a burning sensation at the back of his throat. Before he realized what was happening, the vice president of the United States was retching his guts out. Given that he had barely eaten anything in nearly twenty-four hours, there wasn't much coming up. But that didn't slow down the intense, violent convulsions ripping through his system.

He didn't hear Santini radio for backup or notice agents and medics rushing into the office. He would later notice General Stephens there too, pulled out of a war planning meeting with a dozen other generals in the situation room three floors down. But for the moment, all he knew was that the vomiting wouldn't stop, and he suddenly began to fear for his life.

★ ★ ★

The army Black Hawk helicopter came in low and fast.

It circled the landing pad twice until the pilots received clearance, then touched down amid a platoon of heavily armed Marines.

A colonel rushed out and opened the chopper's side door. *"Chuck Murray?"* he shouted above the roar of the rotors.

"Yes, sir," the former White House press secretary replied.

"Follow me."

Murray grabbed his garment bag, briefcase, and laptop and climbed out of the helicopter, moving quickly to keep up with the colonel and ducking instinctively to keep from having his head sliced off by the rotors, though there was no real threat of that. The colonel gave him a temporary ID badge and coded in at a side door into the NORAD complex. They worked their way through an MP checkpoint, complete with X-rays, metal detectors, and bomb-sniffing dogs, and proceeded down a hallway toward the war room. Exhausted, Murray asked if there was a place he could shower and change before meeting General Briggs and the president.

The colonel stopped in his tracks. "General Briggs?" he asked in disbelief.

"Yes, sir," Murray replied. "I was told to check in with the general as soon as I arrived and then he'd take me to see the president. I know it's urgent, but I'm going to need fifteen minutes or so."

The colonel just stared at Murray.

"Something wrong, Colonel?" Murray asked.

"Actually, there is, sir."

"What?" Murray replied. "Because I can certainly shower and change later if . . ."

"No," the colonel interrupted. "It's not that."

"Then what?"

"You haven't been told?"

"Told what?"

"They're dead, sir."

"Dead? Who's dead?"

"General Briggs . . . and the president."

☆ ☆ ☆

Lee James woke up in General Stephens's private quarters.

He didn't know how long he'd been asleep. He just knew how weak he felt, and how sad and utterly alone. He couldn't shake the images of Bill Oaks being shot to death in that conference room. Or of Bobby Caulfield putting a bullet through his own head. He had experienced more death in the last few days than he would ever have imagined. His tours in Vietnam with the Marines seemed tame by comparison.

James felt untethered, adrift. His love of politics was gone. The thrill of public service had evaporated overnight. He had never planned to serve as the nation's commander in chief. Certainly not in time of war. Certainly not in a nation under an attack of this magnitude. The weight of the responsibility was almost unbearable. How had other presidents handled such moments? How had Truman before Nagasaki and Hiroshima? How had MacPherson before the War of Gog and Magog? Were they this depressed? How could they go forward, day after day?

What was once a few small doubts was now a raging cauldron of confusion and despair. He loathed the thought of betraying his fears to anyone, but they were rising by the second. He feared not only for his own life but for what was coming. What kind of world had he just inherited? The darkness was so dark, so thick, he could barely see beyond the next few minutes, much less the next few days, or weeks. Evil had regathered while the world had slept. Now it was on the move, and James worried it would overtake them all. He didn't simply feel scared. He felt naked and desperately alone in the cosmos.

Where was he supposed to turn? It wasn't military or political advice he craved. What, then? He had never been a religious man. Not like MacPherson. Certainly not like Jon and Erin Bennett. It seemed hypocritical to seek God now. Yet something in him was grasping for spiritual answers. It was a craving so deep it ached, and yet he feared it was, as if by definition, insatiable.

Restless, he got up, steadied himself, and began looking around the general's quarters. He glanced at the collection of family photos on the man's nightstand and thought of his own wife and daughters, holed up at STRATCOM near Omaha, surrounded by MPs, unable to get to him, scared out of their minds. He wanted to call them. He wanted to talk to his wife about what they were planning. But he couldn't. Not now. She didn't have the clearance.

He moved over to the bookshelf and scanned the many tomes in the general's impressive collection. One volume caught his eye. He reached up and pulled out a dog-eared copy of a book by two *Time* magazine correspondents: *The Preacher and the Presidents: Billy Graham in the White House*. He sat down, turned on the desk lamp, put on his reading glasses, and flipped through the well-marked pages. Many sections were underlined and highlighted. There were questions and comments scribbled in the margins. Then he flipped to the back and found several previously blank pages that had been filled with the general's handwritten bullet points and notes.

* ★ *BG preached to 210 million people face-to-face/85 countries/417 crusades/ friends with 11 presidents/"They asked about how the world would end, which was not an abstract conversation." (p. vii, xi)*
* ★ *Churchill: "Do you have any real hope?" (p. 48)*
* ★ *Eisenhower: "How can a person be sure when he dies he's going to heaven?" (p. 52)*
* ★ *JFK: "Do you believe in the Second Coming of Jesus Christ?" (p. 109)*
* ★ *LBJ: "I'm not really sure in my heart that I'm going to heaven." (p. 123)*
* ★ *Graham on Nixon: "I almost felt as if a demon had come into the White House." (p. 219)*
* ★ *Reagan: "I have decided that whatever time I may have is left for Him." (p. 268)*
* ★ *Bush 43 @ Kennebunkport: "How do you become a real Christian?" (p. 329)*

James studied the list. He had all the same questions, and none of the answers. He wished there were time to read, time to think, time to search for answers. But there wasn't, and now someone was knocking on the door.

"Who is it?" he asked.

"General Stephens."

"Come in."

Stephens entered, saluted, and saw the book in the president's hands. "That was a good one," he said softly. "One of my favorites."

James said nothing, just looked down at the questions.

"Kinda wish we could give the ole reverend a call right now, don't you?" the general said with a gentle, easy manner that surprised James.

"Kinda, yeah," he replied.

"Ever meet him?" Stephens asked.

"Graham?"

"Yes, sir."

"No, never did. You?"

"No," Stephens answered, "and I regret that. But I watched him on television a lot, especially when I was based in Germany. And I must tell you, Mr. President, he changed my life."

"How so?" James asked.

"I'd been raised in a Christian home, sir," the general said. "Went to church every Sunday. Prayed before supper. You know, the whole nine yards."

"And?"

"And I got to a low point, sir. I had lost some of my men in Kosovo. My wife had left me. My kids hated me. Everything was going wrong. And the thing was, I thought I was a Christian. And I began to get angry with God. I'd yell at him at night, alone in my room. This went on for months. I was slipping farther and farther into depression. Finally one night, after watching a Billy Graham crusade on television, I yelled at God and said: 'I don't get you. The Bible promises love, joy, peace, happiness. Well, I don't have any of it. So either you're a liar, or I just don't get it.'"

"So what happened?" James asked, genuinely curious.

"Well, that's the thing, sir," Stephens said, reliving the moment as if it had just happened. "It had never happened before. And it's never happened since."

"What?"

"I don't think it was an audible voice, but it may as well have been. I knew it was the Lord, and He asked me, 'Michael, do you ever read the Bible for yourself?' Now, sir, I had read the Bible from time to time, in church, you know. But the real answer was no, I rarely read it for myself. So I said, 'No.' And then He asked me, 'Do you ever really talk to me in prayer?' Again, I said grace before meals, that kind of thing. But the truth was I'd never really understood prayer, much less done it. So I said, 'No, Lord, I don't.' And He said, 'Michael, why should you expect me to bless you when you don't even really know me?' After that, the transmission seemed to end."

61

★ ★
★

James would have expected himself to be skeptical.

Even cynical. But he wasn't. He was trying to process everything the general was saying. He had never heard someone share his story so clearly or so personally, and it didn't anger him as he would have thought it would.

"Go on," he said after a long pause.

"Well, Mr. President, at that moment, I got down on my knees," Stephens continued. "On the one hand, I was so ashamed of myself. I'd been so close to the truth but had never really gotten it. And yet at the same time, I was so grateful that the Lord had spoken to me. He'd told me what I was doing wrong. He was calling me to follow Him. To know Him. To fall in love with Him and stop trying to live my life on my own terms, which obviously wasn't going so well. So I prayed a simple prayer. I accepted Jesus Christ into my heart as my personal Savior and Lord. And I've never been the same since."

"How so?" the president asked.

"Well, sir, I got an immediate assurance that I was going to be in heaven forever when I died, which gave me a new confidence to live life without fear. And I got a hope for the future that I'd never really had before in my entire life. I can't say my life has been perfect since, sir. Lord knows, I haven't been perfect. But I know He's with me. I know He's leading me. I know He loves me, and that's made all the difference."

The room was quiet, save for the ticking of a small clock on the general's desk. No phones were ringing. No aides were bursting in. No Secret Service agents were looking over their shoulders, and James sensed that this, in its own way, was a miracle. God was calling him. Perhaps He always had been, and James had always resisted. But now he knew he was out of excuses.

"Mr. President," the general asked after a pause, "have you ever accepted Christ as your Savior?"

At any other time, under any other circumstances, James knew he would have been offended by someone asking him that question. But not now. He felt strangely warmed inside, as if God Himself had sent this man at this time to tell him what he needed to do.

"No, General, I never really have," James said after a moment of reflection.

"Would you like to, sir?"

"Honestly, General, I'm not entirely sure what that means."

"Would you like me to walk you through it, sir, briefly?" Stephens asked.

James nodded, a bit self-consciously.

The general reached over and picked up the small leather Bible on his nightstand, then, with the president's permission, took a seat on the bed.

"Mr. President, the Bible says God loves us and has a wonderful plan and purpose for our lives. In John 3:16, Jesus said, 'For God so loved the world that He gave His only begotten Son, that whoever believes in Him shall not perish, but have eternal life.' In John 10:10, Jesus said, 'I came that they may have life, and have it abundantly,' that it might be full and meaningful."

The general flipped forward a few pages. "But the Bible also teaches that man is sinful and separated from God, and that's why we don't know Him and experience Him like we want to. Romans 3:23 tells us, 'All have sinned and fall short of the glory of God.' Romans 6:23 says, 'The wages of sin is death.' That's the bad news. The good news is that through faith in Jesus Christ, we can have our sins forgiven. We can know we're going to heaven. We can have a personal relationship with God Himself, all because Jesus died on the cross and rose again from the dead to pay the penalty for your sins and mine."

James thought carefully about the verses he was hearing as the general found another set of passages and began reading again.

"The Bible says, 'God demonstrates His own love toward us, in that while we were yet sinners, Christ died for us.' It also says, 'Christ died for our sins. . . . He was buried. . . . He was raised on the third day according to the Scriptures. . . . He appeared to Peter, then to the twelve. After that He appeared to more than five hundred.' Jesus said, 'I am the way, and the truth, and the life; no one comes to the Father but through Me.'

"But here's the key, Mr. President. The Bible teaches us that it's not enough just to know that God loves us, or that we're sinners, or that Jesus came to pay the penalty for our sins. It's good, but it's not enough. The fact is, each of us must individually receive Jesus Christ as our personal Savior and Lord. Then, and only then, will we be born again into His family, into His Kingdom. Only then can we truly know and experience God's love and His plan for our lives.

"John 1:12 says, 'As many as received Him, to them He gave the right to become children of God, even to those who believe in His name.' And the apostle Paul told us in Ephesians, 'By grace you have been saved through faith; and that not of yourselves, it is the gift of God; not as a result of works, so that no one may boast.'"

Stephens turned the pages of his marked-up Bible one last time, and James noticed he landed in the third chapter of the book of Revelation. He expected a lesson on the End Times. He was surprised when, instead, the general read words of Jesus that James had never heard before. "'Behold, I stand at the door and knock; if anyone hears My voice and opens the door, I will come in to him.'"

The general looked him in the eye. "Mr. President, do you believe Jesus is the only way to God the Father?"

James thought about it and realized that for the first time in his life, he really did. He nodded and said, "I do."

"Do you believe that Jesus died on the cross to pay the complete penalty for your sins?"

"Yes, I do."

"Do you believe that He rose from the dead on the third day, just as was prophesied in the Scriptures?"

James nodded again and said yes.

"And are you sure you're ready to confess to Him that you're a sinner, that you need His forgiveness, and that with His help, you're ready to repent of your sins and follow Him, no matter what it may cost?"

Twenty-four hours earlier, James knew, that wouldn't have been true. Six hours ago, as well. But now it was. His heart was racing. He wanted to give his heart to Christ like nothing else he had ever done in his life.

"I think I am ready," he said.

"Wonderful," the general said.

At the general's encouragement, the two men got down on their knees and bowed their heads. Then Stephens told the president he was going to lead him through the same prayer he had prayed more than a decade earlier.

"Lord Jesus, I need you. Thank you for dying on the cross for my sins. Thank you for rising from the dead. I believe you are the Way, the Truth, and the Life. I believe you are the only way to heaven, the only way to the Father. And right now, as an act of the will, by faith, I open the door of my life and receive you as my Savior and Lord. Thank you for forgiving my sins. Thank you for giving me eternal life. Have mercy on me, Lord. Show me your will. Teach me your Word. Guide me by your Holy Spirit. Take the throne of my life, Lord Jesus, and make me the kind of person you want me to be. In your holy and precious Name I pray, amen."

62

★ ★
★

A day passed, but none of the tension did.

Lee James was struggling to adjust to his new role as commander in chief. Burt Trainor had just been sworn in as vice president of the United States, though James had asked him to continue serving as secretary of defense for continuity. Change was coming fast and furious, but time was running out. They had to make decisions.

General Andrew T. Garrett paced the war room. Deep under Seoul in a reinforced steel and concrete bunker, he was safer than his men. Safer than anyone in South Korea. But unlike any of them, he knew what was coming, and that knowledge was eating a hole through his stomach. He was on medication. It wasn't working. The pain was severe, and it was growing. But he had no choice. Hostilities were going to break out any minute. Either the North was going to strike first or the U.S. was going to unleash the nuclear option and end this thing once and for all. The time to decide was at hand.

He scanned the array of clocks on the far wall, above the satellite monitors and maps of the DMZ. It was now 5:21 a.m. Thursday, September 3, in Seoul.

In Babylon, it was 12:21 a.m.

In London, it was 9:21 p.m. Wednesday, September 2.

In Boston, it was 4:21 p.m.

At Crystal Palace, deep inside Cheyenne Mountain near Colorado Springs, it was now 2:21 p.m. on Wednesday.

In Sacramento, it was 1:21 p.m.

Garrett could barely believe how much the world had changed in the last forty-eight hours, or how much it would change in the next forty-eight. Indeed, it had been less than thirty-six hours since President Oaks had been assassinated by his own body man. Caulfield was dead. Briggs was dead. A Secret Service agent whose name presently escaped Garrett was dead. Now the United States of America had a third president in as many days, and the country didn't even know it yet.

The general and a group of other top military commanders had watched the swearing-in ceremony on secure videoconference. But they had all been sworn to secrecy. At least for now. America was at war. There were national security considerations at stake. A public announcement would be made soon, they'd been told. But as USPACOM commander Admiral Arthurs had reminded them, "loose lips sink ships."

A staff sergeant waved down Garrett's attention. "General?"

"Yes, Sergeant."

"The president and vice president are on the line, sir. So is Admiral Arthurs. They're all ready, sir."

Garrett nodded, took his seat at the head of the enormous conference table, and signaled the rest of his generals to take their assigned seats. The videoconference system was suddenly down—a bad omen, he thought.

He unmuted the speakerphone and began the call. "Mr. President, this is General Garrett at Command Post Tango."

"Good morning, General," the president replied.

It was protocol, of course. There was nothing good about it.

"Do you have your team in place?" the president asked.

"Yes, sir, they're all here."

"Then let's make this quick."

"Yes, Mr. President," Garrett began. "First let me say on behalf of my entire team, U.S. and ROK, we were deeply shocked and saddened by what happened yesterday, and we want you to know that you have our full support."

"Thank you, General Garrett," James replied. "That means a great deal to me."

The ROK's top military commander, sitting beside Garrett, also spoke up. "Mr. President, this is General Soon Young Park. Can you hear me?"

"Yes, General Park. I can hear you well."

"I just wanted to agree with General Garrett. President Woo, my men, and my people are deeply grateful that you are standing with us at this very dark hour, and we want you to know two things, sir. First, we are ready to fight side by side with the American people to bring justice to your people and safety to my own. And second, I want you to know that President Woo and I are devout followers of Jesus Christ. He has known the Lord for many years. But I am from a Buddhist family. I became a follower of Jesus after the Day of Devastation. Anyway, I want you to know that we were on our knees this morning praying for you by name, sir, praying Psalm 32, verse 8, that the Lord would 'lead you and guide in the way that you should go,' and that He would 'counsel you with His eye upon you.'"

James was silent for a beat, clearly moved by the general's simple yet sincere expression of faith.

"Thank you, General Park. I'm touched, and I'll take all the prayers I can get," he finally replied. "Please tell the president how grateful I am, and when all this is over, perhaps both of you and your wives could come for a visit. There is much I would like to discuss with you."

"I will do that," General Park said. "It would be a great honor. You can count on us, sir."

"I'm sure I can, General, and I appreciate it very much."

Garrett thought the president sounded stronger than he had expected. General Stephens at Mount Weather had told him shortly after Oaks's assassination that James had been put on antidepressants and painkillers. But to his surprise, the president seemed to have a new sense of calm and confidence that Garrett found reassuring.

"Now, gentlemen," James said, "let's get to the business at hand. What does the latest intel show?"

"It's not good, Mr. President," General Garrett explained. "The North has two million reservists moving toward the DMZ and two million more being readied for deployment in bases around Pyongyang."

"Do you think they've made the decision to attack?" James asked.

"Strategically, yes, I do, sir," Garrett said. "Tactically, I'd say they are still another twelve to fifteen hours away."

"Which means if we're going to launch a preemptive strike, our window is closing," the president said.

"Rapidly," Garrett agreed.

There was a long pause.

"Are all your assets in place if I were to give a launch order?" the president finally asked.

"We could use another six or eight hours," Garrett conceded. "But yes, sir, we could go now if you gave the order."

"General Park?" James said.

"Yes, sir, Mr. President?"

"I assume you're aware that I have spoken to your president."

"Yes, sir; I just spoke to him myself."

"He is hoping for some kind of diplomatic solution," James said. "But he understands the situation I'm in, and the stakes."

"He does indeed, Mr. President."

"Is it your military assessment that we should strike first?"

"That is not for me to say, Mr. President," General Park demurred. "I am a strong believer in the civilian chain of command."

"I appreciate that," James said. "But do you see a way to prevent massive casualties in Seoul and the South as a whole if we don't strike first with the plan that you and General Garrett have drafted for me?"

"No, sir, I'm afraid I don't."

"Can we win?" the president asked bluntly.

"We can decimate the North with this strategy," the general said. "I'm not sure if that will be a victory. I hate to see it come to this, personally. But it will save my people. I do believe this."

President James paused while considering that, then turned his attention back to his on-site commander. "What am I missing, General Garrett? What are the downsides we're not talking about?"

It was a good question, Garrett thought. They had discussed the military and political implications for much of the past day. James seemed to be warming, however reluctantly, to the conclusion that he had no other choice but to hit the North hard, fast, and with such cataclysmic force that the regime and its forces could never recover.

"The economy, sir," he said at last.

"Go ahead."

"Well, sir, given South Korea's wrenching historical poverty and the devastating war of the 1950s, you really have to think of this country as an economic miracle," Garrett noted. "The ROK's GDP was negligible in 1953. By 2004, it had joined the trillion-dollar-plus club. Now it's the eleventh largest economy in the world and the third largest in Asia. Exports have grown to more than $325 billion annually. Thirteen percent goes straight to the U.S. What's more, this Asian tiger is still roaring. For the past few years, her economy has been growing at 5 percent a year or better, in real terms. The contrast with the North—a $40 billion economy, if that—is as stunning as it is sad."

"And all that's now in jeopardy," the president noted.

"I'm afraid it is, sir," Garrett agreed. "The electronics and steel industries, the chemical and plastics industries, and of course automobiles and consumer goods. All of it could be gone by tomorrow. If the North attacks, it's gone, even if we fight back and win. Our only chance to save the South is to strike the North hard, fast, and now. The implications for the global economy cannot be overstated."

"By hard, General Garrett, you don't see an alternative to going nuclear?"

"No, sir, I don't," Garrett replied. "I wish there were another way, but there isn't. Believe me, Mr. President. I run the war games. I run the models. I eat, sleep, and breathe how to protect the South. I don't relish the idea of killing millions of North Koreans, sir. Not for one moment. But it's them or us. It's as simple as that. Don't forget, sir, we face an enemy who once said he would 'destroy the world' or 'take the world with me' rather than accept defeat at the hands of the Americans and the ROK."

"Do you believe him?"

"I do, sir."

"What about the '61 treaty with the Chinese?" James asked. "What if Beijing comes to the North's defense after we attack?"

"I don't think the Chinese will lift a finger, Mr. President," Garrett said.

"That's what the CIA and MacArthur told Truman in 1950," the president countered. "They were wrong."

"Yes, Mr. President, they were," Garrett conceded. "But Truman didn't go nuclear against Pyongyang. If he had, the Chinese never would have entered the war."

The president noted for the record that he had not made a final decision. But he ordered the U.S. military to do everything necessary to launch a full-scale nuclear attack against North Korea in the next six to eight hours. He specifically ruled out the use of long-range ballistic missiles, for fear that China could misinterpret the launch of ICBMs as an attack on them. Instead, the president ordered that they prepare B-52s and cruise missiles. But both he and Trainor agreed that if they went forward with this plan, they would have to use absolutely overwhelming force and do so with as much speed and surprise as possible to minimize casualties in Seoul and the rest of South Korea.

The president told them to finalize their operations, be ready for his call, and make absolutely sure none of their preparations leaked.

"Everything depends on the element of surprise," he told them. "Everything."

63

★ ★
★

Bennett awoke in a room with no windows.

There was one door. No furniture but a chair to which he was chained. Gray cinder block walls. A filthy white tile floor with a hole at one end that he assumed must be the toilet, though he wouldn't have been able to reach it if he had needed to. And that was it. No color. Nothing to read. Nothing to watch. And it was brutally hot. Humid, too. The cell was bathed in harsh fluorescent light, and the only sound he heard was the electric hum of the lamps on the ceiling.

He was wearing a green prison jumpsuit. His hair was damp, matted with perspiration. Beads of sweat trickled down his back and neck. He was handcuffed with his arms behind his back, but he could lean a little to the left and a little to the right to wipe the sweat of his eyes and face on the shoulders of the jumpsuit. His feet were shackled to each other and to the large wooden chair, which seemed to be bolted to the floor.

Surveying his own physical condition, he found that his stomach and sides ached, and he suddenly had flashbacks of two men beating him while trying to get him off the plane. His head was pounding. His eyes felt a little swollen. He still felt groggy from whatever drugs they had used to sedate him. But as best he could tell, he had no broken bones and saw no blood on him, or on the floor around him.

Then, just as on the plane, the fog began to lift again. He remembered what had happened. He remembered what had been ripped away from him, and he began to convulse with sobs that forced their way to the surface.

☆   ☆   ☆

The press corps was in a frenzy.

America had been attacked, but no one knew by what enemy. The military was clearly preparing for another war, but no one knew with whom. Millions of Americans in four major cities lay dead or dying. Tens of millions more were on the move, fleeing the radioactive hot zones but unsure where to go or what to do next. President MacPherson was dead. President Oaks might be injured, they were hearing. He seemed to have been involved in some sort of violent incident inside the world's most secure military complex. But as of yet there was no central information center, no White House press operation, nor a White House to base it in.

Reporters, editors, and producers kept calling Ginny Harris, who, as the vice president's press secretary, was the highest known ranking media official in the government. But most of the colleagues she had served with in the Communications Department at the White House were dead. She was overwhelmed by the events of the past few days. And no one was giving her direction on what to tell a pack of media wolves as scared as they were hungry for the latest information.

Chuck Murray was finally given permission to speak to President James via telephone. He gave the new commander in chief an earful.

"This is getting dangerous," Murray warned. "The United States government has to have a voice. A message. Answers to people's questions. Otherwise we're allowing a vacuum. It's not that we look pathetically disorganized. It's that we look unable to function."

"Chuck, I get it," James said. "But I've got more than I can handle at the moment. Press relations isn't at the top of my to-do list. In case you hadn't noticed, we're about to launch a war."

"Mr. President, you can't launch a war right now," Murray countered.

"Why not?"

"Because no one knows you're the president."

"I've been legally sworn in," James insisted. "It's legal. It's all constitutional. You saw on the video feed, didn't you?"

"You're not hearing me," Murray said. "Of course you're the president. But no one knows it. You need to get out there, explain what happened."

"I can't. Not yet."

"Why not?"

"I don't want to panic people."

"Too late," Murray said. "They're panicked. And now there're rumors of a gunfight inside NORAD. People don't know if the president is alive or dead. They don't know who's running the country. And it's not just Americans who don't know—North Korea doesn't know; the Iraqis don't know; the Chinese don't know. There's blood in the water, Mr. President, and if the military guys aren't telling you, I will—we're running the risk of drawing another attack because people think the U.S. government really has been decapitated."

★   ★   ★

In time, Bennett's tears slowed.

His breathing calmed. And memories of Erin came drifting back, one by one. He could see her sitting on the steps of the medical clinic back in the camp, surrounded by eight or ten Lebanese and Syrian orphan girls, all sitting in a circle, reading them Bible stories and answering their questions.

He could see her with precious Fareeda, all of nine years old, alone in the world, but always at Erin's side—hanging on her every word, trailing Erin all over the camp, volunteering to do any errand, however tiny and insignificant. Erin had told Jon that in Arabic *Fareeda* meant "unique, matchless, precious pearl or gem," and that's certainly what this little one had been to Erin—a daughter almost, a name and a face and a heart into whom Erin could pour her boundless love and see it matter, see it register.

Fareeda loved to hear Erin tell her about "*Eesah*," Arabic for Jesus. "Tell it again," she would say when Erin would recount stories of Jesus healing the ten lepers or making the blind see and the lame walk. Had anyone told her that he and Erin had left the camp? Did she know what had happened? He hoped not. Everyone that little girl had ever known had died. Bennett could suddenly hear Erin teaching Fareeda to sing "Jesus

Loves Me" in Arabic and English, and that's when he lost it again, dissolving into a bitter wail that echoed through the halls.

Why? The question haunted him. It refused to let him go. *Why had God let it happen? Any of it? Was it really so much to ask that he and Erin be allowed to enjoy a few years together?*

And yet, as much as Bennett wanted to be angry, he knew deep down that he was grateful for every minute the Lord had let him spend with Erin. He hadn't earned her. He hadn't deserved her. She had been out of his league and he knew it. He'd known it from the moment he'd laid eyes on her.

He hadn't been able to figure it out at first. It was a mystery that had taken some time to unravel. It wasn't just that she was the smarter of the two, though that was certainly the case. And it wasn't just that she was braver than he was, though that was true too. It was that she was better than he was. Not to be self-deprecating, but she genuinely loved people more than he did. She loved Christ more passionately than he did. He was learning, no doubt about it. But he was following her lead, though she never made him feel awkward about it. She never held it over him. That wasn't her way, and it made him love her all the more.

Every Tuesday night, she'd bring him to visit a widow and her six kids whom she had met on the other side of the camp. Bennett had constantly pleaded with her to take the night off. She was exhausted and so was he. But she wouldn't listen. She didn't want to just make meals and feed them to thousands of nameless, faceless refugees, even if she was doing it in the name of Jesus in a U.N. camp without so much as a pastor or any other Christian leaders. She wanted to touch real lives. She wanted to help real people meet Jesus. "How else are they going to see Him," she would always say, "unless we take Jesus to them?"

So once a week, she would take this little family candies or toys or some kind of treat. She would bring her guitar and play songs for them. Eventually she helped the mother pray to receive Christ, and then she gave her an Arabic New Testament and bought them a little handheld, battery-operated radio so they could listen to Trans World Radio's Bible teaching in Arabic every night before they went to bed.

At first, Bennett recalled through his tears, it had really annoyed him. They were working twelve- and fourteen-hour days. They needed time to themselves. They were newlyweds, for crying out loud. But Erin was on a mission. She knew she couldn't save anyone. But she could love the ones God put in her path, she insisted. She could be the hands and feet and smile of Jesus for those who had never heard of Him or felt His gentle touch. She said God had once spoken to her during her study of John's Gospel, during their first week in the camp. "You do the loving, Erin," God had said to her, "and I'll do the converting." Bennett had never seen her so happy. She had heard from God. She knew what would make Him happy. And she never looked back.

The ache rose again. The tears began to come again. He had never imagined he could miss someone so much. And all he could ask was, *Why?*

64

★ ★
★

Ninety minutes later, the press conference began.

No members of the media were allowed into the top secret complex. Certainly not in a time of war. But Murray was right, the president had concluded. It was critical to begin communicating directly and consistently with the nation and the world. So at the president's directive, NORAD's acting commander, two-star general George Mutschler—son of the late General Ed Mutschler, who had served as chairman of the Joint Chiefs of Staff under President MacPherson during his first term—made his way to the NORAD briefing room with Chuck Murray at his side. Speaking via satellite to nearly a hundred reporters gathered at a hotel in Chicago, another hundred or so reporters gathered in Boston, and three dozen European editors and network news bureau chiefs based in Brussels, the general began by reading a short statement.

First, he announced that the president would be making a televised address to the nation at precisely 9 p.m. Eastern. He would be speaking from a secure, undisclosed location. There would be no interviews tonight, and no Q and A.

Second, he confirmed rumors of the events that had occurred thirty-six hours earlier inside the NORAD complex. He confirmed three deaths—those of General Briggs, Agent Coelho, and Bobby Caulfield. Then General Mutschler added, "Everyone in the senior leadership of the U.S. government has been shocked and saddened by the event, but the president is committed to leading the country through this crisis and to bringing the perpetrators of the attacks on America to justice."

Not once, however, did the general ever mention the president by name.

Third, he announced that Charles T. Murray had been named the new White House press secretary and counselor to the president. Ginny Harris would serve as the new White House director of communications. The White House itself would eventually be rebuilt, the general noted, but he had no specifics on when or where. Then he stepped aside to let Murray speak briefly and answer questions.

★   ★   ★

The president watched the briefing with General Stephens.

They were joined in the general's second-floor office by their senior staff, with Agent Santini and several other agents standing a few steps away and Ginny Harris still working the phones, lining up logistics for phase two of their media rollout.

The first question to Murray came from Andrea Morris of the Associated Press.

"Chuck, neither you nor General Mutschler explained the state of the president's health and well-being."

"The president will speak tonight at nine Eastern," Murray said.

"But is he okay? Was he injured?" Morris pressed.

"The president will address the nation at nine," Murray repeated. "He will explain what happened. He will then talk about the urgent crisis we face as a nation and how the federal government is going to respond both domestically and internationally. Laura."

Laura Fisher of NBC News was next.

"Is the president going to declare war?" she asked.

James glanced at Ginny Harris, who nodded her approval. Murray was doing well. The press was taking the bait and shifting its focus off the president's health, for now.

"We're clearly at war, Laura," Murray said.

"Is the president going to declare war against a specific country?" Fisher clarified.

"I'm not going to speculate," Murray said. "You'll just have to tune in. Marcus?"

Marcus Jackson, the *New York Times* bureau chief in Brussels, rose in some nondescript hotel conference room and spoke directly into the camera. "Chuck, is it true that two U.S. aircraft carrier battle groups are now steaming toward the coast of Venezuela?"

The question immediately sent a buzz through the entire European press corps.

"Marcus, you know I can't comment on specific U.S. naval activity," Murray said. "But I can tell you that all U.S. military forces are on a heightened state of readiness. I would think that would go without saying."

"Are you denying two battle groups are heading to Venezuela?" Jackson pressed.

"I'm not commenting one way or the other, Marcus."

"What about reports that U.S. special forces are presently using Guyana and Panama as staging areas?" Jackson asked. "Can you comment on that?"

Murray looked uncomfortable. It wasn't that he was getting caught by a question for which he was unprepared. Rather, it seemed that he was squirming with a question he didn't want to even acknowledge, much less answer.

"You're asking me to talk about possible combat operations, and I'm not going there, Marcus."

The buzz intensified.

"One more follow-up, if I may?" Jackson asked.

"Go ahead, Marcus," Murray said. "And while we're at it, please let me extend my condolences and those of this administration on the loss of the *New York Times* staff in Manhattan, D.C., L.A., and Seattle. That goes for all the media outlets who lost colleagues. Our thoughts and prayers are with you guys tonight."

"Thank you," Jackson said, clearly both surprised and even somewhat moved by Murray's comments. "One more question."

"Sure."

"Can you comment on the fact that all U.S. Embassy staff in Venezuela are being airlifted out of Caracas as we speak, and that the Organization of American States has been asked to convene an emergency meeting tomorrow via videoconference?"

Where was Jackson getting this? his fellow reporters wanted to know. Who were his sources, and were they right? Had the military identified the attacks as coming from Venezuela, and were they preparing for a major war in South America?

"No comment," Murray said.

That was all it took. Murray's stiff, almost cagey response suddenly fueled a media frenzy that five minutes earlier hadn't even existed.

General Stephens leaned over to the president. "It's working," he whispered.

"The question is," James whispered back, "for how long?"

"All we need is a few hours, Mr. President," the general said.

James nodded and closed his eyes. He just hoped they had a few hours.

65

★ ★
★

The briefing ended and the general's phone rang immediately.

Stephens answered it on the first ring, then handed the phone to the president. "Sir, it's Vice President Trainor."

James stood, took the call, and began pacing the general's office. He urgently motioned for Ginny Harris to hang up with whatever reporter or producer she was talking to, nodding occasionally but saying little.

"You're sure?" the president asked.

There was a long silence. James kept pacing. Stephens and Harris looked on, waiting for some indication of what was being discussed.

"Fine, talk to Admiral Arthurs and General Garrett," the president ordered. "Make sure everyone is ready. Then call me back in fifteen."

He hung up the phone and turned to Stephens and Harris. "The data from the sniffer planes is in," he said somberly.

"And?" the general asked.

"The preliminary analysis suggests the warheads used in D.C. and L.A. almost certainly came from plutonium enriched in North Korea."

Ginny Harris's hand shot to her mouth.

"The New York and Seattle data, thus far, is inconclusive," the president continued. "More testing is being done. The air force is saying final results won't be available for several weeks. Obviously we don't have several weeks. What's more, the latest satellite imagery shows that heavy mechanized units based northeast of Pyongyang are on the move. They're heading south and setting up a staging area about fifty clicks north of the DMZ."

He looked at Harris. "Is everything set with the network affiliates?"

"Yes, sir," she replied.

"The cable outlets?"

"Yes, sir."

"The overseas networks?"

"It's all been taken care of, Mr. President," Harris confirmed. "Chuck even persuaded China Central Television, the state-run network, to air it."

"Live?" James asked, surprised.

"Live," Harris said. "In fact, all sixteen CCTV channels are going to preempt their regularly scheduled programming to air your address."

"Guess you'd better say something reassuring about Beijing," Stephens said.

James couldn't quite muster a smile under the circumstances.

"They'll delay it by thirty seconds," Harris noted, "to censor anything political they don't like but also to provide simultaneous translation in every major language. And they're not the only ones, sir. It's looking like you'll have live audiences on every continent."

The president began pacing again.

"This could very well be the most watched presidential address in history," Harris said, matter-of-factly. There was no hint of excitement in her voice. She knew the stakes like everyone else. But she was, after all, the new director of communications for a White House that didn't even exist. "Chuck and I expect an audience of no fewer than two billion people, Mr. President," she added.

"Then," James said, "I guess you'd better start drafting something for me to say."

☆   ☆   ☆

Fear has a way of clarifying one's thoughts.

Of reminding you what matters most. And Bennett was suddenly scared.

The temperature in the cell had to be at least a hundred degrees

Fahrenheit. The humidity made it even worse. But some kind of icy cold presence was moving through the room. It felt oppressive. It felt evil. And Bennett was now chilled to the bone. He was no longer arguing with God; he was clinging to Him with a renewed intensity. He no longer felt sorry for himself; he was asking for protection, for the courage to endure whatever was ahead, and for forgiveness for all his doubts and anger. As he prayed, a measure of spiritual vigor began to return to him.

He prayed for the president to have wisdom and discernment in the midst of such chaos, and for his Father in heaven to comfort little Fareeda and draw her close to His heart. He prayed for the Galishnikovs, for Natasha Barak and her cousin Miriam, for everyone he could think of. Then he prayed for Erin.

He knew she was in a better place. He knew the Lord had promised to wipe away every tear from her eyes. But he asked his Father to pass a message on to Erin since she was there at His side—to tell her, simply, that he loved her and that he missed her very much. He didn't know if such a prayer was theologically sound. He couldn't think of a time in the Scriptures when anyone had prayed something like it. But he couldn't help himself, and could it really hurt to ask?

He felt better. Not good, but better. The icy presence had passed. The room was boiling again, and somehow Bennett was glad. New thoughts began to flood his mind. Where was he, and why? Was anyone coming for him, and what would they want? Was he going to die here? And if so, why? What was God asking of him? He was doing nothing. He was chained to a chair at the end of days. Why? What was the point? What was his purpose?

Moving from the horse country of Virginia to the epicenter to do humanitarian work had been an adventure, to be sure. Bennett had to admit that something had felt good and right about selling their house and cars, cashing out their portfolio, giving nearly all of their money to evangelical and messianic ministries operating in Israel and the Middle East, and rolling up their sleeves to care for those who couldn't care for themselves, and to do so in the name of Jesus. But Bennett had also struggled with being so far from the action, so removed from the centers of power and influence.

When he'd worked for the president, he had longed to get off the political bullet train, as he called it. But what he had done for the White House felt important. It was real. It was measurable, and Bennett had always loved to measure. Stocks were either up or down. The same with polls. Oil reserves either were expanding or weren't. Deals either were signed or weren't. It was the same with treaties and executive orders and legislation.

Caring for the poor wasn't measurable—not in a manner that satisfied Bennett, anyway. You could feed five thousand mouths for breakfast. Then they needed lunch. You had barely cleaned up and it was time to prepare dinner. It never ended.

What's more, as time passed since the Day of Devastation, Bennett had noticed that fewer and fewer people seemed drawn by the gospel. There had been such a surge at first. He had preached every Sunday morning in the camp chapel he and Erin improvised, and hundreds had responded to the invitation to accept Christ. Many formed small group Bible studies. He and Erin had been training many of those small group leaders. But over the past several months, the response had dropped precipitously. Spiritual hunger was waning. Apostasy was growing. It had made Bennett restless. He desperately wanted to make an impact. He wanted to make a difference. He wasn't trying to reach a continent for Christ. Just a camp. A single, solitary refugee camp. And now that, too, had been taken from him.

He wasn't mad. Not anymore. Just confused. The world was exploding. The clock was ticking. Christ was coming back. Maybe soon. He desperately wanted to finish well. He longed to hear Jesus say to him, "Well done, my good and faithful servant." But what good could he do here? He didn't even know where "here" was.

66

7:42 P.M. EST—MOUNT WEATHER COMMAND CENTER

Time was slipping away.

There were less than ninety minutes until his televised address, and there was still so much to do. The president sat in General Stephens's office, signing a series of National Security Directives, executive orders, and letters to a Congress still weeks away from being fully reassembled, authorizing an array of emergency and administrative actions.

At 7:42 p.m. Eastern, he signed a letter officially informing the Senate majority leader that he was naming Judge Sharon Summers as chief justice of the U.S. Supreme Court. At 7:45 p.m., he signed a letter officially informing the Speaker of the House and the Senate majority leader that he was naming General Michael B. Stephens as chairman of the Joint Chiefs of Staff. At 7:47 p.m., he signed a letter naming the head of the Chicago Federal Reserve as the new chairman of the Fed, and a separate executive order requiring the Fed to shift all administrative functions from D.C. to Chicago until further notice. Another two dozen documents were waiting to be signed, but suddenly General Stephens had Admiral Arthurs from CINCPAC on the line.

"Mr. President, the targeting packages are being loaded into the cruise missiles and should be ready soon," the general relayed. "Every bomber in Asia is fueled, on the runways, and ready to move on your command, sir."

"Good," James said. "Anything else?"

"President Woo has just arrived at Command Post Tango. He and General Garrett are reviewing final preparations. They would like to do a conference call as soon as possible."

"Very well," James said. "Get them on the line; then get me a number where I can reach Salvador Lucente before I go on the air."

*　　*　　*

David Doron was fast asleep.

So was his wife. She'd drifted off hours ago, but the prime minister hadn't come to bed until well after midnight, consumed as he was with the latest intel from the U.S., Asia, and Kurdistan, not to mention Salvador Lucente's stunning call and surprising offer. Groggy and disoriented, he rolled over, fumbled for the receiver, and found his military secretary on the line.

"What is it?" he groaned, putting on his glasses and checking the clock.

"Sorry to wake you, sir, but Avi Zadok is on the line—says it's urgent."

It was never a good sign when the head of the Mossad was on the phone at 3:09 in the morning.

"Give me a moment," Doron said, putting on his slippers and robe, "then put him through to my office."

"Very good, sir."

Doron breathed deeply, forced himself to his feet, and stumbled to his private study, just off the master bedroom. There he flipped on a small desk lamp, fired up his computer, slumped into his chair, and took the call.

"Avi?"

"Yes, Mr. Prime Minister, it's me."

"What have you got?"

"Several things, sir. Word is President Oaks is going to address the nation at 9 p.m. Eastern."

"He's going to talk about the shooting?" Doron asked, wondering why he'd bother to make a formal address on the topic.

"I'm sure he'll touch on it—he has to," Zadok said, "but rumors are he's going to declare war on Venezuela."

"What? Avi, come on; that has to be wrong."

"That's my reaction," Zadok said, "but the U.S. apparently is positioning two carrier battle groups off the eastern coast of Venezuela and is beginning an airlift of men and supplies to Panama and Guyana."

"What do they know that we don't?" Doron asked.

"Chuck Murray is hinting Caracas may be behind these attacks."

"Have you talked to Trainor?"

"Just did."

"And?"

"He's being pretty tight-lipped," Zadok said. "Off the record he agreed that something is cooking. They've got good intel. They're getting ready to hit someone. But when I pushed him on Venezuela, he said he would call me back as soon as he had clearance to do so."

"Where are they on China?" Doron asked.

"They've ruled China out," Zadok confirmed. "Trainor said Lee James spoke to Premier Zhao less than an hour ago. He assured Zhao that the U.S. does not consider Beijing a suspect, and he urged the Chinese to stand down their forces."

"Do you buy it?" Doron asked, fully awake now.

"You mean Venezuela?" Zadok clarified.

"Right."

"No, sir, I don't."

"Why not?"

"I don't know," Zadok said. "The China thing I can buy. I don't think Beijing did it, and I don't think Bill Oaks wants to start a nuclear war with someone who can shoot back all the way to Colorado Springs, especially when he doesn't have to. But something about this Venezuela thing doesn't seem right."

"You think it's a head fake?"

"Probably, sir."

"So who's the real target?"

"I'd have to think it's Pyongyang."

"Any word from the South Koreans?"

"They're mobilizing as fast as they can," Zadok said. "But it's purely defensive. I don't see any scenario in which they launch a preemptive strike."

"But you still think the North is about to move?"

"I do, sir."

"How soon?"

"If the invasion of the South doesn't begin in forty-eight hours, I'd be stunned, Mr. Prime Minister."

"What about our mole?"

"That's the other thing I needed to talk to you about."

"Why?"

"A communiqué just came in," Zadok noted. "He thinks the Americans are about to strike Pyongyang, wants us to get him out now."

"Do you agree with him?" Doron asked.

"I'm leaning that way, yes, sir," Zadok said. "But there's something else."

"What?"

"Our source says Jon Bennett is in North Korea."

Doron was stunned. "*Bennett?* Why? Where?"

"We're not sure why. Our man's still working on that. But he says Bennett was flown from Jordan to Beijing, taken by truck into North Korea, then flown by helicopter to Yodok."

"Camp 15?"

"Yes, sir."

"How is that possible?"

"It doesn't make sense, I know," Zadok replied. "But our man says he's sure."

"How does he know?"

"You won't believe it," Zadok said.

"Try me," Doron said.

"Remember we sent him a message, asking him to get us more on Indira Rajiv?"

"Of course."

"Well, guess who called his boss?"

"Indira Rajiv called the minister of public security?"

"That's what he said, sir."

"And she talked about Bennett?"

"Apparently."

"What did she say?"

"I don't know. He promised to send more, but only if we agree to get him out of the country. He think someone in the MPS is on to him."

"Why?"

"His boss has launched two separate mole hunts in the last forty-eight hours."

Doron was up now, pacing about his office. "Can we get him out?" he asked after a long silence.

"Our man? Probably. But we'll have to move fast."

"No, no, I mean Bennett," Doron said, the urgency rising in his voice. "Can we get him out before the Americans launch?"

"It might already be too late, sir," Zadok said. "The president's speech begins in forty-two minutes. I suspect the air strikes will begin any moment."

"Do it anyway," Doron said. "I owe him."

"Bennett?"

"Yes—do it now."

"Sir, look, I know Jon is a dear friend to you, but we have an obligation to our asset in Pyongyang."

"Then get them both out."

"We can't, sir," Zadok said. "We don't have enough men or equipment in place. Even if we did, there isn't enough time."

"Then get Bennett."

Zadok protested, "Sir, we can't just cut our man loose. We promised him we'd do everything we could to extract him when he asked. Now he's asking, and I—"

But Doron cut him off. "Avi, I know what he gave us, and I'm grateful. Tell him we're coming. Tell him whatever you need to keep him happy, and quiet. But I'm giving you a direct order: extract Jon Bennett, whatever it takes—*now*."

67

9:16 A.M.—CAMP 15, NORTH KOREA

Bennett was startled by his cell door suddenly opening.

Two men in black hoods entered. Both were armed. One brandished a black metal poker, glowing red-hot at one end.

Bennett's eyes widened. His heart raced. He prayed again for courage, but all he could think of was Erin, how much he loved her, how much he missed her, and how bravely she had suffered at the hands of Mohammed Jibril and Yuri Gogolov. She had never broken, never lost faith. Could he do the same?

The man with the poker walked straight to him. His colleague, meanwhile, moved behind Bennett, grabbing his head like a vise and holding it steady.

"Why?" the man with the poker asked.

Bennett said nothing.

"You only transferred $25 million. We want to know why."

Again, Bennett said nothing. If they had the money, they had the note Trainor had sent along with it. There was nothing more to add.

The man moved the burning instrument closer and closer to Bennett's face. "You were told to transfer fifty million, not twenty-five," he growled. "Why did you break the deal?"

Was this the voice he'd been speaking with on the phone? Bennett wondered. He honestly couldn't tell. And what if it was? *What would it matter?*

"The instructions were very clear, Mr. Bennett. Fifty million, or you'd get nothing. Save the world, or suffer the consequences. You didn't keep the deal. Now your wife is dead. Your mother is dead. And you're next."

Bennett fought for control. It wasn't just fear or grief he was battling anymore. It was rage. Still, he refused to let it master him. He refused to succumb to hate. *Love your enemy. Love your enemy.* He wasn't sure how. He simply kept saying the words of Jesus again and again. He couldn't afford to unleash. Not here. Not now. It wasn't going to change his fate, and any moment he was going to be in the arms of Jesus anyway. And then, before he knew it, he would get to see Erin. He didn't want them to be ashamed of him. So much of his life had been wasted. So much of what he had thought was important for so long in his life was going to burn away at the great judgment. It had all been worthless. It had all been for naught. But not this moment, Bennett decided. If this was the end—if this was his test—he wanted it to count. He wanted to make them proud.

✯   ✯   ✯

The unmarked Black Hawk flew low and fast over the Pacific.

The pilots maintained strict radio silence. The special forces operators checked and rechecked their weapons. They had no idea what the U.S. was about to do. All they knew was that their orders had come directly from the prime minister himself and time was of the essence.

Their commander, Arik Gilad, a twenty-four-year-old Israeli from a kibbutz not far from Kiryat Shmona, near the Lebanon border, handed out 8 ½-by-11-inch printouts of Jon Bennett's photo. Each man on his team studied the photo carefully, then went back to studying the layout of the prison complex at Yodok.

There had been no time to practice this extraction. They had no back-up. No one would be coming to get them if they were captured, or their bodies if they were killed. They put their chances of success at less than three in ten, but Doron had called them personally. He had spoken to them by secure phone in their makeshift training facility in the southern forests of Japan. He had told them how important this was to him and to the nation of Israel. Bennett had found the Ark. He'd found the Temple treasures. He'd stood with the Jewish state when few others had in the days leading up to the War of Gog and Magog. Bennett was, Doron told them, a "righteous Gentile," and he needed their help.

None of the men questioned the order. They all knew who Jon Bennett was. Love him or hate him, they knew his life was now in their hands. What they didn't know was that theirs were in his as well.

"Six minutes," their commander said in Hebrew.

The men checked their watches. They saw the water skimming no more than fifty feet below them. A moment later, they saw the beach and then the forbidding mountains of South Hamgyong rising up before them. This was it. There was no turning back now.

☆　☆　☆

"You will talk, Mr. Bennett. I guarantee it."

The poker was now aimed directly at Bennett's right eye. The heat was unbearable. Bennett shut his eyes, but the second man jabbed something sharp in his back. He demanded Bennett open his eyes again but Bennett refused. He waited for the searing, burning metal to touch his flesh. But something unexpected happened.

Someone yelled, "*Stop!*"

Bennett froze. Then he heard the shuffling of feet. He could feel the air in front of his face begin to cool slightly. The iron poker was gone, and he cautiously opened his eyes to find both of his tormentors standing beside him, one to the left, the other to the right. But they were no longer focused on him. They were focused on a figure on the other side of the room, near the doorway, standing in the shadows. It was Indira Rajiv.

"What are you doing?" Rajiv yelled at the men.

Bennett couldn't believe it was really her, yet in the power play that was unfolding, he didn't dare speak.

"We want our money," said the one on the left. "All of it."

"You'll get what I pay you."

"You promised to get fifty."

"No," Rajiv said. "I promised to try."

"Then try harder," the one on the right said.

Rajiv looked at one, then the other, then stared at Bennett. He barely recognized her. Her long, black Indian hair had been cut short and was riddled with gray. Her once smooth, dark skin now seemed pale and

weathered. Her fashionable suits had been replaced with jeans and a simple black T-shirt. If it weren't for her eyes, he might not be sure it was
really her, though they blazed with an anger he'd never seen before. It
dawned on him that she was the voice who had called him, and now his
anger burned too.

"You asked him to cooperate?" she asked.

"Of course," one of the men said.

"And he refused?"

"That's right."

"Fine. Maybe this will help."

Rajiv suddenly pulled out a sidearm and aimed it at Bennett's head.

"Last chance, Jonathan," she said without emotion. "Help these men
get their money, or die. Make your choice. I'll count to three."

He realized it was Rajiv who had ordered him and Erin to go to Bangkok. It was Rajiv he had refused.

"*One . . .*"

Which meant it was Rajiv who had ordered these men to kidnap him,
and it was Rajiv who had ordered Erin killed.

"*Two . . .*"

Bennett clenched his fists. There was no way he was going to speak
to this woman. She had betrayed her country, set the world on fire, and
robbed him of the only woman he had ever loved. He felt his eyes blaze.

"Fine, Jonathan," Rajiv said at last. "Have it your way."

And then he heard, "*Three.*"

She pulled the trigger, and the explosion echoed through the prison
complex. Then she pulled it again, and everything went black.

68

"It's time, Mr. President."

Lee James looked up from the latest draft of his upcoming address and found General Stephens standing beside him, a leather binder in his hands.

"Are those the orders?" he asked the general.

"They are, Mr. President. Are you ready?"

James nodded. "We don't have another option," he said, taking the binder and setting it on the desk. "And it's not really a preemptive strike. They brought the war to us. We have to respond."

"I believe you are right, Mr. President," the general replied, handing him a fountain pen.

"Doesn't make it any easier, though," James admitted, signing the papers.

"No, sir, I imagine it doesn't."

And the deed was done.

★ ★ ★

His ears ringing, Bennett opened his eyes.

But this wasn't heaven. Nor was it hell. He wasn't dead. The two men who had threatened to torture him were, though, their bodies sprawled out on the filthy white tile floor, each surrounded by a growing pool of crimson.

"They worked for the Legion," Rajiv said, holstering the smoking pistol in her hands and walking over to check their pulses. Convinced they were really dead, she released Bennett from the handcuffs and the leg-irons, then backed away a safe distance toward the door. "In case you're wondering, yes, they brought you here from Jordan."

"Why did you kill them?" Bennett asked softly.

"Because they killed Erin," she replied.

There was a long pause. The fire in Rajiv's eyes was gone.

"I had ordered them not to," Rajiv explained. "I gave them explicit instructions that neither of you were to be harmed. Please, Jonathan, you have to believe me."

Bennett didn't. But he moved on.

"Where am I?" he asked, rubbing the circulation back into his arms and wrists.

"Camp 15," Rajiv said quietly. "Yodok."

The words just hung in the air. Bennett was stunned. Had he heard her right?

"The concentration camp?"

"They prefer to call it a 'reeducation center,'" she corrected.

Bennett had heard horror stories over the years about this place, North Korea's most notorious prison, built in the rugged, forbidding mountains of South Hamgyong province. Surrounded by enormous walls, guard towers, barbed wire, and acres of minefields, it was impossible to escape, and almost as impossible to survive. To many, its very name was evocative of Dachau or Auschwitz. Upward of two hundred thousand religious and political prisoners at a time were typically condemned to serve there. One out of five prisoners died every year, some from starvation, others by freezing to death in unheated cells, the rest by firing squads and hangings.

"Why?" he asked.

"Why are you here?" she asked. "Or why am I?"

Bennett was quiet.

"You're here because I'm here," Rajiv said at last. "I needed to see you—you and Erin. I wanted to tell you what was happening, who was in on it, what was going to happen next. I couldn't do it over the phone. I needed to do it in person."

Bennett wondered how quickly he could get to her before she could pull the gun on him. She was no more than fifteen yards away. But what then? What was he really going to do to her?

"I'm sorry, Jonathan," she said at last, her face sullen, her once rigid posture slowly deflating. "I never meant for any of this to happen—certainly not to you, not to Erin. I never meant any harm to come to you. I just . . ."

Her voice trailed off. She looked away.

"I have a story to tell you, Jonathan," she said, her eyes welling up with tears. "I have a confession to make. When I'm done, you can go. I promise. I have a helicopter and a crew. They'll take you wherever you want. You never have to see me again. But please let me say something first."

☆   ☆   ☆

The first cruise missiles launched at precisely 8:30 p.m. Eastern.

The B-52s, laden with thousands of additional Advanced Cruise Missiles, each tipped with W80-1 nuclear warheads, launched moments later. James privately conceded to General Stephens that he didn't know how to square his responsibilities as president to "preserve, protect, and defend the Constitution" with his newfound faith in Christ and the teachings of the Bible. Was he really supposed to turn the other cheek to America's attackers? Was he really supposed to love his enemies, even if they committed genocide on American soil? He had hundreds of questions with no answers, and he felt a great darkness spreading across the earth.

Chuck Murray called. The networks were in a frenzy over the rumors of a coming war in Venezuela. Coverage of the issue was wall-to-wall. A former U.S. ambassador to Brazil had just gone on CNN to denounce the administration and say that the real threat was Pyongyang, not Caracas. The diversion was working. There was enormous anticipation of the president's upcoming address. Ratings were going to be through the roof. Everyone was going to be watching.

"Is it time to drop the next bombshell?" Murray asked the president over a secure phone line.

James didn't like the choice of words, but as he glanced at his watch, he realized there were only twenty-seven minutes left until his speech. He gave Murray the go-ahead as Ginny Harris entered the room with a new and hopefully final draft of his remarks.

☆ ☆ ☆

"The world is out of balance, Jonathan," Rajiv began.

Bennett just stared at her.

"That's what my parents always told me," she continued. "Their parents hated imperialism. They hated the British. They had done everything they could to drive the Brits out and bring about a free and independent India. But when the war with Pakistan broke out, they fled for Canada and then to the U.S., and that's where they raised their children. My parents met in Berkley in the sixties. They got married during the Vietnam War. They had me after Watergate. My father used to rail against American imperialism, saying it was as noxious as the Brits'. And that's how I grew up, in Haight-Ashbury, hearing about the evils of America every day, every night, in school and in the streets. And I believed it. And I wanted to do something about it."

Rajiv slumped down against the back wall and set her pistol and holster on the floor beside her.

"My grandparents were Hindus," she continued. "My parents were Marxists. But I didn't want to march in the streets or do sit-ins at Harvard or write books or sing folk songs. It was silly, childish, and useless. I wanted to make a real difference. I wanted to bring about real change. So I joined the College Republicans. I voted for Reagan conservatives. I toyed with joining the ROTC, but when Erin came to my campus and recruited me for the CIA, I leaped at the chance. I wanted to work on the inside, and I'll tell you why.

"I don't believe there should be only one superpower in the world. It's too dangerous. A country that is answerable to no one else becomes arrogant. Corrupt. Greedy. Bloodthirsty. And that's what has happened to America. She swaggers about the world as if she owns the place. She invades countries for no reason. She bombs civilians without mercy. She thinks she's superior to everyone on the planet, and it's not right. The world is out of balance, Jonathan, and I decided to set it right."

"How?" Bennett asked, unable to resist.

"I wasn't sure how, at first," she admitted. "I just knew the higher I rose within Langley, the more secrets I would know, the more valuable I would be, and the more effective I could become at humbling the U.S. and helping other would-be powers around the world rise and shake off the arrogance and the corruption of the Americans. For a time, I worked for the Chinese. I think my father, rest in peace, would have been proud. For a time, I helped the Pakistanis. My mother, God rest her soul, would have had her stroke much earlier had she found out. I was a free agent, never beholden to one country, one regime, or one income source. It wasn't about the money anyway. And the people I worked for never knew who I really was. I gave them code names. We worked through dead drops. I parked the money overseas for a rainy day. And then it came."

She picked up the pistol and stroked it gently. "I was working for the Iraqis—Operation Black Box, it was called. We were trying to stop the Israelis from finding the Ark and the treasures, trying to stop them from building the new Temple. Then you and Erin got in the way, and I realized I had pushed the envelope too far. They were going to find me. So I ran."

"You worked for Al-Hassani?" Bennett asked in disbelief.

"Indirectly," she admitted. "But we never spoke."

"Who was your contact?"

"Khalid Tariq."

69
★ ★
★

"This is CNN breaking news."

U.N. Secretary-General Salvador Lucente and Chinese Premier Liu Xing Zhao sat in a small study in a wing of the Great Hall of the People. For the last hour or so they had sipped tea and tracked the latest events and speculated on whether the Venezuela story was real or presidential sleight of hand. But now they were riveted by CNN's exclusive report that President William Harvard Oaks had just "died of injuries sustained in yesterday's gun battle inside NORAD headquarters."

"A high-level administration official who asked not to be named publicly says Vice President Lee Alexander James has been sworn in as president," said a correspondent at Peterson Air Force Base. "CNN has also learned that Defense Secretary Burton L. Trainor has been sworn in as vice president, though sources say he will continue running the defense portfolio as President James rebuilds his Cabinet."

"It sounds like a coup," Lucente said, almost in disbelief.

"It does," Zhao agreed. "But the U.S. has never had one."

"Perhaps they're due," Lucente said.

"What does it mean for us?" the premier asked.

"It depends," Lucente said.

"On what?"

"On whether James is really going to war, and with whom."

"Do you think James wanted to come after us," Zhao asked, "and Oaks was against it?"

"I don't know," Lucente conceded. "But if I were you, I'd call your defense minister and see if there are American missiles or bombers in the air."

Zhao's hand reached instantly for the phone.

★　★　★

"Why did Tariq hire you?" Bennett asked.

"To help them build a world-class intelligence operation," Rajiv explained. "Tariq and Al-Hassani had a plan from the minute they came to power. They were never true democrats. They were opportunists from the start. They wanted to unite the Arabs, the Persians, the Turks. They wanted to protect the Middle East from U.S. imperialism. They wanted to bless their people and give them hope, and they wanted me to help them."

"But why did you say yes?"

"Because the world is out of balance, Jonathan. I hated to see the U.S. running roughshod over the entire Middle East, killing innocent civilians to save a quarter on a gallon of gas."

"How much did Tariq pay you?" Bennett asked.

"Five million a year," Rajiv admitted. "But like I told you, it wasn't about the money. I couldn't even touch the money until I got out. Even now, most of it is sitting in a Swiss bank—twenty million and change. Well, that was before the twenty-five you guys wired the other day."

"Twenty? I don't get it," Bennett said, quickly doing the math. "How long have you working for Tariq?"

"Two years."

"Then you should only have ten million."

"Some of it is from China."

"How much?"

"Three million."

"And the Pakistanis?" Bennett asked.

"Two."

"That's still only fifteen million total," Bennett said. "Where did the other five come from?"

Rajiv hesitated.

Bennett asked again, "Indira, where did you get the other five?"

"It was a bonus," she said hesitantly.

"From who?"

"Tariq."

"For what?"

There was a long, awkward silence.

"For what?" Bennett asked again.

Rajiv took a deep breath, then looked Bennett in the eye and said, "For helping him kill MacPherson."

☆ ☆ ☆

Dmitri Galishnikov and his wife huddled around their TV.

Oil prices were going through the roof. The last he had checked, the spot market had Israeli sweet crude going for more than $416 a barrel, up 6 percent in the past forty-eight hours. The Medexco empire was awash in cash, and the possibility of a war in Venezuela—one of the world's few oil-exporting countries not directly affected by the Day of Devastation—meant the Galishnikovs were fast on their way to becoming the wealthiest couple on the planet.

But in their palatial home overlooking the churning Mediterranean, they were scared. Israel had been saved. For now. But the world was blowing up around them. Their money meant nothing. They felt helpless. They couldn't sleep. They couldn't keep food down. Dmitri, a lifelong avowed atheist, had gone so far as to buy a Hebrew Bible and a yarmulke. When his wife wasn't watching, he was secretly surfing messianic Jewish Web sites, even Eli Mordechai's. *If this wasn't the end*, he thought, *what could it possibly look like?*

"Hold me, Dmitri," his wife moaned as they followed the latest news of the assassination of President Oaks, and he did, trying desperately to comfort this wife of his youth, though he had no comfort of his own. "Tell me everything is going to be okay," she said, her voice cracking in midsentence.

"I wish I could, darling," he replied. "I wish I could."

✫ ✫ ✫

Bennett couldn't believe what he was hearing.

But as livid as he was, something inside him told him not to show it, to keep her talking, to see where this all was leading.

"The attacks on the U.S. the other day—they were your idea?" he asked, fighting to keep his voice steady, not to make her defensive.

"No," she insisted, "they weren't."

"What do you mean?" Bennett asked. "I thought you just said—"

But she cut him off. "I met with Tariq in Rome in early February," Rajiv explained. "I had left Peter. I had left Langley. I was ready to help him build the intelligence network he and Al-Hassani needed to control all of North Africa, the Middle East, Central Asia, and its oil. But the first thing he asked me to do was help him kill the president."

"Why didn't you say no?"

"I didn't want to."

"What do you mean?" Bennett asked, incredulous.

"I knew he was right."

"Who?"

"Tariq."

"About killing MacPherson."

"Yes."

"What for?"

"It was the only way," Rajiv said.

"To do what?"

"To humble the world's only superpower," Rajiv insisted. "To show the American people—and the world—that she wasn't all-knowing, all-powerful, that she had weaknesses too, vulnerabilities."

She paused for a moment and stared at the pistol in her hands. "Tariq said all he needed from me was intelligence—how the president moved, how he was protected, where might be the best place to strike. He said he'd wire me $5 million, and the next day it was there. I knew I couldn't plan an operation like that from Rome, and he didn't want me anywhere near Babylon. He didn't want his fingerprints on this thing. So I came here."

"To Yodok?" Bennett asked.

"Well, to Pyongyang, and eventually to a terror training camp a few kilometers from here."

"But why North Korea?"

"Why not? It's the safest place in the world," Rajiv said. "There are hardly any foreigners here. The CIA doesn't have any assets on the ground here. Satellites can't track me if they don't know I'm here. And who would have expected me to come here? It was the perfect place to hide."

"Perfect," Bennett asked, "or only?"

Rajiv shrugged. "What's the difference?"

70

⋆ ⋆
⋆

Rajiv stared at the ceiling for several minutes.

Then she continued her story. Her words were coming fast now, as if she wanted to get her confession over with as quickly as possible.

"As soon as I arrived, I began building a team," she explained. "I recruited agents from the Legion and DPRK special forces. We mapped out a plan. I paid everyone in cash. It was all going fine. But I swear to you, Jonathan, it wasn't until the last minute that I heard that Tariq and the North Koreans had decided to go nuclear. Apparently Tariq had concluded that he could not only kill MacPherson, he could eliminate the U.S. as a current or future threat to any of the plans he and Al-Hassani were brewing."

"So why did the North Koreans agree?" Bennett asked.

"Because they're psychopaths," Rajiv said. "The leadership in Pyongyang figured if they worked with Tariq to decapitate the U.S., they could clear the way to seize the rest of the peninsula, and then Japan."

Bennett felt the hair on the back of his neck stand up. Something icy was moving in this room again. He wanted out.

But Rajiv wasn't done. "You have to know, Jonathan, about the alliance that is being created behind Washington's back."

"Iraq and North Korea?"

"No, that's just the tip of the iceberg," Rajiv insisted. "Babylon is flush with petrodollars, and they're using them to buy allies. It's not just North Korea. It's China. It's India. It's Pakistan. It's Venezuela. It's the E.U. It's Lucente."

Bennett winced. "Salvador Lucente."

"Bought and paid for by Al-Hassani."

"You sure it's not the other way around?" Bennett asked.

Rajiv shook her head. A cloud seemed to be coming over her at the very mention of Lucente's name.

Bennett wasn't so sure she was right about the secretary-general. Lucente had his own ambitions, he knew all too well. He might be placating Al-Hassani now, but that could all change in the blink of an eye. Still, for now, none of that was relevant.

"So," he asked, "why did you call me?"

Tears began to streak down Rajiv's cheeks. "I told you, Jonathan, I didn't know who else to talk to," she admitted, wiping her eyes but unable to stop crying. "As soon as I learned what was about to happen, I was horrified. But I was in no position to stop it. I never imagined Tariq and the North Koreans would go nuclear. It was never what I wanted. You have to believe me."

"How can I?" Bennett asked. "You've just admitted to masterminding the assassination of the president of the United States."

"But not with nuclear weapons," Rajiv insisted, the tears coming harder now. "I wanted to humble America, not annihilate her. I wanted to bring about some kind of balance, not tip the scales completely."

Bennett sat silently for several minutes, watching Rajiv cry, weighing the implications of what she had said, what she had done, and wondering what might happen next. But the truth was, he had no idea what had been set into motion, or how little time either of them had.

"What have I done?" Rajiv sobbed. *"I have killed my husband. I have killed my best friend. I have brought about such shame . . ."*

She could not finish the sentence. After another moment, she tried to compose herself, but it was a losing battle. She got up, dusted herself off, and walked over to Bennett. He stood as she approached. The closer she got, the more frail she looked, and she was shaking now, shaking and pale. Bennett almost felt sorry for her.

She was holding the 9 mm in one hand. With her other, she reached into her pocket and pulled out a flash drive. She handed it to Bennett. "Here," she said, almost in a whisper. "I want you to have this."

"What is it?" Bennett asked, taking the drive.

"Everything," she said, wiping her eyes again. "Names. Dates. Locations. Amounts. Plans. Digital photos of documents. Bank records. SWIFT codes. The entire conspiracy. I wish it were more. I'm sorry it's too late. But . . ."

Her voice trailed off. Her eyes were glassy, her pupils dilated. "You believe in heaven, don't you, Jonathan?"

Bennett nodded, surprised by the question.

"Do you think Erin is there?" Rajiv asked.

"I know she is, Indira," Bennett replied.

"When you get there, when you see her, please tell her I'm sorry, will you?" Rajiv said, the tears coming again, and harder now. "For everything."

"You can tell her yourself when it's time," Bennett said, suddenly wondering if Rajiv was open to hearing the gospel.

But she shook her head and looked away. "No," she said, though it was almost to herself. "It's too late for me now."

"It's not, Indira," Bennett said. "Jesus loves you. He died for you. He wants to forgive you. All you have to do is say yes."

"I can't, Jonathan," she said, backing away and refusing to make eye contact. "I made my deal. I sealed my fate. I couldn't go back, even if I wanted to."

"It isn't too late, Indira."

"It is," she said, moving toward the door.

"It's not," Bennett pleaded. "As long as you're still living, as long as you're still breathing, you still have time. You can pray with me right now and give your life to Christ."

"I can't," Rajiv said, her body convulsing in sobs.

"You can," Bennett insisted. "I'll show you how. I'll walk you through it."

"*No,*" she said suddenly, with an air of finality that seemed to suck all the oxygen out of the room. "It's too late. It's over. I'm sorry."

And before Bennett could react, she lifted her pistol, stuck it in her mouth, and pulled the trigger.

71

★ ★
★

Automatic gunfire filled the air.

As the unmarked Black Hawk came up over the ridge, the Israelis opened fire first, unleashing rockets into the guard towers, radio antennae, electric facilities, and telephone switching equipment and taking out any guard on the ground who brandished a weapon. A moment later, Captain Arik Gilad slapped his men on their backs and hurried them toward the open side doors of the chopper.

"*Go, go, go.*"

A dozen commandos fast-roped to the ground, six on each side, covered by three snipers still inside the Black Hawk, now rising out of RPG range and circling the compound. Gilad was last man down, but once on the ground he split the team in two and took the lead of "Red Knight One."

★   ★   ★

Bennett stood there in shock.

He stared Indira Rajiv's lifeless body. And the corpses of the two Legion operatives she had shot earlier. He stared at the bloody floor. Then he heard the helicopter and the gunfire, and the room began to spin.

⋆ ⋆ ⋆

Gilad moved quickly.

Using fast bursts of covering fire and tossing two grenades through a nearby door, the daring Israeli captain took his squad into cell block D-6. With thermal imaging from an Israeli spy satellite hovering in geo-synchronous orbit over the Koreas in the lead-up to possible hostilities there, as well as the last transmission of intel supplied by the Israeli mole in Pyongyang, Mossad chief Avi Zadok and his team had narrowed Bennett's possible location to one of five different buildings.

Gilad tossed another grenade around a corner, then did a sneak and peek after it exploded. Seeing no one, he jumped over the bodies of two mangled guards and signaled his men to follow.

He could hear more rockets firing from the Black Hawk and prayed Yahweh would bless their efforts to knock out all camp communications to the outside world. If the DPRK caught wind of what they were up to, they were finished. The prison camp would be swarming with the enemy before they could find Bennett and retreat.

A barrage of machine-gun fire came from somewhere down the darkened hall. Gilad checked his watch and cursed. He'd given himself and his men a mere twenty minutes on site, two of which were for carrying Bennett back to the Black Hawk and loading him in, assuming he was in no condition to walk. For this cell block, he'd allotted six minutes. He'd already used up four and they were encountering heavy resistance.

Using hand signals, he ordered his men to don their night vision equipment, then gave the signal. Gilad and his second-in-command now raced into the corridor, firing at anything and everything that moved. When the shooting stopped, he gave the signal and two more of his men raced down to meet them, while the remaining two held the door.

Gilad looked left, then right. Seeing no more guards, he sent his deputy one way while he went the other, each with a man at his side. Gunfire erupted behind him. He heard a scream. Someone cried out in Hebrew. He had a man down.

He checked his watch again. They were supposed to be on to the next building in forty-three seconds. They weren't going to make it. An intense firefight was now under way in the courtyard. Gilad could hear the Black

Hawk circling again, its M240H cannons shredding everyone in its path. But they had to get their man out, and there was still no sign of the man they'd come to save.

★　★　★

The president was livid.

"What do you mean a Black Hawk just entered North Korean airspace?" he yelled at General Stephens. "How in the world is that possible?"

Stephens admitted he didn't know. According to a U.S. Air Force recon plane, an unidentified UH-60 Black Hawk was spotted 160 kilometers east of Pyongyang, flying a special ops profile, fast and low over the Sea of Japan.

"Was it one of ours?" James fumed.

"We don't think so, sir."

"Think or know—there's a difference, you know."

"We're checking, sir," Stephens tried to assure him. "But no one authorized this."

James was furious, storming around the office and trying to imagine the damage if the North Koreans had the same information he'd just gotten. "How soon until the first cruise missiles hit?"

"Six minutes, maybe eight, tops," Stephens said.

"First impact?"

"Presidential palace, defense ministry, and the DPRK missile command."

"After that?"

"You've got the target package, Mr. President," the general reminded him. "In the next ten minutes, six thousand cruise missiles are going to turn North Korea into a sea of fire."

"Where's this chopper headed?"

"We don't know, sir."

"Where do you think it's headed?"

"Last sighting put it near South Hamgyong, Mr. President."

"What's there?"

"Nothing to speak of, sir," Stephens said. "A lot of military bases. Missile silos. A prison camp or two."

The phone rang. Stephens answered it on the first ring, listened carefully, then slammed the phone down.

"What is it?" the president asked.

"That was Vice President Trainor, sir."

"What's he got?"

"He just got off the phone with Avi Zadok in Jerusalem."

"So?"

"The Israelis have intel that puts Jon Bennett in the Yodok prison camp in South Hamgyong," Stephens said, recounting what Trainor had told him. "They've got a special ops team going in to get him out. Prime Minister Doron wanted to give you a heads-up."

All color drained from the president's face. "You're telling me Jon Bennett is at Yodok?" he asked Stephens.

"It appears so, Mr. President."

James looked at the digital war map on the wall of Stephens's office. He could see the missile tracks converging on six thousand DPRK targets, including South Hamgyong.

"God help me," the president said. "What have I done?"

★ ★ ★

Bennett was stunned to see another living human being.

He was even more stunned to hear one talking with an Israeli accent, and he began to lose his balance.

"Mr. Bennett, my name is Captain Arik Gilad. My men and I are here to rescue you. Can you walk?"

Bennett couldn't speak, couldn't think. He grabbed the man's shoulder for support and nodded.

Gilad's men set up a secure perimeter while Gilad helped Bennett onto a foldout stretcher. Once he was secure, Gilad picked up the back end while one of his colleagues grabbed the front. Two more men provided cover, and they began shooting their way back through the prison.

Breaking radio silence for the first time, Gilad ordered the Black Hawk to land on the roof of cell block D-6. He ordered Red Knight Two to race ahead and secure the landing zone. Then Red Knight One carried Bennett through a hail of bullets up several flights of stairs, heaved him into the back of the chopper, and locked his stretcher to the floor.

Bennett turned and saw another commando being loaded onto the helicopter as well. His colleagues were working feverishly to keep him alive. Blood was spraying everywhere. The Black Hawk began to rise. Bennett could hear more gunfire below. He could hear rounds slamming into the chopper's sides. Someone stuck an IV in his arm and tried to put an oxygen mask over his face. But Bennett furiously shook his head. He had something to say first, though he wasn't even sure if he could.

"Thank you, gentlemen," he said at last, his eyes blurring. "God bless you guys."

The Israeli medic working on him said something in return. Over the roar of the rotors, he couldn't hear a word. But he could read the sincerity in the young Israeli's eyes, and despite all the chaos and bloodshed around him, Bennett suddenly felt safe for the first time in days. He breathed a sigh of relief and turned to look out the window. And that's when he saw it, streaking across the horizon, leaving behind a contrail a hundred miles long. Then he saw a flash of blinding white light, and then he saw Jesus.

72

★ ★
★

"Ten seconds, Mr. President."

The floor manager gestured to the camera he'd be looking into while an aide touched up his makeup and another combed his hair. In all the last-second hubbub, General Stephens slipped James a note that read, simply, "Impact."

"Five seconds."

James nodded, folded the note, and slipped it into his suit coat pocket.

"Four . . . Three . . ." The floor manager stopped the verbal countdown and continued with hand gestures. *Two . . . one . . .*

James cleared his throat and began. "Good evening, my fellow Americans, and to those joining this broadcast around the globe. My name is Lee Alexander James. For the past several years, I served the MacPherson administration as the secretary of Homeland Security. For the last few days, I have served as the vice president, at the request of my dear friend, Bill Oaks. But tonight I am speaking to you as the president of the United States. In a moment, I will explain the terrifying series of events that has led us to this place, and me to this chair. I will explain what our federal government is doing to care for all those suffering in our midst at this hour. But first I must tell you that the United States is at war."

★   ★   ★

Mustafa Al-Hassani and Khalid Tariq watched together.

And smiled. The first that either of them had heard about the slaying of President Oaks was less than thirty minutes before, in a news bulletin on the BBC. Now both men hushed the buzz of the aides around them and called for the volume on the television in Al-Hassani's private office to be turned up significantly.

"Irrefutable and incontrovertible evidence of North Korea's direct and malicious involvement in the atomic attacks against our country has come into my possession," James declared to a global audience that had now swelled to an estimated three billion. "Through the brilliant and determined work of our own investigative agencies and the extraordinary assistance of governments and intelligence services around the globe, I have no doubt that the North Korean leadership planned these attacks in the hopes of decapitating our government and launching a takeover not only of South Korea but Japan as well. Tonight, I will lay out this evidence and the trail of terror that leads directly back to Pyongyang."

Tariq turned and looked at his leader. Al-Hassani just nodded, savoring all he was seeing and hearing.

"But first I must tell you," James continued, "that as commander in chief, I am not waiting to act to safeguard our people from further attacks or to bring retribution to those who have declared war on our people. Operation Asian Justice is under way. At this hour, U.S. military forces—at my direction—have launched a full-scale nuclear retaliation against the government of North Korea."

Al-Hassani reached over and gently squeezed Tariq's hand.

"Over the course of the next hour," the president explained, "I will walk you through as many details as I can. Please understand that our national security needs do not allow me to give every detail. But I want to honestly and forthrightly lay out for you as much as I can. For you deserve to know the truth. You deserve to know—"

Al-Hassani blinked once, and then again. He turned to Tariq, then back to the television.

"What happened?" he shouted. "Where did the president go?"

＊　＊　＊

Lucente's jaw dropped.

He turned to Premier Zhao, then back to the inexplicable visual on the television. There was nothing on the screen but an empty chair. One moment the president of the United States was making a live televised broadcast to the world. The next moment he had vanished into thin air.

"What is this?" Zhao asked. "Some kind of joke?"

Zhao ordered his staff to change the channels, which they did, but every network displayed the same image—a large desk, an American flag, a bookshelf, a credenza, and an empty executive chair from which the president had been speaking just seconds before.

"Where is he?" Zhao demanded. "What happened to the president?"

＊　＊　＊

Command Post Tango was in chaos.

Thousand of missiles and smart bombs were hitting their targets. Satellite imagery showed that everything was on track, on schedule, obliterating the DPRK and catching them completely off guard. But General Garrett had pandemonium on his hands. The president of South Korea was gone. So was the commander of the ROK army. They'd been sitting right beside him. They'd been watching President James's address together, while tracking the early minutes of the war. But no sooner had James vanished than so, too, had the Koreans.

＊　＊　＊

Dmitri Galishnikov slowly rose to his feet.

His eyes were glued to the TV. His wife was bawling. He was shaking. She was terrified of the unknown. He was terrified by what he suddenly knew all too well.

"So," he mumbled, nearly inaudibly, "Eli was right. They were all right."

To be certain, he picked up the phone and called Miriam Gozol, his VP of marketing. There was no answer at her home, so he tried her cell phone. Again, no answer. He called Natasha Barak at home. No answer.

He called her cell. No answer. He called every messianic believer he could think of. None of them answered.

This was it, Galishnikov realized. Everything that Eli and Bennett and Miriam and Natasha had been trying to tell him was true. All of it. Of this he no longer had a shred of doubt. *Yeshua* was the Messiah. He had come for His true followers. He had raptured His church, and Galishnikov and his wife had missed it. Nothing else explained what he'd just witnessed. They had missed it.

He collapsed to the floor and wept for mercy, for himself, for his wife, for his sons. For he knew now with a certainty that nearly paralyzed him that for all the evil the world had just experienced, it was merely a foretaste of the evil that lay ahead.

* * *

A sense of gloom settled over them.

Galishnikov had barely slept in more than a week. Nor had his wife. Since "the disappearances," they hadn't stepped foot in their Medexco corporate offices in Tel Aviv even once, despite the fact that oil prices had shot past a thousand euros a barrel. They had not checked their portfolios or spoken with their accountants or financial advisors—nor had it even occurred to them to do so—despite the fact that gold had already topped twenty-five hundred euros an ounce and most of their holdings were in gold since the Day of Devastation the previous October. Food had lost all taste. They were subsisting on an occasional piece of fruit, a few crackers, and a sip of juice or water now and then, and only because their house-keeper, a Filipino woman who feared for their health, kept insisting.

Locked away in their palatial stucco and glass compound overlook-ing the glistening Mediterranean, they found themselves consumed with watching the news and surfing the Web for the latest developments, talk-ing to their sons and various family members and friends throughout Is-rael and around the world as often as they could punch through on phone lines that were often overloaded and jammed, missing dear friends like Jon and Erin and Eli Mordechai, and studying the Scriptures deep into the night. Together, they had already read the entire New Testament through three times, from beginning to end. On his own, Galishnikov had read it through twice more, while at the same time poring over the prophecies of Daniel and Ezekiel, Jeremiah and Isaiah, desperately trying to make sense of all that was happening and feverishly trying to steel himself for all that was coming. He regretted not having listened to Eli and Jon more while he'd had the chance.

For most of his life he had dreaded attending synagogue on Shabbat, much less listening to the rabbi read the weekly Torah portion. But now he couldn't get enough of God's Word. Indeed, it was only when he read the Bible, or when Katya read it aloud to him, that the pervasive sense of gloom and evil all around them seemed to lift, even momentarily, and he felt any sense of peace at all.

Yet regardless of what else he studied, he found himself continually drawn back the words of the apostle Paul in his first letter to the believers in Yeshua gathered at Thessalonica.

> *The Lord Himself will descend*
> *from heaven with a shout,*
> *with the voice of the archangel*
> *and with the trumpet of God,*
> *and the dead in Messiah will rise first.*
> *Then we who are alive and remain*
> *will be caught up together with them*
> *in the clouds to meet the Lord in the air,*
> *and so we shall always be with the Lord.*
> *Therefore, comfort one another with these words.*

Was this what had just happened? Galishnikov longed to know. Had the true followers of *Yeshua HaMaschiach*—Jesus the Messiah—actually been caught up with Him in the air, just as the Scriptures had foretold two thousand years earlier, just and Eli and Jon and many others like them had predicted over the past few years, and even the past few months? At the moment the American president had disappeared on television, he had thought so immediately, and so had Katya. They had wavered in that initial conviction in recent days, but as hard as they tried, they could come up with no other plausible explanation.

The Internet was full of conspiracy theories and crackpot claims, saying the aliens had finally come, or that the earth had finally experienced the "invasion of the body snatchers." Some insisted it was all a freak act of spontaneous combustion. Others insisted it was all somehow a convergence of global warming and static electricity. But none of that rang true to Galishnikov.

To the contrary, the more he read articles and books online by evangelical Christians and messianic Jews who had been predicting the coming "Rapture" of the Church for years, the more convinced he was that they had just lived through one of the most dramatic moments in Bible prophecy. That meant, of course, that one day—perhaps sooner than they realized—they would have the incredible joy and privilege of seeing Eli's face again in heaven. They would get to walk the streets of gold with Jon and Erin and Natasha Barak and so many other dear ones. And yet such thoughts both comforted and terrified him at the same time, for they also meant that new evils were rising more horrifying than any that had come before.

Then just before six o'clock on the morning of the ninth day, the unlisted phone they kept in their home office began to ring. Galishnikov looked up from his laptop where he had spent the night studying Revelation chapter six and the coming of the "four horsemen of the apocalypse." He rubbed his bloodshot eyes and glanced at the caller ID. A shot of adrenaline suddenly coursed through his body. He picked up immediately.

"Hello?" he said, his voice raspy with fatigue.

"Is this Dmitri Galishnikov?" said a young woman who sounded nearly as tired as he.

"Yes, I am Dmitri."

"Very well, please hold for Prime Minister Doron."

Galishnikov held his breath. Why was he calling? What could this mean?

Katya suddenly tapped him on the shoulder.

"Coffee?" she whispered.

Startled, Galishnikov nodded and gratefully squeezed her hand, and then Doron was on the line.

"Dmitri, is that you?" came the familiar voice of his old friend.

"Yes, David, it's me," he replied, too close to the prime minister for formalities, especially now. "How are you holding up?"

"Off the record?" Doron asked.

"Of course," Galishnikov said.

"Then I would be lying to you if I said I wasn't scared," Doron conceded. "All of our allies are gone, Dmitri. All of them. And I don't know what to do."

"I don't understand," Galishnikov said. "What do you mean all of our allies are gone?"

"I mean Mossad estimates thirty-nine world leaders are missing—and all from countries that are our closest friends," Doron explained. "It's not just the president of the United States. It's the prime ministers of Great Britain, Canada, Australia. It's the president of South Korea and South Africa and dozens more like them all over the world."

Galishnikov felt as if someone had just kicked him in the stomach. He had been tracking such events around the world, but he had been thinking about them in personal terms, about friends and colleagues missing in each of those capitals, and in spiritual terms, about how everything that was happening fit into the trajectory of prophetic events the Bible described. He had not, however, been thinking in geopolitical terms about the big picture, much less in terms of how all these things would affect his own country. But Doron was right. The Israeli leader had just gone from seeing all of his major, immediate enemies consumed by fire—and thus feeling powerful, prosperous, nearly invincible—to seeing all of his major allies vanish into thin air. And the sense of despair in Doron's voice was palpable.

"My God," Galishnikov said finally as the reality of it all suddenly sank in anew and he wished once again Jon and Eli were around to teach him all he needed to know. "Is there anything I can do to help?"

"That's very kind, Dmitri," Doron said warmly. "And that, I confess, is why I'm calling. I'd like you to fly to Rome with me tomorrow, and then to Babylon a few days after that. Katya can come too, if you'd like to stick together."

"I'm sure we would," Galishnikov said, "but why Rome and Babylon?"

"Salvador Lucente has called for an emergency summit," Doron explained. "He's gathering every world leader who's left to discuss how to respond to the crisis."

"What exactly are you hearing, David?" Galishnikov pressed.

"It's absolute chaos out there, Dmitri," Doron confessed. "Avi Zadok has been talking to his sources around the clock, and he's telling me his initial estimate puts the number of missing people worldwide at north of one billion."

Galishnikov gasped. It didn't seem possible.

"Tens of thousands more have died from the chaos created by the disappearances," Doron continued. "And that, of course, is all on top of the fact that four American cities have been wiped off the face of the earth. Manhattan is gone, along with the New York Stock Exchange and NASDAQ. Washington is a smoldering wreckage, along with the White House, Capitol, and U.S. Treasury. The dollar has lost all value. The yen has collapsed. Only the euro is holding, and that's largely because Europe seems to have come through all this pretty much unscathed. I'm not sure how, but they just don't seem to have lost as many people as other regions have. Meanwhile, gold and oil and food prices are soaring. But I don't have to tell you that. The point is, the world is suddenly very unstable and Israel, I'm afraid, is suddenly very vulnerable. Lucente's suggesting we go from Rome to Babylon and have some time alone with Al-Hassani. He wants us to hammer out some kind of fast regional peace treaty—even a temporary one, something that might last five or ten years, or so. He's hoping meeting together we might be able to join forces to get more oil flowing to the world and try to help rebuild the international financial markets. To be honest, Dmitri, given all that's happening, I'm inclined to say yes, and to that end, I'd be deeply grateful for your help."

Galishnikov was suddenly seized with a fear that he had never experienced before. Not in Russia. Not during his time in the Israeli army. Not during all his years in business. Based on his own study of the prophecies, and what he had been reading on Eli's weblog, Galishnikov could suddenly so clearly see what was coming at him like a freight train. Yet there was nothing he could do to stop it, and that thought terrified him even more. Lucente and Al-Hassani were about to persuade Doron to sign a "covenant with the many," just as the prophet Daniel had foretold. The Third Temple was on the verge of being completed. The daily sacrifices were about to begin. Babylon had risen like a phoenix from the ashes. And the church was gone. He and Katya had missed the boat, as it were. They were rushing headlong into what the Scriptures called "the Great Tribulation," which meant the worst was yet to come.

"Give me a few hours, David," he said softly. "I'd like to talk with Katya and I'll get back to you."

"Very well," Doron replied. "But don't wait too long. I need you, my friend. I'm counting on you."

Galishnikov thanked the prime minister and gently hung up the phone.

"What is it?" asked Katya, coming back into the room with two steaming cups of coffee in her hands. "You look like you've just seen a ghost."

Galishnikov could barely breathe, barely think, barely speak. He looked deeply into his wife's eyes and tears suddenly welled up in his own. He had always loved this woman, but now more than ever. From the day they had met as freshmen at Moscow State University, he had always wanted her, always needed her. He couldn't imagine his life without her. He could never have survived this long much less succeeded this much in life without her at his side. Nor would he have ever wanted to.

Far more importantly, though, he shuddered to think of how desperate and alone he would be if Katya had not chosen to follow *Yeshua* in the same moment he had, the very instant they had watched President James disappear before their eyes. Their boys thought they were crazy, and that broke their hearts. The senior executives of Medexco—those who were left, at least—also thought they had lost their senses. But it did not matter, Galishnikov realized. Not anymore. Everything they believed in, everything they valued, had changed in an instant, in the twinkling of an eye. He was only beginning to grasp the horrors that lay ahead. But at least he no longer had any doubt about where the two of them would spend eternity—and the friends that would be waiting for them there—and somehow that gave him a peace he couldn't explain to face what was coming.

Galishnikov took one of the piping hot mugs from his dear wife's hands and asked her to sit down. They had decisions to make, he said, and not much time to make them. He summarized Doron's call and then picked up off his desk the leather Hebrew-Greek study Bible that Jon and Erin had given him at their wedding. He opened to a passage of Scripture he had just studied and underlined a few hours earlier, put on his glasses, and explained to Katya it was from the apostle Peter's second letter to the believers, the third chapter, talking about "the last days" and the coming judgments of God.

"'The day of the Lord will come like a thief,'" Galishnikov began to read. "'The heavens will pass away with a roar and the elements will be destroyed with intense heat, and the earth and its works will be burned up. Since all these things are to be destroyed in this way, what sort of people ought you to be?'"

He paused for a moment, then looked up and took off his glasses.

"This is the only question we really need to answer, my love," he said at last. "What kind of people ought we to be? Peter goes on to encourage us to live holy and godly lives. A few verses later, he tells us to be 'spotless and blameless' and to be 'diligent to be found by Him in peace.' That's all I want now, Katya. I want to be spotless and blameless before our Lord when we finally see Him face-to-face. I don't want Him to be ashamed of us. I don't want to shrink away from Him when we are bowing before Him in heaven."

"Me too," Katya said, tears now streaming down her cheeks.

Galishnikov took her in his arms and held her tight. "I love you, sweetheart."

"I love you too, Dmitri."

"Are you ready for all this?" he asked.

"I don't know," she conceded, her voice catching. "I want to be, but I'm so scared."

"I am too, darling—I am too," he said, and then added, "Someday—maybe soon—I would love to have the awesome privilege of watching our *Yeshua*, the King of kings and the Lord of lords, say to you, 'Well done, Katya, my good and faithful servant. You were faithful with a few things. I will put you in charge of many things. Enter into the joy of your Master.' And I'd love for you to see Him say the same thing to me."

"Then we cannot go to Rome tomorrow," Katya said, as the tears flowed faster. "Or Babylon thereafter."

"Then what are we supposed to do?" he cried, his body shaking now. "What are we supposed to do?"

"Preach the gospel, I think," she replied, holding him tightly. "Preach and pray and use the money He's given us to lift up His name in the time we have left."

"This old Russian Jew ain't much of a preacher, I'm afraid," he said, wiping his wife's tears away. "That was Eli's calling, not my own."

"Who knows, Dmitri?" she replied, a twinkle coming back to her otherwise bloodshot eyes. "We might both be surprised by how the Lord chooses to use us in these final days."

"Maybe so," he sighed. "But where should I start?"

Katya turned and looked at the laptop on the desk behind them. "How about with an e-mail?" she said.

And a moment later, they were composing their first e-pistle, side by side.

TO: *The 9,214 employees of Medexco worldwide*
FROM: *Dmitri and Katya Galishnikov*
SUBJECT: *Discovering the things that matter most*

Dear friends, we have a story to tell you—good news amid all the bad—and we hope you will indulge us for a moment while we tell you something that has changed our lives. Exactly nine days ago today, as the world began spinning out of control, the two of us discovered just how much G-d loves us and what an amazing plan and purpose He has for our lives, and we would love nothing more than for you to discover the G-d who loves you, too. . . .

IS IT TRUE?

★   ★   ★

To learn more about the research used for *Dead Heat*; to track the latest political, economic, and military developments in the Middle East and around the world; to learn more about the Joshua Fund's mission "to bless Israel and her neighbors in the name of Jesus, according to Genesis 12:1-3" and our "Operation Epicenter" humanitarian relief strategy, please visit:

www.joelrosenberg.com
www.joshuafund.net

Also, be sure to sign up to receive Joel C. Rosenberg's free e-mail newsletter with geopolitical updates and analyses and Joshua Fund prayer alerts,
>> FLASH TRAFFIC <<

ACKNOWLEDGMENTS

✭　✭　✭

When you write your first novel, you just hope your parents can find it at a bookstore within a hundred miles of their house. Anything beyond this is a miracle, and I find myself stunned by the miracle of having the privilege of writing not just one novel but five.

Time and space do not even begin to make it possible to thank everyone who has made *The Last Jihad* series so special and accessible to readers in the U.S. and Canada and around the globe. But to all I have named in my previous acknowledgments, please let me say thank you again from the bottom of my heart, especially the entire Tyndale publishing and PR family and Scott Miller of Trident Media Group, my literary agent extraordinaire.

Many, many thanks to our Joshua Fund team for translating our small initial vision to bless Israel and her neighbors into a vibrant and ever-expanding reality: Edward and Kailea Hunt, Tim and Carolyn Lugbill, Steve and Barb Klemke, Amy Knapp, John and Cheryl Moser, and June "Bubbe" Meyers. Thanks to our many strategic allies and silent partners throughout the U.S., Canada, and Europe. Thanks to everyone in the Calvary Chapel family—especially those in Rio Rancho and Albuquerque, New Mexico—for all you've done to help us this year. Words cannot begin to adequately express how much we love and appreciate you all.

Finally, and most importantly, I want to express my deepest gratitude to Lynn, the love of my life and God's greatest gift to me, apart from salvation itself; to my four wonderful sons and prayer warriors—Caleb, Jacob, Jonah, and Noah; to Lynn's entire family; and to my parents, Len and Mary Rosenberg, and the entire Rosenberg team. May we never forget how blessed we are by God's rich mercy and love or cease to do everything we possibly can to bless others in His matchless name.

JOEL C. ROSENBERG

Joel C. Rosenberg is the *New York Times* best-selling author of *The Last Jihad*, *The Last Days*, *The Ezekiel Option*, *The Copper Scroll*, and *Epicenter*, with more than one million copies in print. As a communications strategist, he has worked with some of the world's most influential leaders in business, politics, and media, including Steve Forbes, Rush Limbaugh, and former Israeli prime minister Benjamin Netanyahu. As a novelist, he has been interviewed on hundreds of radio and TV programs, including ABC's *Nightline*, *CNN Headline News*, FOX News Channel, The History Channel, MSNBC, *The Rush Limbaugh Show*, and *The Sean Hannity Show*. He has been profiled by the *New York Times*, the *Washington Times*, and the *Jerusalem Post*, and was the subject of two cover stories in *World* magazine. He has addressed audiences all over the world, including Russia, Israel, Jordan, Egypt, Turkey, and Belgium, and has spoken at the White House.

The first page of his first novel—*The Last Jihad*—puts readers inside the cockpit of a hijacked jet, coming in on a kamikaze attack into an American city, which leads to a war with Saddam Hussein over weapons of mass destruction. Yet it was written before 9/11 and published before the actual war with Iraq. *The Last Jihad* spent eleven weeks on the *New York Times* hardcover fiction best-seller list, reaching as high as #7. It raced up the *USA Today* and *Publishers Weekly* best-seller lists, hit #4 on the *Wall Street Journal* list, and hit #1 on Amazon.com.

His second thriller—*The Last Days*—opens with the death of Yasser Arafat and a U.S. diplomatic convoy ambushed in Gaza. Two weeks before *The Last Days* was published in hardcover, a U.S. diplomatic convoy was ambushed in Gaza. Thirteen months later, Yasser Arafat was dead. *The Last Days* spent four weeks on the *New York Times* hardcover fiction best-seller list, hit #5 on the *Denver Post* list, and #8 on the Dallas Morning News list. Both books have been optioned by a Hollywood producer.

The Ezekiel Option centers on a dictator rising in Russia who forms a military alliance with the leaders of Iran as they feverishly pursue nuclear weapons and threaten to wipe Israel off the face of the earth. On the very day it was published in June 2005, Iran elected a new leader who vowed to accelerate the country's nuclear program and later threatened to "wipe Israel off the map." Six months after it was published, Moscow signed a $1 billion arms deal with Tehran. *The Ezekiel Option* spent four weeks on the *New York Times* hardcover fiction bestseller list and five months on the Christian Bookseller Association best-seller list, reaching as high as #4. It won the 2006 Christian Book Award for fiction.

In *The Copper Scroll*, an ancient scroll describes unimaginable treasures worth untold billions buried in the hills east of Jerusalem and under the Holy City itself—treasures that could come from the Second Temple and whose discovery could lead to the building of the Third Temple and a war of biblical proportions. One month after it was released, *Biblical Archeology Review* published a story describing the real-life, intensified hunt for the treasures of the actual Copper Scroll. *The Copper Scroll* spent four weeks on the *New York Times* hardcover fiction best-seller list, two weeks on the *Wall Street Journal* best-seller list, two weeks on the *Publishers Weekly* hardcover fiction list, and several months on the CBA best-seller list. It won 2007 Logos Bookstores Best Fiction Award.

www.joelrosenberg.com

DISCOVER WHERE IT ALL BEGAN. . . .

TURN THE PAGE FOR AN EXCITING EXCERPT FROM . . .

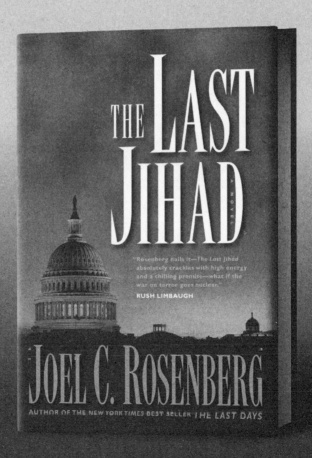

A PRESIDENTIAL MOTORCADE is a fascinating sight, particularly at night, and particularly from the air.

Even from twenty miles out and ten thousand feet up—on approach to Denver International Airport's runway 17R—both pilots of the Gulfstream IV could clearly see the red-and-blue flashing lights of the entourage on the ground at about one o'clock, beginning to snake westward down Pena Boulevard.

The late November air was cool, crisp, and cloudless. A full moon bathed the flat plains below and the Rockies jutting heavenward to the right with a bluish tint and remarkable visibility.

A phalanx of two dozen police motorcycles led the way toward downtown Denver, forming a V, with the captain of the motorcycle force riding point. Then came a dozen Colorado State Patrol squad cars, four rows of three each, spread out and taking up all three lanes of westbound highway with more lights and more sirens. Two jet-black Lincoln Town Cars followed immediately, carrying the White House advance team. These were followed by two black Chevy Suburbans, each carrying teams of plainclothes agents from the United States Secret Service.

Next—one after the other—came two identical limousines, both black, bulletproof Cadillacs built to precise Secret Service specifications. The first was code-named Dodgeball. The second, Stagecoach. To the untrained eye it was impossible to know the difference, or to know which vehicle the president was in.

The limousines were tailed closely by six more government-owned

Suburbans, most carrying fully locked-and-loaded Secret Service assault teams. A mobile-communications vehicle followed, along with two ambulances, a half dozen white vans carrying staffers, and two buses carrying national and local press, baggage, and equipment. Bringing up the rear were a half dozen TV-network satellite trucks, more squad cars, and another phalanx of police motorcycles.

Overhead, two Denver Metro Police helicopters flanked the motorcade—one on the right, the other on the left—and led it by at least half a mile. All in all, the caravan lit up the night sky and made a terrible racket. But it was certainly impressive—and intimidating—for anyone who cared to watch.

A local FOX reporter estimated that more than three thousand Coloradoans had just packed a DIA hangar and tarmac to see their former governor—now president of the United States—come home for Thanksgiving, his last stop on a multistate "victory tour" after the midterm elections. Some had stood in the crosswinds for more than six hours. They'd held American flags and hand-painted signs and sipped thermoses of hot chocolate. They'd waited patiently to clear through incredibly tight security and get a good spot to see the president step off *Air Force One*, flash his warm trademark smile, and deliver one simple, Reaganesque sound bite: "You ain't seen nothin' yet."

The crowd absolutely thundered with approval. They'd seen his televised Thanksgiving-week address to the nation from the Oval Office. They knew the daunting task he'd faced stepping in after Bush. And they knew the score.

America's economy was stronger than ever. Housing sales were at a record high. Small businesses were being launched at a healthy clip. Unemployment was dropping fast. The Dow and NASDAQ were reaching new heights. Homeland security had been firmly reestablished. The long war on terrorism had been an unqualified success. Al-Qaeda and the Taliban had been obliterated. Osama bin Laden had finally been found—dead, not alive.

Forty-three terrorist training camps throughout the Middle East and North Africa had been destroyed by the U.S. Delta Force and British SAS commandos. Not a single domestic hijacking had occurred in the past several years—not since a U.S. air marshal put three bullets in the heart of a

Sudanese man who single-handedly tried to take over a U.S. Airways shuttle from Washington Dulles to New York. And thousands of cell members and associates of various terrorist groups and factions had been arrested, convicted, and imprisoned in the United States, Canada, and Mexico.

Overseas, however, the news wasn't quite as good. The global economy still struggled. Car bombs and assassinations continued to occur sporadically throughout Europe and Asia as remaining terrorist networks—unable to penetrate the U.S.—tried to find new ways to lash out against the allies of the "Great Satan." One newspaper editorial said the U.S. seemed to be playing "terrorist whack-a-mole," crushing the heads of some cells at home only to see others pop up around the world. This was true. Many Americans still felt unsafe traveling overseas, and global trade, though improving, remained somewhat sluggish.

But within the U.S. there was now a restored sense of economic optimism and national security. Domestically, at least, recessions were a thing of the past and terrorism seemed to have been quashed. Presidential promises made were promises kept. And the sense of relief was palpable.

As a result, the president's job-approval ratings now stood steady at a remarkable 71 percent. At this rate he'd win reelection in a landslide, probably pick up even more House seats and very likely a solid Senate majority as well.

Then the challenge would be to move to the next level, to bolster the U.S. and international economies with his sweeping new tax cut and simplification plan. Could he really get a single-rate, 17 percent flat tax through Congress? That remained to be seen. But he could probably get the country back just to low tax rates, say 10 percent and 20 percent. And that might be good enough. Especially if he abolished the capital-gains tax and allowed immediate write-offs for investment in new plants, buildings, equipment, high-tech hardware, and computer software, instead of long, complicated, Jurassic Park–era depreciation schedules.

But all that was a headache for another day. For now, it was time for the president to head to the Brown Palace Hotel in downtown Denver and get some rest. Wednesday night he'd attend a Thanksgiving-eve party and raise $4.2 million for the Republican National Committee, then join his family already up at their palatial lodge, nestled on the slope of the Rockies in Beaver Creek, for a cozy, intimate weekend of skiing and turkey and chess. He could smell the fireplace and taste the sweet potatoes and marshmallows even now.

★ ★ ★

The motorcade cleared the airport grounds at 12:14 Wednesday morning.

Special Agent Charlie McKittrick of the U.S. Secret Service put down his high-powered night-vision binoculars and looked north, scanning the night sky from high atop the DIA control tower. In the distance, he could see the lights of the Gulfstream IV, a private jet chartered by some oil-company executives that was now the first aircraft in the holding pattern and waiting to land. Whenever the president, vice president, or other world leader flew into an airport, all other aircraft were prevented from landing or taking off, and the agency tasked with maintaining complete security put an agent in the tower to keep control of the airspace over and around the protectee. In this case, until Gambit—the code name assigned to the president—was secure at the Brown Palace, McKittrick would maintain his vigil in the tower and work with the local air-traffic controllers.

The holding pattern was now approaching five hours in length, and McKittrick had heard the G4 pilots repeat four times that they were running low on fuel. He hardly wanted to be responsible for a foul-up. It wasn't his fault the flight crew hadn't topped their tanks in Chicago rather than flying straight from Toronto. But it would certainly be his fault if something went wrong now. He glanced down at the radar screen beside him and saw thirteen other flights behind the Gulfstream. They were a potpourri of private and commercial aircraft whose pilots undoubtedly couldn't care less about the White House victory lap or the Secret Service. They just wanted their landing instructions and a good night's rest.

"All right, open 17R," McKittrick told the senior air-traffic controller, his voice suggesting an unhealthy combination of fatigue and fatalism. "Let's get the G4 down and go from there."

He cracked his knuckles, rubbed his neck, and swallowed the last of his umpteenth cup of coffee.

"TRACON, this is Tower. Over," the senior controller immediately barked into his headset. Exhausted, he just wanted to get these planes on the ground, go home, and call in sick the next day. He desperately needed a vacation, and he needed it now.

Linked by state-of-the-art fiber optics to the FAA's Terminal Radar Approach Control facility three miles south of the airport, the reply came instantaneously.

"Tower, this is TRACON. Over."

"TRACON, we're bringing in the Gulfstream on 17 Romeo. Put all other aircraft on notice. It won't be long now. Over."

"Roger that and hallelujah, Tower. Over."

The senior controller immediately switched frequencies to one-three-three-point-three-zero, and began putting the Gulfstream into an immediate landing pattern. Then he grabbed the last slice of cold pepperoni-and-sausage pizza from the box behind McKittrick and stuffed half of it in his mouth.

"Tower, this is Foxtrot Delta Lima, Niner Four Niner, on approach for 17 Romeo," said the Gulfstream. "We are going to increase speed and get on the ground as quickly as possible. Roger that?"

His mouth full, the senior controller thrust his finger at a junior controller by the window, who immediately jumped into action, used to finishing his bosses' sentences.

The young man grabbed a headset, and patched himself in. "Roger that, Foxtrot. You're cleared for landing. Bring her down."

Special Agent McKittrick didn't want to be here any more than these guys wanted him to be. But they'd better get used to it—all of them. If Gambit won his reelection campaign, he might as well open up his own bed-and-breakfast.

★   ★   ★

On board the Gulfstream, the pilot focused on the white strobe lights guiding him in and the green lamps imbedded down both sides of the runway.

He didn't have to worry about any other planes around him, because there weren't any. He didn't have to worry about any planes taxiing on the ground, because they were still in the Secret Service's holding pattern. He increased speed, lowered the landing gear, and tilted the nose down, taking the plane down from ten thousand feet to just a few hundred feet in a matter of moments.

A few minutes more and the long night would be over.

☆ ☆ ☆

Marcus Jackson munched on peanut M&M's and tapped away quietly on his Sony VAIO notebook computer as the motorcade sped along at well over seventy miles an hour.

As the *New York Times* White House correspondent, Jackson was permanently assigned Seat 1 on Press Bus 1. That put him just over the right shoulder of the driver, able to see and hear everything. But having awoken at 4:45 a.m. for baggage call in Miami—and having visited twelve states in the past four days on the president's Thanksgiving Tour—Jackson couldn't care less what could be seen or heard from his coveted seat. All he wanted to do now was get to the hotel and shut down for the night.

Behind Jackson sat two dozen veteran newspaper and magazine reporters, TV correspondents, network news producers, and "big foot" columnists—the big, brand-name pundits who not only wrote their political analyses for the *Times* and the Post and the Journal but also loved to engage each other on Hannity & Colmes and Hardball, O'Reilly and King, Crossfire and Capital Gang. All of them had wanted to see the president's victory lap up close and personal. Now all of them wanted it to be over so they, too, could get home for Thanksgiving.

Some dozed off. Some updated their Palm Pilots. Others talked on cell phones with their editors or their spouses. A junior press aide offered them sandwiches, snacks, and fresh, hot coffee from Starbucks. This was the A team, everyone from ABC News and the Associated Press to the *Washington Post* and the Washington Times. Together, what the journalists on this bus alone wrote and spoke could be read, watched, or listened to by upward of 50 million Americans by 9 a.m.

So they were handled with care by a White House press operation that wanted to make sure the A team didn't add to their generally ingrained bias against conservative Republicans by also being hungry, cold, or in any other way uncomfortable. Sleep was something national political reporters learned to do without. Starbucks wasn't.

A former *Army Times* correspondent who covered the Gulf War, then moved back to his hometown to work for the Denver Post, Jackson had joined the New York Times less than ten days before Gambit announced his campaign for the GOP nomination. What a roller coaster since then, and he was getting tired. Maybe he needed a new assignment. Did the Times have a bureau in Bermuda? Maybe he should open one. Just get through today, Jackson thought to himself. There'll be plenty of time for vacation soon enough. He glanced up to ask a question about the president's weekend schedule.

Across the aisle and leaning against the window sat Chuck Murray, the White House press secretary. Jackson noticed that for the first time since he'd met Murray a dozen years ago, "Answer Man" actually looked peaceful. His tie was off. His eyes were closed. His hands were folded gently across his chest, holding his walkie-talkie with a tiny black wire running up to an earpiece in his right ear. This allowed him to hear any critical internal communications without being overheard by the reporters on the bus. On the empty seat beside Murray lay a fresh yellow legal pad. No to-do list. No phone calls to return. Nothing. This little PR campaign was just about over. Do or die, there was nothing else Murray or his press team could do to get the president's approval ratings higher than they already were, and he knew it. So he relaxed.

Jackson made a mental note: *This guy's good. Let him rest.*

☆　☆　☆

Special Agent McKittrick was tired.

He walked over to the Mr. Coffee machine near the western windows of the control tower, out of everyone's way, itching to head home. He ripped open a tiny packet of creamer and sprinkled it into his latest cup. Then two packets of sugar, a little red stirrer, and voilà—a new man. Hardly. He took a sip—ouch, too hot—then turned back to the rest of the group.

For an instant, McKittrick's brain didn't register what his eyes were seeing. The Gulfstream was coming in too fast, too high. Of course it was in a hurry to get on the ground. But get it right, for crying out loud. McKittrick knew each DIA runway was twelve thousand feet long. From his younger days as a navy pilot, he figured the G4 needed only about three thousand feet to make a safe landing. But at this rate, the idiots were actually going to miss—or crash. No, that wasn't it. The landing gear was going back up. The plane was actually increasing its speed and pulling up.

"What's going on, Foxtrot?" screamed the senior controller into his headset.

When McKittrick saw the Gulfstream bank right toward the mountains, he knew.

"*Avalanche. Avalanche,*" McKittrick shouted into his secure digital cell phone.

✯   ✯   ✯

Marcus Jackson saw the bus driver's head snap to attention.

A split second later, Chuck Murray bolted upright in his seat. His face was ashen.

"What is it?" asked Jackson.

Murray didn't respond. He seemed momentarily paralyzed. Jackson turned to the front windshield and saw the two ambulances and the mobile-communications van pulling off on either side of the road. Their own bus began slowing and moving to the right shoulder. Up ahead, the rest of the motorcade began rapidly pulling away from them. Though he couldn't see the limousines, he could see the Secret Service Suburbans now moving at what he guessed had to be at least a hundred miles an hour, maybe more.

Jackson's combat instincts took over. He grabbed for his leather carry-on bag on the floor, fished through it frantically, and pulled out a pair of sports binoculars he'd found handy during the campaign when the press was kept far from the candidate. He trained on the Suburbans and quietly gasped. The tinted rear windows of all four specially designed Suburbans were now open. In the back of each of the first four vehicles were sharpshooters wearing black masks, black helmets, steel gray jumpsuits, and thick Kevlar bulletproof vests. What sent a chill down Jackson's spine, however, wasn't their uniforms, or their high-powered rifles. It was the two agents in the last two vehicles, the ones holding the Stinger surface-to-air missile launchers.

✯   ✯   ✯

"Talk to me, McKittrick."

Special Agent-in-Charge John Moore—head of the president's protective detail—shouted into his secure cellular phone as he sat in the front seat of Gambit's limousine, his head craning to see what was happening behind him.

Just hearing McKittrick yell, "Avalanche"—the Secret Service's code for a possible airborne attack—had already triggered an entire series of preset, well-trained, and now instinctual reactions from Moore's entire team. Now he needed real information, and he needed it fast.

"You've got a possible bogey on your tail," said McKittrick from the control tower, his binoculars trained on the lights of the Gulfstream. "He's not responding to his radio, but we know it's working."

"*Intent?*"

"What's that?" McKittrick asked, garbled by a flash of static.

"*Intent? What's his intent? Is he hostile?*" shouted Moore.

"Don't know, John. We're warning him over and over—he's just not responding."

Gambit lay on the floor, his body covered by two agents. The agents had no idea what threats they faced. But they were trained to react first and ask questions later. Moore scrambled over them all to get a better look through the tiny back window. For a moment he could see the lights of the Gulfstream bearing down on them. Suddenly the plane's lights went out, and Moore lost visual contact.

Glancing to his right, he could see Dodgeball—the decoy limousine—pulling up to his side as Pena Boulevard ended and the motorcade poured onto I-70 West. Both cars were moving at close to 130 miles an hour.

The question facing both drivers was whether or not they could get off the open and exposed stretch of highway they were now on and get under the interwoven combination of concrete bridges and overpasses that lay just ahead at the interchange of I-70 and I-25. This would make an overhead attack more difficult, though not impossible. The challenge would be driving fast enough to get there and then being able to stop fast enough—or stop and back up fast enough—to get and stay under the bridges and out of the potential line of fire.

But what if the bridges were booby-trapped with explosives? What if the Denver Metro Police and Colorado State Patrol securing the bridges were compromised? Were they escaping an enemy, or being driven into the enemy's hands?

Moore reacquired the Gulfstream in his high-powered night-vision binoculars. It was gaining fast.

"Nighthawk Four, Nighthawk Five, this is Stagecoach. Where are you guys?" Moore shouted into his wrist-mounted microphone.

"Stagecoach, this is Nighthawk Five. We'll be airborne in one minute," came the reply.

"Nighthawk Four. Same thing, Stagecoach."

Moore cursed. The pair of AH-64 Apaches were state-of-the-art combat helicopters. Both could fly at a maximum speed of 186 miles per hour, and both carried sixteen Hellfire laser-guided missiles and 30 mm front-mounted machine guns. But both—on loan from the army's Fort Hood in Texas—might actually end up being useless to him.

After the suicide airplane attacks against the Twin Towers and the Pentagon, the Secret Service had decided that motorcades should be tailed by Apaches. "Just in case" was, after all, the Service's unofficial motto. But the White House political team went nuts. It was one thing to keep the president secure. It was another thing to have military helicopters flying CAP—combat air patrols—over city streets and civilian populations year after year after year. A compromise was reached. The Apaches would be pre-positioned and on standby at each airport the president or vice president was flying into, but wouldn't actually fly over the motorcades. It seemed reasonable at the time. Not anymore.

But it didn't matter now. Moore's mind scrambled for options.

"Nikon One. Nikon Two. This is Stagecoach. Turn around and get in front of this guy."

"Nikon One, roger that."

"Nikon Two, roger."

The two Denver Metro Police helicopters weren't attack helicopters. They certainly weren't Apaches. They were basically reconnaissance aircraft using night-vision video equipment to look for signs of trouble on the ground—not the air. But they immediately peeled off the formation and banked hard to get behind Gambit's limousine. The question was, could they make the maneuver fast enough? And what then?

✯   ✯   ✯

The Gulfstream pilot ripped his headphones off and tossed them behind him.

The tower was screaming at him in vain to change course immediately or risk being fired upon. Why be distracted?

He could see the police helicopters beginning to break right and left, respectively, so he increased his speed, lowered the nose and began bearing down on the two limousines, now side by side.

★　★　★

"Tommy, you got an exit coming up?" Moore shouted back to his driver.

"Sure do, boss. Coming up fast on the right—270 West."

"Good. Stagecoach to Dodgeball."

"Dodgeball—go."

"Pull ahead and break right at the 270 West exit. 270 West—go, go, go."

Agent Tomas Rodriguez imperceptibly eased his foot off the gas, just enough to let the decoy limousine roar ahead, pull in front of him, and then peel off to the right—just barely making the exit ramp.

★　★　★

For the first time, the Gulfstream pilot let out a string of obscenities.

With one limousine peeling off to the right and two Chevy Suburbans going with it, he suddenly doubted the intelligence he'd been given. Which limousine was he after? Which had the president? He was pretty sure it was not the one that had just peeled off. But now he hesitated.

His heart was racing. His palms were sweaty. His breathing was rapid and he was scared. Yes, he was ready to die for this mission. But he'd better take someone with him—and the right someone at that.

★　★　★

"Tommy, how far to the interchange?" Moore demanded.

"Don't know, sir—five miles, maybe eight."

It felt like they were moving at light speed, but Moore didn't like his odds. After all, they were rapidly approaching the outskirts of Denver. He could clearly see the city skyline and the bright blue Qwest logo, high atop the city's tallest building. All around him, industrial buildings and restaurants and hotels and strip malls were blurring past on each side of the highway. In his race to escape, he was drawing the G4 into the city and putting thousands of innocent civilians in danger.

"Cupid, Gabriel, this is Stagecoach. Do you copy?" Moore sure hoped they did.

"Stagecoach, this is Cupid. Copy you loud and clear, sir."

"Roger that, Stagecoach. This is Gabriel. Copy you five by five."

"You guys got a shot?"

"Yes, sir," said Cupid. "Ten miles out—2,500 feet up."

Both Cupid's and Gabriel's eyesight was 20/20 uncorrected. Their night-vision goggles made the G4 impossible to lose against the night sky. Both voices were steady and calm. A former CIA special-ops guy, Cupid was extremely well trained, having lived in Afghanistan for years, training *mujahedin* how to use portable, shoulder-mounted, heat-seeking Stinger missiles in the war against the Soviets in the eighties. Gabriel was nearly as good, having been Cupid's understudy for the past six years.

Moore gripped the backseat of the limousine. He didn't have time to consult Washington. He barely had enough time to give an order to shoot. What if he was wrong? What if he was misreading the situation? If the United States Secret Service shot down a bunch of businessmen in cold blood . . .

☆　☆　☆

"Sir, it's Home Plate—line one," Agent Rodriguez shouted from the driver's seat.

Moore grabbed the digital phone lying on the seat beside him. "Stagecoach to Home Plate, go secure."

"Secure, go. John, it's Bud. What've you got?"

Bud Norris was the gray, stocky, balding director of the U.S. Secret Service, a twenty-nine-year veteran of the Service and a Vietnam veteran who'd driven for U.S. generals and VIPs in Saigon until it fell. In 1981, he'd been President Reagan's limousine driver the day John Hinckley Jr. tried to assassinate the president in a vain attempt to impress actress Jodie Foster. In fact, within the Service, Norris was widely credited with helping save Reagan's life that day. At first, Reagan's agents hadn't realized he'd been shot—until he began coughing up bright red blood on the way to the White House. Told to divert immediately to GW Hospital, Norris slammed on the brakes, did a 180-degree turn into oncoming traffic on Pennsylvania Avenue, and made it to the hospital just moments before Reagan collapsed and slipped into unconsciousness from massive internal bleeding.

Norris was a pro. His agents knew it. And having worked his way up through the ranks from one promotion to another to the top spot just three years ago, Norris commanded enormous respect from his team.

"Sir, we've got a G4 bearing down on us. Broke out of a landing pattern, pulled up its gear, and cut its lights. We're racing for cover but right now we're in the open. Dodgeball broke right but the G4 is sticking with us," Moore told his boss, surprised by the relative steadiness in his voice.

"Range?"

"Twenty-five hundred feet up, ten miles out, closing fast."

"Contact?"

"Not anymore. Tower's been talking to him all night. But now McKittrick's screaming at them to change course and he's getting nothing back."

"Who's on board?"

"I don't know. Charter from Toronto. Supposed to be oil execs, but I don't really know."

"What's your gut tell you, John?"

Moore hesitated for a moment. The full weight of responsibility for protecting the president of the United States sent an involuntary shudder through his body. He suddenly felt cold and clammy. His wrinkled, rumpled suit was now soaked with sweat. Whatever he said next would seal the G4's fate—and his.

"I don't know, sir."

"Make a call, John."

Moore took a deep breath—the first he actually remembered taking in the last several minutes. "I think we've got another kamikaze, sir, and he's coming after Gambit."

"Take him out," Norris commanded instantly.

"We don't know a hundred percent for sure who's on board that plane, sir," Moore reminded his boss, for the record, for the audiotapes being recorded in the basement of the Treasury Building in Washington.

"Take him out."

"Yes, sir."

Moore tossed the phone aside and grabbed his wrist-mounted microphone. "Nikon One, Nikon Two—this is Stagecoach. Abort. Abort. Abort."

"Roger that, Stagecoach."

Both police helicopters banked hard right and left respectively and raced for cover.

"Cupid, Gabriel, this is Stagecoach. You got tone?"

The November air and whipping winds caused by speeds upward of 140 miles per hour created a windchill in the back of the black Chevy Suburbans somewhere south of zero. It also made it almost impossible for any normal person to hear anything. But the agents code-named Cupid and Gabriel wore black ski masks and gloves to protect their faces and hands from arctic temperatures and wore the same brand and model of headphones worn by NASCAR's Jeff Gordon at the Daytona 500. Moore's voice was, therefore, crystal clear.

"Stand by, Stagecoach," Cupid said calmly.

The G4 was now only seven miles from Gambit's limousine and coming in white-hot.

First, Cupid "interrogated" the Gulfstream, pressing the IFF challenge switch on his Stinger missile launcher. This immediately sent a signal to the aircraft's transponder asking whether it was a friend or foe. The answer didn't actually matter at this point. But the procedure did.

Beep, beep, beep, beep, beep, beep.

The rapid-fire beeping meant the answer was "unknown." Cupid sniffed in disgust, turned off the safety, and pushed the actuator button forward and downward. This warmed up the BCU—the battery coolant unit—hooked to Cupid's belt and made the weapon go live. Though it took only five seconds, it felt like a lifetime.

Next, Cupid triggered an infrared signal at the G4 to determine its range and acquire the heat emanating from the plane's jet engines. Instantly hearing a strong, clear, high-pitched tone, he quickly pressed the weapon's uncaging switch with his right thumb and held it in, and the tone got louder. He now had a lock on the G4, just three miles away and down to a mere one thousand feet.

"I have tone. I have a lock," Cupid shouted into the whipping wind and the microphone attached to his headphones. The G4 was now just two miles back.

"Me, too, sir," Gabriel echoed.

Moore was not normally a religious man. But he was today.

"Oh, God, have mercy," he whispered, then crossed himself for the first time since graduating from St. Jude's Catholic High School.

"Fire, fire, fire," Moore shouted.

"Roger that. Hold your breath, hold your breath," Cupid shouted.

Moore and all his agents immediately responded, gulping as much oxygen as they possibly could. But Cupid wasn't actually talking to them. Per his intensive training, he was reminding himself and his driver that they were about to be trapped inside a live, mobile missile silo, and it wasn't going to be pretty. Cupid's driver quickly lowered every other window in the vehicle and threw another switch turning on a small, portable air pump as well. The G4 was now less than a mile back.

"Three, two, one, fire."

Cupid squeezed the trigger.

Nothing happened.

Moore waited, his heart racing, his eyes desperately scanning the sky.

"Cupid, what's the problem?"

"Don't know, sir. Malfunction. Hold on."

"I don't have time to—Gabriel, talk to me."

"Got it, sir. Don't worry. Hold your breath, hold your breath. Three, two, one . . ."

The Stinger missile exploded from its fiberglass tube and streaked into the night sky. The Suburban filled with a flash of blinding fire and hot, toxic, deadly fumes. For a moment, the driver began to lose control of the vehicle. Moore could see the Suburban rock and swerve. But within seconds the smoke and fumes were sucked out of the vehicle and into the atmosphere. The driver could see again. Gabriel could breathe again if he wanted to—but he didn't. Not until he was sure.

McKittrick knew combat firsthand.

He'd been in the Gulf War. He'd seen gunfire and death. But he'd never seen anything like this. Nor would he again. As he watched through his high-powered binoculars from the control tower, he saw the Stinger missile tear the G4 in half. The plane then erupted in a massive fireball. McKittrick fell to the ground, screaming in pain. The explosion was magnified so intensely by his night-vision binoculars that it had burned holes in his retinas, leaving him permanently blinded.

★ ★ ★

Moore was horrified.

Despite all of his training, he was suddenly completely unprepared for what was happening. This was no ordinary charter plane falling from the sky. It was a death machine, packed with explosives for maximum impact. The roar of the explosion was deafening, heard as far away as Castle Rock. The sky was now on fire. Night turned to day. The flash of heat was unbearable. Molten metal rained down on the motorcade.

Cupid's Chevy Suburban swerved hard and barely escaped being landed upon by the disintegrating G4. Gabriel was not so lucky. Moore saw one of the G4's engines slam into the young agent's vehicle and explode into yet another blinding fireball. But what Moore saw next terrified him more than anything else. The fuselage of the G4 was hurtling at him like a flaming meteor, propelled forward by the force of the blast.

"Tommy!" Moore screamed.

Agent Rodriguez began swerving right, heading for an off-ramp and praying desperately the car wouldn't overturn. But it was too late. The G4's burning fuselage crashed into the pavement just behind them and slammed into the back of the limousine, sending Stagecoach careening into the concrete dividers in the center of the superhighway in a series of 360-degree spins. The car rolled over and over again in a fury of sparks and flames and smoke, eventually grinding to a halt upside down below the overpass for which Rodriguez had been racing. Inside Stagecoach— from the moment of impact—airbags exploded from the steering wheel and dashboard, from each car door and even from the roof, a feature designed exclusively for Secret Service vehicles, particularly since no one inside ever wore seat belts.

★ ★ ★

I-70 was ablaze.

The wreckage of the G4 and whatever was inside it was strewn everywhere, on fire and scorching hot. The surviving Suburbans screeched to a halt. Secret Service assault teams immediately jumped out, armed with

M16 rifles and fire-suppression equipment. Cupid regained his bearings and quickly began to check his weapon for the malfunction. He'd personally failed his mission. He had no idea what else might transpire. And he wasn't about to take any chances.

Dodgeball and its security package now reversed course and raced to rejoin Stagecoach. Weaving carefully through the wreckage, the backup vehicles arrived to find assault teams taking up positions in a perimeter around Gambit's car. Two more assault teams quickly joined their colleagues while three agents hauled a large metal box from the back of one of the Suburbans and hurried it to Stagecoach's side. They rapidly removed a specially designed Jaws of Life kit and began trying desperately to get Gambit out of the wreckage.

Colorado State Patrol cars and local fire trucks, along with the motorcycle units, raced to the scene. Overhead, the two police helicopters hovered nosily, each shining powerful search lamps onto the ground below to help the rescuers do their jobs.

☆ ☆ ☆

"John. John. This is Bud. What's your status?"

Bud Norris heard the explosion and the screaming through John Moore's digital cell phone on the backseat of Gambit's car. But now the line was pure static and he feared the worst. Norris grabbed a secure digital phone from the bank of phones in front of him and speed-dialed the lead Apache pilot.

"Nighthawk Four, this is Home Plate. Do you copy?" Norris barked.

"Home Plate, this is Nighthawk Four—we have a Code Red in progress. Repeat, we have a Code Red in progress. Please advise. I repeat, please advise."

"Nighthawk, you've got video capability, right?"

"Affirmative, Home Plate. We've got three systems on board. What do you need?" the lead pilot responded.

"What've you got?" Norris asked, his mind suddenly scrambling to remember the details he needed.

"Sir, we've got the TADS FLIR system, which is thermal imaging. But, sir, you've got two police helicopters here lighting the whole scene with spotlights. It's basically a TV studio down there, sir. If you'd like, we can use our Day TV system with black-and-white video imaging, or the DVO system with full color and magnification. It's your call, sir."

"Can you get it to me through a secure satellite, son?"

"We can get it to the Pentagon, sir. I think they can patch you in, sir, but don't quote me. You gotta check with Ops to be sure."

"I'll do it. Start transmitting, son. I'll take care of the rest."

Norris picked up another phone and speed-dialed the other Apache. "Nighthawk Five, this is Home Plate. You there? Over."

"Nighthawk Five, standing by, sir."

"Set up a perimeter around the crash site and tell the news helicopters they're grounded immediately. I'm scrambling an F-15 fighter squadron to join you in the next few minutes, and I want a no-fly zone over the state of Colorado. Got that?"

"Roger that, Home Plate."

Next, Norris sent out a Code Red on all Secret Service frequencies and gave the word for the vice president, the Speaker of the House, and all Cabinet members—spread out all over the country for the holidays—to be evacuated to secure underground facilities immediately. Moments later Norris was on the phone with the secretary of defense and the Pentagon watch commander. The air force scrambled aircraft to secure the skies over Denver.

Now a live, color, digital video feed from the hovering Nighthawk Four began streaming into the National Military Command Center, the nuclear-missile-proof war room deep underground, below the Pentagon. It was then cross-linked via secure fiber-optic lines to the Secret Service command center in the bombproof basement of the Treasury Department in Washington, the White House Situation Room, the FBI Op Center, and the CIA's Global Operations Center at Langley. Norris could finally see the grisly scene unfolding on one of the five large-screen TVs. His top staff worked the phones around him, gathering intelligence from the ground, alerting other security details and opening a direct line to FBI Director Scott Harris.

"My God," Norris said quietly.

The terrorists had struck again.

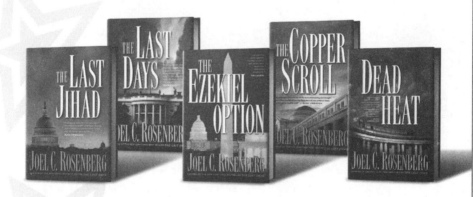